NORTHERN STARS

BRITTAINY CHERRY

Published: Brittainy Cherry 2022, BCherry Books, INC

Editing: Jenny Sims at Editing for Indies, My Brother's Editor, Virginia Tesi Carey
Cover Design: Hang Le
Photographer: Wander Aguiar
Cover Model: Daniel Macedo
Formatting: Champagne Book Design

For my grandparents,
My favorite stars in the sky.

I hope I make you proud.

For the second chances in life:
May we be brave enough to take them.

PART ONE

"Dwell on the beauty of life. Watch the stars, and see yourself running with them."

—*Marcus Aurelius*

ONE

Hailee

Eight Years Old

AIDEN WAS THE KIND OF KID WHO MADE IT EASY TO HATE HIM. "You can't do that!" I screeched at Aiden, annoyed with his stupid face. He'd reached his dirty hands back into the cookie jar with the cookies I'd baked with Mama for later that day. Mama had already given us each a cookie before we played in the backyard. After we came back in, Aiden snuck into the kitchen and climbed onto the countertop. He was breaking all the rules!

"I can do it if you'd shut your fat mouth, chipmunk cheeks!" he replied.

I huffed and puffed out my cheeks, feeling my face heat as my balled-up hands slammed against my waist. "I don't have chipmunk cheeks!"

"Then why do your cheeks look like a chipmunks?!"

"At least my face doesn't look like a gorilla's butt!"

"I'd rather look like a gorilla's butt than have chipmunk cheeks."

"I hate you, gorilla butt!"

"I don't care, chipmunk cheeks!" he shouted back.

Aiden Walters was a pain in my butt. He was always getting himself in trouble, and I was always trying to stop him from doing stupid stuff. Most of my day was spent telling him no, and most of his day was spent ignoring me.

I climbed up on the countertop next to him and yanked the cookie jar out of his hands. "At least my head isn't fat like yours!" I said, sticking my tongue out at him.

He grabbed the cookie jar back and slightly shoved me. "Your head is bigger than mine!"

"No, it's not!"

"Yes, it is! It's so big! It's bigger than an elephant's head!"

I grabbed the jar and tugged it toward me. "Shut up, Aiden!"

"You first, Hailee!" he shot back as he tugged it more.

We went back and forth with a tug-of-war, shouting at one another until Mama entered the kitchen.

"What's going on in here?!" she yelled.

Aiden and I both got so spooked by her voice that we let go of the cookie jar. It crashed to the ground and shattered into a million billion trillion pieces.

Aiden and I froze in place.

Our eyes darted to Mama.

Then to the broken cookie jar.

Then back to Mama.

Then back to the broken cookie jar.

"He did it!"

"She did it!"

We said it in unison as we pointed toward one another, blaming each other for the mess in front of us. Of course, it was Aiden's fault, but he was a big fat liar. I was surprised his pants weren't on fire by how many lies he told.

"I swear, Mama! It was him! He was trying to take more cookies, but I told him not to take more cookies, but still, he tried to take more, cookies, and and—"

"She called me a fat head, Penny, and said I have a face like a gorilla butt!" Aiden said, pushing out his bottom lip and letting his eyes glass over. *Oh my gosh! He's so dramatic!*

"He called me a fat mouth and said I had chipmunk cheeks!" I shot back. "I don't have chipmunk cheeks!"

"Do too!" Aiden mocked.

"Do not!"

"Do too!"

"Do not, not, not!"

"Do too, too, too, tooooooooo!" he sang.

For a boy who was the same age as me, he sure acted like a baby.

Mama didn't look like she cared for our excuses or bickering. She lowered her eyebrows and combed her hands over her afro puff before nodding once. "Get down now, the both of you. You know the drill."

Aiden and I both groaned. "But!" we screeched at the same time. I hated that we did things so much at the same time because the last thing I ever wanted was to be the same as someone like him. I hated our same moments. They made me so mad. Our different moments were the best because if I was different than him that meant I wasn't a fat head gorilla butt.

Mama brushed her hand against her forehead. "No buts. Come on, get down. Then to the living room. Hug-a-thon now." Mama waved her hand toward us both.

We climbed off the countertop and stomped our feet to the living room.

Mama saw a woman talk about a hug-a-thon thing she made her kids do on a talk show. Whenever her kids would get into a fight, she made them hug each other and apologize for whatever they did wrong. The kids had to hug until both apologized, no matter what.

I wished Mama didn't watch TV. It gave her bad ideas.

I hated hug-a-thons, and I always ended up having to do them with Aiden because he was a freaking jerk and always got me in trouble. If anything, Aiden should've been hugging himself. I wanted no part of this. I wasn't eating the cookies!

Still, we were forced to hug one another, and we grumbled the whole time.

When Aiden's mom, Laurie, came over, she noticed us hugging and smiled.

"Another fight?" Laurie questioned.

"You know it," Mama replied. "Just a regular Tom and Jerry over here."

"No apologies yet?"

"Not one."

Laurie glanced down at her watch. "Well, hurry up with it, Aiden, or you won't be able to make it to your acting class tonight."

"But Mom!" Aiden whined.

"No buts. Get on with it," his mom ordered. I liked Laurie, even though her son was a butthead. She always gave me candy when I went to her house and would ask me how my baking lessons were going with Mama.

"I'm sorry for calling you a name, Hailee," Aiden said. He didn't mean it, but he said it. He even seemed to mean it, too, which meant those stupid acting classes must've been working. That was why he almost cried about the cookie jar! Some stupid teacher taught him that trick!

Still, I smirked because he apologized first. Then I felt Mama poke me in the arm.

I grumbled. "I'm sorry for calling you a name, too, Aiden."

"There we go. Was that so hard?" Mama asked.

"Yes," we said at the same time. Another same moment. Gross.

We let go of our hug and dashed away from one another. Aiden and Laurie left to take him to his stupid acting class, and Mama and I made a batch of brownies later that night. They were the best brownies I'd ever made, and when I went to bed, I snuck one into my bedroom without Mama knowing.

I went to my window and looked across, where I saw Aiden sitting in his bedroom, too. I had the most annoying neighbor ever, and I hated that I had to look out my window and see his stupid face.

"Hey, loser!" I yelled.

He looked up and hurried over to the window. He had a grumpy look on his face. "What do you want, bigger loser?"

"Nothing from you, biggest loser!" I shot back.

"Then why did you call me over, huh?"

"Because I wanted to let you know you were a loser. And that I made the best brownies ever tonight, and you didn't get to try them." I held the brownie in the air and waved it around.

He narrowed his eyes. "Give me that!"

"Nope."

He climbed out of his window, snuck across the yard to my window, and climbed into my room. With haste, he snatched the brownie from my hand and hurried back over to his room, where he ate the brownie faster than ever.

Joke was on him, though, because I wanted him to try the brownie and tell me what he thought.

He looked back at me. "You're right," he said with crumbs all over his face. "That is the best brownie ever, and now you don't have it!"

"I hate you, Aiden Walters."

"I hate you, too, Hailee Jones."

I turned off my light and climbed into bed. He couldn't see it, but I was smiling in my bed, too, because Aiden liked my brownies, and even though I didn't want to care, I cared a little about what he thought.

Gorilla butt liked my brownies.

Cool.

TWO

Aiden

Ten Years Old

I COULDN'T BELIEVE HAILEE GOT MRS. ELK'S CLASS, TOO. NOW I didn't only have to look at her stupid self outside of my bedroom window all the time but I also had to sit in the same class with her for a whole year. That was Hailee overload. She was also in my second-grade class last year, and all I did was make stupid faces toward her because it bugged her. But now I was in third grade and didn't want to see her face anymore. Stupid Hailee and her stupid chipmunk cheeks.

When it was time for recess, the whole class headed outside. On our playground was a gigantic map of the United States, and Lars Thomas thought it would be fun to play a game where we'd break into two teams. We'd each get a number, and then he'd call out a number and a state, and each player from each team would have to dash to the state before the other player did.

Dashing States, he called it. It was a stupid name, but I liked to win games.

Hailee was on the opposite team of me. Good. I didn't need her being on the winning team. It made me happy when she wasn't winning.

I was number two. Hailee was number five.

Everyone knew two was better than five.

Lars called out my number and California.

Easy.

I dashed to California and landed there before Peter could even reach Texas.

I smirked as I walked back to the lineup. I gave Hailee a smug look from across the way, and she rolled her eyes. She was annoyed that I had won. I couldn't wait to be happy when she lost.

Lars cleared his throat. "Okay, number five get ready!"

Hailee's eyes narrowed, and she got into her power stance as if she was going to skyrocket to whatever state came out of his mind. Her opponent on my team was Kevin. Gosh, I hoped he crushed her so I could mock her about it forever.

Lars shouted out, "Mississippi!"

The two dashed off, and dang it, Hailee got to the state before him. She looked smug and proud at first. That didn't last long, though.

"She cheated! There's no way chubby hippo beat me there! She was on the wrong state!" Kevin stated as he went and shoved her hard, knocking her down to the ground. Hailee's hands slid across the concrete, and she scraped herself pretty bad.

I didn't know what hurt her more—Kevin's shove or his words.

Her eyes glassed over, and I was almost certain the tears were about to fall. Before they could, I tackled Kevin to the ground and started swinging my fist at the jerk's face. I got in lots of trouble for that, and my parents told me I couldn't use my fists to fight people. But they didn't see Hailee's eyes. They would've fought that jerk, too.

That night, I looked over to Hailee's bedroom from my window and threw a shoe at it to get her attention. "Hey! Hey, loser!" I shouted. She moved over to the window and opened it. I climbed out of mine and walked over to her.

"What do you want?" she asked. Her hand had Band-Aids on it from where she got cut up. I didn't know why, but that made my stomach hurt. If I could, I'd tackle stupid Kevin again for hurting her. I didn't like Hailee, but no one should've ever hurt her.

"Nothing," I muttered, scratching at the back of my neck.

"Then why did you throw a shoe at my window?"

"I didn't."

Her eyes darted to the grass, where my shoe was lying.

I kicked it behind me as if that would stop her from seeing it.

I huffed. "I just came to see if you were all right, okay?"

"Why do you care if I'm all right?"

"*I don't!*" I snapped, but my stomach still felt wound up. Why did I feel so angry? Hailee didn't even say any of her annoying stuff to make me upset. Still, I was mad. I think. I think I was mad. Sometimes I felt like my dad, and I didn't understand my emotions all that well.

"Okay," she replied. She didn't argue. She didn't call me a name. She simply went to close her window, and when my eyes met hers, she still looked sad. Like how sad she looked on the playground. That made me mad. Or sad. Or sad and mad.

"Hailee, wait," I said, stopping her from shutting the window.

"What?" she asked, short and direct.

I stared at her blankly.

I didn't know what to say.

I didn't know what to feel.

All I knew was I wanted to be by her that night, and I didn't know why.

"You're being weird," she told me.

"Am not."

"Are too."

"Am not!"

"Are too!"

"Whatever. Are you okay, though?" I questioned, rubbing my neck. "After what happened?"

Her eyes looked like she was going to cry again, and that made my stomach hurt even more. "I'm fine."

"Oh...okay. Well...I thought I'd just check."

"Okay."

"Okay."

"Good night."

"Night," I muttered. Turning away, I began walking back to my window.

"Hey, Aiden?"

I looked over my shoulder and saw Hailee wiping a few tears from her eyes, which made my eyes kind of sad, too. I didn't know seeing someone else's eyes sad could make mine sad, too. "Yes?"

"Do you think I'm a chubby hippo like Kevin said?"

I was going to rip that jerk's arms off at school tomorrow. Mark my words.

"No. Kevin is stupid and says stupid things because he's stupid. You're good, Hailee. You're not a chubby hippo."

"Promise?"

I nodded. "Promise." I shifted around in the grass, slid my hands into the pockets of my jeans, and shrugged my shoulders. "Some people might even think you're perfect."

She shook her head. "No one does."

"I'm sure someone does."

"Oh...okay."

"Okay."

"Okay."

"Hailee?"

"Yes?"

"Stop crying."

She shook her head. "I can't right now."

"Oh...okay."

"Okay."

"Okay." I cleared my throat. I didn't want to leave her crying alone, so I sighed and gestured toward the grass. "Wanna lay in the grass and count the stars? My mom and I do that sometimes."

She shrugged her shoulders and then agreed.

We lay down in the grass next to one another and didn't talk for a while. Then Hailee began counting. "One... two... three..."

"Four, five, six." I pointed toward the sky.

We got up to thirty-four before Hailee turned toward me. Her eyes didn't look as sad, which made my eyes feel less sad, too.

"You punched Kevin for me," she whispered.

"Yeah."

"You know what that means, right? It means we have to be friends now." She turned back to stare at the sky and pointed up. "Thirty-five."

"You already counted that star."

"No, I didn't."

"You did."

"Didn't!"

"Did!"

"Aiden!"

"What?"

"We're friends now, so you have to agree with me sometimes. Like it or not, that's what friends do."

I grumbled and rolled my eyes, then pointed at the sky at the same star Hailee was pointing toward. "Thirty-five."

THREE

Aiden

Twelve Years Old

I WAS FAMOUS.

Like, *really* famous.

Sure, some people probably thought that sounded dramatic, but what could I say? I was dramatic. And famous.

Did I mention how famous I'd become? Soon enough, I'd have a bodyguard following me around.

"Did you see the commercial?" I asked Hailee as we stood at the bus stop waiting to be picked up for school.

Recently, I landed my first acting commercial as a walking taco, and I was convinced that I was as famous as anyone could ever get at that point.

Hailee was grinning ear to ear, holding the straps of her backpack tightly. "My parents recorded it and played it repeatedly last night. You're famous."

I smirked and patted her two afro puffs. "If you want, I can give you my autograph later."

"That's okay. That would mean you would have to spell your name, and I know spelling isn't your strong point. Or reading. I'm actually surprised you were able to read the script."

"I had no lines in the commercial, so that made it easier."

"That makes sense, actually."

One thing about my best friend was that she was going to sass me. Yup, that was right. Over the past few years, the girl I grew up hating became my very best friend. We'd spent the past two years counting the stars between our two homes.

When we got to school, though, it was the opposite of that. Instead of people thinking I was some acting genius, they were mocking me, saying my dancing made it look like I was humping the bus in the commercial. They also called me the worst actor in the world.

By lunchtime, I found myself hiding in the custodial closet, crying my eyes out from embarrassment. It didn't take long for Hailee to track me down. Even when I didn't tell her where I was, she always kind of knew. I guessed that was what best friends were—people who knew where you'd be and showed up on your worst days.

She came into the closet and closed the door behind her. She didn't talk to me for a while. She just sat beside me and let me cry. I'd be embarrassed to cry in front of most people, but whenever I did with Hailee, she didn't say nothin' about it. Plus, I'd seen her shed a fair number of tears.

After a while, she turned to me and put a hand on my shoulder. "Do you know what my dad says about the critics when they talk about my mama's baking?"

"What?" I murmured, using my sleeve to wipe my snotty nose.

"Fuck them," she stated matter-of-factly.

My eyes widened. "You're not supposed to say that word."

"I didn't say it. My dad said it," she corrected as if that meant the words didn't come from her own mouth.

"But you said it when you were saying that he said it!"

She shrugged, unbothered. "My dad also said words are just words. It's how people use them that makes them good or bad. I wasn't using it in a bad way. I was using it in the way to make you feel better."

"Oh," I muttered.

"Well?"

"Well, what?"

"Did it work?"

"Did what work?"

"Do you feel better?"

"Oh." I shook my head. "No."

She frowned and scratched at her tight curly hair sitting high in two afro puffs. Sometimes, she complained because she didn't have straight hair like the other girls in our class, but that was because she had the best hair. She kind of had the best of everything, from her smile and curly hair like her mom's to her round nose and freckles like her dad. Hailee had the kind of looks that made it easy to look at her. Sometimes I'd find myself looking even when she didn't know I'd been.

She sighed from the realization that I still didn't feel better. "Well, do you want to know what my mama said?"

"Does it use the word fuck?"

She gasped. "You're not supposed to say that word!"

"*But you just said—!*"

"Mama says that first people laugh at you 'cuz they don't understand what you're doing. Then later, they'll be asking you how you did it, so you can't be mad that people don't get it yet. They're just slow."

"What if they don't ever get it?"

"Who cares? We don't like them anyway."

Fair point.

We sat quietly for a while, then she said, "I thought you were the best taco."

It turned out Hailee's opinion of me was the only one that mattered.

FOUR

Hailee

Sixteen Years Old

I KNEW WHAT LOVE WAS BECAUSE OF MY PARENTS. MY FATHER loved my mother in every single way possible, and she loved him the same. It was mutually a quiet love and a loud one. A stubborn love and a docile one. A wild love and a stable one. I grew up in a home blessed with an unconditional kind of love story. Over the years, I'd watched my parents transform in their lives, in their bodies, in their careers in a million different ways, yet the one constant was their admiration of one another.

My mother could gain fifty pounds, and my father still couldn't keep his hands off her. My father could be fired from a job, and Mama would still look at him as if he were the greatest provider in the world. And when each of them had a dream, the other was in their corner as their biggest cheerleader. They championed each other, even if it meant a little disappointment and discomfort in some areas at times. It was an equal love story—one where no one felt unappreciated.

I guessed that was where I got my idea of what it meant to love someone—from my parents.

I guessed that's why I was currently going to champion Aiden in his current situation—even if it meant a little disappointment and discomfort for myself.

"Los Angeles? For how long?" I questioned as Aiden and I sat in the frost-tipped grass wearing our sweatshirts and sweatpants. It was only September, but the cold found its way to Wisconsin. We were in that awkward in-between stage of Midwest seasons where it was freezing in the morning, you were a sweaty mess by midday, and the chills came back by nightfall. Aiden called it the hellhole. I couldn't disagree with that.

"It could be a few months, but they are saying probably over a year," he said.

Those few words broke my heart. Aiden had gotten the biggest acting opportunity of his career thus far. He would be starring in a television show, which would film in Burbank, California.

For over a year.

A year?!

Not to be dramatic, but then again, I was me, so I'd be a little dramatic, but a year without my best friend beside me felt like a lifetime. How would I manage going over three hundred and sixty-five days without him standing at the bus stop next to me? Without him sitting in the grass with me? Without him annoying the living crap out of me?

Who would I count the stars with?

I wanted to cry from the simple thought of it, but I wouldn't. I had to be excited for him, and I was excited. This was the biggest opportunity in the world for Aiden. He was already a part of the previous season of the series, but not as a reoccurring character. This was a huge deal for him. He'd worked hard for it and deserved everything coming his way.

Still…

I'd miss him.

People had many friends and such in life, but not me. I didn't have people. I had a person, and he was leaving our small town to go become a big star.

I knew this day would come. He was too talented, too gifted to not be the brightest star in Hollywood someday, but I wished he could've been in two places at once.

"I don't like saying nice things to you because I know how big your ego gets," I told him.

"Oh yeah, it's massive. And growing by the minute."

"I know. Your head is gigantic from the size of your cockiness. Regardless, just this once, I'll say this nice thing, and if you ever bring it up again, I'll punch you in your jugular."

"Noted."

My fingers fiddled with the frosted over grass, and I shrugged my shoulders. "I'm proud of you. You're going to do amazing things, and you're going to have a lot of fans and stuff, but I want you to know that I'll always be your biggest fan."

He smirked and narrowed his eyes. "Did my Hailee just get emotional?"

My Hailee.

Why did that phrase cause flutters in my chest?

I held up a fist and shook it. "Straight to the jugular, Aiden."

He tossed his hands up in defeat. "Fair enough."

Out of the two of us, Aiden was the more emotional one. I think it helped with his career to be in touch with his emotions. Me, on the other hand? Getting me to open up and be vulnerable was a challenge. We were opposites in so many ways. I was a type A personality. A planner with everything in life. Pie charts and stats were my love languages. Aiden, on the other hand, was a type B personality who went with the flow with any and everything. It drove me bonkers sometimes.

Don't get me wrong, I too could go with the flow. As long as I knew where the flow was flowing and the speed of the flow and the duration of said flow and how chaotic the flow could've been due to elemental equations and the pros and cons of the flow and why in the hell would anyone want to flow anyway when you could plan ahead and account for every mishap that could've happened beforehand?

Anyway. I was cool, calm, and collected. No big deal.

"You know what?" Aiden asked. "I think that's the nicest thing you've ever said to me. It must mean you're going to miss me."

Yes.

I am.

More than words.

I could cry right now thinking of you leaving me.

I rolled my eyes. "Missing is a dramatic term and a weak human emotion that keeps people from focusing on their lives."

Aiden smiled. "I'll miss you, too, Hails."

"When do you leave?" I asked.

"Tomorrow, actually."

Tomorrow?

As in…the day after today?

As in…within less than twenty-four hours?

As in… *Oh no.* My heart. It was starting to feel as if it was being ripped apart. First slowly, then all at a painfully quick speed.

So that was what heartbreak felt like. It amazed me how a heart could break so quietly when others were around. I see why some people avoided the sensation and chose not to love at all. Aiden hadn't even known as I sat in front of him that every piece of me was aching. That every piece of me was in the depths of sadness. I couldn't keep sitting there. If I did, I'd cry. If I cried, he'd feel bad. I didn't want him to feel bad because something great was happening to him. Still, it felt as if the best day of his life was my worst, and I wasn't certain how to deal with that.

Emotions and things. Yuck.

I stood from the grass, dusted off my semi-wet bottom, and started heading toward my window.

"Wait, where the heck are you going? We just got out here."

"I've got some homework to finish."

He cocked an eyebrow. "But…I just told you I'm leaving tomorrow."

"Yeah. I heard you."

"Don't you want to hang out or something? Before my big send-off in the morning?"

In the morning?

I didn't even get until the afternoon?

Tears. They were screaming to fall.

"It's fine, Aiden. Have a nice trip. I'll see you in a year."

"Hailee, wait—"

I didn't. I went into my bedroom, shut my window, closed my blinds, and I cried. Aiden pounded on my window for a little while and texted me repeatedly, but I didn't respond.

Aiden: I leave at seven in the morning. You better be there to say goodbye, Hails. See you in the morning.

When morning came, I still wasn't ready to say goodbye. Mama sat on the edge of my bed, and Dad leaned against my bedroom doorframe.

"You should go say goodbye, Hailee. They are going to pull out any minute now," Mama told me.

Dad nodded in agreement. "I saw them getting into the car."

"It's fine," I told them, hugging my pillow. "I'll see him when he gets back."

"Hailee..." Mama sighed. "You'll regret not getting that hug from him. He's your best friend."

Didn't she know that I knew that? I also knew that a final hug would feel like a final goodbye. After Aiden succeeded, which he would, he'd be given more opportunities and more reasons not to come back. He was leaving me with a wish and a prayer that we might be able to finish our senior year together.

I wasn't real keen on wishes and prayers—they didn't fit into my pie charts.

I listened as I heard the car next door start. My heart began pounding wildly against my chest. Dad walked into my bedroom and sat beside me. He looked like a giant linebacker who could've been the meanest person alive, but he was truly nothing but a big giant teddy bear. He was the gentlest man I'd ever known. From his brown eyes to his soft smile, my father oozed kindness.

"Hailee...Imagine if every time I headed to Los Angeles or around the world to film a movie, I didn't say goodbye to your mother. Don't you think that would hurt her?"

"Of course, it would."

"And wouldn't it make you sad if I never said goodbye to you?"

"Yeah..."

"So why would you do that to Aiden?"

I parted my lips to speak, but only a whisper came out as my voice shook. "I'm scared he might not come back."

"I get that fear. I'm not going to pretend that Aiden isn't insanely talented because he is, but still...he's your person. And you always say hello and goodbye to your person."

"Even when it's hard?"

"Especially when it's hard." Dad leaned in and kissed my forehead.

"You can do difficult things for love, sweetheart. The love is what makes it a little easier."

Love.

Was that what this was between Aiden and me?

Love?

I can do difficult things.

I rose from my bed as my heart pounded within my chest and then began running out of my bedroom, through the front door of my house, and as I stepped foot on the grass, I watched as Aiden's car began to drive down the street.

No.

I felt it as it happened—my heart shattered in my chest.

I broke out into a sprint in the middle of the street. I waved my hands around like a madwoman as I shouted his name. "Aiden! Aiden, wait!" I screamed. My lungs felt like they were inflamed, and my body ached because a runner was the last thing in the world I was. But I ran for him. I ran as fast as I could, pumping my arms, on the verge of tears. The moment I saw the car brake, I came to a stumbling halt as I slammed against the back of the car.

My breaths were erratic, and my heart was pounding against my rib cage as the back door of the car opened. Sweat dribbled down my forehead as I stood in my Nike sweatpants and sweatshirt.

Aiden climbed out of the car. The moment he saw me, he smirked. He placed his hands against his hips, and with his smug face, he said, "Did you just run down the street for me?"

I rolled my eyes, out of breath as my knees throbbed. It was no secret that I didn't have knees like Meg the Stallion. My knees were more like the ninety-three-year-olds down at the nursing home.

I crossed my sweaty arms. "Whatever, Aiden."

He stepped toward me. "Are you here to tell me you'll miss me?"

"What? No. I told you, missing is a dramatic term and a weak human emotion that—"

"Keeps people from focusing on their lives. Yeah, yeah, yeah. Blah, blah, blah." He bum-rushed me and wrapped his arms around me. He was so good at affection. Me, on the other hand? Not so much.

"Aiden, stop. I'm sweaty."

"Give me all your sweat, Hails."

"Let me go."

"Hug me back, and I will."

I sighed. "Okay, but only so you'll let me go." I hugged him back, and the way his hands landed on my back made me want to melt into every piece of him and not let him go.

"ILY," he whispered against my ear. He knew I wasn't good at expressing my feelings, so ILY was the closest we ever got to saying I love you.

Sometimes I felt broken. I came from parents who were so emotionally in-depth, and my best friend had been the same way. Yet, for some reason, I struggled with my feelings.

They never pressured me to speak up, though. They simply allowed me to be me, and they worked around my odd boundaries with ILYs.

"ILY, too," I whispered, blinking away the tears.

As he let go, I missed his embrace.

I missed him.

How could I miss someone who was still standing in front of me?

I rubbed the baby hairs on the back of my neck. "Aiden."

"Yes?"

"What if you get out there and you don't come back? What if you get out there and you change completely? What if Hollywood changes you for the worse?" I blubbered out on the verge of tears. Reality set in now as I saw his car packed up and the engine still running. He was really leaving for a year—if not longer. I was losing the best part of me.

Aiden smiled. "I knew you'd miss me."

"I'm serious, Aiden." I bit my bottom lip, trying to fight back the tears. "What if you get out there and forget who you are?"

"If I forget who I am, then I'll find my way back to you. I'm sure that will do the job."

"Promise you'll find me?"

"Promise."

I shot into his arms and wrapped him in one last hug. He seemed a bit shocked that I was the one to go in for the embrace, but he didn't fight it. Aiden thrived on physical touch. It was his happy place.

"Sorry, Hailee, but we have to get going if we're going to make our flight," Aiden's dad said, stepping out of the driver's seat.

Aiden squeezed me one more time. "We'll make a senior year bucket list, Hailee. I'll call you, and we'll write it out together. I'll be back. I promise."

"Don't make promises you can't keep."

He placed his hands on my shoulders. "I promise."

He headed back to the car and climbed inside. I stood in the middle of the street, watching him pull away. Heading back to my house, I found my parents waiting on the front porch. Mama frowned. "You need a hug, Hailee."

"No. I hate hugs."

"Yeah, we know. But…" Dad brushed his thumb against his nose and nodded. "Do you need a hug?"

Tears streamed down my cheeks, and I nodded slowly. "Okay. Just one."

FIVE

Aiden

Seventeen Years Old

Present Day

SAMUEL **W**ALTERS WANTED TO BE AN ACTOR ALL HIS LIFE, BUT things didn't go the way he'd hoped.

He spent most of his youth in California trying to build a name for himself in the industry. He survived by couch surfing and eating ramen noodles with his cousin, Jake, who liked to party a little more than chase his dreams. If there was trouble, Jake was determined to find his way to it. Still, Samuel was by his side throughout Jake's ups and downs in life. When Jake messed up, Samuel cleaned up his mistakes.

After one too many packs of ramen noodles, Samuel took a small break from his California life to move back to small-town Leeks, Wisconsin, to save up some money. His plan was to go back out to chase his dream, but it just so happened Samuel fell in love with a woman named Laurie. She was a beautiful, intelligent, compassionate woman. The L in Laurie's name mainly stood for loyal and love—the two traits she poured on Samuel throughout their story. Yet, at other times, that L stood for loss and loneliness. After suffering from a miscarriage, Laurie needed her partner by her side.

On his final trip to California, Samuel learned that Jake was having a son with a woman during a one-night stand. When the mother of said son gave up her rights at birth, and Jake knew he could never be the father a child could need, he asked Samuel and Laurie to adopt the little boy.

The only parents I'd ever known were Samuel and Laurie Walters, and Jake was the hot mess cousin who came to visit every now and again. When I was old enough to understand, my parents told me about Jake and my adoption. About how we were all family, but it just looked a little different than others. My biological mother's name and story were the only missing keys to my life.

So many parts of me reminded me of my father. Even though we didn't share the same blood, I was my father's son.

I, Aiden Walters, wanted to be an actor all my life, and things went the way I'd hoped.

I grew up watching all the classic films with my father. By age five, I could quote *Casablanca*. By age seven, I knew *It Happened One Night* inside out. When I was eight and told my dad I wanted to be an actor, he cried. To this day, I still couldn't tell if it was from happiness or sadness. Maybe a little bit of both. He always said he had to give up his acting dream to raise me, and even though he said he had no regrets, I could tell he saw his own dreams coming to life as my career took off. That was why he was so hands-on with my acting journey. He was determined to have it go the way he'd always wanted his to go. Which was why he was struggling with the current situation I'd presented him with.

My father appeared to be suffering from heatstroke even though we were sitting in a room with the air-conditioning blasting.

"Wait, wait, wait, time-out. Rewind. You just won an Emmy, Aiden," Dad remarked as he stormed around our rental apartment in Los Angeles. "An Emmy! Acting roles are flying in weekly for you. There are a lot of opportunities to take you to the next level. How did you decide this was the moment you wanted to take a break? No way."

"I actually think it's a great idea," Mom said as she sat beside me on the couch. "He's been working hard for almost a decade."

Dad grumbled. "But he just broke out, Laurie. There's a difference between working hard and succeeding. He's only now found success. Now's the time to dig our heels in before he rockets off to the next level."

"Or he can go back to Leeks and finish his senior year with his best friend. I'm sure that's important to him. Right, Aiden?"

Dad waved it off. "High school can be finished anywhere. Homeschooling has been working great this past year! He's a straight A student."

"It's not about the grades. It's about the experience," Mom argued. When it came to my work life or my mental health life, my mother was always going to choose the latter. "He can't go back and relive his senior year at school, but he can get other movie roles."

"I'll still fly back for movie auditions if I have to," I insisted. "And if a big role comes up, the role of my dreams, I'll take it, Dad. I just..." My voice began to shake because I saw the disappointment in his eyes. Eyes that I often dreamed looked like mine. "I, um, I..." I began to stutter as my words tangled in my throat. I combed my hands through my messy brown hair and tried not to sound like a rambling fool.

I had an unbelievably strong fear of letting my parents down. I felt myself breaking into a sweat as I tried to make my father understand my point of view. I hadn't even known why I was so nervous. It was just that while I was good at acting, it didn't mean I was happy with it. I felt sadder than someone with my level of success should've felt.

I oftentimes had a lot of thoughts that weren't worthy of being thought. In my emotion-based mind, they made sense, but logically? Most of the things I worried about were ridiculous.

That didn't mean I still didn't worry, though.

Worrying was one of my strongest traits, and hiding my worries from others was my second strongest. Half the time, people could be sitting right beside me, and they wouldn't have a clue I was in a full-blown panic attack.

I once got interviewed and was asked how I could dive so deeply and intimately into the mentally unstable character I was playing.

A part of me wanted to shout from the rooftops that it was easy to play myself in a role.

My father stared at me as if I were seconds away from ripping his heart out. Perhaps, I was.

Over the years, I had an irrational fear that if I let my parents down, they wouldn't love me anymore. It was an intrusive thought with no backing. I hated when those thoughts won. It felt as if you were beaten by your worst fears, which then, in turn, forced you to surrender to them. Logically, I knew my parents would never love me any less if I let them down. If anything, my mom made it clear she'd probably love me even more.

"He wants to be a kid for one last time, Samuel," Mom finished. "I support that decision. Frankly, you should, too. He's worked hard and should have a say in where his life goes next. Regardless of what you think, Aiden is going back to Leeks to finish the school year, and then we'll see what he wants to do next."

Okay, maybe one of my parents noticed my full-blown panic.

Only two people in my life could truly read me. Thankfully, my mother was one of them.

Mom was the most beautiful woman in the world. A stunning Black woman with auburn curls that reached her lower back. Her wide smile made everyone who received it smile in return. Mom's smiles felt like a blanket straight from the dryer—comforting and filled with warmth. Her brown eyes were packed with sincerity and love. When she laughed too hard, she'd hiccup. And when she felt her son shutting down? She'd speak up for him.

"What he wants to do next?" Dad asked in a fiery tone. "He has all the talent in the world to be the next big thing and the road to that is wide open right now. Do you know how many people would kill for this?"

"That doesn't mean it's right for him," Mom said.

He looked at me with a stern stare, but I saw a flash of sadness in his eyes. At that moment, I realized I wasn't living my dream—I was living my father's. Dad and Jake spent a lot of time out in California chasing their dreams of fame. A part of me knew he packed that dream up when I was adopted.

Sometimes I wondered if he was proud of me or envious. I wondered if pride and jealousy could've been roommates in a person's soul. The kind of roommates who fought every day and had no business being around one another.

He crossed his arms. "Do you not want to be an actor? After all this time? After all the sacrifices we've made?"

There it was—the overwhelming desire to go rock in a corner sitting in a puddle of my sweat.

"Don't guilt-trip him," Mom ordered. *Yeah, you tell him, Mom!* At least someone wasn't afraid to speak up.

"I'm not guilt-tripping. I'm asking. Aiden." He approached me. "Be upfront with me. Do you want to be an actor?"

The look in his eyes told me there was only one right answer. Only one answer would make the guilt and panic in my chest ease away. The one answer that wouldn't make me a disappointment in my father's eyes. His dreams, not mine. "Yeah, of course."

Dad sighed with relief. "See? He wants this."

Mom turned to me, tilting her head as she studied me, but remained silent. She knew I was lying, but she wouldn't go against my words.

"I just want to experience senior year for a short time. If a role comes, I'll leave. Dad, I'll stay on top of everything, my career and school. We can make this work."

Dad's brows lowered as his nose scrunched up before he finally surrendered. "The moment schooling interferes with your career, I'm pulling you."

That seemed backward for a parent to say, but I wasn't going to argue it. "Deal."

Right after I finished the talk with my parents, I headed to my bedroom, collapsed onto my bed, and pulled out my cell phone to send off a text message.

Aiden: Guess what?

Hailee: You met Timothée Chalamet and gave him my number?

Aiden: No.

Hailee: Oh. Then there's a very good chance I don't care.

That sounded about right. I skipped right past her snarky remark.

Aiden: I'm coming home for senior year. We can finish our high school to-do list.

At the beginning of our freshman year, Hailee and I created a list of things we wanted to complete in high school before graduation. Unfortunately, we'd only crossed off a few items since I missed a whole year with her. I had a lot of catching up to do with our list. The more I thought about heading home to be somewhat of a normal kid again with my best friend, the more excited I became.

Hailee: Are you really?

Aiden: Yup. I'll be back in the house next door in no time, annoying the living shit out of you.

The three ellipses appeared before disappearing, then showed up again, then disappeared, and did that repeatedly. Which meant Hailee was overthinking her message. My best friend was the master of typing and deleting her messages. She was probably debating on if she should be sassy or sweet. My favorite sweet and sour girl.

Aiden: No reply? Couldn't think of a clever way to sass me?

…

…

…

Hailee: Hurry up already, loser.

A little bit of sassy and a dash of sweet. The way I liked her the best.

SIX

Hailee

HE'S COMING HOME TODAY! *HE'S COMING HOME TODAY!*
Today was the day I got my best friend back. It was almost time for Aiden's arrival, and I was ecstatic. Though, I was trying my best to play it cool.

I kept staring at the clock in my bedroom as if my intense stares would speed up time. Unfortunately, I didn't unlock some hidden superpower of mine, and the clock continued ticking on its own timeline.

Fifteen more minutes.

He'd be home in fifteen more minutes.

The way he was cutting it close by returning to Leeks the day before our senior year stressed me all the way out. But at least he would be home in fifteen—correction, fourteen—minutes.

I'd even had him send me the link to his current location so I could track his drive from the airport all the way home.

I hopped out of my bedroom and dashed to the kitchen as a timer went off, where I had double chocolate chip cookies made for him. There was also a lemon pound cake, a dozen brownies, and oatmeal cookies sitting on the counter. I made all of Aiden's favorites as a 'welcome back, best friend, if you ever leave me again for as long as you did, you'll have hell to pay' treat. I pulled the apple crisp from the oven and set it on the counter.

Did I make too many things?

Yes.

Did I care?

Not at all.

Baking calmed my nerves. Whenever I was overly anxious or overly excited, I found myself in the kitchen whipping something up. I got that trait from Mama. She was the best baker in town, from weddings to baptisms to dog birthday parties. If there was an event, Mama was the one baking all the sweets. She was so close to opening her own bakery with Dad, too. He was the brain behind the endeavor, and Mama was the soul. They worked together like coffee and creamer—just the perfect blend of not too sweet and not too bitter.

We'd even spotted a location in the town square for the shop. I was certain that was where I'd spend a lot of my afternoons helping the family out, but that was a story for another time.

I glanced at the clock on the microwave as I took off the oven mitts.

Twelve minutes.

I was sweating bullets.

Why did I feel nervous? I shouldn't have been nervous. My armpits were drenched, making my white T-shirt equally soaked. I dashed to my bedroom, ripped off my shirt, hopped into my bathroom, bathed my pits in deodorant, then slipped into yet another shirt that I hoped I wouldn't sweat my way through. I checked myself in the mirror and saw every piece of my mother resting against my face, from her brown almond-shaped eyes to her button nose. Our skin was golden brown, which Mama swore made us glow like goddesses in the sun, and our natural hair—well, that differed a bit. Mama's natural curls were always packed with moisture and care. They dangled perfectly down to her bra strap, each one defined and healthy. Mine always became a big, dried-out afro puff because I preferred binge-watching movies on my weekends instead of doing all-day natural hair care routines.

That day, though, I did put some effort into my hair and made two afro puffs. I must've been feeling feisty.

I patted my puffs and shrugged. Good enough.

Each minute seemed to inch by as I lay on my bed, holding my phone over my face, watching as Aiden's proximity grew closer and closer. When it said he was right down the street, I screeched with excitement, skyrocketed from my bed, then dashed to the front door yelling, "He's here! He's here!" so the whole house—also known as my parents—would know.

I booked my way to the front porch right as Aiden's dad pulled the car into their driveway directly next door. I wasn't much of a runner, but you'd think I was running for the Olympics when I made it over to the car. Aiden opened the door and had his big goofy smile on. I didn't even get a chance to really take him in because I dashed into his arms, pulling him into the biggest hug.

As he hugged me back, I noticed his hug felt a little bit different. My hands fell against his chest.

What was that?

Was that...? Did he...?

Is that a six-pack of abs?!

I pulled back away from him, completely thrown off as I studied Aiden. My Aiden! My best friend! A sun-kissed tan on his normally pale body. Contact lenses over his ocean-blue eyes. Arms the size of Marvel superheroes.

Oh. My. Freaking. Gosh.

No. Way.

He got hot!

I slammed my hand against his chest as my excitement shifted into an unexplainable fury. "What the hell?" I spat out. Don't get me wrong, I knew he'd been getting into shape. We'd video chatted, and I saw him on television, but seeing him in person? Feeling him in person? He was a completely different person than when I last saw him.

He laughed.

I didn't.

"Great to see you, too, Hailee," he remarked. "It's good to be home."

Was...was his voice deeper than it sounded on the phone? Who was that man standing in front of me? Where was my best friend?

I clenched my teeth and wrapped my hands around his giant biceps as I released a low growl. *"What did you do?"*

I spent the remainder of the night annoyed, giving him the silent treatment.

Because how dare he do this to me.

How dare he come home looking like *that*.

"You couldn't try harder to look unbothered if you wanted to," Aiden mocked as he walked over to the bus stop the next morning for our first day of school. We hadn't been on speaking terms ever since he'd betrayed me in the most lethal way.

My best friend got hot.

Like *hot-hot*.

I didn't know how it happened, but somehow over the past year, Aiden had transformed from the chubby boy he'd been all our lives into some superhero-type guy. He was tan and had muscles that could convince any person he'd been eating only chicken breasts for the past year while lifting SUVs for fun.

Aiden went to California for over a year to work on a television series, and he came back extremely fit and attractive, which was so freaking annoying. Sure, even before his time away, he'd had some great acting opportunities, but he always came back looking like himself—a bit dorky and a bit chubby in all the right places. He and I were one and the same in that way—both dorks and both chubs. It was our thing! Dorky Chub #1 and Dorky Chub #2.

We'd had an arrangement, and he went against it the day he decided he wanted to come back home from his year in Hollywood looking like that. Our agreement was a simple unspoken one: remain unattractive throughout our high school years so we wouldn't be unattractive alone. Then we'd spend our twenties entering our "glow-up" phase. Aiden hated the term glow-up, which was precisely why I used it religiously to annoy him.

Instead of sticking to our ugly phase, Aiden spent the year falling into his prime steak on a Saturday night at a small-town supper club era, and he became unnaturally good looking like the Hollywood star he was quickly becoming.

What a jerk.

All I gained over the past year was thirty pounds and social anxiety. I did start going to the gym with my dad for the past few months to lift weights, but I didn't get the same results as Hercules over there. Weightlifting helped more with my anxiety and less with my weight. It was what I did when I felt lonely. When I missed my best friend. It also made me feel somewhat like a badass, which was an added perk. But it was clear that Aiden's and my diet were quite different.

Aiden was also taller than when he left me. I knew it to be true because when he hugged me before he left, I'd be able to place my forehead against his cheeks. Now, when we hugged, his chin pressed against the top of my head.

Or maybe he simply stood taller because confidence did that to a person.

Were his eyes bluer, too? Gosh, I missed his blue eyes. At least those didn't gain biceps.

Aiden cocked an eyebrow. "Are you still giving me the silent treatment?" he asked, nudging me in the arm.

I stepped to my right and turned my body away from him. He'd been back in town for almost twelve hours now, and I hadn't said a word to him since I'd seen how he went from looking like Steve Rogers pre-experimental serum from the government to Captain freaking America!!

The freaking nerve!

"Come on, Jerry," he egged on as he began tapping his hand against my arm.

I whipped myself away from his reach. "Don't call me Jerry. Only my best friend calls me Jerry, and you are not my best friend anymore."

Was I being childish? Yes. Was I being overly dramatic? Also yes.

"Don't be dramatic," he scolded.

"You've known me for seventeen years. Dramatic is all I've ever been. I mean, seriously, Tom, this is our senior year. You were supposed to come back chunky with no remorse because since you've been gone, I found twenty-five extra pounds to carry around. You weren't supposed to come back looking like that!"

Thirty extra pounds.

I didn't know why I told him twenty-five.

The subtraction of that extra five pounds made me feel a little better about myself. Mama said a number on a scale didn't define a person, but boy, oh boy, some days, it felt like the only thing defining my existence.

Aiden was smirking ear to ear, beaming with pride.

"Why the smirk?" I grumbled.

"Nothing, it's just… You called me Tom."

Oh crap.

I huffed. "I didn't mean it."

"You did. You meant it because no matter how annoyed you are with my increasingly good looks and toned body, you still consider me the Tom to your Jerry."

"All I'm saying is we had an unwritten rule to come back for our senior year looking fat and ugly, and you failed."

"Not to be the bearer of bad news, but you failed at both of those things, too."

A smile slipped out of me, knocking my stubbornness sideways.

Sweet jerk.

I couldn't stand that man, who I'd stupidly missed more than words over the past year. When we were kids, our moms always called Aiden and me Tom and Jerry because we were always chasing each other back and forth day and night like the classic cat and mouse cartoon. We were glued to one another's hips growing up. He was my Tom; I was his Jerry. We even wore friendship necklaces for it. He wore me around his neck, a little mouse. And I wore him around mine, a feisty cat. Corny? Yes. Us? Completely.

He'd even accepted his Emmy award wearing said necklace. That made me smile.

"Okay, well, if we're going to start our senior year hating one another, at least let me tell you that I missed your bad attitude," Aiden said. His dark brown hair was smoothed back, highlighting his waves. When did the guy start using hair gel? And was that sweet, earthy, oak scent coming from him? What did those Californians do to my best friend? I hated it because, well, I kind of loved it, and it was messing with my head that I loved the changes. My heart was pounding aggressively against my rib cage, and I didn't know why.

"Whatever." I gave him a hard look and shrugged. "I missed you, too."

"Handshake?"

"Aiden, we're seniors now. We can't go around doing our corny handshakes anymore." He began wiggling his fingers in my direction, and I groaned. "Seriously, Aiden. We made that up when we were nine. We need to let it go."

Still ignoring me, he put his hand out in front of him, palm facing me, and began the chant. "Pancake, pancake, up real high."

Without hesitation, I joined in patting my hand against his. "If you toss it, it will fly."

He smacked the back of his hand against mine three times. "If you drop it, it will go."

We both spun once, then faced one another, patted hands, and did a weird body roll as we said, "Down the drains where the creepy clown flows."

When we were kids, we had a sleepover at my parents' house on Halloween, and when it was time for us to go to bed, we snuck downstairs and watched *IT*. Ever since then, we had a thing for creepy clowns, horror movies, and corny handshakes.

The obnoxiously loud pale-yellow school bus hiccupped and skirted in our direction. I silently thanked myself that it would be my last year of riding the banana train to hell.

"Aren't you a famous actor now? Shouldn't you be driving us to school in a Mercedes-Benz or something?" I asked.

"My parents said the same thing, but I wanted to experience the whole school package one last time. You know, one for the road."

"You're a really weird person."

"Says my best friend."

Fair enough.

I climbed the steps of the school bus and took a seat beside the window. Within seconds, I knew it would be an odd year because those on the bus already began whispering about the handsome creature taking Herculean strides behind me.

"Oh my gosh, is that Aiden?"

"No way! He's a total babe!"

"I wonder if he's single?"

"I saw his show a few days ago!"

"He's famous! Did you see his interview with Jacob Elordi?"

"I wonder if he knows Zendaya."

"Is he really going to sit next to Hailee? They can't still be friends, right?"

Great. Just great. I'd prided myself in flying under the radar of other students for the past three years of my high school career. People knew of me, but I wasn't enough of a topic to make fun of or a cool enough person to acknowledge. I was an average Jane, which was fine and dandy in my book. Aiden, pre-Captain America glow up, was underrated in terms of popularity, too.

Now, though? Now they were looking at his double B's—butt and biceps.

Aiden sat beside me, acting completely unaware of the gossiping that was taking place because of his new persona.

He dug into his backpack and pulled out his school schedule as the bus drove off to the next stop. "Swap," he ordered, passing his paper to me. I dug into my backpack, grabbed my schedule, and handed it over to him.

"Oh man, you have crazy Mr. Dom for AP chemistry," Aiden remarked. "With your smart self."

"Says the boy in advanced drawing class." There was almost nothing that Aiden couldn't do, but his ability to draw was just as great as his ability to act. I would even go as far as saying his drawing skills were better than his acting—which was saying a lot. "Also, I find it funny you're in Acting 101."

"Why is that funny?"

I stared at him as if he were insane. "You have a freaking Emmy sitting on your mother's mantel." I swore, sometimes it was as if Aiden didn't realize he was Aiden Walters—Hollywood's next big thing.

"It's just a piece of metal. A million unknown people out there are better at acting than I am but will never get the opportunities I got. Winning an Emmy doesn't really mean anything at all."

"That sounds exactly like the response an Emmy winner would give in order not to sound cocky."

He smirked. "Did it work?"

"Almost."

"I'll keep practicing the speech, then."

"Maybe they can help you in Acting 101," I joked.

By the time Aiden was ten, he'd had a nationwide commercial. By fourteen, he'd starred in three movies, and by seventeen, he had done a television series and received the Emmy. It was no shock that Aiden was Hollywood's newest sweetheart. After spending five minutes with him, everyone fell in love with the guy.

I couldn't blame them. My best friend was like a puppy—ridiculously lovable.

Aiden's eyes darted across the page, and the gleam in his eyes dissipated as he read further into my classes. "We don't have one class together. We don't even have the same lunch period! You're lunch A, and I'm B."

I shrugged. "That's okay."

"That is not okay. How are we not supposed to eat lunch together?"

"Uh, we did it for the past year."

"That was because five billion miles were keeping us apart. Now, it's unacceptable. It's our senior year of high school. I need to have lunch with you for our senior year."

"It's not a big deal."

"Oh, it is. The administration is going to hear from me. Mark your words."

"You mean, mark *my* words."

"That's what I said. Mark your words."

I shook my head. "No. That's not the saying."

"Whatever. Your words are my words; my words are yours."

I rolled my eyes as I leaned against the window. "You have too much energy for seven o'clock in the morning."

"If that's your way of saying you missed me, I missed you, too."

Once we walked into Satan's dungeon, everyone noticed Aiden. He was determined to have a typical senior year before his career exploded even more, which it would without a doubt, but it was clear that nothing about this last year of school would be normal. All eyes were on him.

We were separated early on, but the echoes of people talking about his transformation and his Hollywood success were ridiculous. Just a few years ago, they were mocking him about his dancing taco commercial, but now that he was on the cover of magazines and hanging out with Marvel actors, they were his biggest fans? What a bunch of crappy hypocrites. Sweet Aiden would've welcomed their fake kindness, too. That boy was too wonderful to know when people weren't being genuine. He was the definition of a golden retriever. Loyal to a fault to any and everyone who smiled his way. If he had a tail, that thing would've fallen off from wagging with excitement.

A pit sat in my stomach as I headed to the bathroom before first hour. The popular girls were giggling in the bathroom about Aiden, and I hated the idea of them getting their manicured hands anywhere near him.

The intercom screeched in first hour, reminding us of our broken-down school equipment. Principal Warren's voice broke through the scratchy sounds with the morning announcements, and he welcomed us all back for yet another year of being told to sit down and shut up.

"Last, I want to welcome back Leeks' own Emmy-winning actor, Aiden Walters, to school. We are excited to have his return. Make sure you all stream his Emmy-winning television show *Forgotten* when you get home tonight. Welcome back to school, everyone. Here's to a new year!"

Intercom speeches about my best friend? Normal was the opposite of what our senior year was about to become.

SEVEN

Hailee

I HATED LUNCHTIME. IF I HAD IT MY WAY, SCHOOL WOULD'VE SKIPPED past lunch period and allowed us to get out of prison an hour earlier. Instead, I was left in a cafeteria packed with people I knew but didn't really know, surrounded by individuals who all seemed to have friends to sit with, unlike me.

Ever since I gained weight, I felt even more self-aware when it came time to eat in front of other people. It was almost as if I'd become obsessed with eating things I didn't want to eat because I didn't want others to comment on my choices.

"We should've gotten here sooner. It looks like this chick's gonna take all the food," someone behind me joked. I didn't look back at them. I didn't know who it was, and I wasn't even sure they were talking about me, but I felt as if they were. They had to be talking about me. My thighs rubbed together when I walked. A tire of pudginess that unfolded from the top of my jeans whenever I sat down, which made at least one of my arms always rest against said bulge whenever I sat. Even oversized T-shirts didn't hide the beast.

My hands were clammy around the dull, brown plastic tray that shook in my grip from the unwanted attention.

"Will you just shut up, Robby? I told you, I'm PMSing," a girl's voice replied. I glanced back to see Hilary was the one who the guys were joking about taking all the food.

Well, hell. If her guy friends were bullying her about her diet when she was slim, then I was a hopeless case. All I had to do was try my best not to draw attention to myself.

Sit down. Eat quietly. And don't make a—

"Hailee Jones! Behold!" someone hollered.

My heart shot up to my throat.

I turned to see Aiden standing a few feet away from me, holding a piece of paper up in the air. "I took my grievances to the top tier of authority, and I am officially in lunch A. Victory is ours!" he shouted before he began to hip thrust the air, dancing poorly, reminding me that even though Aiden was famous as heck by society standards, he was still, in fact, my Aiden.

My bad dancing, over-the-top Aiden.

My favorite dancing taco.

I couldn't wait to have lunch with him for one hundred and eighty more days.

"I can't believe you had them change your whole schedule so we'd eat dog food together," I joked as Aiden walked over to join me at our table after getting his food. It was insane how my comfort level shifted the moment I spotted him.

"I refuse to spend my senior year not interacting with my best friend throughout the day. You're the whole reason I wanted to have a senior year. We also have last period study hall together now, too."

I smiled. "We're not allowed to talk in study halls."

"As if we aren't close enough to be able to talk without using words. Like right now." He sat straight and narrowed his eyes at me. "What am I thinking?"

"Nothing."

He tossed his hands up in the air. "See?! You know me."

I snickered, shaking my head. The more he sat with me, the more relaxed I became. All the nerves that I felt before when Aiden wasn't with me had evaporated and turned into joy. Only Aiden had the ability to take my nerves and flip them sideways.

"So should we check the high school bucket list? See what else we have left?" he asked, shoving his chicken patty into his mouth.

I shifted in my seat and nodded. "Yes." I reached into my backpack and pulled out my notebook. I flipped to the first page, where the list existed.

Tom & Jerry's Ultimate High School Bucket List

We'd created the list of goals for our high school experience, and we've made a pretty good dent in them.

- ~~Get on the honor roll for at least two years~~
- ~~Enter the school talent show and lose~~
- ~~Dress up for a full spirit week no matter how corny it is~~
- Both get into a relationship
- Have a Ferris Bueller Day of skipping school
- Have your first kiss
- ~~Dress up for Halloween~~
- Go to a high school party
- Lose our V card
- Aiden introduces Hailee to Timothée Chalamet

The last one was a new edition, but a worthy one.

So far, we'd nailed the nerdy honor roll goal for the past three years. During our sophomore year, when no one really knew who we were, we performed during the talent show and sang "Total Eclipse of the Heart" by Bonnie Tyler—and lost. Check, check. We'd dressed up for spirit week, even during the week when we weren't together, and we FaceTimed our outfits to one another. Check, check, check.

He arched an eyebrow. "So we are both still lip virgins?"

"You kissed that Samuela Lee in that show."

"That was acting. It doesn't count."

"It definitely counts."

"No, I'm talking about a real first kiss. The kind you remember forever. I don't even remember the Samuela kiss."

"Go watch the show on any streaming service. I'm sure you'll recall it."

"Jerry," he groaned.

"Tom," I replied.

"I switched my schedule to eat lunch with you. You can at least give me this."

With a dramatic sigh, I agreed. "Fine. Neither of us has had a first kiss. I'm sure it won't be much of a challenge for you to get a girlfriend this year," I grumbled as girls kept walking past and whispering about Aiden. It didn't shock me that he was so unaware of the attention these girls were giving him. Aiden had never had much attention from the opposite sex up until now, so he probably assumed they were talking about someone else.

My sweet, naïve, idiot of a best friend.

Soon enough, girls would be lining up to kiss him.

"We also have to pick out our Halloween costume," I said. "Last year was sad because we couldn't do themed costumes together. And since this is our last year, we must go all out. I was thinking a badass duo or—"

"Hey there, Hailee. I haven't seen you all day!" a voice said, cutting into the conversation. I looked up to see Carlton walking our way, and the happiness on Aiden's face evaporated and shifted to confusion as Carlton walked up to our lunch table.

Carlton wore his thick-framed lime-green glasses, vibrant orange Adidas jumpsuit, and red Converse. He was also rocking a cheap gold chain that he probably got from a Run DMC costume. For lack of a better word, he was weird. Not that weird was a bad thing. I was weird, too, in my own ways.

He was the oddball who did extremely embarrassing things in front of people just for attention. He had a strange desire to be liked by the popular kids, but he was so out there that any popular person was simply using him to get a laugh. They didn't respect him at all. He dressed ridiculously every day and would tell terrible jokes as if he was a sixty-year-old dad. People would laugh, but he never realized they were laughing at him, not with him.

Surprisingly, when Aiden was away, Carlton made me laugh at his stupid jokes. If it wasn't for him and his weirdness, last year would've been that much lonelier for me. Unlike others, I laughed with Carlton, not at him.

I sat straight. "Carlton. Hey. I thought you had a different lunch period?" I said, feeling the tension in the space, or maybe it was just my anxiety-ridden mind. Wait, no. Aiden was shooting daggers toward Carlton.

"I did, but I wanted to switch lunch periods to be able to eat with you." He looked toward Aiden. "Even though it seems you already have a lunch buddy."

"Oh no. There's room for all of us," I said, patting the spot to my left. "Right, Aiden?"

Aiden didn't say a word. His brows were arched in a perplexed way.

I kicked him under the table, and he snapped out of it, clearing his throat. "Yeah, totally. Sit," he muttered, still a bit baffled.

Carlton didn't even pick up on Aiden's confusion. He sat and began talking nonstop about whatever came to mind. After his random ramblings that didn't really connect, he looked over at the notebook.

"What's that?" he asked.

Aiden shut our bucket list and shoved it into his backpack. "Nothing."

"We were trying to decide on our Halloween costumes for this year," I said to Carlton.

"Oh! Sweet! We should totally do a triplet costume or something."

Aiden shook his head. "It's a Hailee and me thing."

"It was a Hailee and me thing last year. I was Superman, and she was Wonder Woman."

Aiden shot me a stunned look before he leaned over to whisper to me. "You dressed up with him last year? Why didn't you tell me you dressed up with him last year? Since when are you and Carlton friendly-friendly?"

"It just so happened we showed up that way. We didn't plan it. And we're friendly-friendly since last year when my best friend left me alone with the wolves," I whispered back. "Play nice."

"Your wish is my command," Aiden stated, still baffled but going along with it.

Before the conversation could expand, Cara, the homecoming queen for three years running, came bouncing over to our table. She'd been Aiden's ultimate crush for the past seven years. She slid onto the bench right beside Aiden and flipped her hair over her shoulders. Then she batted her long eyelashes at my best friend.

"Hi, Aiden," she sang as if her interaction with him was the most normal thing in the world. It should be noted that Cara, Aiden, and I have been in the same classes since kindergarten, and Cara Simmons had never made it a point to converse with either of us. She was always too good to talk to people outside her friend group—at least that was how it read to me.

Aiden must've felt the same oddity from the situation because his eyebrow cocked up high, and his voice stayed low. "Uh, hi?" he said in a questioning tone. "What's up?"

"Nothing. It's so good to be back in school, isn't it? Speaking of school, we missed you last year," she said.

I'm sorry, we?

We?!

We missed who?

Who is this we you're speaking of?!

The nerve.

"Uh, yeah. Thanks?" he said, confused.

Carlton and I sat frozen in place, unsure of what we were supposed to do. Did Cara even notice us? Doubtful. We weren't hot, popular, or rich enough to be on her radar.

"Welcome." She smiled, and her dimples deepened as she crossed her legs and leaned in closer to Aiden. "So I'm having a party next weekend."

Aiden nodded. "Cool."

"You should come," she said nonchalantly.

"Who, me?" he asked, pointing at himself.

"Yes, silly, of course." She poked his chest with her finger, and his skin didn't bounce back a lick. All rock-hard body. I probably stared too long at his chest in amazement.

"Give me your cell phone," she ordered, holding her hand out toward him. He didn't because I think he was stunned at the unfolding situation.

"Aiden"—Cara snapped her fingers—"your phone."

He shook his head, coming back to reality, and grabbed his phone. He placed it in her perfectly manicured hands, and she gladly typed her cell phone number into his contacts.

Then she placed it back in his grip, stood from the table, and gave him her teeth-whitening-commercial perfect smile. "Okay! See you Saturday. Normally, it's bring your own booze, but don't worry. I have a

VIP section with your name all over it." She winked at him before bouncing away. No, really. She bounced.

Our table of three stayed quiet.

Our eyes darted back and forth with one another until Carlton said, "So was that a group invite, or…?"

It wasn't a group invite. Carlton and I weren't famous enough.

After school, I found Aiden surrounded by people at his locker. He was smiling and talking up a storm, but I saw the slight trembling in his hand as he tapped his pinkie finger against his leg. His invisible golden retriever tail was not wagging. It was between his legs.

I went into full-blown bodyguard mode. I dashed toward him, breaking through the sea of bodies. I wrapped a stern hand around his wrist and pulled him around the corner, yanking him away from the crowd. I slung the janitor closet open and pushed him inside, shutting the door behind us. I pulled the dangling string attached to the light on the ceiling and lit up the space.

"What are you doing?" he asked.

"Saving you."

"What?"

"You're having a panic attack."

He blinked a few times, looked down at his trembling hands, and nodded. "Oh."

I knew my best friend inside and out. I knew when he felt overwhelmed by such small changes in his body language. Most people missed his slight transitions, but I could read that man like a book. He was my favorite novel. One I'd repeatedly reread if given the chance.

"You don't owe these people any part of you, Aiden."

"They're being nice."

"They're being gremlins who are trying to suck you dry. Stop talking. It doesn't help. Just breathe."

He lowered his head, and I took his shaky hand into mine to steady it. We stayed there for ten minutes, not talking. Sometimes words didn't help a situation. Sometimes you just have to let time pass on by.

"We're going to miss the bus home," he mentioned.

"It's fine. We can walk. Look at me."

His blue eyes rose, and they didn't look as overwhelmed anymore. He was coming down from the intensity of being bombarded by people all day long.

"You're good," I told him.

"I'm good." He cleared his throat and brushed his hand against the side of his face. "Can I walk you home now?"

I nodded.

He held the door open for me, and after I stepped out of the closet, he followed.

"I know you're too nice to tell people to leave you alone, so I just want you to give me permission to throat punch anyone who crosses your boundaries," I said.

"I don't think throat punches are needed."

I frowned and patted him on the back. "I know. That's because you're painfully sweet."

"Are you really good friends with Carlton?" he asked me out of nowhere.

I raised an eyebrow. "Yeah. He's nice."

"Is he? Or were you just lonely last year?"

"What's that supposed to mean?"

He shrugged. "He just rubs me the wrong way. He's always trying too hard to win people's approval. Do you know after lunch, he tracked me down to offer me money if I'd get him into Cara's party? It's weird."

"He's quirky."

"There's quirky, and then there's desperate. He also has a crush on you."

"What?" I laughed. "He does not."

"Yes, he does."

"How do you know that?"

"Because not only did he try to pay me for a party invite, but he went on and on about how he was into you."

It almost amazed me how the idea of Carlton didn't make my emotions do anything at all, but if Aiden's arm brushed against mine? Butterflies. Every single butterfly.

I shook my head. "Boys don't have crushes on me."

"What? Why would you say that?"

"Because I'm me."

"That's exactly why Carlton likes you. Because you're you."

I shrugged. "He's not my type."

"Oh? And what exactly is your type?"

You.

Then you.

And maybe, on Sundays, you.

Whoa.

Where did those thoughts come from?

The palms of my hands grew sweatier, and I clenched them into fists as I said, "I told you. Timothée Chalamet."

He smirked, and I felt his smile deep within my heartbeats. "That's it? No one else?"

"Nope." I picked up my pace as I tried my best to shake off my nerves. I couldn't look him in the eyes because he could read me the same way I was able to read him. I couldn't allow him to take in the new development chapter about the odd sensations I felt whenever he stood around me.

Besides, whatever I was feeling for Aiden was a temporary thing. It had to be. He was my best friend, after all, and I would never want to jeopardize that by, oh, I don't know, falling in love with him.

Still, I thought about it a little. Okay, I thought about it a lot. I thought about what it would be like to fall in love with a guy like Aiden. They were pointless thoughts, though. I'd read enough romance novels in my life to know how those things went.

Guys like Aiden ended up with girls like Cara. Never with girls like me. I was forever going to be the best friend side character, while Cara received my leading hero.

Aiden upped his pace to keep up with my strides. "So about that party…"

EIGHT

Aiden

"**T**HERE'S NO WAY IN HEAVEN, EARTH, OR HELL I'M ATTENDING that party," Hailee said as we walked home. It was quite a bizarre first day for me. The number of photographs people asked me to take with them—teachers included—was odd. My jaw hurt from smiling so much. It was even odder that I was being asked by the people who mocked my first acting ventures when I was a dancing taco.

I vividly remembered hiding in the custodial closet and sobbing my eyes out from being bullied. Hailee was the one who found me, and she skipped the rest of her classes to sit with me in said closet. The only time she left was to go get us some lunch. By the end of the day, she had me laughing again, too, because Hailee had a way of making shitty days less shitty.

Now those same bullies were asking for my autograph. Life was odd. People were odder.

The one consistent thing? Hailee Jones saving me from the masses and pulling me into closets to remind me to breathe.

I gripped the straps of my backpack. "What? Why not? It's on our bucket list."

"I figured that would be one of the items we wouldn't achieve."

"But we will! We got a clear as day invite."

"*We*?!" she remarked. "That was definitely a solo invite."

I paused, pulled out my cell phone, and began texting.

"What are you doing?" she asked.

My phone dinged, and I smiled as I held the phone in her face.

Aiden: Can I bring a friend to the party, too?

Cara: Sure! Bring whoever you want.

Hailee rolled her eyes. She was a Master of Fine Arts when it came to her eye rolling. Her skill was unmatched. "She doesn't know that the friend is me. It wasn't as if I was personally invited."

"Of course, she knows it's you." I wrapped my arm around Hailee's shoulders and pulled her into a sideways hug. "You're the only friend I've got."

Being back in my hometown felt better than I thought it would feel. For the first time in a while, I felt like myself again. From the outside looking in, I had everything when it came to my acting career. From the inside looking out, I felt empty. Coming home was the first thing that made me feel like somehow everything would be all right.

I had a few secrets that had been eating at me since I'd gotten back to Leeks, secrets that I wanted to reveal sooner than later, but I wasn't exactly sure how to go about it. Two secrets that would undoubtedly change everything for me.

Secret number one: I didn't want to be an actor anymore. Being away from home for a whole year came with a heavy dose of homesickness that I didn't expect. Sure, before the past year, I'd filmed things for a few months here and there, but being gone for such a long time was a lot harder on me than I thought. I missed my normal life. I missed my family and Hailee.

Which brought me to secret number two: I. Missed. Hailee.

Throughout our friendship, waves of unexplainable feelings hit me whenever I was around her. There were times when she'd hug me, and I'd have the urge not to let her go. Sometimes she'd laugh, and I'd dream about the sound. There were times when she was doing the most mundane thing, and I'd look at her, and all I'd want to do was cover her face in a thousand kisses. I always thought those were fleeting feelings. They came fast but would always dissipate when I thought about how if I did have a crush on my best friend, it could ruin our friendship forever.

Then I went to California for a year. It was almost as if I truly realized how special Hailee was when I was forced to be away from her. People surrounded me nonstop in Los Angeles, but I wasn't surrounded by *my* people. My person.

I was determined to tell Hailee about my feelings and then proceed to make my senior year the best year ever with her. I just hadn't built up the courage yet. Which meant I only had one secret worth focusing on at that time—my growing hatred of acting.

My parents had put a lot of time and money into my acting career. When I was young and said I wanted to be an actor, they supported it to the fullest. Dad made sure I gave it my all, and I did, but now I didn't have the same passion I once held for it. Being around Hollywood somehow made me jaded. I felt as if I was losing parts of my roots, and even though I didn't know what I wanted to do, I knew I didn't want to continue down that road.

Having that conversation with my parents wasn't going to be easy, but I figured dinner that night would be a good time to just blurt it out. Rip the Band-Aid off.

When I approached the dining room, Dad was already standing, putting food on each plate. He looked up at me and raised an eyebrow. "You and that phone are attached at your hip so much lately. No phones at the dinner table unless it's for business."

Dad and his dinnertime rules.

Mom walked into the room and kissed my forehead. "Hey, baby."

We started eating, and it felt both great and nerve-wracking to have one of Mom's home-cooked meals. My mother was a fantastic chef, one of the best in the Midwest, if not the world. Her restaurant in Chicago was thriving. It was the reason she couldn't spend as much time in Los Angeles with me as Dad did. So coming home to her home-cooked meals felt like being spoiled.

My agent said I should've avoided certain foods to keep my physique, but I couldn't pass up Mom's cooking. All I knew was if I could have a few days not eating chicken and rice, I would celebrate it. Before the past few years, I'd never worried about my weight, but over the last year, when I had to get cut for a role, it was all I seemed to ever think about. I didn't talk about it to anyone, though, because I would've sounded like a little bitch complaining about getting a six-pack and getting paid to act in movies and shows. *What a hard life, Aiden.*

Therefore, I kept my struggles to myself.

I hated that one of the first things that I did when I got home was weigh in, too. Then the following morning, I weighed myself again. It was as if the number on the scale and the image in the mirror were one of the most important things to me.

Before I left Leeks, I didn't even own a scale. Now, I could look down and guesstimate how many macros were sitting on my plate. Another reason I wanted out of that industry. Insecurities ran rampant.

"How was your first day?" Mom asked, shaking me from my thoughts.

"Good. I was able to switch lunch so I could have mine with Hailee. The teachers are all nice, too."

"Are people excited to see you?" she questioned.

"A little too much. It's weird how people are paying attention to me. I got invited to parties by people who've never talked to me before."

"You should ignore their advancements. It's easy to celebrate when people think you are successful. You must be careful and smart with individuals," Dad warned.

"Yeah, it's just weird is all."

Dad placed his fork down and clasped his hands together. "I want to make sure we are on the same page about this school year, Aiden. You know I was against the return because being a public figure makes it harder for you to be a normal teenager. Like you said, people are already treating you differently. So let's just keep things clean and cut. In and out, do your homework, get your good grades, and report home. Do you understand?"

I nodded. "Yes, sir."

"And have fun," Mom said, leaning over to squeeze my forearm. "You're allowed to have fun, too. It's your senior year!"

Dad grumbled a little but didn't disagree with Mom. She seemed to be the only person alive who didn't get his sharp tongue.

"Actually, I was hoping to talk to you about something," I said. My hands were sweaty, and my nerves were skyrocketing through the roof, but I figured I might as well put it out on the table. Just a few simple words: I don't want to be an actor anymore. Easy. Effortless.

"One second, Aiden. Don't you have something else to tell him, Sam?" Mom asked. "What were you telling me earlier?"

Dad shook his head. "We can save that for another time."

"Samuel," Mom sternly stated. "Now's a perfect time."

He released a weighted sigh and sat up straighter as he looked at me. His brows were knitted. A knot formed in my chest as he gave me his hard stare. The same stare he'd always given me when he was disappointed in something I did. When he parted his mouth, he said something that almost knocked me backward. "I'm proud of you. Of the work you've done in the past year and the opportunities you're creating for yourself in the entertainment industry. I've seen how much work you've put into it, and it doesn't go unnoticed. You've also changed my life by giving me the opportunity to be your manager. I couldn't live out my acting dream because your mother and I took you in, but watching you shine means the world to me. It feels as if my dreams have come true. I'm happy because of you, and I am proud of you."

I stood there frozen in place, completely stunned by his words. "Uh, what?"

"I said I'm proud of you."

"Yeah, I heard you… It's just…" I scratched the back of my neck. "Uh, thanks."

Well, crap.

He gave one head nod. "Just don't falter. Now's the time when you will be tempted to sway or lose your balance. Millions would kill to have your level of success, and it will only keep building, Aiden. Keep your eye on the prize. You've got this."

He shifted the conversation, but my mind stayed on that speech well after dinner was finished. My father, my stone-cold, emotionless robot of a father, just told me he was proud of me.

I'm proud of you.

Seventeen years, and all I'd ever wanted to hear were those words from that man. That he was proud of me. That he believed in me. That what I was doing was worth it. That night he gave me those words, and I knew I'd have to keep working to advance my career in order to keep him proud. No part of me wanted to be an actor, but every part of me wanted to make my father proud.

The sound of knocking on my bedroom window was a sound I had missed. I moved over there to find Hailee standing there with her arms crossed tightly. I opened it, and she scrunched up her nose. "Fine," she blurted out.

"Fine what?"

"Fine, I'll go to the stupid party with the stupid people."

I smirked, tossing my legs over the window ledge and taking a seat. "What changed your mind?"

"The ultimate high school list lacks completion, and who knows when you might be swept off to Los Angeles again before the year is over. Figured we might as well knock off the easiest tasks on the list."

"I'm not going to argue with you because if I do, I know you'll change your mind."

"You're right." She sat on the other edge of my windowsill. Her leg brushed against mine, and I silently prayed she wouldn't move it.

She cleared her throat. "But—"

"Of course, there's a but."

"Don't sass me, Tom."

"Lay it on me, Jerry. What are your terms?"

"I don't want to stay at the party the whole time, but I don't want to arrive early, either. I need you to go before me, scope it out, give me updates, and then when I show up, you meet me outside to take me inside the house."

"Okay."

"That's not all."

I sighed. "Of course, it's not. Continue."

"You take Carlton with you right away."

"No way."

She grimaced. "Come on, Aiden. It will be a good chance for you to get to know him."

"I don't want to get to know him."

"Yeah, I know, but…" She took a deep breath and released it slowly. "It's important to him. He begged me to come."

I tilted my head toward her in complete dismay. "You're really friends with him, aren't you?"

She laughed and shrugged. "I am. You don't understand. When you were gone last year, I was lonely. I had no one to talk to, and Carlton was there when I needed… a person. Plus, this party is kind of a dream of his. He's always wanted to be invited. I figured if he walked in with you, he'd get a few cool points with everyone."

"Cool points? What makes you think I have cool points?"

Hailee placed her hands against my shoulders. "My sweet, naïve, stupid best friend. It's cute how you don't see how you instantly became the coolest person at our school today. You have the coolest points that there are to collect."

"They don't mean anything. Those people don't know the real me."

"Yes." She nodded. "But I do. And I know you'll do this for me because I'm your person, and best friends do uncomfortable things for one another in order to make each other happy."

I narrowed my eyes. "Are you really playing the best friend card?"

"I'm playing the best friend card."

"Wow." I blew out a cloud of smoke. "That's not fair."

She smiled.

Crap.

That smile would've caused me to do anything she wanted.

"Fine," I grumbled. "But this means you owe me."

"Sure, sure. Whatever you say." She stood from the ledge to head back to her window, and my eyes tracked every inch of her from behind. Was her butt always that plump? Did it always sit that high? Did her thick thighs always appear so kissable? When did she become so… perfect?

"What do people wear to parties?" she asked, looking over her shoulder toward me as she almost caught me checking her out. "Do I have to wear a dress? I hate dresses."

I laughed. "You can wear whatever you want, Jerry."

"That's not a helpful answer."

"I'm not a helpful person."

"Fair enough."

She went and climbed into her window as I climbed back inside mine. She smiled my way and said, "Welcome home, ugly."

I cocked an eyebrow. "Ugly?"

"With everyone else blowing smoke up your butt, I figured I should keep you humble and grounded."

I laughed. "Thanks, beautiful," I said, knowing compliments made her extremely uncomfortable.

"Shut up, Aiden," she said, followed by her slamming her window closed.

I missed that, too.

Slamming windows and Hailee's attitude.

NINE

Aiden

NEVER IN MY WILDEST IMAGINATION DID I ENVISION MYSELF going to a party with Carlton by my side. Then again, never did I imagine Hailee befriending someone like him. It was the oddest pairing in the history of pairs. That was what I got for leaving her alone for a year. My best friend had officially lost her mind.

"Can you do me one big favor?" I asked Carlton as we stood on the front porch of Cara's house.

"What's that, buckaroo?" He pulled out a pack of mints and tossed a handful into his mouth.

"Once we get inside, go off on your own and have the time of your life."

He smirked ear to ear. "You got it, dude," he spat out, hitting me in the face with one of the many mints sitting in his mouth. He took his hand and wiped it across my face. "My bad."

Hailee owed me more than she knew.

I'd never been so irritated showing up to a party before. Sure, it wasn't my first party. I'd been to a handful of gatherings in Los Angeles, but it was my first high school party. I was excited to see how much

Hailee hated the party. That would be the most entertaining part of the evening.

As we walked into the house party, it was well underway. Carlton burst into the living room with his arms wide open. "Hello, party people!" he shouted. He went left, I went right, and I'd hoped we wouldn't run into one another again.

I spent the first thirty to forty-five minutes of the party taking photos with people and having them record videos of me saying hi to their random family members. The joys of being semi-famous. The second hour was spent with me talking about what acting was like and the different celebrities I'd interacted with. I'd turned down about fifty drink offers. The last thing I needed was for someone to post a picture of me drinking underage. My father made sure that I was very aware of my surroundings since I was a public figure. Underage drinking was not something I needed to get caught doing.

Even though I knew all the people at the house party, I was playing a role of sorts. They weren't allowed true access to me because the more people I let in, the more people could turn on me or use information against me. Another tactic I'd learned from father dearest. The only people I could be myself around were my family and Hailee—who pretty much was family.

As I sat on the living room coffee table, going on and on about how sweet and great everyone was in La La Land—a lie, but I didn't need my schoolmates knowing about my Hollywood enemies—Cara stepped into the crowd surrounding me.

"How about you all get off his dick so I can slide on it," she said, winking my way.

Well damn.

A quite forward approach.

Cara looked striking. It wasn't shocking. Cara had been beautiful since grade school. She was my first ever crush. She moved with a confidence a lot of people couldn't carry and just seemed to always get anything she wanted without much effort. Her biggest downfall? She wasn't Hailee.

Cara held her hand out toward me and tilted her head. "Do you want a tour of the property?" she asked me.

"Uh, yeah. Okay."

The tour led us to her bedroom, and she locked the door behind her. The music from downstairs was still loud as ever, and Cara pulled out a bottle of liquor from behind her bed. She took a swig from it and then held it out toward me.

I shook my head. "No thanks."

She raised an eyebrow. "Don't be a pussy, Aiden. I know you've partied it up in Hollywood."

It was the opposite of that. I worked, I had a teacher who homeschooled me, and then I worked some more. The last thing my father would've allowed me to do was to go off to some Hollywood parties—unless networking was involved. Each party I'd gone to was a business trip. Plus, I was given an opportunity of a lifetime. I wasn't going to blow it for some booze and bad decisions.

Which unfortunately made my current situation a lot less appealing than I'd hoped it would be. Aiden from five years ago would've been freaking out about being in Cara's bedroom with the door locked. The Aiden I currently was? I was on the brink of a panic attack, thinking about what would've happened if my father had found out about this situation. It would look scandalous, and the tabloids loved a good scandal. I wished I could've shut off my father's stern judgments from every decision I'd made, but he was the Jiminy Cricket on my shoulder telling me not to make bad choices.

Plus, he was proud of me. Damn him and his pride.

"Maybe we should head back downstairs," I offered, standing up from her bed, where she'd placed me. She walked over to me, stumbling a bit before taking a seat. On my lap. *Oh boy.*

"Or we can have some alone time."

It was clear she had a bit to drink. "I don't think that's a good idea."

"Why? Are you and that Hannah girl screwing?"

"Hannah?"

"Yeah. That girl who follows you around like crazy."

"You mean Hailee?"

"Sure, okay." She picked up the bottle of alcohol and took another swig. "Are you two fucking?"

"What? No. We aren't. She's my best friend."

Have I thought about the possibility of having sex with Hailee? Sure. Yeah. Often. Twice a day. Maybe three times on the weekends. Whatever.

Cara scrunched up her nose. "Why, though?"

"Why is my best friend my best friend?"

"Yeah. I mean, don't get me wrong, you're hot and famous, and she's… nobody."

Within an instant, any kind of attraction I felt for Cara sizzled up and died. I removed her from my lap and stood. "I'm going to head back downstairs," I shortly stated as her phone dinged. She reached over and grabbed it, ignoring my comment.

"Oh my gosh, did you see crazy Carlton?" Cara asked. "He's going off downstairs about Hannah."

"Who's Hannah?"

"Your Hannah."

"Hailee."

"Whatever."

I stood and grabbed her phone from her hands. On the video was a drunk Carlton on a table, swaying back and forth with a bottle of liquor in his hand. "No way. You think I like Hailee Jones?!" he spat out. "Hell no. Have you seen her? It's like she swallowed the Doublemint twins," he slurred, mocking Hailee's weight. "Honestly, I just hung out with her cuz I felt bad for the chubby cupcake. She had no friends, really." He went on and on and on, because the crowd gave him the laughter and attention that the addict craved.

I could feel the blood boiling beneath my skin.

I was going to murder the asshole.

I pulled out my cell phone to text Hailee, but it seemed she'd already seen the video.

Hailee: I'm not coming.

Hailee: This is humiliating.

Shit.

"Where the heck are you going?" Cara asked.

"To check on Hailee."

"Who cares how she's doing? Besides, it's funny. Laugh a little. She's not even on our level."

Our level? As if Cara and I were the same in any way, shape, or form. That made my rage grow stronger.

"We're not on the same level," I muttered, walking toward the door.

Cara dashed in front of me and blocked my exit. "I swear to God,

Aiden, if you walk out of this room to go check on that loser instead of having the best night of your life with me, then you are dead to me. Do you understand me? We are over if you leave. You'll be dead to me. DEAD!"

I swallowed hard and stood tall as I cocked an eyebrow and locked my eyes with hers. "RIP."

She gasped, stunned. "You'll regret this, Aiden Walters. Mark my words. I'll make sure of it."

I pushed past her and left the house. I started running home as nerves shot through my system. The moment I approached the Joneses' house, I repeatedly rang the doorbell.

"Is she okay?" I asked, my voice cracking when it left my throat as Hailee's parents answered the door. They looked up to see me, and the hurt in their eyes made my own chest ache even more. Fuck. What kind of assholes would hurt someone as soft as Hailee? She was the definition of kind. At that moment, I wanted to track down everyone who posted, reposted, and mocked my best friend. I wanted to tear them limb from limb and make them feel like the complete trash they were.

"Not right now," Penny said, her eyes glassed over. I wasn't surprised that Penny was on the edge of her emotions because her daughter was her heartbeats. When Hailee hurt, Penny hurt even deeper. That was what moms did. They felt their child's pain as if it were their own.

"Can I talk to her?" I asked.

"Did you know?" Karl asked. His brows were knitted, and his face was stern. Unlike Penny, he wasn't sad. No, he was pissed off. "Did you know they were going to mock her?"

"No. Of course not."

"Going to that party was your idea. I swear to you, Aiden, if you knew—"

"Karl," Penny cut in, grabbing him by the fabric resting against his forearm. She looked at me and frowned, seeing the hurt in my eyes that Karl couldn't see because he was too busy dealing with the hurting of his daughter. She shook her head. "He didn't know."

"How can you tell?" he asked.

I respected Karl more than my own dad. When it came to being a father figure who could be soft and gentle yet stern and tough, Karl had it in tenfold. My father wouldn't know how to be soft and gentle if his life depended on it. I really appreciated that about Karl—how balanced he was as a parent. But, at that very moment, if he didn't get out of my way and let me go see his daughter, I was going to bum-rush past him, and I wouldn't even care if he fell to the floor.

"Because he's Aiden. He's her person," Penny said, moving out from in front of the door. She nodded toward Hailee's doorframe and gave me a broken smile. "So go check on our daughter, all right, Aiden?"

"Yes, ma'am," I muttered, nodding once.

Karl gave me another hard look, but he didn't say anything. He stepped to the side, which was more confirmation than any words he could've given me.

I placed my hand on Hailee's door and turned it as my heart twisted in my chest. As I opened it, I found her sitting in a floral dress, cross-legged, with her back toward me as she stared out her bedroom window.

"Jerry," I said, closing the door behind me. She didn't move an inch. I wasn't exactly sure what to do. Her hair wasn't in an afro puff. It was styled with perfect loose curls. Even from only being able to see her from behind, I knew she looked beautiful.

She didn't say anything.

I shifted around in my sneakers. "Can I sit by you?"

I waited a few seconds, and when there was no reply, I frowned. I bent down, untied my shoes, took them off, walked over to her, and sat beside her, cross-legged. Because when you were a best friend, you didn't need an invitation to be there for your person. You just showed up and stayed.

Her makeup was ruined as tear stains left marks from their departure from her eyes. Still, she looked good. I'd seen Hailee in some of her worst states. When she had food poisoning from our favorite Chinese buffet a few years back, she looked like the walking dead. She couldn't do anything except walk to the bathroom, where she'd thrown up nonstop.

I held her hair back during her vomiting, and then she'd crawl back to bed, and I'd sat with her talking about bullshit that didn't matter just so she didn't have to be alone.

Carlton being an asshole wasn't worse than when she had food poisoning, but I knew it twisted up Hailee's stomach just as bad. My stomach was in fucking knots, so I couldn't imagine what hers was doing.

I stared out the window with her, looking at the big oak tree sitting in front of it. We stayed there for a few minutes, silent and still. I only knew she was still alive due to her blinks every few moments.

"I put on a dress," she finally said.

"I know."

"I hate dresses."

"I know."

"I also did my hair."

"I know."

"I hate doing my hair."

"I know."

She turned her head in my direction, and her eyes were bloodshot, and fuck, if hearts could break from moments, mine shattered right then and there.

"I thought he was my friend," she whispered.

I sighed. "I know."

I patted my left shoulder, and she lay her head against me. I placed my head on top of hers, and we went back to staring out the window. Her makeup smeared on my shirt, but I didn't care at all. If she wanted to use my whole outfit as a rag, I'd let her.

"I'm going to kill him," I told her. It'd been the only thing I'd been thinking about since I'd seen the video of Carlton being a complete shithead. When I saw him, I was going to murder him.

"No, just… let it be." She sighed and lifted her head from my shoulder. "Don't you have a party to be getting back to, anyway? I'm sure Princess Cara is freaking out about you being gone."

"I don't care what she thinks."

"Please. She's the only thing you've cared about for years. Plus, going to a party is on our high school bucket list. At least one of us can check it off."

"I'm not leaving, Hailee."

She looked my way and frowned. "I think I need you to go, though, because I feel like I'm going to cry."

"Which is why I need to stay."

"You don't need to see me cry, Aiden."

"Why not? I've seen you cry a million times before. You've cried an unrealistic number of times before. Remember when we watched *Bambi* for the first time? Waterworks."

"This is different. I've never cried like this before."

"Like what?"

Her lips trembled as she stared down at her hands, which were linked together, and she began slightly shaking as she choked out her words. "Like everyone is laughing at me because of how I look. Because of my weight. And I just thought… I thought he was my friend, and I don't know why he'd say those things just because someone mocked him about us being friends, and… and… and…" She began sobbing into the palms of her hands, and I was definitely going to murder that fucking asshole.

"Please, Aiden? Please just go? I want to be alone right now."

"Swear?" I asked.

She nodded. "Swear."

I sighed and stood from the bed, but before turning to leave, I wrapped my arms around her from the back and held her tight. "I know you're sad, Hailee, and I know you're hurting, but even though you want to be alone right now, you aren't alone. I'm right next door. Okay? I'll be right here, too, if you need me to be."

I walked out of the room and closed the door behind me. Instead of going home, I had another thing to tackle. So I headed to the living room, where Hailee's parents were sitting on the couch, talking about what had happened to Hailee.

"Penny and Karl?" They looked up at me with concerned expressions, and I gave them a broken smile. "Do you think you can help me with something?"

TEN

Hailee

"**D**AD, WHAT ARE YOU DOING HERE?" I ASKED, CONFUSED as my father stood in front of my bedroom door in a tuxedo, looking as dapper as ever.

"I'm your chauffeur for the evening, my lady," he said, holding his arm out toward me for me to loop around.

"My chauffeur?" I giggled, even though I was far from the mood to laugh. But I'd cried so much that I wasn't certain I had any tears left in me. I'd already wiped all of my makeup off and tossed on my oversized sweats, ready to binge-watch *The Vampire Diaries* and eat Ben & Jerry's like a good heartbroken girl. I arched an eyebrow at Dad. "You're not wearing shoes. You're going to drive with no shoes?"

He tipped his invisible hat and smirked. "Where we're going, we don't need any cars. Now come on, your date is waiting."

I was too intrigued to ask more questions, so I looped my arm around Dad's. He walked me through the house, and my alertness rose as I saw Mama standing at the front door with a goofy grin on her face.

"You look beautiful, Hailee," Mama said, snapping pictures of me.

I glanced down at my gray sweats and cocked an eyebrow. "Where?"

Dad placed a kiss on my forehead. "Everywhere. You look beautiful everywhere."

What in the world is going on?

Dad looked down at his invisible watch and then snapped his fingers. "Not to be rude, but we've got to get a move on, folks. We have a tight schedule to adhere to, so come on, Hailee. Let's get going."

"Get going where?" I urged, but they ignored me.

"Have a wonderful night, sweetheart," Mama sang before giving both Dad and me kisses on the cheek.

Dad walked me outside into the chilled night air. We didn't go far at all. Just right next door to Aiden's house, where Dad walked me to their backyard. The minute we went through their gate, I gasped when I looked around.

White lights were dressed throughout the yard, twisting in the trees and bushes, lighting up the space like never before. To my left was a folding table set up with two chairs. On said table sat a huge bowl of spaghetti and meatballs, a plate of garlic bread, and a tossed salad.

To my right was another folding table with a record player on it, which was playing a Taylor Swift soundtrack. Aiden despised Taylor but knew that I was a deep Swiftie, so for him to have her music playing meant more than words. Beside the table were cardboard boxes lying on the ground with the words dance floor written across them.

The broken pieces of my heart were surprisingly still able to beat as Aiden walked out of the house, smiling my way.

"Hey, Tom," I whispered.

"Hey, Jerry."

"What's going on?" I asked as butterflies swirled in my stomach. Since when did that happen? Since when did I get butterflies from my very best friend?

"We are checking off one of the items on our high school bucket list tonight. We are going to a house party together. Well, our version of a house, that is. A backyard edition."

He took my hand into his and pulled me over to the table of food. "First up is dinner, which we should probably eat now. Otherwise, it's gonna get cold. My mom picked it up about an hour ago, and even though it's been in the oven to stay warm, it's not top-notch. I got your favorite things, spaghetti and garlic bread. Here." He pulled out the chair for me, and my cheeks hurt from smiling so much from my best friend's act of kindness.

I took a seat, and he pushed me in. Then he walked over to his chair and sat down.

Red Solo cups were filled with soda. I looked around and couldn't stop smiling to myself. It was funny how emotions worked. How only a few hours ago, I was at my lowest of lows, but then Aiden managed to make me smile when all I wanted to do was fall apart and be sad. That was my favorite thing about best friends—how they could make the dark days shine with splashes of light.

"I don't think people eat fancy dinners at high school house parties," I mentioned.

"That's because they aren't cool enough."

"You didn't have to do all of this," I told him.

"I did."

"You should've been at the party with the girl you've been obsessed with all these years."

"I know," he agreed. "Which is why I'm here."

My heartbeats.

They fumbled, skipped, and flipped in my chest.

I looked down at my hands and tried to collect my thoughts, but Aiden wouldn't let me.

"Don't overthink, Hailee. Just eat your favorite foods and enjoy the night," he urged.

"I'm actually not eating carbs right now."

Aiden's eyes bugged out. "Bullshit. Why not?"

Never in my life did I feel uncomfortable talking about anything to Aiden. Heck, he was the first person I told when I got my period for the first time, and instead of being grossed out, he went to the corner store and bought pads for me. Were they the size of Mars? Yes. Regardless, he didn't get thrown off by much.

Yet telling him about my weight gain and eating problems felt more humiliating than anything else. While he became extremely attractive, I was going in the opposite direction, no matter the amount of time Mom and I spent in the gym together over the last year.

I hated that my first thought the moment I saw the video of Carlton and people laughing about my size was that I had to diet. Not that they were assholes, and they were being jerks, but that I had to diet because there was something lacking within me that made me an easy target for their insults.

I shook my head. "Just not into them anymore."

He frowned, looking at the plate filled with carbohydrates. "I can order something—"

I shoved a piece of garlic bread into my mouth and forced out a laugh the moment I saw how sad he had grown. "I'm just joking. Pass me the pasta."

His hands flew to his chest. "Oh, thank God." He shook a finger at me. "You had me in the first half, not going to lie."

"You know me, jokes on jokes." When was someone going to hand me over my Emmy award?

"Yeah, well, shut up and eat before it gets cold."

So I did exactly that. We ate all the food on the table, and I loved the fact that I felt comfortable enough to stuff my face in front of the boy who'd been there for me since day one. I never felt comfortable enough to do that around Carlton. Once last year, he mentioned how much bread I was eating at lunch, and it kind of stayed in my head a little too much. I was embarrassed by myself, and ever since then, I've watched my carb intake.

I couldn't stop laughing at Aiden's lame jokes during our meal. Every girl deserves a best friend like Aiden. The world would be a lot easier to live in if they had someone like him.

After dinner, Aiden brought us wet naps to clean our hands. Then he moved over to the record player and put on another song.

"All right, it's time to get that first dance out of the way. So come on down and move your hips to Hailee's favorite Disney song as she takes the dance floor for the first dance." Aiden held his hand out toward me. "Can I have this first dance?" he asked.

I took his hand into mine, and he smiled as he walked us to the dance floor.

Just then, the song "Beauty and the Beast" came on, my favorite song from my favorite Disney movie.

I smiled a little. "I don't know if this is what people are really doing at house parties, Aiden."

"Are you kidding? This is exactly what was happening before I left earlier tonight."

I gave him a broken smile. "Thank you."

"Always."

I lowered my head. "I'm still sad," I confessed. Every now and again, Carlton would cross my mind, and I'd be filled with an extreme amount of embarrassment. But then, I'd shift my thoughts to Aiden, and things would seem a little bit better. "But I'm happy, too. I don't know how I can be both things all at once."

"I'm not surprised. Nothing about you has ever been simple, Hailee Jones."

I smirked. "True."

"You look beautiful, Hails."

I felt my cheeks heat. I was convinced that more men like Aiden needed to exist. Men who called women beautiful in all their states of being.

I leaned in and rested my head against Aiden's shoulder as we swayed back and forth to my favorite song. "Thanks for being you."

After we danced the night away and drank way too much soda from the Red Solo cups, we lay down in the grass and looked up at the stars sprinkled across the sky. Aiden kept making corny jokes, and I kept laughing. We talked about everything, and the conversation always came easy. After a while, we stopped talking, and even our silence came easy. We listened to the music on the record player, and before I knew it, I was falling asleep with Aiden by my side.

"Cinderella," a voice whispered, waking me from my sleep as I was lifted into the air.

"What's going on?" I mumbled, rubbing my eyes as I looked up to see my father carrying me in his arms.

"The clock struck midnight. Time for bed," he said. I yawned and wrapped my arms around his neck. No matter my size, no matter my age, I was always going to be my father's little girl.

Dad walked over to Aiden, who was still sleeping, and he lightly nudged him with his foot. "Hey, Prince Charming, bedtime," Dad said, his voice much sterner than when he woke me up.

Aiden yawned and stretched out as he rubbed his eyes. "Okay, Karl."

He stood to his feet and looked in our direction with his sleep-drunk goofy grin. "Best. Party. Ever."

I couldn't help but agree.

"Night, Tom," I said as I yawned and lay my head on Dad's shoulder.

Aiden tousled his messy hair and then brushed his hand against the back of his neck. "Night, Jerry."

Dad carried me the whole way to my bedroom, even when I told him he could've put me down because I was too big to be carried to bed by my dad. He lay me in bed and smiled as he kissed my forehead.

"I'm sorry about what happened earlier, Cinderella," he said. "Sometimes people are stupid and make stupid choices, but that has nothing to do with you. Those people's words do not get to define you. Only you do. Do you understand?"

"Yes."

"And their actions have nothing to do with your self-worth, right? They don't get to tell you that you're good enough—you do that. Do you understand?"

"Yes."

"And you are the most beautiful, smart, and powerful woman alive. Do you understand?"

I smiled. "Yes."

He kissed my forehead. "Get some sleep. I'll make you and your mother waffles in the morning. Love you forever."

"Love you longer than that," I replied, something we'd been saying to each other for as long as I could remember.

I fell asleep that night, unable to control my dreams, but I wasn't mad when they went to Aiden. Dreaming about him always seemed easy.

ELEVEN

Aiden

THAT MONDAY AFTER THE PARTY, I COULD TELL HAILEE WAS nervous about going to school. We sat on the bus, and I could feel her energy was off.

"You good?" I asked.

She nodded. "I'm good."

"Liar."

"Yeah."

I squeezed her kneecap. "You'll be good, though."

"Swear?"

"Swear."

"Do you think he feels bad?" she asked as the bus pulled up to the school building, speaking about Carlton. The little amount of respect I had for the asshole completely evaporated after what he'd done on Saturday. Truthfully, I always knew Hailee was too good for him. There was nothing about Carlton that read "good enough" to me. Not even for friendship.

"If he does feel bad, he's too much of a little shit to admit it. If he doesn't, he's more of a dick than I imagined."

"I bet he doesn't feel bad. Now, all the popular kids are talking to him because it's funny."

"It's a weekly trend. They'll drop him just as fast as they picked him up."

"I hope he bruises when he falls," she muttered, disdain in her voice. Her afro was pulled into a big puff that morning, and she wore an oversized sweater with leggings and tennis shoes.

"If you want, I can make sure that he bruises," I offered, a tad joking but mainly serious. All I wanted to do was pound my fists into Carlton's head and make him feel an ounce of the pain he'd put Hailee through. I knew she was hurting even more than she was letting on. Hailee did that often—kept her biggest hurts to herself.

"No, Aiden," she sternly stated, looking my way. She gave me a hard, authoritative glare and pointed a finger my way. "Do not do it."

"I was joking." I snickered, tossing my backpack higher on my shoulder.

"No, you weren't."

No. I wasn't.

"He's been staring at you from a distance all day," I groaned, finding Carlton, yet again, creeping on Hailee from a distance. He hadn't had the balls to walk up to her and apologize, and I'd even seen him trying to play it off with some football assholes who mocked the whole situation. He seemed more excited about getting attention from people who didn't give a damn about him than the attention from the girl who would've given him the best friendship he'd ever have.

I wondered how many other idiots threw away something good to be deemed as cool.

Color me shocked when Carlton approached Hailee and me at her locker after last period. He didn't seem as cocky as he had when talking to the football players and cheerleaders, though. He seemed more like his normal, wannabe cool self.

"Hey, Hailee. Yo-You think we can talk?" he asked, scratching his fingers against his neck. I didn't know why that annoyed me so much, but it had. Everything about the guy annoyed me, but it wasn't my place to tell him to fuck off. That was all in Hailee's hands.

Please tell him to fuck off.

She shifted in her shoes, grabbed some books from her locker, then shut it. Pressing the books to her chest, she held on to them tightly as she stood tall beside me. She shook her head. "No."

One word. One solid word from my best friend, and I'd never been so proud.

That's my girl.

Carlton's brow knotted, and he looked perplexed. "What? I mean, we should talk. You are my friend, after all."

Hailee huffed. "Ex-friend, you jerk. I have nothing to say to you, so leave me alone."

He reached out to grab her arm, and she flinched when he did so, which made me automatically step between the two of them.

"Back off, Carlton. She said she didn't want to talk to you, so how about you respect that?" I growled, feeling my blood begin to boil.

"This has nothing to do with you, Aiden," Carlton said, standing up tall—well, as tall as he could at five-foot-seven. "You've always been a bit too involved in Hailee's affairs anyway. How about you mind your own business?"

In Hailee's affairs?

Who talked like that?

I took a step toward him because he was starting to really piss me off. Hailee put a hand in front of me to halt my advancements because Hailee Jones never needed anyone to speak on her behalf. She was strong on her own. I was just there for extra protection because I was an over-protective best friend, and I wanted to pound my fist into Carlton's face.

"We have nothing to say, Carlton. You showed me your true colors, and it would be stupid for me not to trust them."

"What happened this weekend isn't who I am," he urged, making me roll my eyes harder than ever before. "And now, some people look at me as if I'm this jerk who tried to hurt you."

"You should've thought about that before you got on camera and called me all those names," Hailee said matter-of-factly. "So if you'll ex-cuse me, I have nothing else to say to you."

She pushed past him, and I gave him a mocking smirk because fuck that guy. Hailee left him with his tail between his legs like the idiot he had been.

As we began to walk away, I heard some popular kids, including Cara, talking to Carlton. "You're really going to let someone like Hailee Jones embarrass you like that? Oh my gosh, I didn't know you were so weak," they mocked.

They kept egging him on, mocking him, making fun of how a girl just walked all over him like he was nothing. I could feel the tension building up from the situation as I glanced back and saw Carlton growing more and more intense and nervous from the rude remarks.

"Tell her how you really feel, Carlton! Or are you just a weak little punk?" Brad Gates egged on. And if there was anything about peer pressure, it always engulfed the weakest links.

Carlton cleared his throat, stood taller, and shouted. "Whatever, Hailee, it's not my fault I didn't want to fuck you because you got fat over the past year."

My jaw hit the floor.

Hailee's footsteps paused, and I saw the color as it drained from her face. Every insecurity that lived within her spilled out of her eyes. The pain of Carlton's words ran deep, and as she turned to look at him, I saw a moment of guilt flash over him before everyone around him broke out into laughter.

"Hell yeah! You tell that fatty who's the man," someone said.

Carlton blinked, released a smug chuckle, and shrugged. "I mean, I couldn't even find where to put it because of her stomach rolls. Can you blame me for not wanting to have sex between two ham hock thighs? Honestly—"

He hadn't had a chance to finish his thoughts. I rushed at him, knocking him to the floor within a few seconds. My fist began to pound into his face as a bigger crowd began to form around us. Carlton got one good hit to my left eye, but that was all I would allow him to have. My knuckles ached from the contact to his face, to his gut, to his soul, but I didn't stop. Because Hailee was hurting due to his words. If she had to hurt emotionally, he had to hurt physically. An eye for an eye or something like that.

Carlton didn't know what he was signing up for when he decided to bully the good girl with a best friend like me.

Anyone who dimmed Hailee's light had to deal with her shadows, and I was the motherfucker standing there, all dressed in black.

"Break it up, break it up!" a voice hollered, an authoritative tone to the sound. I wasn't surprised when I saw two teachers yanking me off Carlton, who was balled up like a jerk.

"Mr. Walters, Mr. Holmes! Principal's office—now!" Mr. Jacobson shouted, holding me by my collar as Mr. Thompson went and scraped Carlton up from the floor.

My eyes connected with Hailee's terrified stare as Mr. Jacobson dragged me past her, off to face my doom.

"You okay?" I mouthed.

Her eyes flashed with emotions, and she nodded slightly. "You okay?" she mouthed back.

I gave her a half grin, and it dropped the moment she was out of eyesight.

All I could hear in my head was my father's voice, telling me that I was a fucking idiot.

"Are you a fucking idiot?" Dad grumbled as I sat in our living room with Mom. Well, Mom and I sat. Dad stood tall with his arms crossed.

"Sam, the tone," Mom said, cutting in. At least I had one parent in my corner.

"Screw my tone. Your son pummeled his fists into another boy's face and got suspended for the rest of the week. We're lucky I was able to talk to the principal into not expelling him. Who do you think you are, huh? Attacking another kid like that? You think that makes you tough? You think you're a big man on campus because you can use your fists?"

I sat with my shoulders rounded forward and fingers entangled. I didn't speak to him because I knew whatever I said would've been seen as an excuse, and my father didn't believe in excuses. He believed in the Walters standard. We didn't act out in public. We didn't behave like savages. We didn't create scenes.

We stood in line. We fought for important issues. We obeyed the law and never disrespected authority—my teachers and the administration of my school being the authority in this situation. If we did, the tabloids would report on it, and God forbid that happened.

"Oh, so you're deaf?" he snapped, walking toward me. "Get off the couch."

"Samuel—"

"Laurie, if you don't see the disrespect he's feeding me right now, then you aren't looking hard enough." He turned his attention back to me and away from Mom. "Get. Up."

I stood, and I felt his intimidation wash over me. I stood at least four inches taller than my father, but still, whenever he was around me, I felt three feet tall.

"Lift your head," he ordered.

I did as he said.

"Now look me in the eyes."

I did as he said.

"Don't say a word because I know whatever you say is going to be covered in excuses. All you do now is listen. Do you understand me?"

"Yes, sir."

"You will never act out in such a way again. Do you understand me?"

I swallowed hard. "Yes, sir."

"You are in the public eye now, too, Aiden. This could've ruined any career opportunity if this got out to the press. Don't you get it? You're not allowed to behave like a regular kid because you are not regular. You are more. Do you understand me?"

"Yes, sir."

"You could've ruined everything I worked for," he said.

"Everything *you* worked for?" Mom asked in a sarcastic tone.

Dad grumbled. "Everything we worked for. You know what I meant." He cleared his throat. "And you will apologize to that boy. I will take you to his house, and I will make sure it happens."

"What?! No fucking—"

"Language!" he barked.

Fuck you, I silently replied.

I wished I had liked my father at that moment. I loved him, yes, but I wished I liked him.

In his eyes, I was my father's biggest failure, and if anything, he hated the idea of failing.

He went on with the punishments and then left the room, leaving Mom and me sitting there alone. The space felt lighter whenever my father wasn't around.

"He's a dick," I muttered.

Mom moved over and placed her hands on my cheeks. She looked at me with a smile soaked in sadness and gently touched my eye. I tensed up from the pain. "We need to ice that."

"It's fine," I huffed. I had so much pent-up rage inside me that I felt as if I was going to burst.

"Your father loves you," she claimed, getting up to get an ice pack from the kitchen. When she returned, she had it wrapped in a cloth. She sat back down and held it against my face. "He just has a hard time showing that kind of love."

"He acts like I wanted to fight."

"Did you?" she questioned.

"No. Of course not."

She arched an eyebrow. "Did you?"

I sighed. "He called her names."

"Called who names?"

"Hailee."

Mom's face softened as she pulled the cloth away from my eye for a moment. "What did he say?" She looked horrified when I told her and shook her head. "That's disgusting. And familiar. I once had a guy who used to get caught up in fights for my honor, too."

"Dad?"

She nodded. "More than once. His motto back then was punch first, talk later."

I grumbled.

Hypocrite.

Mom smiled. "It wasn't his right to do it, either. There are more ways to stand up for a woman you love than using your fists."

"Yeah," I agreed. It just seemed easier at that very moment.

Later that night, after dinner, the doorbell rang. Dad answered it to find Hailee standing there.

"Samuel, hi." Hailee's voice was coated in sweetness, something it always seemed to be. "I wanted to stop by and tell you that what happened at school wasn't Aiden's fault. If anything, he was protecting me from a jerk at school."

"Now, Hailee, I know you're always going to try to get Aiden out of trouble, but—"

"He was calling me fat and ugly and gripped my arm hard, Samuel. He was humiliating me in front of the whole school. I know that fighting isn't the right answer ever, and I know Aiden made a mistake, but he made it for me. At the end of the day, I know you taught your son to stand up for what he believes in, for the right side, and that's what Aiden did today. He stood up for me when no one else would. I hope you understand that."

She glanced toward the hallway leading to my bedroom and locked eyes with me for a second before a small smile found her lips. When she smiled, I smiled, too. Kind of a thing we did together.

"Thank you for the information, Hailee. I'll take it into account," Dad replied.

I rolled my eyes. "I'll take it into account," I quietly mocked.

Hailee kept smiling. "Of course, sir. I also made you my special chocolate-chocolate chip cookies. Your favorite ones that I make for Christmas time each year."

Dad grumbled a bit and crossed his arms. "With the big chocolate chunks?"

"The biggest ones, sir."

He took the bag from Hailee as he thanked her for stopping by with more details on the incident that took place. Before she left, she looked up toward me once more. When I smiled, she smiled, too.

"Good night, Hailee," Dad stated sternly, yet I knew his cold heart had thawed a little. If anyone was good at softening up my tough father, it was Hailee.

After Dad shut the front door, I hurried back to my bedroom and slid into my desk chair to make it appear as if I was working on my homework. It only took a few minutes for Dad to stand in my doorway holding the container of Hailee's cookies.

He furrowed his brow and kept the hard look in his eyes. His shoulders were lower than before when he scolded me, and he looked a bit more relaxed—which didn't say much. My father's form of relaxation appeared like someone stressed out to the core.

He nodded once. "You're still grounded. Do you understand me? No television, no cell phone, no internet."

"Yes, sir."

"But it might be best to avoid the apology at this time. Focus on your studies. You'll need your grades to be good for the year. Plus, we want your image to stay unstained for your acting career."

And that, folks, was how my father apologized.

"Yes, sir."

"And don't go causing any trouble for Hailee, you hear?"

"Yes, sir."

"And keep protecting her."

"Yes, sir."

"Just not with your fists."

"Yes, sir."

He wiggled his nose and looked toward my bedroom window. "No climbing out of the window, either."

The ultimate punishment for me. I was now unable to open my bedroom window to sneak over to Hailee's and vice versa. I couldn't even open my window to talk to her, which felt like the biggest punishment.

He cleared his throat. "Our choices in life have consequences. Think about that the next time you use your fists instead of your brain." He turned to walk away.

Feeling brave, I called out to him. "Can I get a cookie?" I asked, knowing exactly how good Hailee's baking skills were.

And with one word, he replied flatly as he continued his descent from my room. "No."

The following week, I met Hailee at the bus stop where she held the straps of her backpack. We'd hardly communicated over the past few days, due to my punishment.

"How long are you grounded?" she asked.

"For five more days, but I don't have to apologize to Carlton, thanks to your cookies. Speaking of cookies…"

She smiled as she reached into her backpack and pulled out a container for me. "I figured your dad wouldn't share with you, so I made you a new batch."

"That's my girl."

We took our seats on the bus.

"Hey, Aiden? Thanks again for standing up for me," Hailee said, leaning her head against the slightly frosted window.

"I hate the fact that he thought he had the right to say that crap about you because you didn't want to give him another chance."

"I saw a phrase for that online. It's called S.D.E."

"S.D.E.?"

"Small dick energy."

I snickered. "Makes sense."

"Which would mean that you had B.D.E. for how you stood up for me." I glanced up at her and saw her cheeks flushing over with nerves. "I'll let you assume what that stands for."

TWELVE

Hailee

AFTER THE INTERACTION CARLTON HAD WITH AIDEN'S FIST, HE didn't give me any more trouble. And as the weeks passed, the popular kids got bored with him, and he went back to his previous social standing.

Then there was the newest issue at hand—my newfound crush on my best friend.

After the house party he threw for me and the punches he also tossed around in my honor, I couldn't get him off my mind. Even sitting beside him on the school bus as he yapped away about any and everything as he drew was a bit too much for me. I felt uncomfortably sweaty whenever he'd look my way, and those blue eyes locked with mine.

Had his eyes always been that blue? Had he always made me feel this way?

Over the past few weeks, we celebrated our eighteenth birthdays together. As I blew out the candles on my cake, I wished that I'd stop feeling the feelings I'd felt for Aiden. When Aiden blew out his candles, I'd made the same wish.

It didn't work.

I'd only felt more feelings for him.

Would the butterflies I had for him pass over time?

Of course, they would. It was just a silly, passing crush.

Nothing more, nothing less. I was fine. Totally fine.

No, no, no, no, no.

My heart was beginning to beat out of order when Aiden approached me at the bus stop. It'd been behaving odder and odder each day that passed whenever he showed up.

What was that smell?

Was that Aiden? Why did he smell like that? Did he always smell that good? It was like he was soaked in the universe's favorite cologne, and it was making me insane. His scents were overwhelmingly delicious, like a baked citrus scone on a rainy Sunday afternoon. I wanted to bathe in Aiden's scent. Oh yes, I wanted to swim in a pool of his aroma and dip my pillows in the same smell so when I fell asleep, I could dream of him and breathe him in against my pillowcases.

Wait, no.

Act normal, Hailee. Don't be awkward.

"What do you think?" Aiden asked as I sat beside him on the bus.

"Huh?"

He narrowed his eyes at me. "The acting role I'm up for. Do you think I should audition for it?"

Wait? Were you talking this whole time? I was too busy staring at your lips. Were your lips always that full and moisturized? What kind of ChapStick are you using? Was there always a rosy tint to them?

"Hailee?!" he called out, snapping his fingers in front of my face.

I grumbled and shook my head, breaking my stare from his smackers. "What?!"

"Dude. Did you not sleep last night? You're grumpy."

"I'm not," I spat out, sounding remarkably grumpy indeed. At least he saw it as grumpiness instead of what it really was—me being hot and bothered. Luckily, he thought I was solely bothered. I cleared my throat. "Sure, take it," I said about the movie role.

"Really?"

"Yeah, why not?" Confession: I had no clue what he was asking me about because, for the past fifteen minutes, I'd been deeply engrossed in his lips and scents. Scents and lips. *Oh my gosh, you're staring at his lips again, Hailee. Stop it!*

I moved my stare to his eyes, and that was no better than before.

My heart pounded erratically against my chest as we made eye contact. When did his eyes get like that? Were they always that blue? I wanted to swim in his irises and bathe in his thoughts and—

What the heck, Hailee. Snap out of it.

Aiden made a goofy grin, and I loved it. Dang it, I wanted to bathe in that, too. "I mean, they want me to play a gorilla most of the flick. I just don't think that's the road I want to go down. It's not the best script."

"Then don't do it," I quickly snapped. I didn't mean to snap, but my nerves were all over the place.

Aiden didn't seem to take any alarm at my oddities. He nodded. "Do you want me to buy you ice cream after school?"

"Huh?"

He narrowed his eyes and glanced around before leaning in toward me. "You know, for your thing." He nodded toward my lap. ,

"What? What thing?"

"You know. The thing that comes at the end of a sentence. Your monthly lady friend. You always get extra snappy around that time, and I know you like ice cream so—"

"Oh my gosh, Aiden, I'm not on my period!" I whisper-shouted, smacking his arm.

He rubbed his arm jokingly as if I hurt him, and my gosh, how I wanted to rub his rock-hard arm, too. "My bad, my bad. Just wanted to make sure you're all right."

"Don't do that."

"Do what?"

Be so thoughtful. Thoughtfulness was a turn-on, too.

"Nothing. Never mind. I'm fine."

"Are you sure?"

"Yes. Just didn't sleep well last night."

"Fair enough." He nudged me in the arm, and those bluest of blue eyes looked deep into mine. Was there a longing in his stare, too? Did he ever look into my eyes and want to swim in them? Or was this a one-way crush?

He went back to his drawing, and I fiddled with my sweaty palms, wiping them against my gray sweatpants, leaving sweat stains. Sweat stains, which now, after seventeen years of Aiden knowing me, made me feel embarrassed. Did he think I was a sweaty beast? Did he wonder why I was so tomboyish? Of course, the crush was a one-way street. I'd seen the people he fell for, and I didn't fit that prototype. I was the opposite of every single girl he'd ever wanted.

I went to my first few classes and tried to focus on my studies, but for some reason, my mind kept wandering to Aiden. It didn't help that every girl in our school had a newly developed crush on my best friend. How cliché. Gosh. I was cliché because I, too, fell into the crushing on Aiden territory. I found myself scribbling in my notebook, writing his name and crossing it out, and trying to shake him from my thoughts. I wasn't thinking about him too much, I told myself. I was thinking about him just as much as I thought about everyone.

As I walked down the halls toward the cafeteria, I held the straps of my backpack tightly. I moved past my classmates and noticed them, too. Just as much as I noticed and thought about Aiden, really. Aiden did not get special treatment inside my noggin. Nope. Just normal, everyday thoughts of my very best friend.

There was Erika Wells. She smelled like strawberry shampoo whenever she walked past me. And Tommy Henry smelled like cigarettes and hairspray. Kelsey Smith smelled like bad decisions and roses. And—

Lemon drops.

He smelled like delicious, sensational lemon drops.

"What's that smell on you?!" I aggressively barked at Aiden as he set down his lunch tray to join me.

He didn't seem fazed by my outburst. He smiled, and gosh, was his smile always like that? Did he always slightly nuzzle his bottom lip before talking? "A brand sent me a free collection of their colognes." He held his arm out in front of me. "This one is called Bliss. Do you like it?"

I want to drown in you, Aiden Walters.

I swatted his arm away even though I wanted to rub my nose against his wrist for the remainder of the day while inhaling his lemon drop scent.

I shrugged and cleared my throat. "It's fine."

Like you.

You're fine, Aiden.

So, so unbelievably fine.

He took a long sniff of his wrist and nodded. "I like it."

"I like you, too," I replied.

"What?"

"What?" I echoed. I shook my head. "I mean, I like it, too. The smell. I was talking about your cologne."

He narrowed his eyes. "Are you sure you don't want me to buy you ice cream after school?"

I grumbled and grimaced but didn't want him to think I was acting strange for any other reason outside of perhaps being on my period. "Ice cream would be nice."

THIRTEEN

Aiden

WELL, I'LL BE DAMNED.

Hailee had a crush on me.

Unlike me and my top-notch acting skills, my best friend was terrible at trying to hide her feelings. Hailee Jones wore her emotions on her face as if they were stitched in place against her skin. It was one of my favorite things about her—how easy it was to read her. Sometimes, I wondered if everyone could read her the way I could or if I'd just become ultra-tuned in on every little curve that fell against her face.

I couldn't think of anything better than this outcome. I'd been walking around with the secret that I had feelings for my best friend, so to discover that she had feelings for me was a dream come true. Now, I wasn't too self-conscious about bringing it up to her, either, because it was clear she felt the same way.

I couldn't wait until morning to tell her exactly how I felt.

FOURTEEN

Hailee

THE NEXT MORNING, I WAITED AT THE BUS STOP. AIDEN CAME bouncing out, extremely excited and wide awake.

"Too much energy," I muttered to him, still rubbing the sleep from my eyes.

"Never too much energy," he said, grinning widely. "You look beautiful today."

"What?" I asked. Was I hallucinating? Did I pass out at some point and end up in a deep coma? Do people dream while in a coma?

"I said you're beautiful, Hailee."

"Oh." I grimaced and narrowed my eyes. "Why did you say that?"

"Because it's true."

"Oh." He had a goofy smile on his face. I cocked an eyebrow. "What is it?"

"I've been thinking."

"That's a very harmful thing for a brain like yours."

"Yeah, not going to lie, it's been a rough few hours. I wonder if people get headaches from thinking too much."

"Probably just you."

He smiled. Gosh, I loved his smiles the most.

"What are you thinking about?" I asked, trying to shift the conversation to make my butterflies disappear.

"Skipping school today."

I snickered. "Yeah, right."

"With you," he added.

I looked at him, confused. For a second, I thought I imagined the softness in his eyes, the somberness to his stare, the honesty in his words. Yet when it stayed longer, I swallowed hard, noting that the butterflies affecting me only grew in intensity.

"You want to skip school today?" I echoed his question.

"Yes."

"With me?"

"Uh-huh."

I narrowed my eyes. "Did you kill someone or something? Do you need an alibi?"

He laughed. "No. I just want to go on a date with you."

"I just don't see why—" Wait. Pause. Did he say date? Like D-A-T-E? Like date-date? With me? With me-me? "What did you just say?"

"I want to take you on a date."

I blinked at him so repeatedly that I was shocked that my eyelashes didn't fall off. "Like, a friend-date?"

"Yeah, sure. Or… more? A more-date."

Oh my gosh, I was in a deep coma.

"But, if you wanted to go on a more-date with me, that would mean you like me more than a friend-date."

"Yeah."

Why was he acting so calm, cool, and collected about this? Why weren't his eyes bugged out like mine from this reveal? How long had he been sitting on these feelings?!

"Why would you want to go on a date with me?!" I barked. My nose flared with irritation. I didn't even know why I said it so aggressively. It was as if my emotions didn't even know how to act anymore. I was malfunctioning in the worst of ways right in front of Aiden. My mind, body, spirit, soul—all those things that made me who I'd been were under major attack. Every inch of me was starting to sweat. Was my tongue sweating?

No, Hailee, that's your saliva, idiot.

"Because." He shrugged. "You're the person I think about when I'm not thinking at all. You're also the person I think about when I'm thinking too much. You kind of just live in my thoughts when they are calm and wild. Like, some people have thoughts, and I have Hailee. So I want to go on a date with you."

"Is it opposite day?" I asked.

"It's not opposite day."

"Oh."

"Yeah, oh."

"Tom," I breathed out.

"Yes, Jerry?"

I didn't know what to say or do. I felt frozen in my spot because he was saying the things I'd wanted him to say, but for some reason, that scared me.

"Hailee." He glanced down the street again. "I really want to spend today with you and go to the movies and to lunch with you. And cross off the *Ferris Bueller's Day Off* bucket list item with you. And look at you. And date-date you. But if we do this, we have to go now."

"Now?"

He looked down the road and then back to me. He took my hands into his and moved in closer. We were holding hands as a more-type holding hands, or maybe it was a friends-type holding hands. Who knew anymore? Not me, not I, not Hailee Jones.

"Now," he echoed.

I said the only thing I could think to say. "Okay."

With that confirmation, Aiden yanked me toward his backyard, where we hid out until after our school bus left without us. His parents were already out of the house for the day. His dad had gone into Chicago to network with others in Aiden's industry until later that night.

Aiden grabbed the keys to the spare car in their driveway, opened the door for me, and we were off to watch a movie at eight in the morning.

"When we get there, you can have anything you want. I've got you covered," Aiden said.

"I can pay for my stuff."

"That would be a friend-date. This is a more-date, remember?"

"This isn't the 1920s. A woman can pay for her own date."

"Do you want to pay for your own date?"

"Of course not. Why would you even ask that? I'm old-fashioned in certain ways, Aiden."

He laughed. "You're the most confusing person I've ever met."

"You already knew that and still decided you wanted a more-date with me. Who's the real confusing person here?"

"Fair enough."

I got comfy in the car, leaning my seat back as Aiden said, "Will you split a dog with me and share the popcorn?"

"I'm not that hungry."

"Liar. I hear your stomach growling. Please don't tell me you don't like hot dogs and popcorn anymore. I can't take much more heartbreak."

I snickered. "I do like hot dogs and popcorn, but you do know what a hot dog is made of, right?"

"As a guy who eats the school chicken patties, I can assure you that I am not too worried about what's in a hot dog."

I glanced over at him to find him with that stupid smirk that I loved. "I'll split a popcorn and dog with you." We arrived at the theater, and I realized an important detail that was missing. "What movie are we seeing anyway?"

"I don't know. Whatever's playing at eight in the morning."

"You lead, and I'll follow," I said, allowing him to pull me along. "Oh, by the way, in the past thirty seconds, I came to a realization."

"And what's that?"

"I want my own hot dog. No splits."

The movie was long and boring, and Aiden and I were the only ones in the theater. That somehow made it even more fun. We talked through the whole thing and laughed the whole time. I didn't know when it happened, when I became so comfortable being around him, talking, saying more than "yeah," but I was glad that it did. Hanging out with Aiden that morning would be a core memory of mine. I didn't know my heart could feel like that. I didn't know I'd ever be able to unlock a new level of happiness.

Aiden didn't finish his hot dog, but he didn't look at me sideways when I finished it for him. He didn't judge my appetite or mention me shoving handfuls of popcorn into my mouth. He just looked at me with those blue eyes that read nothing but kindness. When I looked into those eyes, it was as if they gave me permission to be myself wholly and completely.

He felt safe to me. I didn't know a haven could be a person until that very morning.

We watched two more movies after that. The last one being the worst.

"That movie was awful," I remarked as I walked out of the theater in a giggling fit.

"It was pretty bad," Aiden agreed after he tossed out our popcorn container. "But somehow, it was still the best movie experience of my life."

"Me too. I now understand why people skip school." I spun in a circle. "This feels free. Do you feel it?" I took his hands into mine and began spinning with him. "Free!"

We spun faster and faster, chuckling like kindergarteners during recess until I lost my footing a bit. Aiden was quick to pull me in closer to him to steady my unstable steps. He pulled me into his chest and held me close. Our spinning came to a halt as we stood on solid ground, yet somehow I still felt as if I were spinning round and round. His eyes were dilated as he stared at me. I watched as his stare moved from my eyes to my lips. My eyes fell to his mouth as it parted, and he whispered, "Free."

His hands moved to my lower back, and I grew a little closer to him. My hands landed against his chest as I stared up at him once more. "Free," I softly replied.

Were our thoughts the same?

Was he thinking about kissing me the way I was thinking about kissing him?

Was his heart beating forward, then backward, then sideways, too?

Were his thoughts still spinning at full speed ahead?

Were his lips soft?

Did he know I wanted him to be my first kiss?

Did his heart want to know mine the same way my heart wanted to know his?

"Hails," he breathily sighed. Our faces were so close that his word warmed my skin.

"Yeah," I breathed back, my stare on his lips. His full, plump lips.

"I'm thinking about doing something right now." His fingers slightly massaged my lower back, creating a wave of rippled nerves throbbing between my thighs.

"Yeah?"

"Yeah." His teeth slowly grazed against his bottom lip. "Are you thinking about it, too?"

I nodded. "Yeah."

"Yeah?"

I giggled, but this time it was nervously. My butterflies were intensifying, my nerves were a wreck, my anxiety was heightened, and he smelled so much like lemon drops, which was my new favorite scent. "Yeah."

He brought a hand up to my mouth and gently brushed my bottom lip with his thumb. "Hailee, I—"

"Are you Aiden Walters?!" someone blurted out, making me jump what felt like five feet away from Aiden. Our intimate moment was ambushed by three girls, squealing like crazy over Aiden.

"It is him! Oh my gosh! You are so hot," one of them breathed out, jumping up and down.

The other one, the redhead, told him that he was the most talented person in the world. Then they all begged him for photographs. Aiden's whole body shifted into a different demeanor, and he turned up his charm factor. He instantly went into actor mode and was so kind to the girls, giving them the photographs and autographs which they begged for.

Shouldn't you people be in school?

Wait, I should've, too. Still, they just ruined what was bound to be the best moment of my life.

"I'm sorry, ladies, I'd love to chat more, but we have a meeting to get to," Aiden said, stepping over toward me.

The girls looked in my direction, and the redhead blurted out, "Is that your girlfriend?"

"Of course, it's not," the other replied.

What was that supposed to mean?

The way she eyed my body up and down with a look of disgust

showed exactly what she meant by her commentary. Within an instant, I regretted eating that popcorn and the hot dogs.

Aiden's reaction was the opposite of mine, though. His wasn't shame; it was anger. "What's that supposed to mean?" he demanded, his kind persona fading as his nostrils began to flare.

"No offense." The girl giggled. "She just doesn't seem like your type."

"My type?" he barked. His tone made it out as if he were about to snap at these strangers. Before he could, I put a comforting hand against his shoulder.

"Let's go," I whispered.

"They're assholes," he mumbled under his breath.

"Yeah," I agreed. "But let's go."

He did as I said as I tugged him away. By the time we reached the car, Aiden was still sitting in an energy of rage, but still, he opened the passenger door for me. Even in his anger, he was still so gentle with me.

He climbed into the driver's seat and shut his door. His hands gripped the steering wheel, and he shut his eyes as he released weighted breaths of irritation.

I sat in silence for a moment. "Aiden, it's okay. I—"

He held a finger up to silence me, then went back to holding the steering wheel.

When he was ready, he turned to me, and his eyes were packed with so much emotion and sincerity that I felt tears pushing to the forefront of my eyes.

"Everything about you keeps me in awe, Hailee. From your face to your waist and from your hips to your thighs, you are remarkable. Every inch of your being is something I long for. But it's not just the physical stuff either, even though holy fuck, your physical stuff," he groaned in delight as he bit his fist jokingly, making me laugh.

Then he grew more somber as he continued. "Your body, mind, and spirit, I want it all. You're the most beautiful person I've ever met, Hailee Jones, and I'm in love with you. You're the kindest, funniest, most caring person in this world, and I'm in love with you. You have the most stunning brown eyes I get lost in, and I'm in love with you. You have a smile that I dream about constantly, and I'm in love with you. You're gentle and strong, and I'm in love with you. And every time someone disrespects you, it sets off a rage inside me because you are the most incredible person I've ever met, and I'm in love with you."

He had tears rolling down his cheeks from either rage from the others or from his love for me. Maybe it was a mixture of both. Aiden didn't cry often, and he didn't cry easily, so the fact that he felt safe enough to show that side of him in front of me made me feel so much joy.

I wiped his tears before leaning toward him and placing my forehead against his. "You're my best friend, Aiden." My mouth was millimeters away from his. My heart was racing faster and faster, pounding wildly against my rib cage. I leaned in, brushing my lips against his. "And I'm in love with you."

FIFTEEN

Aiden

As Hailee and I pulled up to our houses, we had a nice surprise waiting. Two sets of parents sitting on their front porches with looks of annoyance plastered on their faces.

"Oh boy. Do you think we got caught?" Hailee asked.

I put the car in park. "Judging by the way my father's nose is flaring, all signs point to yes."

Hailee tilted her head toward me with a big smile on her face. "We are about to be grounded for life."

"Yep."

"Worth it?"

I laid my head against the headrest and grinned. "Worth it." I squeezed her hand before we both climbed out to face our punishments. We went our separate ways, and even though I knew Hailee's parents might've been a little tough on her, I was certain my father would take the cake on the rage factor.

I already felt my panic rising as I walked over to my parents. "Hey, Mom. Hey, Dad."

"Don't 'hey, Dad' me. Why weren't you at school today?"

"I...um, well..." I stuttered, feeling like an idiot because finding words always seemed hard whenever I was confronted by my father. "We, uh—"

"Spit it out," he ordered.

"Maybe we should move this inside," Mom said, walking over to me. She glanced down the street at our nosy neighbors. Then she placed a hand on Dad's shoulder. "Inside, Sam."

He grumbled, and the three of us walked into the house.

I rubbed the back of my neck. "How did you even find out?"

He pulled out his cell phone and held it in front of our faces. "It turns out when your son is a celebrity, people take videos of him and post them all over social media. Plus, news flash, if your kid is missing from one period, the school calls and notifies the parent," Dad barked, his veins popping out of his neck. His irritation was high, and my unease grew with each passing second. I shouldn't have gone to the movies that day. Even though it was the best day of my life. Even though I felt free for the first time in a long time. Even though I was in love with Hailee Jones, and she loved me, too.

Holy shit, she loved me, too.

Still, I shouldn't have gone because I let him down.

"Plus, what about that audition you were supposed to film and submit last night?" he asked me.

Oh, crap. I forgot about that. I scratched at my hair and muttered an apology. I felt sweat building at the brim of my forehead. My mouth parted to speak, but no sounds were produced. I felt frozen in a sea of anxiety, unsure of what to do or say next.

Mom noticed my panic and placed a gentle hand on my arm. "Go to your room. Your father and I will discuss your punishment, and we will go from there."

"You're being too easy on him," Dad warned.

Mom shot him a harsh look. "And you're being too cruel." She turned to me. "Your room. Now."

I did as she said. I went to the bathroom and let out a heavy sigh as my panic attack escaped from my chest where it had been sitting. "I'm okay, I'm okay, I'm okay," I repeatedly told myself as my heart pounded against my chest as if it were trying to escape. "I'm okay, I'm okay, I'm okay," I said again, trying to add calmness to the wildness of my thoughts.

Dad looked at me as if he hated me. He stared as if I was the biggest disappointment in his life.

How did I forget to send that audition in? How did I drop that ball? He was going to be so pissed at me for that. I was trying my best to be what he wanted me to be. I was trying my best not to let him down. But today... I needed today. I needed to feel like I could be me for a little while and not who my father wanted me to be—him.

I splashed water on my face, feeling on the verge of vomiting. I hated how shaky my body felt as the panic rippled through my nervous system. I hated how it felt as if every inch of me was seconds away from shutting down. I hated how my mother could see how close I was to the edge and pull me back, but my father didn't notice my struggles. He couldn't see me.

He can't see me.

He only saw what he wished to see, and whenever I shifted his perspective of being his perfect son, his disappointment made me want to fade into the void of life.

"What's the verdict?" I asked Mom after she knocked on my door and came into my bedroom. I'd been sitting on my bed, waiting to hear the outcome of the day. She and Dad had been talking for the past forty-five minutes about me, and I turned my music up to tune it out.

"Three weeks grounded. Unless you have an audition coming up and need to travel. Outside of that, you go to school and then come home."

"Fair enough."

She walked over to my bed and took a seat beside me. "It's not like you to lie and skip school like that."

"Yeah, I know."

"What's going on in that head of yours?"

"It was on Hailee's and my bucket list."

Mom smiled a little. "Tom and Jerry being Tom and Jerry, huh?"

I scrunched up my nose. "I told her I had feelings for her today," I mentioned.

Her eyes widened, but she didn't seem too surprised. "And she...?"

"Feels the same way."

She smiled. "Took you two long enough to figure that out."

"Wait, you knew?"

"I'm your mother, Aiden." She kissed my forehead. "I know everything."

"Dad's not going to forgive me for this, is he?"

"Your father will get over it. He's just in a mood right now. I'm not worried about that, though. I'm worried about you, Aiden. I see how hard you're working to keep your father happy, but I just don't know if you're happy."

"I'm okay," I lied.

"Aiden Scott Walters. Try again."

"I needed a break. I've been a bit overwhelmed and saw a way to escape for a few hours with a girl I really like. It was stupid, but—"

"You had fun."

I nodded.

She leaned in and smiled. "Good. You deserve more of that."

"You're not mad at me like Dad is?"

"Mostly, I'm mad at myself for not creating a space where you felt as if you could come and tell me these things. I'm upset with your father for being so stern with you. We'll do better, Aiden. Your mental health is important, and I see that. I don't want you to slip into a dark place where you feel like you can't share these things with me. Okay?"

"Okay."

"Next time you need a break, let me know. I can write you a get-out-of-school-free pass."

"Dad won't like that."

"Luckily, he doesn't make all the rules in this house." She narrowed her stare. "He gets to you more than I realized. I'm sorry, A. I'll talk to him. But do know, you being upfront with your feelings to us will help avoid these outcomes. Honesty is best even when it's hard, okay?"

"Okay."

Before she left, she kissed my forehead. "I love you, I love you, I love you, I love you."

She tossed a few extra "I love yous" into the mix because I think she knew I needed it that evening. I gave her four "I love yous" back because she deserved every single one.

I closed my bedroom door and walked over to my window. After I climbed out, I walked over to Hailee's and knocked two times. She came over and smiled. She climbed out of the window and then sat on the ledge. "Are you grounded, too?"

"Three weeks. You?"

"Four!" she exclaimed. "Until Thanksgiving."

"Our parents are dramatic. It's not like we skipped school, drove a car to a different city, and hid it from them or something," I joked, sitting beside her. She didn't laugh at my stupid joke, so I nudged her arm. "You okay?"

"I'm in love with you," she blurted out, almost sounding upset about it.

"Yeah. I thought we came to that conclusion already today."

She turned to face me a little more and sighed. "No, Aiden. I mean, I love you a lot, and now you're saying you love me back, and that's scary."

"How is that scary? I thought two people loving each other was a good thing."

"It is for most, but you're my best friend."

"Which makes it even better."

"Or worse. We should make pie charts of the pros and cons of us dating."

"We aren't making pie charts."

"What if we don't work out as a relationship?"

"Then we'll go back to being friends."

"What if it's a messy breakup?"

I snickered. "Why are we already talking about breakups before we've even gotten to the dating part?"

"Because we have to think this out."

"Or we can just let it happen." I took her hand into mine and led us to the grass, where we sat.

"Why aren't you overthinking this like me? Why aren't you freaked out?"

"Because I know this is right. Because I know we were always supposed to get to this point. Because you're you, and I'm me, and we've always made sense. Because I know it can only get better from here. If I can love you this much as a friend, I can only imagine how much love I can have when I'm yours. Plus, I promise I won't do it."

"Do what?"

"Break your heart."

"I promise I won't break yours either," I swore.

He smiled. "I know, Jerry."

"How do you even like to be loved, though?" she asked.

"I don't know. I was hoping you could show me."

She smiled and took my hands into hers. We sat between the houses with the stars perched above us in the sky. My heart pounded wildly against my chest as I stared at our embraced hands.

"This is nice?" I questioned in a whisper.

"This is nice," she replied.

I pulled her hands up to my mouth and kissed her palms. "This is nice?"

"This is nice," she agreed.

I bit my bottom lip and inched my body closer to hers. My mouth grazed against hers. "This is nice?" I asked.

"This is nice." I went to lift her onto my lap, and she paused. "Wait, no. I'm too big for that," she said. I saw it, too, the quickness of her insecurities hitting her stare.

I ignored her as I settled her onto my lap, and she wrapped her arms around my neck. She hovered over me, not placing all her weight against mine.

"Hailee?"

"Yes."

"Sit."

"But—"

"Butt." I moved my hands to her hips and yanked her down a little. The shyness hit her cheeks, but she relaxed against me. It felt like the missing piece of my favorite puzzle sliding into its rightful place.

I placed my forehead against hers as I wrapped my arms around her waist. "This is mine?" I asked so quietly as our mouths rested against one another.

She nodded. "This is yours."

I kissed her so slowly, and every inch of me felt it. Her eyes began to water as we crossed the barrier into a new territory with one another. The invisible lines between friends and lovers began to somehow tangle. We didn't have to lose one for the other. We could create our own story where we loved one another both within our friendship and within this newfound relationship. Maybe that's why it would work for us. Maybe the best love was the kind built with the strongest friendship.

One kiss sealed the deal.

She was mine, and I was hers, and it felt so good that I had to kiss her again.

- ~~Have your first kiss~~
- ~~Both get into a relationship~~

Felt good to cross those off our list. I couldn't think of a person I'd rather share that task with, either.

She laid her head against my shoulder. "I think I'm going to like this."

"Like what?"

"Being loved by you."

SIXTEEN

Aiden

THE MORNING AFTER HAILEE AND I SHARED OUR FIRST KISS, WE met at the bus stop like we always did.

"Hi," I said.

"Hi," she replied.

Her cheeks were sitting high, and I could tell she was a bit nervous.

"Handshake?" I asked, hoping that would make her feel a bit more normal because we were still us.

She put her hand in front of her, palm facing me, and she began the chant. "Pancake, pancake, up real high."

Without hesitation, I joined in patting my hand against hers. "If you toss it, it will fly."

She smacked the back of her hand against mine three times. "If you drop it, it will go."

We both spun once, then faced one another, patted hands, and did a weird body roll as we said, "Down the drains where the creepy clown flows."

She laughed until I took her hand into mine to hold.

She hesitated. "Wait."

"What?"

"You're going to hold my hand? In front of people? Like at school?" she timidly asked.

I smirked. My best friend was nervous. No, wait, correction: my girlfriend was nervous. Wait, no. That still wasn't right. Hailee was my best girlfriend. Yes, that was what she was now—my best girlfriend. The ultimate position in my life.

"I've been waiting seventeen years to hold your hand," I said matter-of-factly. "So yes, I'm going to hold your hand in front of the whole world if that's okay with you."

"Oh." She grumbled a little, doing that overthinking thing she did where her nose crinkled up. She then took my hand into hers, her perfect chipmunk cheeks rose and blushed over, and she replied, "Okay then."

Okay then.

That was what she said when she couldn't over analyze a situation. When her brilliant mind couldn't come up with a scenario for things not to work out. Whenever I received an okay then from Hailee, it felt like the biggest victory.

I knew it was odd, but I loved her cheeks so much when they rose with her smiles.

She had three freckles that sat on her right cheek and seven that sat on her left, and each time she smiled, I somehow counted every single one. I wanted to kiss those cheeks day in, day out.

For now, though, it felt good to simply hold her hand.

So many good things were going on for me lately that I wasn't shocked when Jake reached out to me.

Jake was one of the biggest disappointments in my life. You know how some people were bursts of sunshine on cloudy days? Jake was the complete opposite. He walked into the sunny days, and somehow, the sky always darkened.

When everything seemed to be going good in my life, my biological father always liked to show up to shake things up for me. I was somewhat surprised when I received a text message from him asking me to meet up because I hadn't seen Jake in almost a year. The last time I saw him, he was drunk at Thanksgiving and going on and on about how he was going to get sober. He promised the following morning to take me shopping for Black Friday. I waited for hours on my front porch for him to come.

That was what Jake did—made promises he couldn't keep. I couldn't count the number of times as a kid I'd waited on my front porch for Jake to take me out for bonding time. He'd hardly ever shown up, and when he did, he was too wasted to drive.

Jake was a sports guy. He'd tell me all about his favorite teams, so as a kid, they became my favorites, too, because I wanted to have something in common with him. During the holidays, I'd buy him jerseys for the teams he loved and matching ones for myself. He'd talk about how he'd take me to games down in Chicago, and I'd sit on the porch wearing those jerseys waiting. And waiting. And waiting.

Over time, I started waiting less, but I still waited, just like that afternoon. He called and asked if I wanted to catch a movie with him, and a big part of my mind told me to ignore him. Unfortunately, my stupid heart said to give him one more try.

Dad was always vouching for me to give Jake chances. After all, he was his cousin. Dad said family mattered more than anything. Mom said family only mattered as long as they didn't do you dirty. Clearly, my parents had different viewpoints on Jake being in my life.

I sat on the front step of my porch, and I was somewhat shocked when I saw Jake pull up in a car. Not only did he show up, but he had a nice vehicle in tow. Normally, he'd ask to borrow one of Dad's.

"If it isn't my favorite kid," Jake said as he walked toward me. I didn't like when he called me his kid. It reminded me of how he and I were somewhat connected forever.

He held his arms out with enthusiasm, and even though I worked hard not to get excited about seeing that man, my inner child was doing cartwheels. A part of me still craved a connection with him. I felt wanted when he showed up. I felt unwanted when he didn't. The scale of wanted and unwanted with Jake was tipping heavily in the unwanted direction.

"Hey, Jake," I said, pulling him into a hug.

"Holy shit, man. When did you turn into the Incredible Hulk?" He pounded his hands against my biceps. "I need you to train me in the gym."

"We could do that," I quickly replied. My mind instantly started daydreaming about what it could've been like to get Jake into the gym with me.

Damn that hope. It still existed.

"Yeah, man. You look good." He patted my arms. "You want to head to a diner for some lunch?"

"I thought you wanted to go see that new movie."

"Definitely. My schedule is a bit more jam-packed than I thought it would be. I have an interview for a job that I gotta make later this afternoon."

"Oh, okay. Yeah, let's grab a bite. I didn't know you had a new car."

Jake walked over to it and put his hands on the top of the hood. "Yeah. Your old man hooked me up with the down payment for it. I'm gonna pay him back once I get this job."

"My husband did what now?" Mom said, walking out onto the front porch to catch the conversation with Jake. She crossed her arms, wearing her "I'm annoyed" expression.

"Shit, I wasn't supposed to mention that. Hey, Laurie. You're looking good as always."

"Mm-hmm," Mom groaned. "Where are you taking my son?"

"How about some wings?" Jake said, snapping his fingers toward me. "You still like barbecue wings from West's?"

I hadn't been to West's since I was twelve years old. That was the last time Jake and I had a one-on-one situation.

"Yeah, love it there," I agreed.

"I'll have him back in no time, Laurie," Jake promised.

"I'm sure you will," she replied as she walked over to me. She pulled me into a hug and held on tight. "Call me if you need me."

"I won't need anything. I'll be back soon. Love you, Mom."

"Love you, too. Have fun and be safe." She kissed my cheek, and then Jake and I were off and away.

As we drove, Jake was distracted by any and everything. He had one cigarette dangling from his mouth, one hand on the steering wheel, and the other messing around with the radio. "You want a cig?" he offered.

"I don't smoke."

"Yeah, of course. Smart. I was just teasing, anyway. This shit is bad for you. Just say no." He snickered. "So what's new with you? If I knew you were back in town, I would've swung by to hang out sooner." That was a lie, but whatever. He was the kind of person who lied so much that he believed his own falsehoods. "I saw some articles online about how you had yourself a girl?"

"Yeah, Hailee."

"Oh, no shit? How did you guys meet?"

I stared at him blankly. "It's Hailee. My best friend, Hailee. You've met her at most holidays and—"

His phone started ringing, and he looked down at it as he pulled up to the diner. "Oh, shit," he muttered as he held a silencing finger up toward me. He hopped out of the car and answered his phone quickly.

As I climbed out of the car, he was talking hush-hush on the phone. When he hung up, his mood had shifted a bit, but he gave me a half grin and opened the door to the diner. "Ready, buddy?"

"Yeah, sure."

Being around Jake felt like being around a stranger. I didn't know why there was a part of me that longed for a connection with him in some way. I had wonderful parents. There was no reason I should've even thought about Jake, let alone, my biological mother. I didn't even know her name, but she still crossed my mind every now and again. I hated that, too. It felt like I was betraying my own mother in some odd way.

We sat with our wings and talked for a while as Jake's phone kept going off. He grumbled a bit after one message and sat back in the booth. "Hey, I just got called into work. So I might have to dip out earlier than planned. Like, now."

"I thought you had the interview today. I didn't know you got the job already."

"Right, yeah. I mean, it's like a done deal. I am getting the job. It's just all the bullshit paperwork and stuff, you know? They need me to come in earlier than planned." He brushed his thumb against his nose and leaned in. "Listen, kid, this is embarrassing, but things have been a bit tight. I was wondering if I could get a loan from you for a short period. Just until I can get up and on my feet. Things are turning around. I know they are. You know, I ran into a psychic last week, and she said things were going to start slow, and then boom! I'm on a rocket ship toward win after win. But, for the time being, if you could help me out, that would mean a lot to me."

That hope that still showed up within my gut? It was slowly being ripped to shreds.

"I, uh, I didn't bring cash."

"That's fine. They've got an ATM right over there. You can take out cash right now." He gestured behind him and then gave me a smile that looked like mine. I hated that. I hated how we had the same smiles. Unlike mine, though, his felt sleazy. I couldn't believe that I thought Jake was any different than before. It was embarrassing how I thought that this time would be different all because he showed up. Turned out, he only showed up so he could get something out from me.

I brushed my hand through my hair. "How much do you need?"

"I don't know. An Emmy-winning boy like you? Maybe you can get by with giving your old man like eight hundred or a thousand?"

He didn't see my heart break at that moment, but of course he missed it happening. He knew nothing about me. How would he know how to notice my pain?

I slid out of the booth and headed to the ATM to get the money out. The second I handed it to him, he took a twenty and put it down on the table. "You can find a ride home, yeah? Lunch is on me," he said. I wasn't sure if he was being ironic or not. He then collected his things and headed out, leaving me stranded.

I sat there for an hour longer, too embarrassed to call my parents that early on to come get me. After that time passed, I called Mom to pick me up. She pulled up within ten minutes.

I climbed into the passenger seat and didn't say anything. I didn't have to tell her anything, though, because Mom was too good at reading me.

"Hey, look at me," she urged, shoving me in the arm.

"I'm fine," I swore, staring out my window.

"Aiden, look at me right now," she ordered.

I sighed and turned toward her. She locked her eyes with mine. I wished my eyes looked like my mother's. I guessed that was too much to ask for.

She placed her hands against my cheeks and cradled my face as if I was still that little boy waiting on the front porch for Jake to love me.

"You are remarkable, Aiden Scott Walters. You are a great person with an extraordinary heart. You are kind, and good, and true. Don't let anyone else's bullshit steal your joy from you. It's yours. You own it. No one else gets to have the rights to it. Do you understand me?"

"Yes, ma'am."

She tapped my cheek before leaning in to kiss it. "Okay. Let's get you home."

That night, Mom and Dad got into the biggest argument over Jake. I listened from my bedroom. My mother was the calmest of souls. She never raised her voice or cussed until someone pushed one of her triggers. I was her biggest trigger, and that afternoon, it had been pushed.

"And you didn't think I deserved to know you were handing Jake a car, Samuel? I mean, are you shitting me?" Mom blasted. Cuss words from Mom meant she was pissed.

"It was a loan. He said he'll pay it back," Dad argued.

"Yeah, he said the same thing last time, right before he crashed the vehicle."

"He's doing better now."

"Oh, is he? Is that why he abandoned our son at a diner? Because he's got his shit together? I don't want that man in our lives anymore. He's no good, and he's proved that fact time and time again."

"What do you want me to say, huh? You want me to ditch my cousin?"

"Yes! You don't owe him anything. You are not your cousin's keeper."

"He deserves to have a connection with Aiden."

"No, he doesn't. He doesn't deserve an ounce of my son's love, especially with how he keeps abusing it. I'm disgusted that you think he does."

I had enough of listening to them argue. I felt my panic coming back as I scratched at the palms of my hands. I headed to my window and climbed outside. It was almost December, and the weather showcased it. The chilly breeze brushed against my face as goose bumps formed on my forearms.

I knocked on Hailee's window, and she came over smiling. The moment she saw me, her grin dropped. She opened the window, and she could hear my parents arguing. She didn't say a word. She just stepped to the side and let me climb into her room.

I lay on her bed, and she shut off the lights and climbed in beside me. "Do you want to talk about it?"

"No."

"Are you sure? You can tell me anything."

I grimaced. "I'm not the best at talking about the hard stuff. My mind gets too jumbled trying to speak the words out loud."

"Oh, okay. Well, how can I help you tonight?"

"Just be here with me. That will be enough."

She snuggled into me, and she fell asleep in my arms.

Oh.

There it is.

The way Hailee Jones loved me… that was it.

That was exactly how I wanted to be loved.

I didn't need anything from her. I just needed…her.

SEVENTEEN

Hailee

AFTER OUR NEWFOUND ROMANCE, AIDEN HAD TO HEAD OFF
to Los Angeles for some business work for two weeks. I
dreaded having him gone, but I kept my head down and
counted the days until his return. During his trip, he was busy, but
there wasn't an evening when he didn't make time to call me. Each
morning before I went to school, he'd send me a text message saying
he hoped I had a great day. When I called him out about the two-hour
time difference, he told me he set an alarm to tell me good morning,
then he'd hit snooze on his clock and go back to sleep.

Aiden Walters, ladies and gentlemen. The boy who set the standards.

Each day at lunch, I'd sit alone at my table. Carlton noticed me one
day, but he didn't dare walk over to me. He knew we had nothing to say
to one another. The popular kids had already ditched him, too, seeing
as how they'd had their laughs. That didn't mean they were done mocking me yet, though.

"Hey, Hailee, how are you doing?" Cara asked, sliding into the lunch
booth across from me. She had two followers with her, and they sat on

either side of her. They were smiling as bright as ever, which was enough of an alarm for me.

They were smiling, but it didn't seem like a peaceful approach. I was on high alert.

"Hi?" I said as a question.

Cara grinned and leaned in toward me. She took my hands into hers. "I think it's great that you and Aiden have officially become official. I mean, who doesn't love a friends-to-lovers trope, am I right?"

I remained silent.

For the past few weeks, Cara and her friends still mocked me over my weight. I didn't tell Aiden about it, though, because him being Aiden, he would've flipped out.

"I think it's so brave of you to date him," Cara's friend, Elizabeth, stated.

"So, so brave," Natalie echoed. "Like, so brave," she swooned.

Brave?

What was so brave about me dating Aiden?

I knew I shouldn't have, but I took the bait. "What do you mean?"

Cara kept smiling. "The article just came out this morning. You have to read what people are saying about you online."

My heart rate picked up as chills ran up and down my spine. "What people are saying?"

Cara lightly gasped, but I was all but certain she wasn't surprised. "You haven't seen? Here, let me show you." She pulled out her cell phone and tapped against it a few times before holding it in my face. There was an article on one of the biggest tabloid websites titled: Everything we know about Aiden Walters's Plus-Sized Girlfriend.

Under the headline was a picture of Aiden and me holding hands, followed by even worse photographs of me in the most unflattering angles that someone took of me during the school day. I was slouched at a desk in one, picking up a dropped notebook in another, and getting my food in the lunch line.

People were taking candid photographs of me at school.

People were taking candid photographs of me at school and giving them to the paparazzi.

People were taking candid photographs of me at school and giving them to the paparazzi, and were all mocking me about it.

"I was nice enough to send them some pictures for their article. You're better than me, honestly," Cara said, picking up the spoon on my lunch tray. "Because if it were me, instead of using this spoon to put food into my mouth…" She turned the handle of the spoon to her mouth and opened it wide, "I'd be using it to get food out of me. But then again, I'm not so brave like you, Hailee."

Tears sat at the back of my eyes, but I didn't want them to fall in front of her and her followers.

I climbed out of the booth, grabbed my backpack, and took off running out of the cafeteria.

"Guys! Hurry! Get video of the hungry-hungry-hippo running," Cara shouted as I made my exit.

Everyone was laughing at me. Not just everyone at school, but everyone online, too. I sat in the janitor's closet in the complete dark as my cell phone shone in my face. I read every article about me, every comment, every trending post.

Aiden's into Black girls? No fucking way.

If she spent half the time doing her hair that she did eating, she could be cute.

There's no way that thing is dating Aiden Walters.

Dear God, I've seen what you've done for others…

How did she get the sexiest guy alive, and I'm still single? Clearly, looks don't matter.

Someone doesn't skip meals.

One burger away from a heart attack.

Mooooo!

This has to be photoshopped.

My phone began ringing as Aiden's name flashed across the screen. Tears fell against the phone as my hands shook repeatedly. My stomach sat in knots as I rejected his call. He called again and again, and I rejected every single one.

Aiden: Answer, Hails.

Aiden: Please. Answer the phone. I saw the articles. They're bullshit.

Aiden: You're perfect. They're idiots and haters and trolls.

Aiden: Please, answer. Hails. Please.

Aiden: I'm coming home on the first flight out. I'm coming.

I headed home that day to find my parents speaking with Laurie in our living room. The second they saw me, it was clear that they, too, had read the online articles.

Dad shot to his feet. "Cinderella," he started.

I shook my head. "I'm fine. I'm going to study."

"Baby girl," Mama began, but I didn't give them a chance to continue. I shot to my bedroom and locked the door behind me. I collapsed onto my bed and cried into my pillows. Every inch of me ached. My head was pounding from crying for so long and so hard.

"Cinderella, we're going to give you the space to feel what you have to feel for a few hours, but then I promise you, I am going to kick this door down and hold you," Dad said from outside my door.

He meant it, too.

I unlocked my door and had dinner with my parents. I could almost feel their concern as Mama made my plate for me. Why did she put so much food on my plate? I didn't need that much food. I shouldn't have been eating that much. My hands sat in my lap as I stared at the mountain of food Mama was giving me as the words of the strangers around the world echoed in my ears.

Fat ass.

Disgusting.

He's cheating on her.

Did you see the size of her thighs?

The dinner conversation was fine, and I told them I was okay. I had to tell them that. Otherwise, they would've worried and felt bad. I didn't want them to feel bad. It wasn't their fault that my body looked the way it did.

After dinner, I went to the bathroom attached to my bedroom and stared at myself in the mirror. I took off my T-shirt and slid out of my sweatpants. I stood there in my bra and panties as tears rolled down my cheeks. My hands moved across my body, across my skin, and gripped the extra weight. I pinched it, I bunched it up, I hated it. I hated it. I hated it.

Me.

I hated myself.

Fat ass.

Disgusting.

He's cheating on her.

Did you see the size of her thighs?

I pulled out the scale from under the sink and dusted it off. I stepped onto it. Two hundred and forty-five pounds. I was two hundred and thirty when the school year started, not that long ago. How did that happen?

Fat ass.

Disgusting.

He's cheating on her.

Did you see the size of her thighs?

I threw up.

I hugged the toilet seat as everything inside me came up. I threw up until I was dry heaving. Until my eyes watered. Until everything felt dizzying.

I stood from the floor, brushed my teeth, then tossed mouthwash into my mouth and wiped the tears from my eyes. I spat out the mouthwash.

I stepped back on the scale.

Two hundred and forty-four pounds.

One pound down?

How was that possible?

I put on my pajamas and climbed into bed. Aiden hadn't stopped texting me. He'd already booked a flight and was on his way to the airport. He kept updating me about when he would get home. It was two in the morning when there was a knock on my window. I went to open it to find my best friend, my person, standing there with the most heartbreaking stare I'd ever seen in my life.

I turned on my lights, then opened my window. The chilled breeze brushed against my face.

"Hey, you." He smiled, but I felt his sadness.

"Hey, you," I replied.

"Can I...?" He gestured into my room.

I stepped to the side. "Yes."

He climbed through my window. He stood beside me and wrapped his arms around my body. I tried to wiggle out of his embrace, uncomfortable with the idea of him feeling my rolls through my pajamas. It was silly because he had held me many times before, but now my mind was jumbled with other people's thoughts that didn't belong to me.

I always thought I was enough. The rest of the world was trying to convince me otherwise. I hated that they were winning, too. I hated that their thoughts in my head were louder than my own.

"I'm sorry," he started.

"It's not your fault."

"It is. It's happening to you because of me, and I hate that." He took off his jacket, followed by his shoes. He rolled up his sleeves. "They're idiots. People who feel loud and proud behind a keyboard are total dicks who just type bullshit to get likes from other miserable people."

"Yeah, but..." My voice trembled.

"I know. It still hurts."

I nodded. "It still hurts."

"They made you insecure."

"Yes."

It wasn't a secret to me that I was plus size. I lived in my body day in, day out. I saw all the things in every situation that non-plus size individuals probably never even thought of. When we went to restaurants, I noticed the chairs. I wondered how I would fit in them, or if it would be an embarrassing situation if said chair snapped beneath me. I never sat in lawn chairs at parties for that exact reason. I loathed airplanes, because sometimes I'd have to ask for a seat belt extender. I overthought what the strangers beside me thought about being seated beside me on the flights. I've walked into shopping malls and had the biggest sizes be too small. I've cried in dressing rooms. I've cried into my pillows when most of the fashion choices I'd had looked like something my grandma would wear.

But also, I'd danced in my body. I'd moved it and flourished in it. On my best days, my body was there for me. On my worst days, it carried my sadness around. I knew my body. I knew its pros and cons. I knew how it squatted and how it stretched. I knew of its abilities, its strengths and weaknesses. It wasn't a new relationship—the one with me and my body. We had our ups and downs, but that was the thing—it was ours.

Now, it felt as if the rest of the world had a say on my body without knowing the history behind every single inch and every single pound. That brought about a whole new level of uncertainty. My body and mind hadn't even had the time to figure out how to process the whole situation.

Society made me doubt myself in a way that I'd never had. Sure, I'd had bad days in my body, but I also had great ones. Yet the world judged me from a few photographs. They didn't know me but pretended to know my body.

Fat ass.

Disgusting.

He's cheating on her.

Did you see the size of her thighs?

It was the world that created a new set of insecurities within me, and I hated that they were silencing out my own inner voice. Their voices were growing louder and louder as mine became muted.

Aiden grimaced. "Okay. What are they?"

"What are what?"

"What are your insecurities?"

"Huh?"

"Your insecurities, what are they?"

I covered my stomach with my arms. *There's one.* A woman online said I should've been embarrassed about my gut. "I'm not going to tell you that."

He grew closer, making my heart rate increase. He placed a hand against my leg, sending a wave of sensation through my whole body. He wouldn't break his eye contact either as he spoke to me. "I want to know each insecurity they created, so I can tell you why they are all wrong."

"Aiden, I'm not going to—"

He took my hands into his. His warmth soothed me. "Tell me one insecurity, and we'll go from there," he requested. My lips parted as he stole my next breath. My thighs began to tingle from the smallest touch he gave me. "Now, Hails. Tell me now."

I went to argue, but before I could, he leaned in, brushed his mouth against mine, and nibbled on my bottom lip before gently biting it. "Do you trust me?" he asked.

Butterflies. "I do."

"Okay. Then take off your clothes."

The way he ordered me… the way his blue eyes stared straight into my soul…I had no choice but to give him the information he demanded.

"Can we turn off the lights?" I asked.

"Absolutely not. We are going to starve out every single insecurity with the lights on. So"—he gestured toward me—"remove the clothes."

With a pool of nerves in my stomach, I removed my pajamas. I stood in front of Aiden, baring not only my body but my soul in a way, too. Standing in front of him like that made me feel a heavy level of embarrassment. That was until I met his stare. It was filled with nothing but admiration.

How did he do that?

How did he look at me and somehow make me want to love myself a little more, too? How did one look from Aiden silence out a million comments from strangers?

And I am in love with you…

"Where do I start?" I asked him.

"Wherever you want. I'm here, and I'm listening."

"My cheeks. They talked about how chubby they are."

He took my hands into his. He brought me close to him, then caressed my cheek with the back of his hand. "I love your high cheeks and how you have three freckles on your left and seven on your right. I love how they rise so high when you smile and how the left one has a small dimple that appears ever so slightly when you laugh." He kissed them, the left cheek three times for each freckle and the right seven times.

His kisses felt like a calming balm he laid against my soul.

"What's next?" he asked.

I shut my eyes, feeling trembles growing. Not from fears, though, from the odd sense of comfort he was delivering to me.

"My arms," I told him. "They said they are ugly and fat and only used for stuffing my face."

He moved to my arms and began massaging them with his fingers, then he placed his arms around my lower back, pulling me into a hug. I hugged him back without any thought, and he sighed with relief as he whispered against my ear. "These arms are my favorite things in the world when they're wrapped around me. They make me feel safe." He then made sure to kiss every single inch of both.

The butterflies intensified with every touch he gave me.

I rubbed my hands against my stomach. "They talked about the size of my stomach. And my thighs. The roundness of my face."

He lowered himself to kneel before me as if he was in a state of worship. That was exactly what he did, too. He worshipped every single inch of my body, running his hands over them, telling me why he loved my stomach, why he craved my thighs, why my face was what he dreamed up whenever he was lonely, how my body was a temple, and how if he could, he'd pray to said temple for the remainder of his life.

When we covered all my insecurities, he laid me in my bed. My heart pounded as I kissed him long and hard. The tabloids, the strangers, the kids at school—they all began to fade from my mind. At that moment, it was just him and me. At that moment, all I wanted, all I ever wanted, was for Aiden to stay with me.

As we kissed, I removed his shirt. His pants came off next. As his body pressed against mine, he paused and locked his blue eyes with my brown. "Tell me what you're feeling."

"Scared," I confessed.

"Yeah." He nodded. "Me too. We don't have to do this, Hails. We can wait and do other things, or we can just go to sleep and I can hold you."

I shook my head. "No. I just… just be scared with me, okay? We'll be scared and nervous together."

"Okay. Yes?" he asked against my lips for what was to come next.

I nodded my head and held him closer. "Yes."

Once he had his permission, I was swept away in his embrace. It was a first for us both. Every time he touched me, I became tethered to his soul. Every emotion rushed through me as I made love to my best friend for the first time ever.

Fear.

Excitement.

Pain.

Bliss.

Happiness.

So much happiness.

I cried because it felt so right. He felt so good. He felt... like mine.

I made love to him after he soothed every insecurity and shut off the outside noise for a little while. How could I not? He was my haven in a very hard world.

That night, I gave him every piece of me, and he gave me even more of himself.

EIGHTEEN

Aiden

LOSE YOUR **V** CARD.

That went over well… again, and again, and again. Still, even though Hailee and I were doing well together, I worried about her.

Since everything went down with the tabloids over the past few weeks, she'd been saying she was fine, but I had a hard time believing her. My overprotective nature with Hailee was surreal. Whenever I had to leave town for work, I felt as if I was leaving her to be an open target for the jerks at school. She seemed to be taking it the best she possibly could, though.

Each day, it seemed that we were falling more and more into one another.

We had routines that we did together. Since I was getting in shape for an upcoming role opportunity, I was in the gym each morning, and Hailee started joining me each day. She'd look good as hell working out, and half the time, I wasn't hitting my goals because I was too focused on her hitting her own.

For the most part, we fell into our relationship with nothing but ease. The only drama that seemed to come toward us was from others who had no business being involved in our business. People didn't stop bullying Hailee, though. She told me it didn't bother her, but I could tell it did.

I became hyper-focused on her and everything she did. Every day during lunch, she'd make small comments about counting calories or how wild it was that something had so many grams of carbohydrates in it. After lunch each day, I'd walk her to her next class, but I noticed after leaving her, she'd go around the corner to the bathroom instead of going into her class.

At the gym, she pushed herself too hard to the point of concern.

"We should get going so we can get ready for school," I told her one morning. We both were dripping in sweat, and I was beyond exhausted. Hailee went ten times harder than I had that morning.

"Let's get in a fast run on the treadmill before we head out."

I chuckled and shook my head. "After leg day? No way."

"Come on, don't be a wimp. Ten minutes tops," she said, breathing heavily as she held the side of the treadmill.

I narrowed my eyes at her. "Hailee, let's go."

She hopped onto the treadmill and waved me off. "It's fine. You go ahead. I'll catch up with you on the way home. I'll…" She paused and gripped the sides of the treadmill. She placed her head down and took a few breaths.

I rushed to her side. "You're seconds away from passing out. Did you eat this morning?"

"Yeah, I did. Big breakfast. I just feel a bit faint."

I hopped on the treadmill in front of her and took her hands into mine. "Time to sit down for a minute."

"But the run—"

"Hailee. Sit."

She sat down on the treadmill. I grabbed her water and handed it over to her. "You've been working out a lot more lately. Are you sure you're eating enough?"

"Yeah, I'm fine. I'm just tired."

I wanted to believe her, but I struggled to do so. As an actor, part of my job was studying characters. Understanding how they moved, how they interacted, how they existed, and how they lived.

Something was off with Hailee, and that terrified me because after I collected all the pieces, I knew exactly what I had to do. Each year, our families celebrated Thanksgiving and Christmas together. We went back and forth between the houses. My family oversaw the main meal, and the Joneses handled dessert and cocktails.

When Thanksgiving came, my eyes were glued on Hailee. She hadn't been eating a lot. If anything, she'd become a professional at pushing food around on her plate. She also wouldn't use the bathroom at my parents' house. She'd go over to her private bathroom attached to her bedroom, then she'd come back. It was suspicious as fuck, and she went every single time we ate anything throughout the day. So after dinner, I made the choice to follow her.

I snuck into her bedroom window without her knowing and listened to her from outside the bathroom. My chest ached as I stood and listened to her throwing up. She washed her hands, and when she came out of the bathroom, she was wiping at her mouth, and she gasped when she saw me.

"Aiden, what are you doing?"

"What are you doing, Hails?"

She raised an eyebrow. "Using the bathroom?"

"Hailee."

"What?" She laughed nervously. "You're acting weird."

"I heard you."

"You heard what?"

"You in the bathroom."

She pushed past me and shook her head. "You're being super weird. Let's just go back to our parents' and—"

"Are you forcing yourself to throw up?" I blurted out.

"Excuse me?"

"Are you—"

"I heard you the first time, Aiden!" she snapped at me. She snapped. Hailee never snapped at me. She grew irritated from time to time, but she never yelled. "Listen, I'm not going to sit here and have you lecture me. Okay? I'm fine."

"Hails…"

"No," she ordered, holding a hand up to me. Her eyes glassed over. "You don't get to do that. You don't get to look at me like I'm broken."

"I'm not."

"You are. I see it. But you don't understand. I'm down sixteen pounds, Aiden. I'm losing weight. And it's going to be fine, and people aren't going to say things about me in articles, and you won't have to be embarrassed to be seen with me. I was eating too much before, anyway. This is working for me. I know it is. It's fine, and I'll stop once I get to my goal weight. Everything's fine. This is just temporary."

It was as if she reached into my chest and ripped my heart out. The panic and fears were pouring out of her as she spoke, and I knew it was my fault. I knew if it wasn't for me and my stupid career, Hailee would've never had to doubt herself in the way she was doubting.

"We can get you help, Hails. To do this in a healthy way, but this isn't it. Your parents can—"

"You can't tell anyone. I swear to God, Aiden, if you tell anyone, I will never speak to you again. I have this under control."

I narrowed my eyes in confusion. "You don't. If you did, you wouldn't be doing something like this. I can't keep this from them. Not if it's hurting you."

"It's not! It's helping me. Don't you see? I'm happier now," she said as tears streamed down her cheeks. "I'm getting skinnier."

"That shit doesn't matter, Hailee. You were perfect the way you were. Your weight doesn't define you."

"Tell that to the internet!" she cried, tears falling faster and faster.

Before I could reply, I heard the front door of her house open as our parents walked in. "Dessert time!" Dad shouted. "Karl, I hope you're making me an old-fashioned to go with dessert."

"You got it," Karl replied.

Hailee quickly wiped her eyes and cleared her throat. She looked at me and grabbed my arm. "Promise me you won't say anything to anyone, okay? Promise me not as my boyfriend but as my best friend."

"Only if you swear you'll stop."

"I swear."

Her bottom lip twitched.

She was lying.

I hated that she felt as if she had to lie to me. I hated that she was struggling. I hated that she was dealing with demons I'd help place in her mind. I also hated that I had to break her heart by telling her parents.

"I'm sorry, Hailee," I muttered before leaving her bedroom.

"No, no!" she shouted, chasing after me.

I hurried to the kitchen where Karl and Penny were preparing dessert, and I called out to them. "Karl, Penny, there's something you need to know."

"He's lying!" Hailee stuttered as she reached the room. "He's lying!"

"Wait, wait, wait, what's going on?" Karl asked.

"Aiden, don't," Hailee begged.

I didn't want to hurt her. I didn't want her to be pissed at me. But even more so, I didn't want to lose her. And with what she was doing, there was a chance I could lose my best friend. My person. My Jerry.

I turned to her parents and said, "Hailee's been throwing up after all her meals."

"Aiden," she pleaded, but I continued.

"I've been watching her closely, and I noticed something was off for a while now, but I wasn't sure until tonight. Well, I caught her in the act. I just thought that was something you should know."

Penny's eyes shot to her daughter. "Is this true, Hailee?"

"I, it, I-I-I'm, it's fine," she stuttered over her words as the tears fell from her eyes. She shrugged her shoulders. "I'm fine. I'm fine."

Her parents rushed to her and caught her as she began to fall apart.

My parents walked over to me and told me to come home with them, to give the Joneses time with their daughter.

I felt sick to my stomach as I sat in my bedroom after everything went down. Mom came into my room after a while and sat on my bed beside me. "What you did today for Hailee took a lot of courage. You did the right thing by telling her parents."

"Then why do I feel so awful?"

"Because sometimes the right thing is the hardest thing." She kissed my forehead. "Hailee will be okay, and you both will be okay together. Just give it time."

"She's going to hate me."

"No. She'll be upset, but that's expected. I know for certain she could never hate you, though."

"Why?"

"Because you're you, Aiden. Because you're you."

Hailee texted me after Thanksgiving telling me she was pissed at me but still loved me.

I was almost certain she'd made a pros and cons list of never talking to me again, so I considered that a win. I could deal with her being mad at me. I couldn't handle her not loving me anymore.

After Thanksgiving, she'd missed a few days of school as her parents worked to help her.

Each day at school when I walked by Cara, she'd give me a smug expression. As if she was proud of what she'd done. All because I didn't want to date her. All because I chose Hailee over her and her egotistical ways. All because I said no.

Imagine being so bitter and sad with yourself that you felt compelled to ruin someone else's life. I didn't even understand why people cared what others looked like, big or small, tall or short, but they did. It was as if they tried to make themselves feel better about their sad, pathetic lives by belittling others. Because if others felt unworthy, then maybe their sad existence would've felt more fulfilling to them. It was ass backward, and it took everything in me not to cuss Cara out for her tactics, but I knew that would only make things worse for Hailee. Plus, my mother told me never to get into big altercations with women. Even though I hated Cara, I wouldn't disrespect her. My mother taught me better than to ever disrespect a woman. But when a guy had the nerve to say something slick about Hailee?

Well, the gloves came off in those situations.

"Another fight?" Dad asked as I walked into the living room after school. Some asshole was going on about how Hailee would've been hot if she'd developed an eating disorder, so I rearranged his jaw. It seemed fitting. My fist was still red from the interaction.

Mom sat on the couch, looking extremely disappointed. That made me feel bad, but I couldn't muscle up the ability to feel guilty for what I'd done.

"Did you know that this time people got the fight on camera? And that it's trending on social media?" Dad questioned. I could see the anger rising more and more in his eyes. I glanced at the clock on the wall. Hailee was still at her therapy appointment, so she probably hadn't heard about the fight. I was already thinking about ways to keep her from hearing about it.

Her parents had her remove all social media from her phone in order to avoid seeing any negative comments, so I knew I was safe from that. She didn't have to know I was defending her honor. It would've pissed her off.

"Aiden, are you listening to me?" Dad barked. "Or have you completely lost your mind?"

"I hear you. But he called Hailee—"

"Hailee," he said back. "Hailee this, Hailee that. Have you realized how obsessed you've become with her? I get she's been going through a hard time, but it's not your battle to fight."

I raised an eyebrow. "It is my fight, Dad. If someone hurts Hailee, they have to deal with me."

"That's ridiculous."

"So you'd let someone talk about Mom that way?" I challenged.

His brows lowered as he crossed his arms. "Excuse me?"

"I'm asking if you'd let people talk about Mom that way. Because she told me, you used to get into fights all the time to defend her honor."

"She told you that?" Dad looked toward Mom. "You told him that?"

"It's the truth." Mom shrugged. "And you still haven't answered his question."

She seemed oddly calm, even bored with the conversation. She and Dad had been fighting more and more lately. Sometimes I was surprised they were in the same room with one another based on how much they argued.

"I didn't answer because it's a stupid question. You're my wife. Hailee has been your girlfriend for what? Two minutes."

"She's been my best friend for seventeen years. I think that trumps your two minutes."

"Since when did you start doing this backtalk, huh? And since when do you not tell me about the roles you've been offered?"

I paused.

Dad cocked an eyebrow. "That's right. I know." He gestured toward me. "He got the leading role in the big Spielberg movie. They offered it to him before the holiday. I heard about it from his agent today."

Mom's eyes widened. "You got the role?"

"I was going to turn it down," I explained.

"The hell you are. I already booked our tickets to Los Angeles for the meetings."

The palms of my hands were sweaty as my anxiety built more and more. "I'm not going. Hailee needs me right now."

"Baby…" Mom started, but I shook my head.

I stood. "Do whatever you want. Lock my window. Ground me. Tell me how much of a fuckup I am, but I'm not taking that role. I don't care about it. I don't care about any of that crap. I'm not leaving her."

There was no way in hell I was getting on a plane when Hailee needed me more.

NINETEEN

Hailee

I'D BEEN OUT OF SCHOOL FOR A FEW DAYS AS MAMA AND DAD signed me up to talk with a therapist who could help me with my heavy thoughts. I was somewhat surprised when Samuel stopped by the house to speak with me.

Samuel smiled my way. "Hey, Hailee. Are your parents home?"

"They ran out to check out a property location for their bakery. I can tell them you stopped by..."

"No. Actually, I was hoping to talk to you for a second?" he asked.

"Sure, of course. Come in."

He walked into the house and closed the door behind him. He smiled, but it felt a bit cold. Colder than I was used to from Samuel. Normally, there was a level of gentleness and protection when he was around me.

His arms crossed, and he cleared his throat as he looked down at me. "How are you holding up, kiddo?"

I shrugged. "I'm okay. I'm sorry about Thanksgiving. It was a lot."

"That's okay. I just hope you're okay." He wiggled his nose and shifted his feet. "We've been praying for you."

Prayers were weird. I wondered if they were ever answered or if there was just a sky packed full of unanswered requests floating throughout the atmosphere.

"Is there something wrong?" I asked. My stomach felt tangled up, and I hated that I didn't know why.

"Uh, yes. Can we sit?"

I nodded and led him to the living room. We sat across from one another, and he still seemed tense, which made me feel even worse.

"So I know Aiden and you have been having a hard time lately," he stated.

"Oh. Yeah. It was more me dealing with myself than him. Honestly, if it was the other way around, I would've done the same. I was hoping to talk to him tonight and—"

Samuel held a hand up and halted my words. "You're a good girl, Hailee. I've known you for a long time, and I have no questions about the type of person you are."

I swallowed hard. "What's going on?"

Samuel frowned.

My heart cracked.

He clasped his hands together. "He has a bright future. His dreams are finally coming true. And in order for him to fully step into his future, he has to let go of all things from his past. He cannot have one foot in Leeks and the other in California. You need to break up with him."

"What? No. We can figure everything out. We can—"

"He got in another fight, Hailee."

"What?"

"At school. He heard people talking about you. He got into a fight, and it was leaked to the media. People in town are not only talking but people in the industry are questioning if he has what it takes to build an actual career or if he's just some kid who got lucky." Samuel took off his glasses and pinched the bridge of his nose. "My son is a lot of things, but he's not lucky. He's hardworking, and I refuse to allow the world to label him as a one-hit wonder."

Why didn't Aiden tell me about the fight? Why didn't he mention that there was a fight? A fight over me? Why would he keep that from me?

My voice cracked as I spoke. "I can say something. I can speak out on his behalf and let people know—"

"No." He shook his head. "No offense, Hailee, but you speaking up for Aiden will only worsen the situation. Any involvement, even a friendship, will be harmful to my son."

Even a friendship?

What?

"Samuel, what are you asking…?"

"You're his kryptonite, Hailee. Aiden will do anything and everything for you, to the point of his own destruction. You're a great girl. You know how my family feels about you and yours, but… this isn't healthy. Not for you and not for him. This level of codependency is toxic."

My eyes began to glaze over because I knew exactly what he was asking me to do.

He was asking me to let go of Aiden. Not just as my boyfriend but also as my person. As my best friend. My Tom. He wanted me to let go of my other half.

"You must understand, Hailee, this isn't easy for me to say. You have always been a shining light in my family's world, and I would not wish what you are going through with the bullying and the tabloids upon my worst enemy, but Aiden is my son. So you must understand me asking this of you. You must understand that you cannot be a part of Aiden's life from this point on. Not if you love him. If you truly love him, and I know you do, you will let him go."

Was it true?

Was I the harm in Aiden's life that he needed to be protected from?

The tears fell down my cheeks, and I seemed to choke on each inhalation I took. My body broke out into trembles as I shook my head. "He's my best friend," I muttered repeatedly. "He's my best friend, Samuel. He's my best friend."

He's my person.

He's my one and only person.

Without him, I had no one.

Without him, there were only dark days without an ounce of light in the sky.

Samuel's eyes were glassy, as if he was on the verge of a breakdown, too. I'd never seen Aiden's father grow so close to tears. That fact alone broke my already shattered heart.

He sniffled and cleared his throat. "Hailee, you must understand.

He's going to lose everything because of you. His dreams will end if he keeps going with you. Your struggles are too big for him to carry. You can't expect him to do that."

My chest felt tight.

My mind was in a state of dizziness and confusion.

The worst part of it all? I knew Samuel was right. My association with Aiden wouldn't bring about any positivity of sorts. People would always have something to say about me, which, in turn, would make Aiden feel as if he needed to protect me. The last thing I wanted was for Aiden's acting career to end because he was trying to look after me.

"I think you should go, sir."

"Sure. Of course. Just consider everything I'm saying. We're supposed to fly out later this week for a big opportunity. He's already refusing to go because he wants to make sure you're okay. I'm sure Aiden will stop by to see you tonight. If you could do me a favor and kill any hope he might have of continuing this thing between the two of you, then that would be great."

This thing.

As if our love was nothing more than a fling.

Samuel turned and walked away. He walked away as if he hadn't just shattered my already damaged heart into a million little pieces.

How did I do it?

How did I break things off with the only person I never wanted to let go of?

When Aiden tapped on my window for a visit, I'd already played out the conversation about to take place in dozens of different scenarios. I'd broken down the emotional damage that could be unlocked and every reply he could give to me in an attempt to make us work. I'd gone through the ups and the downs, the hopeful and the dreadful outcomes. I'd considered him thinking I was joking. I considered him falling apart. I'd even considered him being numb.

I still wasn't ready. I'd never be ready to break his heart.

He climbed into my bedroom and gave me the biggest hug the

moment he saw me. I let him hold on a bit longer than normal. I didn't know the next time I'd be able to be wrapped in his arms.

"Are you okay?" he whispered against my ear.

"You didn't tell me you got the leading role for a Spielberg movie. Why didn't you tell me that?"

He narrowed his eyes. "How did you know that?"

"Your dad stopped by and told me. He brought me flowers." And heartbreak, but whatever.

"Oh. Yeah. I was offered the role but I didn't take it due to the time-line issue."

"What's the issue?"

He narrowed his eyes at me as if I were insane. "I can't leave you when you're struggling like this. I need to be here for you."

There it was. The truth that his father worried deeply about. Aiden was turning down huge opportunities to watch over me.

"You can't do that, Aiden. You can't turn that down. You have to do the movie."

"But…"

"I'll be fine."

"I know you will be, but I want to be here for you through it all."

I wanted to cry, but I couldn't. I couldn't let him see how much this situation was breaking every piece of me. "Aiden, I'm sorry. I don't think I can do this anymore."

"Do what?"

"This." I gestured back and forth between us. "Us. I can't do this right now. I can't have you giving up opportunities for me. That would never be okay with me."

"Okay, fine. Then we'll be long distance for a while. It will take work, but we will be proactive, and I'll make sure that no matter what, you're the first priority in my life."

I love you, I thought.

I need you, I thought.

"I don't want to do long distance. We crossed pretty much every-thing off our bucket list. We accomplished what we wanted to do during our senior year, so now you can get back to your real life."

"My real life?" He narrowed his eyes at me. "What is this? What's going on in your head? What are you really thinking?"

"Everything I'm thinking is what I'm saying."

"No, it's not. This isn't you."

"It is me."

"No, it's not. Who's in your head?" My chest tightened from the question. "Are you still mad at me for telling your parents?"

"No. I'm not upset about that at all. I was, but I get it. If it was the other way around, I would've done the same."

"Then what is it? What people are getting in your head, Hails?"

My lips parted, but no words came out. How did I tell him? How did I inform him that the person getting to me, the whisperings in my ear, were from his father? I couldn't do it. I couldn't speak that truth. Even though I wanted to say it. I wanted to tell him that I loved him, and my fears, though warranted, were not my own.

"Aiden, it's no one else," I lied.

He blinked, and his eyes were packed with tears. He took my hands in his, and I wished he hadn't because whenever he touched me, I felt as if I was stepping into forever. But I couldn't have forever. I couldn't have him.

I pulled my hands from him, and that motion cut him deep. "I'm breaking up with you, Aiden. I'm sorry. We both have our own things we are dealing with. I can't be with you as I work on myself, and you have to work on yourself and your career."

"Come on, Hailee! Fuck the career!" he shouted. I knew it would shift. From sadness to confusion to anger. I knew Aiden would go through an array of emotions. I planned for it. Yet behind each emotion, it was clear that they all developed from the same expression: heartbreak.

I was breaking his heart.

The heart I promised to take care of for the rest of my life.

"You can't do this right now. You can't push me away when we just got to this new place. You promised if we took the risk, you promised if we decided to be a 'we' that you would not run away when things got hard. You promised no matter how much our lives changed, we would not. You promised me we would stay the same. You promised you wouldn't break my heart. You promised!" he hollered. His voice cracked as he spoke to me. I felt his pain in every single syllable that left his mouth.

"Aiden, I know I made those promises, but things have changed. I mean, look at my life. Look at the struggles I've dealt with over these past few weeks, over these past few months. My life is currently a mess, and I refuse to let it interrupt yours. You're going to change the world. You'll create films with meaning and heart, and I'll still be your biggest fan. But I can't... I mean, I can't..."

"Love me." He released the harsh breath and rolled his shoulders back as the anger began to subside and realization set in. A new sadness washed over the space. It was a type of sadness I'd never experienced before. The kind that made your own blood feel chilled as your whole body began to tremble. "You can't love me."

I didn't know what to say because those words were a lie. There were only a few things I knew how to do in life. I knew how to read books for hours. I knew how to bake pastries. And I knew how to love Aiden Walters. Loving Aiden came as easily as taking a breath each morning. The love I had for him was one of the only constant things in my life.

"We will still be best friends?" I promised him. As it left my mouth, it came out as more of a question. As if I doubted that was even a possibility. I doubted everything lately. I doubted my own mind and my own thoughts and my own feelings because my world had been turned upside down so quickly that I hadn't had a chance to even catch up.

"No. You don't get to say that. You can't be my best friend after breaking my heart. You have to either love me or let me go. This in-between bullshit isn't going to work, Hailee. So if you can't be with me, you can't be my friend either. So say it. Say we aren't best friends anymore, that we aren't together anymore so I can get it through my thick head and move on."

Our worlds that once collided as one were beginning to separate. We were moving in two different directions, and it was time for me to cut our cord. To sever our connection. He had to get on the plane tomorrow without a drop of hope that we could be us again. He had to believe that we were finished so he could truly start his life.

"For fuck's sake, say it, Hailee!" he shouted, making me jump in fright. "And don't be a wimp about it. If you want to break my heart, look me in the eyes when you do it. Don't half-ass this. If this is what you want, what you really want, then say it with your fucking chest."

I shook off my nerves the best I could and stood tall. I rolled my shoulders back and said the words that would break his heart. They'd break mine even more. I told the biggest lie I'd ever told as I looked deep into his eyes. "I don't want to be your best friend anymore, Aiden."

The flash in his eyes at the sternness of my words shattered me. I saw his hurt, yet it was my soul that ached. That was how connected we were, how connected we'd always been. When I was sad, he felt it. When he was broken, I collapsed, too.

His mouth parted to speak, but he paused. He then wrapped his hands around his Jerry necklace and ripped it off. He dropped it to the floor and looked me dead in my eyes. For the first time in our whole lives of knowing one another, his blues looked hollow. As if any emotion he had attached to me vanished in an instant. His cool blue eyes were now cold as he parted his lips and said, "Fuck you, Hailee Jones. I never want to speak to you again."

TWENTY

Aiden

I GOT ON THE STUPID FLIGHT.

"Are you okay?" Mom asked as she sat beside me on the airplane.

My hand gripped the armrest, and I'd been tapping my foot non-stop. I didn't feel like talking to her. I didn't feel like talking to anyone. But I did feel.

I felt so much that I felt as if my heart was going to explode from my chest and crumble into a million pieces. I felt rage. I felt sadness. I felt loneliness. I felt betrayed. Then I felt her.

I didn't know how, but I still felt Hailee within my chest.

I didn't want to feel that. I didn't want to feel her because she had no business remaining in my mind, in my psyche, in my fucking shattered heart.

I stood by her! I stood by her side through all her hardships, and the moment she got the opportunity to throw me to the side, she did it without any effort. She went on and on about how if we started dating, we wouldn't ruin our friendship, and then she did this.

"I'm fine," I murmured, reaching into my backpack underneath the seat to grab my script. I was going to pour myself into my craft.

I was going to immerse myself into every character that came before me because if I focused all my attention on the characters, I'd have less time to focus on myself. On my feelings. I didn't want to feel anymore, so I did the only thing I could think to do—I shut off that corner of my soul.

I locked up my emotions and threw away the key.

I'd spend the rest of my life dedicated to the characters in my movies so I wouldn't have to face the hole that Hailee left within my chest. It was easier that way. It was easier to become someone else instead of being the heartbroken kid from Leeks, Wisconsin, who had enough nerve to fall in love with his best friend.

I sat in the bedroom of our rental property in California, having a full-blown panic attack. My body was drenched in sweat, and my heart felt as if it was being tossed through a paper shredder. The room was pitch black, and the only noise heard was the spinning of the ceiling fan above me. I felt nauseous as I replayed my last words to Hailee.

I never want to speak to you again.

Why did I say that? I didn't mean that. I was angry. I was hurt. I was confused and blindsided, but I didn't mean that. Of course, I didn't mean that. She was my person. I needed her. My heart ached without her.

I couldn't breathe at a steady pace as I reached for my cell phone and texted her.

Aiden: I didn't mean what I said, Jerry. I'm sorry. I love you.

Aiden: It's late, so I know you're sleeping, but please, call me in the morning.

Aiden: I shouldn't have gotten on the plane. Fuck, Hails, I'm sorry.

Aiden: Even if we are just friends, that's fine. I can do that.

Aiden: I just need you in my life, okay?

Aiden: I need you.

Aiden: Call me in the morning.

Aiden: I love you, Hailee. I love you.

She didn't text me the next morning. She didn't text me that following week.

She didn't write me back for weeks until she did.

Hailee: I'm so sorry, Aiden. Our lives are heading in different directions. Maybe we can still be friends, but I think it's best if we don't talk for a while.

And just like that, the sun of my life faded to darkness.

PART TWO

"Love is so short and forgetting is so long."—Pablo Neruda

TWENTY-ONE

Aiden

Five Years Later

WAS CONVINCED MY HEARTBEATS WERE BUILT ON LONELINESS.
They thrived in the darkness of my solitude.

Everyone who surrounded me probably didn't even notice the
seclusion leaking from my spirit. They'd never came close enough to
exam the real me. They only knew the character I'd presented myself as.
To them I was Aiden Walters, Hollywood's it boy. The happy-go-lucky
people-person who thrived in crowded rooms. Yet my true self was the
complete opposite.

I was Aiden Walters, the lonely boy. The boy who'd become too
great at covering up his panic attacks on red carpets. The boy who'd become a chameleon based on whoever he was interacting with. People
thought they liked me because when they talked, I listened without in-
serting my thoughts and opinions. I laughed when they laughed. I grimaced when they did, too. It would amaze you how many people wanted
someone to simply listen to them and not give them feedback.

People liked me because they didn't know me. If they knew me, they'd probably be turned off by the level of sadness inside my soul. Then again, who was I to be sad? I had fame, money, and success. How dare I even question my mental health when I'd been given so many blessings. At least that was how my father made me feel on the subject.

"You're living everyone's dream. You're living my dream. Be grateful," he'd say.

It turned out, living everyone else's dreams didn't make your own come true. It made you an overlooked side character in their life's story.

My mind was spinning as my stomach rumbled like thunder.

I'd made it to where so many people wished to be.

I was sitting in the front row at the Oscars.

Cue the excitement.

It was hot in that room. It also smelled like overpriced perfumes and uptight egos. A big part of me didn't feel as if I belonged in that room. Don't get me wrong, I was glad to be invited. They said, "it's an honor to be nominated." Blah, blah, blah.

That summed up exactly how I felt—blah, blah, blah.

Every inch of my body dripped in perspiration.

My stomach rumbled like an old car engine trying to get a jump start.

The person sitting to my left glanced over at me with a raised eyebrow from the wannabe tune-up.

"Bubbly guts," I murmured, patting my stomach. Right as I gave it a pat-pat, I burped on accident.

For the love of…

My body was shutting down on me as my old-school panics started to resurface.

Nerves.

You have to control your nerves, Aiden.

My parents were upset I didn't bring one of them as my plus-one. Mostly Dad was upset. Mom was worried. She knew back then I said if I'd ever made it to the Oscars, my plus-one would be Hailee because Mom was my plus-one at the Emmys.

Hailee.

Shit. My fucking nerves.

I smiled brightly and focused my attention on the stage in front of me. Rob Gregory was presenting. He didn't look nearly as nervous as I'd felt, but then again, Rob had attended these events for over sixty-some years. He was one of the best actors in the industry. Hollywood royalty, if I may say. The guy was pushing mid-eighties but didn't look a day over sixty. He must've had solid genetics. Or an extremely talented personal trainer and cosmetic surgeon.

My stomach howled once more.

Rob held an envelope tight in his hand and said, "And the Oscar for best actor in a leading role goes to..."

Blah, blah, blah...

"Aiden Walters."

Wait, what?

The crowd burst into a roaring celebration.

Aiden Walters.

That's me.

I did it.

At the age of twenty-two years old, I'd won my first Academy award.

I was going to vomit.

No, wait. I was going to walk on stage. Correction, I was walking on stage. Somehow, my feet managed to take one step after another as my brain became dazed and confused about what was happening. I felt light-headed as I made my way toward Rob Gregory. Then Rob Gregory hugged me, congratulated me, and handed me the Oscar. My Oscar.

For fuck's sake, I won an Oscar.

Rob stepped to the side, leaving me in front of a microphone with dozens of my colleagues and heroes standing in front of me. Hundreds of thousands of others watched the greatest moment of my life happen right before them. It was time for me to speak, yet at that very moment, it was as if my tongue was tied.

Bubbly guts and twisted tongues.

I cleared my throat. "This is quite the shock. For starters, thank you to the Academy for the ultimate gift. I am blown away that this is happening to me. A huge amount of gratitude for the other artists in this category. These men are some of the most gifted individuals in this industry, and I want to apologize to you all for them somehow picking me over you. Clearly, they don't know talent," I joked, getting a bit of laughter from the audience. I thanked everyone involved in the making of the movie and then moved on to those who meant the most to me.

"To my father, who pushed me into this industry and told me I'd one day be standing right here. Thank you for believing in this moment when I couldn't see it. To my dearest mother, the woman who raised me, the woman I first loved, the woman who taught me all about life and the beauty of living it to the fullest… Thank you, Mom, for always being my right-hand woman. Dad's a lucky bastard to have you." I paused. "Can you say bastard at the Oscars, or are they bleeping that out?"

Another eruption of laughter. As I worked through my speech, a woman's name popped into my head.

Hailee.

Thank Hailee.

Screw her for showing up in my thoughts at that very moment. As a kid, I'd always practice my Oscar acceptance speech while holding my mother's hairbrush in my hand. I'd performed the talk countless times in front of my best friend, correction ex-best friend. Hailee Jones was always a part of my life. She was my very first friend, then she became my first love. She followed that up with becoming my first heartbreak, too.

Back then when I practiced my speech, I always thanked her. If you had told me she wouldn't have made it into my acceptance speech many years later, I would've called you a liar. In my mind, I always figured she'd be a forever piece of my story. I figured she'd be the woman sitting beside me in the audience, smiling at me with that big smile. Staring at me with stars in her deep brown eyes from the pride she felt for me.

I tried my best to shake off my nerves and stared out into the audience. I thanked the cast and crew and directors, yada, yada, yada.

After winning an Oscar, your world moved on autopilot. People directed you around to pose for photograph after photograph. You did press conferences. Then, there were the parties. The Vanity Fair gathering. The socializing. The smiles that were both fake and genuine, depending on who you were conversing with. I interacted with everyone who came my way. My personal assistant was close by, too, telling me who certain individuals were as they approached so I could appear as if I didn't have the most forgetful mind.

Afterward, I got into a car, and I was driven home.

My chaotic world grew quiet.

I poured myself a drink and sat alone with my thoughts.

Winning an Oscar was supposed to mean something. It was

supposed to have some kind of meaning behind it, yet after the win, I felt empty and alone.

I sat on the floor of my darkened living room with a bottle of bourbon in my left hand. In front of me on the coffee table was that damn statue. My parents had called me multiple times. I talked to them, of course. But everyone else? My agent, manager, and publicist? Fellow actors and people in the industry?

I didn't answer their calls.

I didn't want to talk to anyone.

I didn't want to see anyone.

Well, there was one person who crossed my mind.

Pissed me right the hell off that she kept crossing my mind, too, seeing how she was supposed to remain in my past after she ended things all those years ago. Yet that was the thing about Aiden and bourbon being mixed—buried memories began to unlock. The words she'd spoken in our youth all flooded back to me as I stared at my award.

"When you win your Oscar, I better be your date or the first text or call you make," she'd say. *"After your parents, at least."*

"Of course, it would be you. Who else would I message?"

"Promise?"

"Promise."

I pulled out my cell phone and flipped through my contacts. There she was. Her name in my phone? It was clear as day: **DO NOT TEXT OR CALL WHEN YOU'RE DRUNK AIDEN.**

A long name but an honest one.

I opened our text messages from five years ago. The last thing she said to me still stung a piece of my heart. That pissed me off. I hated that after all this time, this woman could still hurt me in an odd way. I guessed that happened when your best friend ended a seventeen-year friendship over a text message.

Hailee: I'm so sorry, Aiden. Our lives are heading in different directions. Maybe we can still be friends, but I think it's best if we don't talk for a while.

It had been a while.

Five years, eight weeks, and a handful of change.

Not that I was counting.

Back then, I tried to reach out, yet she all but ghosted me. Over a decade of friendship and one season of love down the drain for no real reason other than her thinking our lives were going in different directions. What a pile of horseshit.

I began typing out a new message even though her name in my phone told me to do differently.

Aiden: I won an Oscar. I'd promised you'd be the first person I'd text about it after my parents. So there you go.

I blocked her before she could reply.

Then I unblocked her to see if she'd replied.

Then I blocked her again because screw her.

Then I unblocked her *because screw her.*

I went back to my bourbon and pity party for one. It was odd to me how I could be in Hollywood's spotlight, surrounded by people most days, yet still feel so eerily alone.

I'd spent the next few months in that same strange feeling of loneliness. I kept busy because that was the best way to keep her off my mind, but when I returned to my quiet house, too many thoughts would flood my mind.

So more bourbon, more quietness, more thoughts.

I felt as if I was going to go insane. That was when my mother called me and said she saw an interview with me from the week prior. She'd told me she saw it in my eyes—the sadness.

"I'm fine," I lied.

"You're not," she argued. "You're going to play Superman, Aiden, and this is a huge deal, but still… you're sad."

"No one else has mentioned me looking sad."

"No one else is your mother, so come home for a while. Take a break. Winning the world over isn't worth losing yourself, so please… come home."

I disagreed for a while until I realized that she was right. I didn't know who I was anymore. I felt so far from myself that I saw a stranger when I looked in the mirror. I didn't even see a glimpse of who I used to be.

So I packed my bags and headed back to Wisconsin.

TWENTY-TWO

Hailee

SIX MONTHS AGO, AIDEN TEXTED ME.

He won an Oscar.

My hand shook nonstop as I saw Aiden's message come through my phone.

Of course, I knew he'd won the Oscar. Aiden was quite the trending subject after his epic win. As I watched it unfold in front of my television screen, I felt my heart bursting with excitement. My heart also burst a bit with sadness, because I saw the slight panic attack he was living on that stage. Over the years, he'd become better at hiding his panic attacks. I'd watched all his videos online, though, and could still spot them. Nobody studied that man more than me—even from a distance.

My poor Aiden...

Not mine, Hailee. Not mine.

Still... I missed him.

I thought the missing aspect would dissipate over time, but it didn't. It only grew quieter.

Even though it had been over five years since we'd stopped talking, I still loved that man. It was a quiet love that moved throughout my life as a whisper. I sometimes wondered if he could ever feel my love for him when the wind brushed against him. I always sent him the best with my thoughts. At some point, we could read one another's thoughts without issue. We were that close.

Now, he was nothing more than memories that floated around within my mind every now and again. Since I still lived in the small town where we grew up, not a day passed when Aiden didn't cross my mind. Every little crack of every sidewalk held a memory that he and I shared. I was almost certain that for the remainder of my life, Aiden would live within my thoughts.

Yet seeing that text message pop up?

That caused me a wave of emotions I wasn't quite ready to deal with.

I read it over a dozen times throughout the past few months. I talked to my therapist about it probably one too many times. I could almost hear his voice, hear his conflictions and tones through the sentence. I could tell he'd been drinking. Of course, he'd been drinking. I doubt that message would've come through if he'd been sober.

It was a good thing I hadn't been drinking, too. Otherwise, I might've texted him back, and I knew I had no right to answer. Even though I wanted to. Even though my heart still ached for him after all this time. Even though all I wanted was to give him a hug after the biggest win of his career.

But the world I currently lived in wasn't the same world I resided in when Aiden was in my life. That version of Hailee that he knew was long gone. I've changed, and I was certain that he had, too. I couldn't currently be a part of his triumphs because years prior, I chose to become his pain.

So I sat in my silence and didn't reply. I wondered what it must've been like for him nowadays, always surrounded by people. His world seemed so magical, packed with color, while mine was so ordinarily… ordinary.

Don't get me wrong, it wasn't a bad life. I liked the world I'd created.

I'd spent my whole life in the same small town with the same small-town people talking about the same small-town things day in, day out. Over the past few years, most of my time was spent alone reading my romance novels, or with my parents, or working at the Starlight Inn, or with my friend Kate. Those were the ins and outs of my life.

I'd graduated from college last spring with a bachelor's degree in psychology, and I was currently applying to colleges for my master's degree in child psychology and development. I didn't get into any of the programs I'd tried for before, but as Mama always said, "Try again and again until you get the result you're searching for." So, I was still going hard for my goals. In a way, not getting accepted to the programs lit a fire beneath me. Giving up on myself wasn't an option. I didn't care if it took me twenty more years to get my master's, followed by my PhD. I was going to become one of the best children's therapists in the country.

I had a vision, and it was crystal clear. Yet until then, I was working nonstop to pay for that college tuition.

Overall, life was beautiful because I worked hard to make it that way.

"Don't tell me you're on your way already. I just clocked in," Kate said, fixing her name badge. She was one of the housekeepers at Starlight Inn where I worked and a saving grace in my life. I didn't have many friends in town, all of which I could count on one hand—four fingers, if I were honest, but Kate was one of them. She was a stunning Asian woman who came into town a few years back. Since then, we'd connected once we started working together. We were complete opposites—which meant we worked out perfectly. She made me be more social when I was stuck in my introverted cave of reading. While I'd got her to start reading historical romances and cozying up with a book on Friday nights. I called it a win-win friendship.

"You should start working earlier," I joked. "I'm off to help my mom bake for a few hours, then filling out more master program applications and reading."

"You're going to stay up all night reading the book and finish it before me, aren't you?"

"Guilty." Kate and I started our own romance book club, and she always complained about how I finished the books in one day while it took her a week. I blamed it on my inability to go to bed without knowing if the book ended with a happily ever after. Spoiler alert: they always did.

She blew out a cloud of hot air. "When do you even sleep?"

I glanced down at my smartwatch and held it up toward her. "Apparently, I get some good deep sleep between two and six o'clock."

"And still not a bag of exhaustion under your eyes. I hate you."

"You know what they say, genetics help. Plus, there's the fifteen-step facial routine I partake in each morning and night."

Kate rolled her eyes at me and waved me off. "Too much work. Just give me a bar of Dove soap, a washcloth, and a prayer to Jesus, and I'm good to go." Reaching into her pocket, she pulled out a Tootsie Roll, unwrapped it, and popped it into her mouth. "Call me tomorrow. Maybe we can go to that festival together."

I scrunched up my nose. "I'm not going to that festival tomorrow. Besides, I think I work."

"Oh, come on. It's not every day an Oscar-winning actor returns to his hometown. Aiden Walters's return is the talk of the gossiping town."

"Don't remind me," I muttered as I pushed my curls behind my ears. "I already have an appointment with my therapist to talk to her all about it. My anxiety is going crazy."

"Or is it butterflies about seeing an old high school love?" Kate gave me a goofy grin. "What if there's a chance for old flings to be reunited? Just think about it. High school lovers separated for years, then forced back together after growing up and realizing they just need to be together."

I narrowed my eyes and pointed a stern finger at her. "I'm not going to get back with my ex-boyfriend just so you can meet Bradley Cooper."

"But it's Bradley Cooper!" she exclaimed, clutching her hands to her chest as if the idea of her and Bradley falling in love was something she played over and over in her head. To be fair, Kate probably did play that scenario on repeat.

"Good night, Kate." I laughed, walking off, leaving my friend in the most dramatic state as she shouted back.

"I'll take Sebastian Stan or Manny Jacinto! I'm not picky!"

"I said, good night!"

"Sinqua Walls! Oh, sweet heavens, the way I would love to lean against Sinqua's walls!"

A few years ago, Mama and Daddy opened their dream bakery in town. Hailee's Bakery. If I ever doubted that I was spoiled, having them name a bakery after me was enough proof that I was forever loved. They'd even converted the space upstairs into an apartment for me to live in during my undergrad years. They'd wanted me to be able to focus on my studies and save up my money from my job at Starlight Inn instead of worrying about rent. My gratitude for my parents was through the roof.

Plus, living above a bakery wasn't the worst thing in the world. It always smelled like heaven. After years of hard work and dedication, they'd made their dreams come true. The bakery was an instant success in town. So much so that Mama had to hire more workers. With the big festival happening the following day, I volunteered to help Mama with the baking the night prior. I knew she'd probably had her hands full, and she never wanted her employees to work overtime.

Walking into Hailee's Bakery always felt like walking into Willy Wonka's factory. The sweet aromas could be smelled hundreds of feet before you even reached the store. The quite large and spacious location sat right on Lake Michigan's coastline.

Something about walking into the shop and smelling the baked goods was so reassuring. It was a sign of perseverance of sorts. Mama and Dad waited years for the right location and finally got it.

"Is that pumpkin loaf I'm smelling?" I asked as I guided my way through the shop and landed in the kitchen, which looked like a culinary war zone. Flour and pots were everywhere. The countertops had been transformed into a decorating area with frosting, piping tools, and sugar cookies galore.

I sniffed the air. "And lemon bars!" I gleamed, walking over to my favorite dessert ever. As I reached down to grab one, Mama slapped my hand. "Don't you dare, Hailee Rose. Those are for the festival."

I pouted and took a seat on a barstool at the counter. "You didn't make one extra pan of lemon bars?"

She narrowed her eyes toward me, took off her gloves, and walked into the pantry. When she reappeared, she came out with a tray of lemon bars and placed them right in front of me. "Only eat one if you haven't had dinner yet. You'll spoil your appetite."

I grinned ear to ear and rubbed my hands together. "These are dinner."

"Hailee, don't you dare eat all that sugar and no real meal. Speaking of… you should go get yourself dinner. You didn't need to come and help me. I've got this covered."

I glanced around at the destruction of Mama's house and smirked. "You do know you need all of this done by tomorrow, right?"

She placed her hands against her hips and sighed before wiping the back of her hand against her forehead. "I am a little overwhelmed. Your dad was helping, but you know he can't bake to save his life. He burned two pans of cookies. I sent him to the office to do some admin work."

"Well, let me underwhelm you and help."

Relief washed over Mama's dark-brown eyes as her shoulders dropped. "Great. You're on sugar cookie duty. You are filling in the Oscar-shaped cookies, writing quotes on three dozen cookies, and then doing the edible stickers of Aiden's face on three dozen." She paused and wrinkled up her nose. "Are you okay doing this, sweetheart?"

"What do you mean?"

"You know…spending the next few hours plastering Aiden's face on cookies."

I smiled and shoved a lemon bar into my mouth. "Anything for an up-and-coming baking company," I joked, trying to push off the thoughts of staring into the edible blue eyes of my first and only love.

Was it going to be awkward? Yes.

Was it going to be *really* awkward? Absolutely.

Would I do anything for my parents? One hundred percent. Even when it came down to sticking edible prints of Aiden onto her world-class cookies.

"It's fine, Mama. It's been years since Aiden and I were even a thing. He's moved on. I've moved on. It's nothing but ancient history." Minus the random text message from a few months ago, but she didn't have to know about that.

She walked over to me, kneeled a bit, and stared me in the eyes, searching for any truths I was hiding from her. Detective Penny Jones was on the case, searching for any reminisces of heartbreak that I still carried around with me about a relationship that ended years prior. Then she smiled, kissed my forehead, and thanked me for being the best daughter ever.

I reached down to grab another lemon bar, and she teasingly patted my hand again. "No more sweets until after dinner. I'll order Chinese. Go tell your father food will be on the way soon."

She walked out of the room to order food, and I shoved yet another piece of a lemon bar into my mouth. Then, I headed to the back office, where Dad seemed to live lately.

"Knock, knock. Hey, Dad."

He looked up from his paperwork and smiled wide. "Well, if it isn't my favorite daughter."

"Your only one."

"I'm pretty sure if I had more kids, they wouldn't come close to comparing to you."

I chuckled as I walked over to him and kissed his bald head. "Mama said to tell you she's ordering Chinese."

"Sounds good." He sat back in his chair and studied my face. Detective Karl Jones was now on the case, searching for any off emotions I might've been hiding. "How are you, baby girl?"

"I'm good. I'm applying to a few more grad schools tomorrow and am about to help Mama with the baking."

"You know dang well that's not what I'm asking about."

I sighed and leaned against his desk, crossing my arms. "I'm good, Daddy."

"It would be okay if you weren't. You don't always have to be good, but you should always be true. Any feeling is warranted, especially when it comes to Aiden."

Even hearing his name sent chills down my spine. I couldn't lie straight to Dad, so instead, I pushed myself from the desk. "I'm going to get back to helping Mama, and I'll come get you when the food is here."

He smirked. "Good on you for not lying to me. Love you forever."

"Love you longer than that," I replied, giving him another kiss on the forehead.

After we all ate dinner together, Mama and I got to work decorating the cookies.

I was a bit stunned that Mama bought my speech about Aiden being nothing but ancient history and me being fine with his return to Leeks. If anything, my nerves were a mess. I could hardly stop making up scenarios of what would happen if we ran into one another. For the past week, I'd been having fake conversations with myself as if I were speaking to Aiden for the first time in years.

"Hey, dude. What's up? Want to do that weird handshake we always did?"

"Hey, Aiden, how goes it?"

"Well, look what the cat dragged in. Get it? The cat? You were my Tom. I was your Jerry. Meow!"

Clearly, I was screwed.

My stomach had been in knots, and those knots tightened even more as I plastered Aiden's face against the sugar cookies. A face I once loved so much. I still loved it, to be honest. Aiden Walters was the kind of man that a woman never truly got over. My biggest fear about seeing him was that those feelings of longing would come rushing back at me, and I wouldn't be able to stop myself from diving straight into his arms.

For that reason alone, I needed to avoid him at all costs.

I didn't have a clue how I would avoid seeing Aiden tomorrow, but I knew I had to try my best. With the way my heart and mind were tangled up, it was clear the results of our interaction may vary.

Sure, I was able to play cool with my parents about the idea of coming face-to-face with Aiden. Yet I wasn't certain I could do the same when it came to him being right in front of me. That night I'd take semi-tricking my parents as a victorious win.

And the Oscar for best performance of getting over one's ex in a mature and appropriate fashion goes to Hailee Rose Jones.

Best performance ever.

TWENTY-THREE

Hailee

"H̶E'S HERE! HE'S HERE!" PEOPLE CHATTERED AROUND THE
Starlight Inn the following morning as I organized the
bookshelves in the sitting room.

Those words alone made my heart pound faster within my chest.

The people surrounding me hurried from where they were socializing and dashed out of the building. I knew exactly where they were
going—to the clock tower to see the golden boy of Leeks, Wisconsin.
The man of the hour. The Oscar-winning celebrity who was born and
raised in our town. The one, the only, Aiden Scott Walters. America's—
correction, the world's—heartthrob.

I couldn't believe the day had finally come.

The news of Aiden returning to our small town had been all anyone had been able to talk about since Laurie informed everyone of the
news about three weeks ago. It had been five years since Aiden stepped
foot in our town, and a lot had changed for him since then. He'd been
a star in an Emmy-winning drama series. Last year, he starred in three
blockbuster films, and just recently, he'd won his first Oscar.

It was hard to believe there was a day and time when he was my

Aiden. My best friend, my other half. My person. Now, we were nothing more than strangers. People didn't talk enough about the shift from friends to lovers and then to strangers. It cut a little deeper than most heartbreaks, and that wound never completely healed.

At one time in my life, I thought Aiden would always be in my corner, and I'd be in his. I was his biggest cheerleader, and he was mine. That was why when I broke his heart and ended things with him, I also shattered my own.

"Hailee! Hailee!"

I turned around as I held Shakespeare's collection of sonnets in my hand to find Henry standing behind me. He shook with excitement as he stared at me through his thick-framed round glasses. His shaggy blond hair was swept across his forehead, and he brushed his hand through it, making it messier.

"Yes?" I asked.

"Did you hear the news? Aiden Walters is here!" he exclaimed as if he'd come dashing into the room to reveal that Santa Claus was, in fact, real and came to town a few months early.

I smiled at his joy. "I think everyone heard."

"He's right in the town square by the clock tower. Rumor has it he's signing autographs!"

"Oh?"

"Yeah!" Henry stood there blinking at me repeatedly. I blinked back with a lack of expression. I'd pushed all my emotions deep down that morning, hoping nothing would let my feelings come out that day. It turned out Henry felt enough for us both at that very moment. He was grinning ear to ear like it was Christmas morning, and his happiness was enough to make my day not suck. Henry was a gentle soul. He was a nerdy sixteen-year-old who'd just started working at the inn a few months prior. He'd been bullied a lot for just being himself, which infuriated me. He didn't fit in a lot with people, something I could relate to.

Henry always had a lot on his plate, but still, he found more than enough reasons to smile each day. I hoped the world wouldn't steal that away from him—his joy. All in all, Henry was a good kid. He worked hard, never complained like the other employees, and he always was quite the gentleman whenever I crossed his path.

"Go, Henry," I said, waving him off. "Go meet America's sweet-heart. Take the whole day off."

"Oh no, I won't take the whole day. I need the pay. I want to buy that new virtual reality game in a few weeks! I just need like fifteen min-utes or so, and I'll be good."

"I'll cover for you and make sure you get the pay. Besides, the big festival for Aiden's return is happening tonight. You should go enjoy it with your friends."

"Then you'll come, too?"

I laughed a little. "I can't. I'm going to be busy."

"Dang. I was going to win you a stuffed animal," he joked. "Well, if you're really okay covering for me," he said, already backing up and taking off his name tag. "Thanks, Hailee! I'll get a picture for you if you want! I'll see you later! And maybe we'll run into one another at the fes-tival if you get a bit of free time! People said there will be fireworks!" He excitedly skipped away as I was left there in the solitude of a now completely silent inn.

A part of me wanted to dash outside, too. I wanted to see Aiden—hug him, hold him, and tell him that I'd thought about him repeatedly over the years—but I couldn't. I wouldn't. I was determined to do my best to stay out of his way over the next few weeks. The less interaction I had with him, the better.

I went back to organizing the bookshelf for a while, glancing out the window every now and again toward the clock tower. The crowd was massive, and I couldn't help but feel my heart start racing faster as I set my eyes on Aiden.

That man.

My heartbeats.

How were they still controlled by him after all this time?

It turned out that that heart of mine was still somehow connected to the man who stood only a few hundred feet away from where I worked. I wondered when that feeling would fully fade away, or maybe when you once had love for a person, reminiscences of that love would always tug at one's heart. Perhaps I'd always be tethered to his essence in some way. My racing heartbeats were proof of that the moment I saw Aiden grab his suitcase and start walking in the direction of the inn.

Wait.

Why was he walking toward the inn?

What?

No.

"You have got to be shitting me," I breathed out, completely distraught as to why he was heading my way with a train of groupies and townspeople behind him. "You better not come in here, Aiden Walters, or so help me…" I grumbled to myself, placing my hands on top of my head in a state of complete shock.

He didn't hear my order as he walked right into the inn. My boss, Mr. Lee, sat behind the front desk, and the moment he saw Aiden, his eyes lit up with joy.

"Well, well, well… if it's not Leeks's superstar!" Mr. Lee said, leaping up from his chair. He hurried over to greet Aiden and pulled him into a tight hug. "Welcome back home. Welcome to your home away from home!"

Did Mr. Lee know that Aiden was staying at the inn?

The worst trait about Mr. Lee, bless his loving, bald head of a soul, was his ability to forget to tell me the most important things. Like the fact that my ex was staying at the inn where I spent the majority of my time. Why was he staying here? Why wasn't he staying with his parents?

Aiden seemed somewhat surprised by Mr. Lee's warm embrace but melted into the hug. It was no secret that Mr. Lee gave the best hugs in all of Leeks. I knew I hadn't seen much of the world outside of our small town, but I had no doubt that he might've had some of the best hugs in the whole world.

"It's good to see you, Mr. Lee. It's been a long time," Aiden said. His voice was deep, and strong, and oh-so kind. That hadn't changed much. What had changed was the fact that he was built like no other. Aiden was always a good-looking guy. He had the kind of smile that made it easy to fall head over heels.

"I was surprised to hear you wanted to stay at the inn instead of with your parents," Mr. Lee mentioned.

You and me both, Mr. Lee.

It was fine. I could deal with one weekend of avoiding Aiden.

Aiden grinned, and my heart almost exploded. "No, sir. I have a few work commitments and business calls I'll be taking throughout the next few months. Figured it would be best to have my own space."

Months?

I'm sorry, did he say months?!

He was giving me heart palpitations. My stomach was twisting and turning. Now for a fun game of "is it gas or is it anxiety?"

Probably both.

Mr. Lee nodded toward Aiden in understanding. "Makes sense. We have more than enough room for you here." He placed his hands on his hips and glanced around. "Let me get someone to help with your suitcase."

Not it!

I took a nosedive behind the couch in the sitting area before their eyes could locate me. My breaths weaved in and out as I placed my hand over my mouth to somehow muffle my state of panic. I wondered if they could hear my erratic heartbeats, too. My heart pounded against my rib cage as if it was trying to escape to Narnia. Far, far away where Aiden would never find it. Where was a cupboard to walk through when you needed one?

"Don't you worry, Mr. Walters, I'll help you with your bags," Henry said, probably tripping over his feet as he hurried back into the inn. "My name's Henry J. Peterson. I am the bellhop for Starlight Inn. Anything you need, I'll get it for you. If you'd like, I can even give you my cell phone number. You can dial me up day and night, Mr. Walters. Truly. I am at your beck and call."

"Fewer words, more working," Mr. Lee told Henry, waving him away. "Take Mr. Walters to Room thirty-four. Best room in the inn, Aiden."

A wave of nausea hit me as I realized that for the next few months, I'd be working for my famous ex-boyfriend. Or even more so, my ex-best friend.

Good grief.

"I appreciate that. Thank you," Aiden said to Henry. He sounded so grateful for the help, and I knew he meant it. Aiden was one of the humblest guys in the world. When people in the tabloids called him one of the kindest guys, I knew it was true and not some role Aiden was playing up. Gratitude could've been his middle name.

As Henry started rolling Aiden's suitcase toward the staircase near the sitting area, I held my breath once more as they chatted their way up the stairs, allowing my cheeks to look as if they were storing nuts for a great winter harvest. A sigh of relief hit me as I heard Aiden thank Henry before he closed the door behind him.

"What are you doing?"

I jumped out of my skin as I turned to see Mr. Lee staring at me behind the couch. I stood and smoothed out my outfit. "Dusting."

"Dusting the... carpet?"

"Yes."

"With your body?"

"Uh-huh."

He narrowed his eyes as if trying to figure me out. *Good luck, Mr. Lee. I can hardly figure myself out.*

He shifted his weight to his left side and crossed his arms. "Are you okay, Hailee?"

I pushed out a fake grin. "I'm dandy."

"Great. I need you to be on top of your toes these next few months with Aiden staying here."

"Few months?" I questioned, trying not to sound too nosy. "I actually wasn't aware he was staying here."

"I know, right? I logged him into the system under a fake name. Totally what Hollywood actors do, you know." He winked my way as if he pulled a fast one on me. "I never thought I'd get to do that. Pretty cool, huh?"

"Yeah, totally neat," I muttered, pretending that my panic wasn't rising with each passing second. "He can't really be staying for months, though, right? He's a busy actor. He must have to go back to California at some point."

"Who cares? As long as he's here, it's great for us." He looked toward the front window of the inn, where a crowd was still stationed due to the arrival of Aiden. "We'll need to make sure his stay is safe, with all the fans around. Do you know what this could do for our business? Having an Oscar-winning actor staying with us?"

"Oh, I don't know, give me a heart attack," I muttered.

"What was that?"

"Nothing, Mr. Lee. I'll make sure everything goes as smoothly as possible for Mr. Walters's stay."

He smiled, pleased. "Great. I'll let you get back to work." He glanced back over his shoulder toward me and narrowed his eyes. "By the way, for future reference, we do have vacuums. You don't have to dust the carpet with your body."

"Right. Vacuums. Funny how I didn't think of that."

"You're a smart girl who just had a dumb moment. Happens to the best of us."

He walked away, leaving me alone with the silent storm forming in my head. Aiden Walters was staying in town for the next few months at the Starlight Inn.

How was I supposed to avoid him when I was also in charge of making sure he was comfortable?

TWENTY-FOUR

Aiden

PLAYING THE ROLE OF THE SOCIAL BUTTERFLY OUTSIDE completely drained my energy. The moment I reached my room at the inn, I collapsed onto the bed. Shockingly, the mattress was one of the most comfortable beds I'd ever laid on, and I'd slept on a lot of beds. Especially during my last worldwide tour press conference.

I rubbed my hands over my face and sighed. Being back home felt odd. I hadn't visited my hometown in over five years. Some would say I made it a mission of mine not to make it back home. By "some," I meant my mother, but I saw her often enough. I spent pretty much every day with my father since he was my manager. Mom would've been out in Los Angeles with us, but she had her restaurant in Chicago to tend to. Still, she flew out often for visits.

A part of me never wanted to come back to Leeks. I felt like a complete asshole when I arrived in town with all the fanfare shown to me by the townspeople. My face was plastered all over the town's shops, and there were celebratory decorations across our downtown. The streets were blocked off for a huge festival happening that night to welcome me home for the next few months.

My father hated that I wasn't staying at their place, but the idea of being in town and sleeping in my childhood bedroom seemed like a personal nightmare. Especially if Hailee was right next door at any point in time.

Hailee.

Just being in town made her come to my mind often. I couldn't walk down the street without a collection of memories shooting through my brain.

A knock on the door broke me out of my thoughts, and I was thankful for the interruption. I opened the door to find Henry, the bellhop, standing there with a huge welcome basket in his hands. He wiggled his nose and tossed his head back a bit to try to push up his falling glasses.

"Hey, Mr. Walters. Sorry to bother you, but I wanted to bring you a welcome basket for your stay. I read online that you're allergic to tree nuts—just like me—so I checked and double-checked all the ingredients in each product. If you want anything else, I can run to the grocery store and pick it up for you, no matter what. Day or night, sir. I mean, school is starting back soon, so I'll mostly be here at night, but I can skip classes if you need me to."

I took the basket from him. "No need to skip school, but thanks, Henry. I appreciate it." I set the basket down on the nearby table, then reached for my wallet to give him a tip.

"Oh, no, Mr. Walters. It's fine, truly. I just wanted to drop it off. You don't have to pay me a cent. Honestly, just being able to be in your presence is a gift. I don't know if you know this, but"—he pushed his glasses up the bridge of his nose—"I'm your biggest fan. I've seen every movie you've done and watched every interview. I don't think anyone out there could be a better Superman than you, and I know you'll do the next trilogy justice. I know people can say a lot of negative crap online, but I hope you don't let it get to you. I know you'll kill those roles in the best possible way. Internet trolls are just jealous jerks."

I liked this guy.

He had heart.

"Thanks for the reminder, Henry." I handed him a couple of

twenty-dollar bills. "And you can call me Aiden. I'll be here for quite a few weeks, so we might as well be on a first-name basis."

Henry's eyes bugged out of his head as if I'd just asked for his hand in marriage. He nodded rapidly. "Of course, Mr. Wal—er—Aiden. Thank you. Also, there are two people downstairs who were hoping to see you. Mr. Lee made it clear that no one should be able to bother you, but—"

"I figured your parents were worth breaking those rules for," a familiar voice said, walking up the staircase down the hall.

I smiled wide as I saw my mother coming my way, with my dad not far behind her. Henry excused himself, leaving me with my greetings.

I held my arms out for a hug from Mom, and she swatted my shoulder with her purse. "Aiden, how dare I find out you made it to Leeks through the gossipy women in town. How did you not stop by our place before prancing through downtown? My goodness, you were out here hugging strangers before your own mother."

I pulled her into the hug she was fighting against and held on tight. I kissed the top of her head as her small figure settled into my embrace. "Sorry, Mom. I was hoping to come straight to the inn but got noticed."

Mom returned the hug, then pulled back and playfully tapped my cheeks with her hands. "Of course, you were noticed. You're Superman!" Her eyes started tearing up as she said those words. "You're Superman, Aiden!" she exclaimed. I hadn't seen my mom in person since the news came out that I'd be the next in line tackling a worldwide favorite fictional character.

"Don't cry, Mom."

"I'm not crying," she said as she wiped away the tears leaking from her eyes.

"Telling your mother not to cry is like telling water not to be wet," Dad said, interrupting the hug Mom and I were sharing to pull me into an embrace of his own. Unlike Mom, I didn't tower over him. Even though I'd put on a good amount of muscle mass over the past few years, Dad still had me beat in height.

He pulled away from me and nodded once with a smile on his face. "Superman."

"I still haven't wrapped my head around it yet. I can't believe it."

He placed his hands on my shoulders and squeezed. The small affection spoke volumes of his thoughts. It was his way of saying he was proud of me. Then before he could get overly emotional like Mom, he pulled back. "I wish we would've talked about this temporary break you and your mother came up with behind my back," he said. "I've been doing a lot of behind-the-scenes stuff to make sure it works."

"And it does," Mom argued quickly. "Filming for the movie doesn't start until next year. He earned this break."

"That's not exactly how this industry works, sweetheart," Dad told Mom.

"Well, I don't care. My son needed a break, so he's taking one."

I smiled. Mom would always go to war for me.

"I was hoping to come over to your house before the festival tonight for dinner," I said, trying to turn the topic around.

Mom combed her hair behind her ears. "Of course, you were. I already have dinner planned out. But for the time being, we are going to lunch at the diner. I've got our corner booth already reserved for us."

I laughed. "Since when does the diner take reservations?"

"Since my son became Superman. Now, you get ready and meet your father and me downstairs."

She headed downstairs as Dad stood in my hotel room, looking around. His brows were knotted as he crossed his arm across his broad chest. "You sure you don't want to stay with us? We have more than enough room."

"It's no big deal."

"This inn gets a bit drafty sometimes, I've heard."

"It's fine. I've got blankets."

"Sure, sure. Makes sense." He brushed his thumb against the bridge of his nose. Something was eating at him.

"What is it?"

"Nothing. I get you want to take a break, Aiden but... Just don't take your life for granted. Many don't get the level of success you have. If I were you, I would've eaten these opportunities up. If you change your mind about this long hiatus, I can get us up and running quickly. You have something millions of people would dream of, Aiden."

He reminded me of that on the regular—to count my blessings. In a way, I was living out his own dream, so I felt a responsibility to give it my all, even when I didn't love my career as much as I should've.

"Is this my 'with great power' speech?" I joked, nudging Dad in the arm.

"You're Superman, not Spider-Man, which is kind of disappointing. I'm more of a Marvel guy." He chuckled, shoving me. "I'm surprised you chose to stay at this inn," he mentioned, shifting the conversation.

"Why is that shocking? It's the only place to stay in town."

"Yeah, but I figured once your mother told you…" He narrowed his eyes and grumbled. "Your mother didn't tell you, did she?"

"Tell me what?"

"About Hailee?"

My whole body tensed up the second the name rolled off his tongue. A wave of anxiety hit me as I packed down the feelings that were trying to unleash from a simple name. Shakespeare once said, "What's in a name?" Well, a lot of trauma and heartache, Mr. Shakespeare. That was what was in a name. Especially when that name belonged to the girl who took my heart and hammered it into a bloody pulp.

"What about her?" I shortly asked.

Dad grumbled under his breath and shook his head. "I knew I shouldn't have left it to your mother to tell you. The woman is always forgetting something if it's not written down on a Post-it Note."

"What about her?" I repeated, trying to act as if my mind wasn't spiraling already from her mere mention.

"She works here."

"At the inn? Since when?"

"Few years now. She worked part-time while she was in school, then this summer she became the manager after the former one quit. She pretty much runs this whole place since Mr. Lee is getting older."

Shit.

The last person I wanted to see was the woman who broke my heart and never looked back all those years ago. She was dead to me. I didn't need for her to have a resurrection of sorts. I could've gone my whole life not hearing her name again, and I would've been just fine. Sure, I drunkenly texted her a few months back, but outside of that, I never thought of the woman.

The lies we tell ourselves daily.

"It's bothering you," Dad mentioned.

"It's not," I said through clenched teeth. How could Mom forget to tell me that? Seemed like a big fact to misplace. She was able to tell me all about the importance of organic products and about how the small-town dog Skipp just went through hip surgery, but she somehow forgot to drop the bomb that the place I was staying was the same place Hailee managed and lived?

I doubted it was due to her forgetful mind. If I knew one thing about my mother, it was her love for love. She probably had it somewhere in her mind that if Hailee and I reconnected, some old love story would resurface. A second chance romance of sorts.

Not a chance in hell. Hailee Jones and I would never be endgame. She killed all possibilities of that when she crushed my soul.

"Guys, you must come try this flavored water the inn has! Mr. Lee added pomegranates!" Mom hollered, breaking us away from the conversation of Hailee. We headed downstairs, went out to lunch, and talked about everything under the moon except for Hailee. Yet being back in town and knowing she worked at the inn was eating at my mind. Knowing that she was working at the inn unlocked an avalanche of connections we once shared. Everything around me reminded me of her. Hailee was soaked in every aspect of the small town that raised me. From the candy shop on the corner of Riley Street that we broke into freshman year to Cole's Ice Cream Shoppe where she'd eat only the bottom of her cones.

Every single inch of Leeks reminded me of Hailee.

She was now freshly on my mind.

TWENTY-FIVE

Hailee

"I **TOLD YOU I WASN'T GOING TO THAT FESTIVAL, KATE.**" I'D BEEN reading my newest book in my apartment for the past few hours since I'd gotten off work, and Kate was determined to pull me away from my introverted ways.

"You told me you had to work," she replied, plopping onto my couch. "But I just saw Mr. Lee, and he told me you had the evening off, like the rest of the staff due to the festival, and that he was running the front desk."

I groaned. "Mr. Lee talks too much."

She reached across to me and shut my book. "Get off your bum. We're going to the festival. It will be fun! They have all kinds of rides and stuff."

"It's a festival dedicated to my ex-boyfriend. Why don't you see why that's weird?"

"Oh, I see why it's weird, but there's deep-dish pizza and fried cheese. I'd go into a dungeon with all my exes for some deep-dish pizza and fried cheese."

"I guess we all have our limits," I joked. I went to reopen my book, and she slammed it closed.

"Don't get me wrong, I love a good romance book, thanks to you getting me addicted. But hear me out. How about for the next few hours, you stop reading about fictional characters living life and start actually living *your* life?"

My nose scrunched up. "Tempting, but where's the fun in that?"

"I'm glad you asked." She stood and walked to the backpack she brought over. She unzipped it and pulled out two matching forty-ounce black Yeti water bottles. She handed one to me.

"Don't tell me this is a mixed drink."

"It's not. Drink it."

I took a sip and cringed.

"It's straight vodka! It's not mixed at all!" She laughed. She reached into her backpack and pulled out a jug of lemonade. "Now we mix it."

I should've known. "Or we can just read books about people getting drunk."

"Hailee. We're in our twenties. Soon enough after your gap year, you'll be in getting your masters followed by your PhD, and you'll have babies and crap, and your life will become packed with baby vomit and dirty diapers. So, we have to live in the moment. You have to get drunk on a Saturday night with your friend. Plus, I never have Saturdays off, so this is a very rare, unique occasion, and my boyfriend is busy tonight."

"You don't have a boyfriend."

She pouted and whined. "I know, which makes this so much more depressing. I heard some local band is headlining the stage with their country music tonight."

"It's like you're trying to get me not to go," I joked.

"Come on, Hailee. This is our Coachella."

"You do realize how sad that is, right?"

"We live in Leeks, Wisconsin. Sad is our middle name. Which is why we must take every good moment, grab it by the balls, and milk that sucker until the cows come home. What do you say? Let's get drunk, go to a festival dedicated to your ex-best-boyfriend by a town of lunatics, and ride the Tilt-A-Whirl?"

I smirked. "Stop with the puppy dog eyes."

"I can't until you say yes," she whimpered, nudging me in the arm with the bottle of lemonade.

"Fine. But you're buying me fried cheese."

"I'll toss in a corn dog, too, if you play your cards right." She untwisted the top on my water bottle and poured lemonade into the cup, then did the same to hers. She held the bottle in the air and toasted. "To our twenties and bad decisions!" she declared.

I took a long drag from my bottle and cringed at the realization that not nearly enough lemonade was mixed into the drink, but oh well.

Bottoms up.

It seemed as if everyone in town was at the festival that night, conversing, laughing, and partying it up like it was indeed the Coachella Music Festival. I'd never seen so many people in our town at the same time, not even for the annual chili festival. The festival was taking place right on Lake Michigan, and the weather was perfect.

I had to admit, getting out of my apartment was the right thing to do. I was glad Kate pushed me out of my comfort zone.

"Is that your ex-best-boyfriend's face on a cookie?" Kate asked me in complete awe as we walked over to the bakery stand where Mama's goodies were all displayed.

"That is definitely his face on a cookie," I said as I pulled out my cell phone and took a shot of Mama's display. "I made them myself."

"You had to make ex-best-boyfriend cookies?"

"Yup, all night last night."

"Your life is oddly traumatic. I hope you tell your therapist that."

"Trust me, she knows," I joked.

"We have to buy one," Kate ordered as she dragged me into the long line. "It's a must."

I wanted to argue, but then again, it supported my parents, so I went along with it. As we reached the front of the line, Dad gave us both a grand smile. He wasn't allowed to bake the goods because he was a professional at burning things, but he sure could sell them.

"Hey, ladies. Welcome! What would you like to get your hands on?" he asked.

"Two Aiden Walters faces, please and thank you," Kate said, pulling out her cash.

"You're in luck. Those are the last two here. They've been selling like hotcakes. I guess that's what happens when they are made by the best baker in town," Dad said about Mama as he gave me a slight wink. Gosh, he loved that woman so much. It would've been gross if it wasn't so cute.

We grabbed the cookies and walked to the side to eat them. Kate stared down at the sugar cookie in complete awe.

"What is it?" I asked.

"Nothing, nothing. It's just… very realistic."

I laughed. "I think that's the point."

"No offense, Hailee, because I know he's your ex and all, but Aiden Walters might be the sexiest man alive."

"That's what the magazines seem to think," I agreed.

"I mean, look at him. Those blue eyes! Those luscious waves of brown hair."

"You're drunk."

"Tipsy." She giggled. It was no secret that my friend was a light-weight, just like me. I felt a nice buzz going on. "But that doesn't change the fact that everything I'm saying is actual and factual. Never in my life did I want to sit on a cookie just to know what it would be like to sit on Aiden Walters's face."

"Kate!" I gasped, laughing as I linked my arm around hers and pulled her away from the crowd that overheard. "You're ridiculous."

"Did you do it, Hailee?" she asked, eyes wide with hope. "Did you ever sit on Aiden's face?"

My cheeks felt flush, and I shook my head. "I refuse to answer that question."

Kate gave me a devilish smile and nodded. "You little freaky freak. What other kinds of stuff did you do? Reverse cowgirl?"

"This conversation is over."

She bit into the cookie and moaned, having the most orgasmic bite of her life. She closed her eyes and waved her hand in the air as if she'd died and gone to heaven. "This is the best cookie I've ever eaten."

That made me happy. I took a bite of mine, too. Just as great as the night before. "It's amazing," I agreed.

"It's not the first time you shoved Aiden between your lips, huh? I bet he's quite the mouthful."

"I'm done with you."

She grinned and took a sip of her lemonade. "Never."

We moved around the festival as the sky darkened over our heads and sparkled with stars. The more we drank, the less worry I had about running into Aiden. Liquid courage and all. The amount of confidence bursting from my seams was ridiculous, but I didn't care. I felt good. Life was weird, sometimes, so whenever there was an opportunity to feel good, I bathed in the joy.

Kate kept up the good time by buying me way too much fried food, and when our water bottles ran out of drinks, she purchased us alcoholic slushies. My toilet was going to have hell to pay come tomorrow morning, from either the top end of me or the bottom, but I didn't care. I felt like a kid again.

"Aren't you happy you came out tonight?" Kate urged after she drunkenly won me a stuffed tiger from a carnival game. She was leaning on me because her steps were zigzagging, and I leaned back on her because mine were doing the same. "We didn't even run into—oh shit," she muttered as we turned the corner, and without looking, I ran straight into a person, spilling my pink slushy all over them.

"Oh, my goodness, I'm so sorry I…" My words faded as I looked up to meet the person's stare.

Not just any person.

My person.

Correction: my ex-person.

Aiden.

There he was, right in front of me, looking at me square in the eyes. Those blue eyes that seemed to match the deepest parts of the ocean. Those blue eyes that I'd loved since I was a little girl. Those blue eyes that made my heart shatter into a million pieces right then and there.

A white cotton T-shirt hugged his body, showcasing his toned arms, a T-shirt that was now stained pink.

"Oh gosh, I'm sorry, I, um… I…" I'd played the situation of us meeting face-to-face in my head a million times before. I'd had played almost every outcome out in my head, but shockingly, spilling my booze-filled slushy all over his chest was not one that crossed my mind.

Without thought, I started rubbing at his shirt with my hands, smearing the mess even more, feeling his rock-hard abs beneath the fabric. "I'm so sorry, Aiden, I didn't mean to—" My stomach flipped as my nerves bubbled up. Now for another round of was it gas or anxiety?

Answer: it was neither. It was nausea.

I pulled back for a beat to try to push the rising sensation away, but as I parted my lips to apologize, vomit flew out of my mouth and landed onto Aiden's shoes.

Oh goodness. I threw up on my famous ex-best-boyfriend.

I covered my mouth with my hand from shock as I looked up at Aiden wide-eyed. I was humiliated. If I could go hide under a rock, I would.

"Aiden—" I started, but my words stopped as he released a low growl.

Yup.

That was right.

He growled at me.

He took a step back. *"Don't,"* he whisper-shouted, his voice low, rough, and controlled.

I looked up at him and saw those blue eyes that I once loved, and they seemed so different. Filled with… hatred? Was that hatred that flashed across his face?

He stepped out of his vomit shoes and slid off his socks, leaving them there in front of me.

He then turned his back toward me and wandered off completely barefoot, leaving me there drunk and embarrassed, and with a dash of heartbreak, too. I didn't know what to expect from our first interaction, but it wasn't that.

It was at that moment of him saying one word to me that reality set in for me.

Don't.

One word was enough to break my heart. Even though I'd played out a million scenarios in my mind, it was clear that I'd secretly only wanted one. I wanted him to hug me. To hold me. To tell me he missed me. To tell me he'd thought about me every single day for the past few years. I wanted him to still long for me in the same way I secretly dreamed of him.

Don't.

It was cold, harsh, and truthful. He didn't want anything to do with me. That crushed my soul a little bit more than I was prepared for it to do.

"Holy crap. I didn't know Aiden Walters could look pissed off.

Did America's puppy dog just give you the evil eye?!" Kate murmured, stunned by the cold, harsh look Aiden shot my way when we made eye contact.

"I think so," I said, a bit shaken up by the expression delivered my way. Chills raced up and down my spine as I tried to push away the odd feeling.

"You didn't tell me you two had a bad break-up to the point that he hated you."

"I didn't know it was to the point that he hated me."

"Don't cry."

"I'm not gonna cry." I shrugged, rolling my eyes.

"Then why are your eyes leaking?"

Because I'm so deeply sad.

I brushed at the falling tears and choked out my words. "I'm drunk and lost my slushy. That's why I'm crying."

"Hailee," she said so softly. She must've sobered up from my painfully awkward situation. "You still love him."

"What? No. No. We were a thing such a long time ago," I muttered, starting to walk ahead. I waved my hands around in a dismissive way. "Ancient history. Nothing to see here," I blabbered. "Anything I felt for him is long, long gone!" I declared. I stood as straight as I could. "I feel great! The tears are happy tears. I didn't even like that slushy."

Kate gave me a concerned look. "You're lying, aren't you?"

Through my clenched teeth.

I held my hand out to her. "Can I go home now and read romance books?"

"Yeah." She nodded. "Let's get you home."

TWENTY-SIX

Hailee

"I CAN'T BELIEVE YOU THREW UP ON SUPERMAN'S SHOES," Henry said the next morning at the front desk of the inn. I slouched in my chair, hungover and dumbfounded about how my night turned out. I didn't even want to go to the stupid festival.

"I didn't throw up on Superman's shoes. I threw up on Aiden Walters's shoes."

Henry frowned as he walked over to the coffee table we'd set up for guests. "I hate to break it to you, Hailee, but they're the same person." He grabbed a cup of coffee, added sugar and cream, then brought it over to me. "I'd be so embarrassed if I were you."

"Don't remind me," I groaned, taking a sip of the coffee. "Thank you for this, Henry."

A noise was heard at the top of the stairs, and I sat up, alert.

Henry reached across to me and patted my hand. "Don't worry. Superman already left. He headed out to the gym for a workout. You don't have to face your humiliation until later."

Goody.

"I'm not humiliated," I urged.

"Hailee, I think you're great. Really, I do. One of the best people I know, but if there's one thing you're bad at, it's lying."

"Shouldn't you be getting to work?" I asked.

He glanced around the inn and shrugged. "Nobody needs anything."

"Maybe you should vacuum the floors for something to do." The pounding headache I was nursing wasn't leaving much space for me to socialize with anyone at all. Not even sweet Henry.

"You got it, boss lady."

He hurried off to do the task as two women walked into the inn with their suitcases. They looked about my age, maybe a little bit younger. They were giggling and whispering to one another as they approached me. Then the blond turned my way with a big smile on her face.

"Hey, there. How are you doing?" she asked with a little Southern twang to her voice. She was not from around these parts, that was for sure. Our town didn't have many passersby. Most people just kept on their way for another forty-five minutes and headed straight to Chicago.

I pushed out a smile and tried to ignore my flipping stomach. "I'm doing good. How are you? How can I help you?"

"Well, yes. My name is Marna, and this is my best friend, Violet. We have a room booked for the next few weeks. I know we are a bit early to check-in, but we were hoping we could maybe get in early."

"For sure. Let me get your ID and a credit card so I can pull up your reservation."

She handed me her goods, and I noticed her charm bracelet. It had little charms of books, cats, and hearts. "Oh, I really like that."

"Thanks, my mom gave it to my when I was a kid. I never take it off," she explained.

I touched the piece of jewelry dangling around my neck. My Tom necklace. I hadn't taken it off, even though Aiden took his off all those years ago. It oddly gave me comfort during my hardest days.

After I shook off my emotions, I found their reservation. As I typed in their information, they whispered to one another as if I couldn't over-hear them.

"Stop, I'm not going to ask her that," Violet said to her friend.

I smiled at them both. "You can ask me anything."

She sighed and brushed her hands through her long, red hair. She

glanced around the inn and then leaned in toward me. Her voice lowered, and she whispered, "Is it true Aiden Walters is staying at this inn?"

I sat up straighter, stunned by her question.

Oh my gosh.

Were they groupies?

I cleared my throat and returned to entering the card information.
"I'm not allowed to share guest information like that."

"That means yes!" Marna said, slapping her hand against her leg.
"Can we get a room near his?" she questioned.

When pigs fly.

"We actually have a great room for you on this floor right down
the hallway." I handed them the keys. I rang the bell sitting on my desk,
and Henry came over within seconds. "Henry, can you show these ladies
to their room? Welcome to Leeks, ladies. I hope you have a great stay."

Henry was quick to grab their suitcases and chat their ears off as
they walked off toward their room. Mr. Lee wasn't kidding. Having a
celebrity staying at your inn was very good for business. By the end of
the night, all our rooms were booked. That fact alone gave me anxiety.
I doubted Aiden came to the inn in hopes that a ton of fans would be
checking in.

I'd remember how bad his panic attacks could be. I didn't want these
people giving him any kind of trouble.

When I was done working for the day, I headed out to pick up
some very important items, and I headed back to the inn with them in
my grip. I'd been going back and forth with the idea of saying something to Aiden, but I also knew I couldn't avoid him forever. And who
knew? Maybe what I read as cold and distant the night before was just
my boozed-up mind playing tricks on me.

I headed to his hotel room door, took a deep breath, and knocked
on it four times.

When he came to open it, my breath got caught in my throat, and
I started choking on my own air. I turned away from him and tried my
hardest to clear my throat. My eyes began to water as panic began to
rise in my mind. I began coughing hard, unable to cover my mouth due
to the box within my hands. Was I choking? Oh gosh, I was choking in
front of Aiden as he blankly stared my way.

"Sorry," I said, forcing myself to swallow as a few more coughs slipped through. Once I gained my composure the best I could, I looked at him and smiled. "Hi." If you looked up the word awkward in the dictionary, my photograph would be plastered there.

Aiden stared at me coldly, and a chill raced up and down my spine as he didn't say a word.

I cleared my throat—again. "I wanted to apologize for throwing up on you last night. I normally can hold my alcohol better, but the mix of fried cheese and slushy, and—"

"Is that all?" he harshly cut in. His eyes were unamused, and his stance was hard as he crossed his arms. Was his chest always that broad? Regardless, it was clear that I didn't dream up his standoffish appearance the night before like I'd hoped. He wasn't the same gentle boy I fell in love with.

"I, well, no, I, uh—"

"Words, Hailee," he ordered. "Use your words like a grown-up."

Well.

That's rude.

I shook my head and held the box out toward him. "I bought you new shoes. You're still a size thirteen, yes? They're probably a lot cheaper than the ones I ruined last night, but I figured it was the least I could do to make up for it."

"I don't want your shoes."

The flurry of butterflies in my stomach was having their wings ripped off one by one. I inched the box closer to him, glanced around the hallway, and whispered, "Just take the shoes, Aiden."

"I don't want them," he repeated. He stepped back into his room and went to shut the door, but I put my foot in place to stop it from closing.

"Aiden, please."

"What do you want?" he snapped, his eyes packed with hatred. A hatred I thought I'd daydreamed the night prior. A hatred that I thought I'd never see come from him. A hatred that broke my heart.

"I... I—"

"Words," he barked in a low scowl. His harshness threw me for the biggest loop. Never in my life had Aiden been so rude to me, even when we ended things. Sure, he texted me being confused, and I ignored his messages, but he was never rude. Just hurt.

Plus, he treated everyone else in town as if he was a golden retriever, the nicest man alive. Why was he being so painfully rude toward me after all these years? Besides, he moved on! He had his dream life. His rudeness was uncalled for.

People break up in life, Aiden. That doesn't mean you have to be a total dickhead.

"What's the matter with you?" I shot back. "I'm trying to be nice."

"You should stop trying. It's not working."

I narrowed my eyes. "You're being a dick."

"Good. Then maybe you'll leave me alone."

"I—"

"We aren't doing this."

"Stop cutting me off!"

"Then finish a fucking thought!" he hammered back, his veins popping out of his neck.

"I would if you wouldn't cut me the heck off! Geez! I came to bring you a pair of shoes, you jerk. You don't have to be like that. I figured after all this time, we could maybe be on good terms, but—"

"We aren't."

"Stop cutting me off," I said once again.

His brow knitted, and he glanced at my foot blocking him from closing the door. Then he looked back at me. "Move your foot."

"No."

"Yes."

"No."

"Hailee," he sternly said. Hearing his lips say my name? It was a new kind of heartbreak because he used to say it so gently. "Move. Your. Foot."

I moved it.

He slammed the door in my face, leaving me standing there with a shoebox in my grip and my ego buried six feet under.

As I walked away, his door swung open, and he called after me again. I turned toward him, hopeful that he'd come to his senses and was ready to apologize to me for being so cold and nasty.

He approached me slowly, and with each step he took, my heart began pounding faster and faster within my chest. He was so close that my mind made up a crazy idea for a second that he would lean in and kiss me right then and there. That he'd been fighting a war in his mind, and his outburst was just because he didn't know how to act around me after all this time. That his lips missed my taste so much that he was going to fall back into me.

Fall into me, Aiden.

He hovered over me. His blue eyes narrowed, and his chest puffed out. His full lips parted as he whispered, "I am in town for the next few months, and I want to make something extremely clear, okay?"

I swallowed the lump that sat in my throat. "Okay."

He moved in closer. His hot breaths brushed against my skin as every hair on my body stood straight. "I want nothing to do with you. I don't need you checking in on me just because you work here, I don't need you buying me shoes because you can't hold your liquor, and I don't want to reconnect and talk about the good ole days with you, Hailee. You are nothing to me, and I am nothing to you. We are strangers, and I am not interested in knowing anything about you at all. Am I clear?"

My lips parted as I tried to keep my composure. "Crystal," I replied, standing as tall as I could, which somehow still left me feeling so little.

He released a low grumble of annoyance before turning and walking back into his room, leaving me there to gather the small bit of dignity I had left.

When did that happen? When did the sweetest boy I'd ever known turn into such a cold, cold man? The rest of the world would've been shocked to see how harsh Aiden could've been to a person, to me. But I guessed that was why he had his Oscar. His acting skills truly showed his range.

"It was that bad?" Mama asked during dinner at my parents' house. Recently, we'd been rewatching *I Love Lucy* once a week at my parents' place while Dad was doing some accounting work down at the bakery.

"I threw up on his shoes, and then today he told me he wanted nothing to do with me. In a very mean way."

"That's so hard for me to imagine. Aiden was always the sweetest boy."

"Well, that sweet boy was stung with asshole serum."

Mama shook her head. "He's probably not sure how to handle being around you. The same way you don't know how to be around him."

"But I wasn't a jerk to him!"

"Yes, but you were the one who broke his heart all those years ago."

"It's not like I wanted to hurt him. Besides, that's ancient history," I repeated like the robot I was becoming when it came to talking about Aiden.

"Just because it happened a long time ago doesn't mean the healing has come full circle, Hailee."

I pouted. "Whose side are you on?"

"Yours. Always yours." She laughed and stole one of my french fries. "All I'm saying is, your break-up had to be hard on Aiden. I'm not saying how he's acting is right, but I'm saying I can understand how he feels. Especially with how you went about the break-up…"

"Okay, can we not relive that?" I asked. I'd already spent long enough feeling guilty about the way I ended things with Aiden all those years ago. Could I have handled the break-up better? Yes. Did it crush me to my core to crush him? Of course, but I was young, stupid, and thought I was doing the best thing for us both. I'd already felt crappy enough for the past twenty-four hours. I didn't need to feel even worse about my past mistakes.

"Sorry. What is it you want me to say?" Mama asked.

"Men are stupid, and your daughter is the best."

"Men are stupid, and my daughter is the best," she echoed.

Loyalty was Mama's middle name.

Before we could continue, my cell phone rang. Mr. Lee's name flashed on the screen, and I was quick to answer. "Hey, Mr. Lee. What's up?"

"Hailee. Hey, how are you? I'd hate to do this to you, especially last minute, but the bar and grill is packed tonight, and Sarah went home sick. Do you think you can come in and cover for her?"

"The bar and grill is never packed on Sundays."

"It is when an Oscar winner is staying at our inn. I told you Aiden would be great for business!"

At least one of us was thriving from Aiden's arrival.

"I see. Yeah, sure. I'll be over in about fifteen minutes." I hung up the phone and told Mama what was going on.

She grimaced. "I have a feeling it's going to be very hard for you to keep your distance from that boy with him staying at your inn."

Who was she telling? I was in a constant state of sweatiness from the situation due to my shot nerves.

When I arrived at the bar and grill, I hopped behind the bar to get to work. I wasn't the best at making cocktails, and whenever I had to cover for a person back there, my anxiety rose to new heights. I'd never seen the bar and grill that crowded. Leading the crowd was the man of the hour and the man who gave me the dirtiest of looks.

I stood behind the bar, feeling my chest tighten as Aiden's eyes locked with mine. His smile evaporated, and the coldness came back as the lines on his face tightened, and the veins in his neck popped out. If love was based on smiles, and hate was based on frowns, I was the girl most hated by the boy most loved.

He blinked and moved his stare away from me, stepping back into the role he seemed to be putting on for the townspeople. A big smile hit his face, and he shouted, "Drinks on the house from me!"

No, Aiden. Don't put me through this hell.

The crowd cheered, I all about cried, and then I got to work as the orders started rolling in. He'd made it clear that he didn't want to have anything to do with me earlier. What he didn't make clear was that he also wanted to make my life a living hell.

As people crowded the bar, I poured beer after beer, shot after shot, and my stomach repeatedly turned from the smell of the alcohol. After last night, I'd be okay going a long time without having a drink.

At the end of the bar, Aiden sat with Tommy Stevens, the journalist for our town's paper. I'd overheard Tommy going on and on about a manuscript he'd written and how he wanted Aiden to read it. Aiden engaged as if he was interested, and Tommy kept going on and on about how Aiden would be the perfect hero for his movie idea.

The more Tommy drank, the more touchy-feely he was growing with Aiden. He kept patting Aiden on the shoulder, lightly shoving him in the chest to express his point as he grew louder and louder.

When most of the crowd headed home, Aiden and Tommy were the last two remaining.

"You have to read it," Tommy drunkenly slurred. "It's an

Oscar-winning kind of script!" He then turned back to me. Lying across the bar, he snapped his fingers. "Jones girl! Get me another."

I saw a slight twitch in Aiden's lip and then looked at Tommy. With a knot in my stomach, I gave him a smile. "Sorry, Tommy. I think we need to cut you off for the night."

"What? We're just getting started! Seeing how Mr. Hollywood is covering the tab. Right, Aiden?" he said, patting Aiden's chest. I swore he'd touched him more in the past hour or so than I had during our whole relationship.

"I think I'm actually gonna call it a night," Aiden said, standing. "It seems as if the bar is ready to close anyway. Most people have wandered home. You can close out my tab and charge it to my room," he ordered me. He turned to walk away, but Tommy didn't follow.

"Well, shit. I'll pay for my own drink," Tommy stated.

"Sorry, Tommy. I can't serve you any more. It's just a rule. But I can call you a ride to get you home if you need it." I turned to walk to the cashier to ring Aiden out, but before I could, Tommy reached across the bar, grabbed my arm, and yanked me back toward him.

"I said I want another drink, woman," he drunkenly expressed, spitting profusely as he spoke. "It looks like you never cut yourself off from the pleasures of life judging by your size, so how about you take your fat ass over there and get me one?"

A slight chill raced down my back. There was a time in my life when his comment would've made me spiral into a fit of insecurities, but I'd worked hard enough to know my worth over the years. Tommy's words were just that...words. They didn't get to stick to my soul unless I brought out the superglue myself.

Before I could even blink, Tommy was on the floor. Aiden had slammed his fist into Tommy's face, knocking him out with one swing. Thankfully, no one else was in the bar. Otherwise, I was certain cameras would've been going off like crazy, filming Hollywood's sweetheart being violent.

"What the hell?" I blurted out, stunned. It happened so fast.

"What's going on in here?" Parker, the cook, asked, emerging from the kitchen. He looked at me and noticed that I was shaken up, then looked over at Tommy, who was still on the checkered floor. Then he looked at Aiden, whose chest was rising and falling.

"Go home, Hailee," Parker said as he walked toward me. "I'll handle this mess and lock up."

I parted my lips to speak, but no words came out.

Parker gave me a lazy half grin. "Go home. I'll handle Tommy."

I nodded, grabbed my purse, and headed straight out the door.

The moment the autumn breeze hit my face, I choked out a sob as tears began falling down my cheeks.

"Hailee, wait," Aiden called out. "Wait up."

I whipped around and stepped toward him. "What's your problem?" I barked, frustration fuming from my words. "What do you think you're doing going around punching people like that? And why? It's clear you've been going out of your way to avoid me. You've literally crossed the road to be far out of my reach, and then, out of nowhere, you're defending my honor? What the hell, Aiden?"

He looked confused as ever, as if he hadn't even known what came over him. He raked his hand through his hair out of frustration. "I don't know what came over me in there. All I know was Tommy was treating you like shit, and—"

"And it's none of your business. You made it clear that you wanted nothing to do with me."

"I know, all right? I get it. We're strangers."

"We aren't strangers, Aiden. We will never be strangers. I mean… I'm even open to a friendship again if you are." He huffed in disgust, which made me frown. "When we ended things, I didn't think it would leave you hating me."

"When *we* ended things? There was no we in that equation."

"I know how it looked…"

He parted his mouth to speak, but no words came. He shut his mouth and clenched his jaw.

What, Aiden? What were you about to say?

"Say it," I urged.

"No."

"Say it," I repeated.

"It's not worth it."

"Of course. Close yourself off to having a grown-up conversation."

"What the hell is that supposed to mean?"

I narrowed my eyes. "You've been treating me like crap since you got back here. Acting very childish and rude and—"

"*You broke my fucking heart!*" he shouted, pain in his vocals as he tossed his hands up in defeat. "First in person, then via text message! Why the hell would I want to talk to you, Hailee? You made it clear as day that you wouldn't give me another chance. You made it clear that we were over. Why the hell would I want to converse with you, let alone be nice to you?"

"I don't know, maybe because before we were in a relationship, we were best friends since we were kids?"

"That didn't seem to mean anything to you when you ended things." He huffed, rage burning in the back of his eyes. "You even said maybe we could remain friends, but it was best we didn't talk for a while. Then I waited. I waited for you to reach out again, Hailee. A while passed by, and you still stayed away. Or do you not recall the text message you sent me?"

"Aiden…" My voice cracked. Guilt filled me up to the brim.

"I want to be strangers," he said. "I need you to be a stranger to me."

I hated that. I hated it so much, but also, I understood. If that's what he needed, it wasn't fair for me to get in his way of healing. Like Mama said, healing had its own timeline. It wasn't right of me to step on Aiden's when I was the one who hurt him in the first place. I'd respect his wishes—even if it broke my own heart. "If that's what you really want, I'll stay out of your way until you leave town."

"Fine."

"Great."

"Splendid."

"Wonderful."

"Okay."

"Fan-freaking-tastic," I spat out.

"Do you really have to get the last word in? Are you that childish?" he grumbled like a grumpy old man.

"Says the man who goes around punching people. That's real mature, Aiden. We aren't kids anymore. We don't go around throwing punches."

"He disrespected you."

"And why do you care?"

No. Really. Why do you care?

His nostrils flared, and he raked his hand through his hair as he paced the sidewalk. "Call it an old reflex. We're done here."

He turned to walk away and paused halfway in the middle of the road. His head lowered. His steps moved to turn back around to face me and the anger that lived within his stare was gone. For a moment, he looked like his old self. The boy I once loved. For a moment, he stared at me as if he still cared, and he said, "Do people do that often?"

"Do what?"

"Comment about you like that?"

"Of course not. Tommy was drunk, and he's an idiot," I said. "We're not in high school anymore. People aren't out here slinging insults at me."

He grimaced. "Of course, they aren't. Sorry. I just…I can't think clearly around you," he whispered. His shoulders dropped, and a shift overtook his entire body. It was at that moment that I saw it—Aiden's truth. He didn't hate me. He wasn't angry or bitter like his words were coming off. He was…sad.

Aiden was painfully sad. I saw it within those blue eyes when they locked with mine.

How had I missed it before? Was I too deep in my own thoughts to notice his evident pain? Was he that good at shielding his sadness? How long had he been hurting so quietly? How long had he been in the depths of that pain?

It was a kind of sadness that was deeper than just our separation. It was the kind of sadness that lingered throughout someone's entire existence. It crept in every crevice of a person's soul, melting pain and struggle into their spirit.

I could only spot that level of sadness in his eyes because I'd lived it before, right when Aiden left town five years ago. Those demons of sadness were the hardest to rid myself of. It shattered my heart to know that Aiden was sitting in the eye of his hurricane, in the middle of his despair, and not a single person seemed to notice. Not even me.

Yet now that I saw it…

My chest ached. "Aiden…"

"Do you feel bad?" he asked. "For how you ended things between us?"

Yes.

Repeatedly.

All the time.

"You already know the answer to that," I told him.

"I need you to say it."

"I feel guilty every single day."

"Then why did you do it? Why did you let me go?"

"I knew it had to be done. I do wish I could've handled it differently. I was young and scared. All I want to do is start with a clean slate with you, Aiden. That's all." I wanted him to let me back into his world so I could help walk beside him. I knew depression. I wouldn't wish for my greatest enemy to walk with that anguish all on their own. Let alone Aiden.

"Clean slate," he huffed, disgusted by the idea. He didn't give me another word. His somber look deepened, and he slid his hands into the pockets of his jeans before he turned and walked away.

TWENTY-SEVEN

Hailee

THE FOLLOWING MORNING, I WAS A ZOMBIE WHEN I WENT TO
work. Kate couldn't feed me enough coffee to keep me on
my toes. I'd spent most of the previous night worrying about
Aiden. At least it was a slower day. When Aiden came out of his room,
he kept his head down and avoided me at all costs. My sensitive heart
ached as I prayed for him to look my way.

Around one in the afternoon, the front door opened and in walked
Tommy. His eye was black and blue from Aiden's fist making contact
the night before. Tommy had clearly sobered up and walked over to the
front counter as if his tail was between his legs.

"Hi, Hailee," he said, pushing out a small smile. He raked his hand
over his head. "I wanted to stop in and apologize for being a drunk asshole last night. I was out of line. You didn't deserve that nasty comment."

The apology was… odd. Sure, Tommy said something awful the
previous evening, but truth be told, he'd made much nastier comments
throughout the years about others in town. Tommy was known for his
rudeness toward people when he drank too much. If anything, last night's
comment was tame for him.

I arched an eyebrow. "Okay."

That was all I could think to say.

He narrowed his eyes. "So… you forgive me?"

"It doesn't matter."

He glanced toward the front window and then back at me. "It does kind of matter. I need to hear you say you forgive me."

"Why does it matter?"

"Because I need to hear you actually say it, all right?" he snapped. The thing about assholes was they couldn't keep their tempers at bay for long. Tommy's was already slipping out. "Just say it, Hailee."

"No." I shook my head. "You can't force someone to forgive you. That's not how forgiveness works."

"Stop being dramatic, okay? Just say it."

"No."

"Don't be a bitch, Hailee. Just say it!" He kept glancing toward the window.

I finally looked over and saw Aiden standing outside with his arms crossed. When he noticed that I saw him, he stepped out of my view.

"Did Aiden put you up to this?" I asked Tommy.

"He said he'd read my manuscript if I apologized."

Oh, Aiden.

He still controlled my heartbeats.

"Fine, I forgive you," I blurted out to Tommy. Did I truly forgive him? No, of course not. I despised that man. Yet if it got him to leave me alone, it was good enough of a lie for me to tell.

Tommy walked off confidently, and I rolled my eyes as I sat back in my chair. I stared out the window and watched Tommy hand Aiden his manuscript. They talked for a while, Aiden nodding at whatever Tommy was saying, and the moment Tommy walked away, Aiden tossed the manuscript into a nearby trash can.

I smiled a little.

That was a very Aiden thing to do.

It wasn't long before he walked back into the inn to head to his room. He didn't look my way, even though I'd wished he had. I wanted to see his blue eyes again so I could read more pieces of his soul he'd kept to himself.

He said he wanted to be strangers, but his actions and words were so out of sync.

"Hey, Hailee, can you run up the room service tray to Aiden's room? I'll watch the front desk," Mr. Lee requested.

I raised an eyebrow. "What? Can't someone from the bar and grill do that like they normally do?"

"Carly was the only runner here and went home sick."

What kind of bug was going around the inn?

I grumbled a bit. "Can Henry take them?"

"He's out back. Go, please. I don't want to keep him waiting." Mr. Lee waved me away, so frustratedly, I did my job. I carried the tray up the stairs. Seconds before I knocked on Aiden's door, my stomach twisted into knots. When he opened the door with a smile, it hurt to see how fast it faded from his face when he realized it was me.

"What do you want?" he barked.

"Nothing. You're the one who requested room service, so here it is."

He grumbled something under his breath. "Fine."

"Would you like me to set it down on your table?"

He stepped to the side to let me in. My skin felt tingly from being in the intimate space with him. I set the tray on the table, uncovered his meal, a burger and fries, and poured his beer into the chilled glass. "There you go. If there is anything else you need, you can let me know or—"

"Ketchup." He cut me off. His new favorite habit.

"Oh. Right. Okay. I'll be right back."

I hurried down the steps and shot to the kitchen, then came back up with the ketchup. "Here you go."

"How did you forget mustard?" he rudely asked.

"Um, maybe because you didn't mention mustard?"

"I did. I said ketchup and mustard."

"No." I stood taller. "You said ketchup. Since when do you even like mustard?"

"Let's not act as if you know who I am anymore."

Here we go again. Don't take the bait, Hailee.

I gave him a bright smile. "Let me go grab that for you."

I hurried downstairs—again—and came back up with yellow mustard.

He scrunched up his face. "You don't have Dijon?"

"You have got to be kidding me right now, Aiden. Just take the mustard." I shoved the bottle against his chest.

He shoved it back. "I want Dijon."

"I"—*shove*—"don't have Dijon."

"Well, I don't want this," he growled back, shoving it back toward me.

"Aiden, stop." I pushed it toward him, and he pushed back.

"You stop."

Neither one of us would. We pushed back and forth until Aiden accidentally squeezed the bottle, and the mustard exploded all in my face.

"Ahh!" I screamed, dropping my hold on the bottle.

"Fuck, sorry," he muttered. Rushing to the bathroom, he grabbed a towel and started wiping my face. I yanked the towel from his hand.

"I got this," I muttered, wiping the mustard from my face. It was in holes where mustard didn't belong. My nostrils, my ears, my eyes.

"It's in your hair, too. Let me get it," he said. "Shit," he breathed out. "I'm sorry, I'm sorry," he repeated.

I didn't know why, but I started laughing. I began giggling like a fool over the whole situation. There was mustard everywhere. In my hair, up my nose, under my fingernails. I became hysterical in a fit of laughter, and Aiden began to laugh, too. Oh, how I missed his laughter.

When was the last time you laughed, Aiden?

For a moment, we felt like us again. Him picking mustard out of my hair, me wiping it out of my eyelashes. We laughed together, and my soul felt healed. It felt right laughing with him, which was exactly what led to me falling apart within the next few seconds. My hysterical laughter transformed into hysterical sobs. My tears intermixed with mustard as they rolled down my cheeks.

"Hailee, don't," Aiden pleaded, his voice cracking as he stood before me.

I covered my mouth with my hands and shook my head. "I'm sorry."

"Don't do that."

"I'm sorry. I didn't mean to make the mess, and I should've just gone and got the mustard and—"

"No." He let out a weighted breath. His hard expression was softer now, gentler. His eyes reminded me of the boy who once loved me. "That's not what I mean."

"Then what do you mean?"

"I mean, don't do this to me." He palmed the nape of his neck, appearing conflicted. "Don't cry."

"Why not?"

"Because if you cry, I'll want to comfort you, and I can't comfort you... so please don't. Don't make me stop hating you, Hailee. I've spent a lot of years building up this hatred for you, and it's not fair for you to just come along and knock it down."

I took a step toward him. "Aiden, I..."

"Please," he begged, holding up a halting hand in my direction. "Because every time you come near me..." A deep growl of irritation escaped his lips as he shook his head. "Just keep your distance, all right? And I'll keep mine." He walked to the door to open it for me to leave.

"Why do you hate me?" I blurted out, my voice trembling. I knew he ordered me to stay away, but I couldn't. I marched toward him and blocked the door.

"I don't want to talk about it."

"No. Really. When we ended things, we weren't even together that long."

"You can't be serious right now."

"I am serious. Plus, before we decided to date, you said we wouldn't let it ruin our friendship. You said—"

"I know what I said," he hissed. He moved his hand above my head and placed it against the door. I felt my body heating as he hovered over me with his rock-hard posture. "Move, Hailee."

"Aiden. Please. We'll be running into one another over these next few months. I'm going to be delivering things to you. It's best if we just nip this in the bud now."

He grimaced, unamused. "Nip it in the bud?"

Clearly, that was the wrong thing to say. "Clean slate" and "nip it in the bud" weren't his favorite phrases from me, that was for certain.

"Whatever issues you have with me, let's just bury them now so we can both stand being in the same room as one another without it being awkward."

"But I can't."

"You can't what?"

"Stand being in the same room as you."

My heart hurt from those words. I narrowed my eyes and shook my head. "But why?"

"*Hails!*" he shouted, tossing his hands up in defeat. "Dammit, you can't be that naïve! You honestly can't think I'd want to come back to this town and be anywhere near you, could you? It might be ancient history to you, something that you just nip away, but that shit between us, you and me, that was real for me."

"It was real for me, too." *It's still real. It's still so, so real.*

"That's funny because you didn't seem to have a hard time abandoning it."

"That's not fair, Aiden. You have no clue how hard it was for me to let you go."

"Nobody told you to let me go," he scolded.

If only he knew the truth.

"I'm sorry. I never meant to hurt you, Aiden."

"Keep your apologies. I don't want them. All I'm saying is there's not going to be a situation where I can be around you."

Tears kept falling down my cheeks. It felt selfish to cry when I was the one who broke his heart. "But why?" I asked. "We could even work to build a friendship again."

"Friends? You want to be friends with me?"

"Yes, I do." *So much more than you'd ever know, Aiden.*

"No," he spat out, crushing any small hope I'd had.

"Why?" I questioned again. It seemed like I was a child asking why to everything that left his mouth.

He placed his hands against the door, boxing me in. My back was pressed against the wooden door as my nerves sat tangled up in my gut. "Because I can't be near you without feeling crazy. When I'm near you, my mind gets fucked up. I don't know how to act around you. I want to cuss you out and call you names for the shit that went down between us, and then…" He sighed and shut his eyes, his face inches away from mine. His hot breaths fell against my skin, sending chills of sensation down my back. "Then I want to push you up against this door, rip your clothes off and take back what was once mine. I want to hold you, Hailee. You have no clue how much I want to fucking hold you and never let you go again. So I'm sorry. Either I hate you or I love you. There's no in-between for me. Therefore, it's best if I hold on to the hate because we already know what happens when I love you." He opened his eyes, and his lips were millimeters away from mine. If I leaned forward, I could taste him. If I bent two inches forward, he'd be mine again.

His hand moved to the doorknob, and he began to twist it. "Move, Hailee."

I wanted to argue with him. I wanted to beg for him to understand that I never wished to let him go. I wanted to ask if he was all right. I wanted to take his sadness and put it in my own soul. He didn't deserve it. He didn't deserve to be so hurt. I wanted to hold him, too. I wanted to fucking hold him and never let him go again. Instead, I stepped to the side. He opened the door, and I left. He shut the door in my face, and I wiped my tears away.

"Are you okay, Hailee?"

I looked up to find Carly there, holding a tray of food.

"Carly. I thought you went home sick after getting the same stomach bug Sarah had?"

She raised an eyebrow. "Stomach bug? No. Mr. Lee sent Sarah home early yesterday for some reason. I've been here the whole time." She walked over to me and narrowed her eyes. "You have mustard in your ear."

"Yeah. I know."

"Okay, well, as long as you know. I'll see you later. Gotta get back to the bar and grill."

She hurried away, and I took off, too, to get to the bottom of the issue at hand. "Mr. Lee!" I shouted. Sitting at the front desk, he was relaxed as ever with his feet propped on the countertop.

"Oh hey, Hailee. Ready to take over again?"

"You tricked me!"

One thing about Mr. Lee was that he had no poker face. He lied like a three-year-old who stole an extra cookie. "Who me? I would never lie! What have I lied about? I haven't lied!"

"I just ran into Carly, and she told me Sarah wasn't even sick the other day, but that you sent her home."

"Oh." He sat up straighter. "Those lies."

"Mr. Lee!"

"What? What?!" He tossed his hands up in surrender. "I'm an old man. You can't yell at an old man."

"What exactly is going on? Why have you lied about these things?"

"I told her you were too smart. I told her you'd figure it out."

"Figure what out? Who's her?"

"Laurie, Aiden's mother."

"What does she have to do with this?"

Mr. Lee waved his hand in a dismissive fashion. "You know mothers. They are always sticking their noses in their children's business. She wanted you and Aiden to make up. To rekindle some old flames. To force you into proximity." He sighed and swooned, placing his hands against his cheeks. "It's kind of romantic if you think about it. But then again, what do I know? I'm just an old man. I'm going to go take a nap." He stood and started walking away but paused and turned back to me. "You glow different, you know."

"What?"

"For years, you've walked around unassuming. You keep your head down in your books and don't really show many emotions. I know you're happy, but at the same time, your aura feels muted. Yet when he walks into the room… you glow different. You glow bright. You know how I can spot it in you?"

"How?"

"Because it's the same glow I used to get whenever I was around my late wife. It didn't matter if I was happy with her or pissed off at her. Whatever I was feeling showcased through my glow whenever she was around me. Do you know why? Because she made me feel alive. Life is short. So many people are walking around like zombies. Most people's souls are dead as they move through life. But when you find that person who makes you *feel*? When you find someone who makes you glow? Stay around them. Anyone who makes you feel alive in a dark, lonely world is worth fighting for."

After work, I found myself knocking on the Walters's front door. When Laurie answered, she gave me the biggest smile. "Hailee. What a lovely surprise. What are you doing here?"

"Don't play innocent, Laurie. I just left work, and Mr. Lee told me everything."

Her sweet, sweet smile dropped a little as guilt filled her brown eyes. She then stepped to the side and gestured toward her living room. "Samuel is on his way home from Chicago. Do you want to come in for a glass of wine?"

I walked into their house, and it felt so odd. Walking through their hallways felt like a time capsule. I couldn't help but smile when I saw pictures of Aiden and me still hanging in their living room.

"Take a seat. Are you into red wine or white?" Laurie called out from the kitchen.

"White, please."

"Coming right up."

She brought out two glasses, handed one to me, and sat on the couch across from me. "I bet you're wondering what's going on."

"Uh, yeah. You could say that."

"Aiden is miserable."

"You've noticed, too?"

She nodded. "It kills me to see how sad and broken my son has been over the past few years. He's not himself. He hasn't been himself in a long time. I selfishly figured that if you came back into his life, a bit of light might come back to him. So I placed him at the inn after I convinced him to come home for the holiday season. I wanted to get him around you to remind him how you both need one another. There's no Tom without Jerry."

"Laurie… he doesn't want anything to do with me."

"That's not true. I know my son." She placed her glass of wine on the table and reached across to touch my arm. "Aiden, he's been numb. He's so closed-off, but over the past few weeks, whenever I get a glimpse of you two together, he comes to life again. Sure, he might be angry, but that's better than the numbness he's been displaying for years. He's feeling something again, and I know he hasn't felt alive in a very long time. You light him up in a way he hasn't been lit in a very long time. You two are meant to be together."

"I think he hates me," I confessed.

"There is no way my son hates you, Hailee Rose Jones. You're his best friend."

"I'm not. Too much time—"

Laurie took my free hand into hers and squeezed it. "You're his best friend."

Tears washed over my eyes as her words settled into my soul. "You think so? After all this time?"

"The love you two have for one another was made for an eternity. Now, I just need you to figure out how to get him to stop being so stupid so you two can reunite already."

"Laurie…"

"I'm not telling you to fall in love with him, Hailee, but if there is ever a window of opportunity to be his best friend again, please take it. I feel his saddest parts would be healed if that happened."

"I'll try my best." I pushed out a tight smile before I finished my white wine in one gulp. I stood and smoothed my hands over my outfit. Laurie smiled, knowing full well that my nerves were wreaking havoc on me. "Thank you for the wine, Laurie."

"You know it was always you for him, right, Hailee? You were his leading lady." She stood and pulled me into a tight embrace. She whispered against my ear, "It was always you."

TWENTY-EIGHT

Aiden

I WAS OFFICIALLY LOSING MY MIND.

The mental war taking place in my head had been nothing but exhausting after running into Hailee over the past few days. And now seeing her emotional and covered in mustard in my room? *Fuck me sideways, and just let me love you, Hailee Jones. Except don't. Don't let me love you.*

See what I mean? I was going insane. I felt like a tug-a-war was happening between my emotions, and I had no control over them. I hadn't felt so much in such a long time.

A part of me wanted to be able to forget what went down between us, but it was still so fresh in my mind, even after all these years.

Nip it in a bud? *Bite me, Hailee Jones.* Honestly, I'd probably like that. I hated how great she looked. She was a more grown-up version of her always beautiful self. Her hair was done up in micro braids that fell below her waist, and her skin still glowed in the sun without a drop of makeup. She didn't wear sweats like she did when we were kids. Nope. She went with the much more form-fitting dresses and tight jeans that made her ass that much more apparent. And even with the pathetic hate I had, my eyes still wandered. My dick still twitched. If only my dick could've gotten the memo that Hailee Jones was off-limits, then I'd be a happy camper.

Hailee had a newfound confidence, too, that was new to me. She was more than comfortable in her own skin, and that was such a turn-on to me. I wished it hadn't been, but seeing her authentically happy in her body, in her life made me proud of her. Even if I hated her.

Hated her. I wondered if that hatred would be real one day. It didn't seem likely. My stubborn heart still beat for her.

I tried my best to shake off my nerves when Mom texted to request I bring her some baked bread for dinner that evening. She sent me the address, and the moment I arrived, I stood in front of the storefront in a state of shock.

Hailee's Bakery.

Because of course, my mother sent me to the Jones's bakery for a few loaves of sourdough. Why was I starting to think Mom had her own motives for sending me out for bread? I walked inside to find Penny behind the counter, ringing up a customer's order. She looked up at me when she finished, and the biggest smile fell against her lips.

A smile that was identical to her daughter's.

"Well, if it isn't Mr. Hollywood himself," she said, walking from behind the countertop. "I hope you have a hug to offer up."

I pulled her in for an embrace. Penny's hugs always felt like fresh baked cookies on a Sunday morning. I didn't know how much I'd missed her hugs until that very moment.

She pulled back and patted my cheeks with her hands. "You've grown up a bit. Facial hair and all."

I chuckled a little and rubbed the stubble against my chin. "I should probably shave soon."

"Don't. It looks good on you." She walked back around the counter and rubbed her hands together. "Your mother told me you'd be stopping in to pick up her order. I have it all packaged and ready to go. Let me run in the back and get it." When she came out, she had a brown paper bag wrapped with yellow ribbon and a sticker with their logo on it.

"How much is it?" I asked.

She shook her head. "Friends and family discount. It's on the house today."

"Penny, I can't let you—"

"You can, and you will, young man," she ordered.

I smiled and looked around the shop. "It's good to see you guys doing so well. The shop looks amazing. I'm happy for you and Karl. I know how long this dream has been in the works for you both."

She glanced around with a smile filled with pride. "It's not much, but it's ours."

"Trust me, it's a lot. It's more than most people could ever dream up."

She crossed her arms and kept giving me that gentle grin. I didn't know smiles could feel like home. "How are you, sweetheart?"

"Me? I'm alright."

She tilted her head and narrowed her eyes. "How are you, sweetheart?" she asked again.

I couldn't lie to her again.

"Yeah"—she nodded—"I sense that. You know, your mother worries about you. I do, too."

"I guess that's what mothers do."

"It's the hardest part of the job. Worrying about our babies." She shifted in her shoes. "I heard you've crossed paths with Hailee since you've been back in town."

I felt my body tense up at the mention of her. "We've had a few run-ins."

"How did that go?"

"She didn't tell you?"

"She did, but we all see situations from different viewpoints. I'd love to hear yours."

I grimaced. "It hasn't gone the greatest."

"You two have a very strong history. It's no surprise that your first interactions after all these years are a bit rocky. I hate to see you kids struggling through it."

"Yeah, well, she made it clear as day all those years ago that she wanted nothing to do with me. It's probably best I keep out of her way."

"Oh, Aiden." Penny shook her head and sighed. "You don't really think my daughter wanted nothing to do with you, do you?"

"Of course, I do. She broke up with me."

"Yes, but it wasn't as if she wanted to. Her hands were tied, and your father made a very solid selling point when Hailee was dealing with her own issues, and—"

"My father?" I asked, alert. "What do you mean?"

A look of shock found her eyes as she realized that I lacked a few key details in Hailee's and my break-up. "Sorry. That was a slip of the tongue. You better get that order to your mom and—"

"Penny," I urged. "What are you talking about?"

She looked down at her hands and swallowed hard before speaking. "Your father asked her to stop seeing you. Hailee only told me after she had one too many drinks on her twenty-first birthday. She made me promise not to tell anyone, but my big mouth just let it slip."

My dead heart found a few faint beats. "Why would he do that?"

"He figured it would damage your career after Hailee's issues. He thought you were focusing too much more on her than your own career, so he told her how selfish it was of her to stand in your way." She shook her head with defeat. "I'd never seen Hailee struggle so much with a decision, Aiden. I need you to know that giving you up was the hardest thing she's ever had to do. She loved you more than you'll ever know, and—"

"My father did this? Told her to stay away?"

She frowned. "I didn't mean to let that slip out, Aiden. I wouldn't have told you if—"

"Sorry, Penny, I have to go."

"Aiden, wait."

"Yes?"

She sighed before rubbing her hand against the back of her neck. "Hailee lives in the apartment right above the bakery." She gestured toward the ceiling. "If you need to have another run-in with her."

"Thank you." I grabbed the paper bag and stormed out of the bakery. I felt sick to my stomach as I replayed Penny's words repeatedly in my mind.

When I arrived at Mom and Dad's place, I pounded on the front door. Mom opened it, giving me her wide smile. "Hey, sweetheart. I see you've got the bread—"

"Where's Dad?" I cut in, marching past her into their foyer.

"He's in the kitchen. What's going on?"

I didn't reply to her as I headed through their house. The second my eyes spotted my father, I barked his way, "Is it true?"

He turned to see me with the same kind of smile that Mom had. "Is what true?"

"About Hailee. Did you tell her to break up with me because it would've damaged my career?"

The smile evaporated from his face, and his eyes grew somber. That was enough of an answer for me.

He pinched the bridge of his nose and looked down to the floor before looking back up at me. "Now, listen, Aiden…"

Mom stood in shock. At least it appeared she wasn't in on this bullshit. "That can't be true, Samuel. You wouldn't—"

"He did." I gestured toward my father, the man I trusted most in my life. The man who'd betrayed me. "Tell her what you did."

He sighed and crossed his arms. "I thought I was doing the right thing. I thought having you involved with her while she was going through her own issues when your career was taking off would've been detrimental to your success."

"You told Hailee to break up with him all those years ago?" Mom questioned, flabbergasted. "Sam, that broke his heart. You've watched it, too. How could you?"

"I was trying to do the right thing. You must understand, Aiden. I was doing what I thought was the best and—"

"Fuck you," I blurted out, rage building inside me as I realized what really happened between Hailee and me.

"Aiden, watch it. I'm still your father," he ordered as if that meant anything to me anymore.

"No. You're nothing to me."

"Now, Aiden. Wait. We need to clear our heads before we say something we don't mean," Mom warned, trying to keep the peace, but there was nothing to be kept.

I loved Hailee.

I loved her to my core, and my father stepped in, thinking he knew better. Then he'd watched me be heartbroken over it for years, but he didn't care because career-wise, I was at my best. Even if that meant my soul was dying.

I shook my head. "I mean everything I'm saying. I'm done with you. She was my world, and you convinced her to walk away from me. You forced her to close that door when she was already vulnerable, and then you kept that secret from me for years!"

"Aiden," he pleaded.

"*I've been drowning!*" I shouted as my voice cracked. Emotions overtook me as the realization settled into me more and more. "I've been drowning for years, lost and confused, and you could've pulled me up, but instead, you shoved me deeper under the water."

He cussed under his breath.

Mom stepped toward me, but I held a hand up. "I can't do this right now. I have to go."

"Where are you going?" he asked.

I thought that was an easy enough question for him to figure out on his own, so I walked out and slammed the door behind me.

Where was I going?

To find her.

TWENTY-NINE

Aiden

I ARRIVED AT HAILEE'S PLACE BEFORE SHE MADE IT HOME. PENNY was on her way out for the night as I showed up. She let me in, so I sat on the steps inside the bakery that led up to her apartment. My feet tapped rapidly against the wooden steps as I waited for her. I created different scenarios of the conversation we'd have once she arrived. Of how I'd convince her to give me a shot again, to give us a real chance. How I'd give up everything, every penny, every dime of my career if it meant I could have her forever.

That was all I wanted—forever. Forever with her.

I wasn't thinking straight. Why was forever even crossing my mind when I should've been trying to make it to our next conversation? Why did the idea of forever always show up when it came to Hailee Jones?

When she arrived, she had a bag of groceries in her hands. She looked confused as she stared my way. "Aiden. What are you doing here? You shouldn't—"

"I'm pissed at you," I blurted out.

She arched an eyebrow. "That seems to be a reoccurring event between the two of us lately. Can I ask why you're pissed this time around?"

"Why did you break up with me?"

She raised an eyebrow. "I thought we decided we weren't going to rehash that anymore and—"

"Why did you break up with me, Hailee?"

Her bottom lip trembled. She was nervous. She looked down at the floor, unable to hold eye contact. "Aiden…"

"Did my father tell you to end things with me?"

Her shocked expression when her head rose told me everything I needed to know. The way her eyes glazed over and emotions hit her spoke volumes. "After that Thanksgiving years ago, things were hard. My life was messy, and your father thought with my messiness, I'd screw up your world. That was the last thing I ever wanted to do, and when you mentioned you were going to turn down that role to stay back with me, I knew had to break up with you."

"You didn't have to."

"I did." She nodded. "I wasn't going to let you ruin your career because of my issues."

"I would've quit acting."

"Which is why I did what I did. I wasn't going to be the reason your dreams didn't come true."

I groaned and pinched the bridge of my nose. "I'm pissed off. Mostly because I know if the roles were reversed, I would've done the same thing. I would've wanted you to have your dreams come true. I just wish you had realized that my dream wasn't acting. It never has been and never will be."

"What? Of course, it's your dream."

"No. Hailee… my dream was you."

Tears streamed down her eyes as realization settled in that the greatest dream I'd ever dreamed was the one with the two of us together.

She parted her lips, but before she could speak another word, I took the bag from her hands, set it down, then wrapped my arms around her and pulled her into a kiss. I kissed her hard so she could feel my soul. I kissed her to apologize for all the kisses we missed. I kissed her for so long that I no longer knew if we were two separate beings. I pushed her against the stair railing and kept kissing her.

The best part about it? She kissed me back.

She kissed me with the same intensity, with the same heat, with the same love.

Love. It was there. She didn't have to say it, and neither did I, but the love was there, and it was strong. It was no secret that Hailee and I were made for one another. I'd be damned if I ever allowed the universe to create another second when we were not together.

Before we knew it, our clothes were being tossed to the side. I tasted every inch of her skin against that staircase, and she tasted every inch of mine. My heart was racing fast, pounding erratically against my chest. I unhooked her bra with two flicks of my fingers and let it fall. She unzipped my jeans and slid them and my boxers down in one movement. My cock was hard as a rock, ready and willing for the opportunity to slide deep inside her.

Next came her pants, followed by her panties. I pressed myself against her, rubbing her clit with my dick that was wide awake, awaiting permission to proceed. I wrapped my hands around her ass cheeks and lifted her against the stair railing. Our eyes locked and without words, she gave me one nod. Permission granted.

I slid into her and groaned from her tightness. The way she squeezed against me made me feel like I'd entered the greatest euphoria, and I had no desire to leave.

Her hands fell against my chest.

My hands stayed tightly wrapped around her.

It was everything I wanted.

All I wanted was to hold her…

Making love to Hailee against that staircase felt like every daydream I'd had over the past five years. My mind couldn't stop focusing on how good it felt. I couldn't slow down my thrusts. I couldn't stop myself from…

"Shit," I said, squeezing my eyes shut. "I'm sorry, Hailee, I can't hold back. I'm going to…"

"Come now," she ordered, wrapping her arms around my neck. She ground against me as we locked eyes. "Come for me, Aiden, please," she begged, and well… *As you wish, my everything.*

I came hard and fast, sweat dripping down my body as I held her against me. I trembled as I kept thrusting after my own pleasure had been met. I kept sliding in and out for a few strokes, seeing how much she was still enjoying it.

When I reached my limit, I slid three fingers inside her. She moaned, tossing her head back a little to rest it against the wall. She took both her hands and gripped the railing to steady herself as my fingers went to town inside her. My thumb rubbed her clit as I pressed my mouth against hers.

"Now it's your turn," I ordered, my voice hoarse as my fingers worked their magic. "Come for me, Hailee," I commanded. Nothing was better than seeing her like this. Nothing was better than pleasing her and watching her enjoy every single moment of it.

"Aiden," she breathed out, her voice dripping with need, with want. "Right there, right there, please, yes, right there," she moaned, shutting her eyes.

I felt her core grip my fingers as she let out a loud scream when she climaxed. My fingers pulsed with her body as she let herself unfold against me.

After she finished, I removed my hands from her body.

"Geez... that was..." I was out of breath as I lowered Hailee's body to the steps. I sat beside her, trying to collect the words for what it was that I'd just felt. "That was—"

"That was, uh, okay. That's not what I expected."

"Yeah," I sighed. "I agree."

"Okay, well. I have to go."

"Wait, what?"

"That, this..." She waved her hands around, gesturing toward her and myself. "This was a lot, and um, I think my brain is overheating. Therefore, I need to take a second to process this all because, uh, yeah." She started gathering her groceries. "Okay. We'll talk later. Okay? Okay. Yeah. Okay."

"You're freaking out."

"I am not freaking out!" she shouted. She paused, then took a breath. "Okay, I am, but that's completely okay. I'm okay. I'm okay. I'm okay."

"Here, let me help you." I started to reach for one item, and she snatched it up before I could grab it.

"No!" she ordered, shaking the beef kielbasa stick my way. "Stay back."

Something about her shaking a sausage stick at me was oddly humorous, but I didn't laugh due to her current panic attack. "Why do I have to stay back?"

"Because when you come near me, I can't really think straight. And in order for me to process this, I have to think straight."

I snickered a little. "You're being dramatic, Jerry."

Her eyes widened and glassed over. "Don't do that."

"Do what?"

"Don't call me Jerry."

"Why not?"

She swallowed hard. "Because it makes me want to cry after not hearing it for so long."

That tugged at my heart.

Slow down, heart. You haven't beat this much in years.

"Please don't cry," I urged.

She pushed out a smile. "Okay, I won't."

"Jerry," I whispered. "You're crying."

She lightly chuckled. "Let's not act like it's shocking that I'm emotional." I took a step toward her, and she halted me again. "Please, Aiden. I need a little time to process this. That's all."

I pinched the bridge of my nose. "Take all the time you need." I'd waited five years to hold her again. I could wait a little bit longer.

"All right. Well, uh, it was great seeing you. You look great like, uh…" She waved her hand, gesturing toward my body. "You look great. Okay, cool. Have a good night. Goodbye." Her words were soaked in awkwardness as she scurried into her apartment, slamming the door shut behind her.

There I was, completely butt naked on the steps of the Joneses' bakery, feeling like I'd been spun around in a hurricane of emotions. Yet the strongest one I was feeling after the interaction with Hailee was happiness. I didn't know I could still feel such a thing.

"Fucking hell," a person muttered.

I looked up to find Hailee's father standing in front of me with his hands full of loaves of bread. "Oh shit!" I shouted, reaching across the steps and grabbing my T-shirt to cover my privates. "Hey, Karl," I muttered, probably fifty shades of red. As if that day couldn't get odder.

"I've had nightmares that started this way," he grumbled. "It looks like you and Hailee are reconnecting. Unless you're just waiting on her steps naked for some reason."

"No, I mean, yeah, I mean, I, uh, I'm going to get dressed and go now."

"Probably a solid idea. I'll make sure to sanitize the steps once you're gone." Karl began walking to the back of his bakery but called out my name. "Aiden?"

"Yeah?"

"Don't break her heart, or I'll have to rip yours out."

"She was the one who broke my heart last time."

"I hear you, I do, but that girl is my heartbeats. So again. Don't break her heart, or I'll have to rip yours out."

Fair enough.

"And Aiden?"

"Yes, sir?"

"Put on your damn boxers. People can walk by the windows and see your balls."

"Right, of course. It's good to see you again, Karl," I said, reaching out a hand toward him for a shake.

He narrowed his eyes and shook his head. "There's no way I'm touching your hand. I'm honestly going to go bleach my brain and pretend this interaction never happened so I'm able to sleep tonight."

Fair enough.

THIRTY

Hailee

"You banged Aiden Walters on the steps leading up to your apartment last night?" Kate gasped as we sat at the front desk of the inn during Kate's evening break. I'd just finished my shift and was filling Kate in on the craziness of the past twenty-four hours.

"I banged Aiden Walters on the steps leading up to my apartment last night."

"Oh, my goodness." Kate sighed, flopping back against the couch. "How romantic. That's some *The Notebook* making out in the rain type of love. You two were pulled together like force-packed magnets, and the wind ripped your clothes off, and his Special K accidentally slid into your Lucky Charms."

I arched an eyebrow. "Are you hungry?"

"Starving, and I'd just finished stocking the cereal for the morning. I really want some Froot Loops."

"You're losing focus."

"What can I say? I'm a Pisces. My mind floats away. Okay. Continue. What happens next between the two of you?"

I shrugged. "I'm still processing it and trying to figure out what this means."

"What? No, no, no. You two just reconnected in the most romantic way. Now is not the time to be logical!"

"It's very much more romantic in your mind than it actually was, I think."

"Hailee Rose Jones. Aiden screwed you on a staircase after telling you that you are his dream come true. You cannot tell me that's not romantic and sexy."

"I'll admit, it was a little bit sexy when he lifted my body up on the railing and, well, railed me. He did it so effortlessly, too. As if I weighed nothing more than a feather."

"You were light as a feather, and I bet that man was as stiff as a board where it matters most."

"Kate!"

"I'm just saying!" She narrowed her eyes. "How long was this board of his?"

I felt my cheeks heat as I bit my bottom lip. "I'm not answering that."

"That means it's a long, long board." She smirked. "If you don't marry this man, I will."

I stood and shook my head as a slight chuckle left my lips. "I'm done talking to you. I'll see you later."

"I hope you run into some Special K on your walk home!" she hollered.

As she shouted that, an elderly woman named Joan overheard, and she said, "I could really go for some Special K."

"I bet you could, Joan," Kate agreed. "I bet you could."

The next few days were a comedy of errors while I tried to avoid Aiden. Whenever he'd show up at the inn, I'd duck and dive out of his view. Sometimes we'd make eye contact, he'd smile, and I'd quickly shut my eyes like a paranoid freak. He didn't show any annoyance, though. I needed time to process the situation. I wanted to make sure I was in the right frame of mind to be for Aiden what he needed me to be. I didn't want to stumble into a conversation about us without a clear mind.

I did everything in my power to stay out of his way, but when Mr. Lee came up to me and told me that Aiden requested me to take him some towels, I was stuck between a rock and a hard place.

"I feel like you're lying to me again," I told him.

"No, really. I need you to take him some towels."

"Can't Henry do it? I know he loves working with Aiden," I urged.

"He's busy with another task I gave him. Besides, Aiden requested you." Mr. Lee handed me a stack of towels. "So if you could deliver these, I'd be happy."

Freaking A, Mr. Lee.

Can't you tell I'm in the middle of a quarter-life crisis when it comes to seeing Hollywood's dreamboat?

I smiled and took the towels from my boss. With a stomach packed full of annoyance and nerves, I headed to Aiden's room. Before I could knock, I noticed the fangirls who'd been staying at the inn for a little too long hanging out near his room with their ears pressed to the wood door.

How were they even affording to stay for so long? I'd be broke.

"Marna, Violet, what are you doing?" I asked.

They looked over, giggling when they saw me. "We think Aiden's having sex."

The knot in my stomach tightened as those words left their mouths.

"He's groaning and moaning." Marna giggled, covering her mouth.

Was Aiden in there hooking up with another woman? After hooking up with me? I felt like vomiting. Yet I tried my best to keep my composure as I stood straight. "Ladies, if you continue disturbing our other guests, we will have you removed from the inn."

"What? No! It's fine. We were just leaving," Violet explained. "It's just funny, is all. The girl must have your name, too. He keeps saying, 'Hailee, Hailee, ohhh Hailee.'" She laughed like her friend had been chuckling nonstop. The two girls walked off in a fit of laughter as I stood there feeling ill.

Was he really screwing someone with my name?

Was it some weird Hailee kink?

Psh. Whatever. I bet she spelled her name like Haley. Or Halee. Or Hailey. Or—

Why did I care how a woman spelled her name? That had nothing to do with anything. But realistically, if she was spelling her name like Halee, that meant she was trouble, because why?! Anyway. It was none of my business. None of what Aiden Walters did was my business.

Still, I somehow found myself walking over to his door and placing my ear against it to listen in. Oh my gosh, I deserved to be fired for this. I was losing my mind. Still, I listened in, and I heard… nothing. There was no sound. No moaning and groaning. Especially no other woman's voice coming through.

"Hey, Hailee, what are you doing?" Henry asked, interrupting my snooping.

"What? Nothing!" I gasped, dropping the towels. I scrambled to pick them up, and Henry walked over to help me.

"Let me give you a hand," he offered.

"Shhh!" I shushed him, hoping not to draw attention to Aiden inside that room. Luck wasn't on my side, though, as the door opened, and I found a shirtless Aiden standing in front of me wearing gray sweatpants. As I kneeled, my eyes made perfect contact with his crotch, and for some unknown reason, I kept my gaze aimed right there. Eyes on the prize. I hated how my body became a traitor at that very moment because the thought of the night before on the stairs came flooding back to me as I stared at Aiden's crotch. Thoughts of him lifting me in his arms and going to pound town. I'd never had a man lift me before, and for some reason, that was an odd turn-on for me.

My legs trembled with pleasure from the memories hitting my mind, and my stomach filled with a pool of heat.

"Oh great, you brought the towels," Aiden said, smiling down at me. I looked up at him and gave him the meanest look I could muster. My brows tucked in, my grimace was grimacing to the tenth degree, and I growled at him as I stood—trying to shake off the longing my thighs were feeling for his touch.

"I've got it from here, Henry. You can head out," I told him.

He did as I said and scurried away.

I placed the towels in Aiden's hands. "You know, before you were telling me not to show up at your door."

"Funny how one night can change everything. I thought it would be a good way to get us to talk, seeing as how you've been avoiding me like the plague."

"Not like the plague; just like a slightly viral cold."

He frowned a little. "Are you mad at me for the way I treated you before I knew the details? I owe you a big apology, Hails. You didn't deserve that—even without the knowledge I've learned about the breakup. I'm truly sorry."

"I appreciate that and accept the apology."

"Is that why you've been staying away?"

"No, not at all. I'm just processing this whole situation."

He narrowed his eyes. "Did you make a pie chart over the stair incident?"

I huffed and puffed. "No!"

He gave me a knowing smirk. "Are you sure?"

"Only a small one."

"Hailee—"

"What?! This is a big deal. I still need to figure some things out."

"Is this like a five-to-ten business day processing situation or…?"

"Tom, you can't just rush my overthinking." His grin stretched far. "What? What is it?"

"Nothing…it's just…you called me Tom."

I felt my cheeks heating. "I guess I did. Anyway. If you need supplies, you can let housekeeping bring them to you. You don't have to request me." I glanced into his room, somewhat hoping to see Haley. Or Hailey. Or Halee. *Gosh, I hope it's not a Halee.*

Aiden arched an eyebrow. "What are you looking for?"

"Nothing."

"You definitely were looking for something."

"Your groupies were at your door. They said they heard you… um…" I shrugged a little. "You know. With another person."

He narrowed his eyes. "What does 'you know' mean?"

I leaned in closer to whisper. "You know… having the sex with someone."

"The sex?" He chuckled. I wanted to slug him in the arm for laughing. Stupid jerk. "I wasn't having the sex with a person. They probably heard me… um…" He shrugged a little, clearly mocking me. "You know. Having the sex with my hand."

"Oh gross, Aiden. You can keep that to yourself," I said, shoving his arm.

"Do you want to know who I was thinking about while I did it?"

"Don't say it."

Me.

It was me.

Oh gosh.

He held his hands up in surrender. "We should talk about what happened last night," he urged, "but I won't rush you. When you're ready, bring me some towels."

THIRTY-ONE

Aiden

FIVE YEARS. I'd missed five years of having Hailee in my life. I knew I couldn't go another five years without her. I didn't see the drama of my father telling Hailee to end things with me coming to center stage. I came to town with a chip on my shoulder, ready to avoid the woman who broke my heart, only to learn that she'd broken my heart because she thought she was saving my dreams.

Noble Hailee.

That was very much in line with her character. Which was another reason I'd always been crazy about her. She'd always tried to do the right thing, even when it was hard.

I'd give her the space to process her feelings while I did my best to avoid mine. It appeared that over the past five years, Hailee had grown into herself. She still had my favorite parts to her soul, but she seemed more mature. More confident. More…healed.

I envied that. The only thing I'd developed over the past five years was more trauma. I wasn't sure how to start facing any of it, but before

I could even try, my mother showed up at the Starlight Inn to add a bit more shit to my trauma suitcase.

The moment I opened my door to find her, I grimaced. "Look, Mom. I'm not ready to talk to Dad or about what happened. I know you're used to playing the peacekeeper role, but—"

"This isn't about your father, sweetheart," she said, teary-eyed.

My concern grew instantly. "What is it? What's wrong?"

"It's nothing bad. Well, depending on how you look at it. Can I come in?"

"Of course. Come on." I stepped to the side and let her in. She sat down on the bed and hugged her purse to her chest. I sat down beside her and placed a comforting hand against her shoulder. "What's going on, Mom?"

"Mom," she echoed me and burst into tears. She placed her face in her hands and cried. At that very moment, every piece of me shattered.

"Shit, what happened?" I urged, pulling her into a hug.

"Watch your language," she sobbed as she trembled in my arms. "It's fine, really. I'm just emotional. It's silly." She released herself from the hug and wiped her eyes. "I'm just glad I didn't wear any makeup today."

"You never really need it."

"Still." She sniffled and tried to gain her composure. She then shook her head and rolled her shoulders back. "I've thought about this day for over twenty-four years, and it's now here." She reached into her purse and pulled out an envelope. "It's a letter."

"I see that."

"From your mother."

I arched an eyebrow. "Why did you write me a letter?"

"No." She shook her head. "Your biological mother."

My heart dropped. I immediately felt sick to my stomach as she placed the envelope into my hands.

"It showed up at the house today. A part of me thought about not giving it to you, and I know how awful that sounds, but..." She smiled as tears welled up in her eyes. "I had a brief moment of fear, but you deserve that letter. So I brought it to you."

I didn't know what to say.

I didn't know how to react.

Within my hands were words from the woman who put me up

for adoption. I'd be lying if I said I hadn't thought about her time and time again. I'd be lying if I said I hadn't wondered who she'd been all my life. Yet my thoughts always felt like a fever dream. Like something that would've never come to life. I figured my thoughts would be just that—thoughts.

Now, she felt real.

That envelope made it real.

"Your father doesn't know I gave you the letter. He'd probably try to talk me out of it," Mom explained.

"Yeah, well, he's known for making shitty choices on my behalf."

She frowned. "You two are going to have to figure out your issues."

"Maybe." I wasn't ready to deal with that fact, though. I was still processing that white envelope in my hands.

"I have to get to work. I just wanted to drop that off for you." She stood from the bed, and I followed her. She walked to the door and opened it, moving quickly. Before she could escape too fast, I pulled her into a tight hug and held on for dear life.

"You can let me go at any time, Aiden," she told me, laughing lightly.

"No, I can't."

We didn't look alike. Her skin was brown and mine was olive. She was a beautiful Black woman with chocolate eyes and high cheekbones. Her hair was kinky, and her smile was mesmerizing. We didn't look alike, but she was my twin in so many ways. We felt feelings the same way. We celebrated and grieved in the same fashion. We had the same laughter. We both felt our hurts deep in our souls, too. Laurie Walters was my twin, and I was hers.

I placed my hands against her shoulders and locked my eyes with hers. "You are my mother. You will forever and always, no matter what, be my mom."

She sniffled a bit as a few tears slid down her cheeks. "And you are my son."

I kissed her cheek, and then she kissed mine back.

She patted my face with her hands. "And since I am your mother, it is my job to tell you to call your father. You two must figure it out."

"Spoken like a true mom. I do have a question for you."

"Shoot."

"Are you happy with Dad?"

The flicker of emotion that hit her stare from my question rocked her a little before she caught her composure. "What an odd question."

"What an odd response."

She smiled. "Call your father. I love you, Aiden."

"Love you, too."

After she left, I picked up the envelope and stared at it for the longest time.

I didn't open it.

I wasn't ready to read what was written inside.

THIRTY-TWO

Aiden

AFTER I TOOK A QUICK SHOWER TO SHAKE OFF MY NERVES, I heard a knock on my door. I wrapped one towel around my waist and started to dry my hair with another as I went to answer it.

Hailee stood there with a stack of towels in her hands and a goofy grin on her face. The moment she saw me in the towel, her cheeks rose high as she blushed. "Uh, hi there."

"Hey." I glanced down at the towels, then back toward her. "You brought me towels."

"Yeah. You mentioned when I was ready to talk to bring you towels, but now that I think about it, you were probably being sarcastic and didn't really want towels. Let me run these back down and—"

I wrapped my hands around the towels before she could make a dash for the exit. "I appreciate this."

She smiled. I smiled back. It felt good to smile at Hailee and have her smile back. Reminded me of the us we used to be. A small glimpse of who we used to be.

"You're ready to talk?" I asked.

"Yes. Well, not now, because I'm heading home for the day. My shift is up, and I'm exhausted."

"Can I walk you home? Or take you out for a drink? Or…" *Love you? Can I love you again, Hailee?*

She looked at me confused and shook her head. "No."

Silly me for thinking we'd gotten past our issues. "Right. Of course."

She stood tall with her hands in her pockets. "You can take me to dinner."

"Oh. Now?"

"No. I promised my mom I'd help her at the bakery tonight, but how about tomorrow."

A sliver of hope from Hailee? I'd take it. "It's a date."

"It's a meal," she corrected.

"Sounds a lot like a date."

"Maybe it's a two-people-considering-a-friendship-again kind of date."

"Or hear me out… it could be a more-date."

Her cheeks blushed. "It's not a more-date. What happened on those stairs was a one-time thing."

I smirked, seeing how hard she was trying to fight off her feelings. I knew she wanted to be more than friends solely based on how she kissed me.

"I'm still banking on a more-date, Hailee."

"No offense—"

"I'm going to take offense—"

"But I would never go out on a date with you."

"Offense taken, but also, why not?"

"Because no matter what, I can't date you."

"In what world?"

"Reality."

"Reality's stupid."

"Yet still, it exists."

"Right. Of course, but you want to go out for a meal with me?"

"I really love a good two-people-considering-a-friendship-again kind of date."

I had little to no desire to only be that woman's friend…

"You really will never date me again, huh? Because of my dad telling you that you'd ruin my career?"

"No, that's not the reason anymore."

"Oh? What's the reason?"

"Well, you do a weird nose crinkle when you're in deep thought. You fake laugh too loud during online interviews. No joke is that funny, Aiden. You smell like oak trees with hints of lemon. Pull back on the cologne, buddy. And not to be rude, but to be rude—you're ugly."

Was she…? Yeah. She was being playful. Teasing Hailee was back. Oh, how I missed her.

"I was being considered for *People's* hottest man of the year. I think I can see myself as attractive."

"That's because most people are programmed by what society tells them is attractive. Sure, you have a head full of luscious hair, biceps that flex without you flexing, a quote-unquote perfect smile, and you stand over six-foot-three. That's just mediocre surface-level attractiveness that we were told was the be-all and end-all. The truth is, attractiveness runs much deeper." She tapped the side of her head. "Having a sexy mind is where true attractiveness lies. Looks change over time. I'd like to rest my head on the shoulder of a man with a sexy brain."

"I have a sexy mind," I offered.

Her laughter was cold but with a hint of flirtation as she waved me off. "Your brain is as sexy as a lima bean. You're pretty much a dick for brains, if I'm being honest. Now come on, wannabe Casanova, are you coming or going? I'm not gonna hold this door open for you all night."

I smiled at her level of sass. I didn't know a woman calling me a dick for brains was a turn-on until the words left her mouth. Did I have a shame kink that Hailee somehow unlocked for me? *Call me a dick for brains again, Hails. I think I felt a twitch in my jeans.*

"Good night, Tom." She turned on her heels and began to walk away.

"Night, Jerry." I called out to her. "You sure I can't walk you home?"

"Are you kidding? I can't be seen with you in this town. People will talk."

"People are already talking. Besides, a long time ago, a girl gave me a nice saying about people who don't matter."

"Oh? And what was that saying?"

"Fuck them."

Her cheekbones rose, and all I wanted to do was kiss those chipmunk cheeks that I always loved. "Yeah... fuck them." She grew bashful for a few seconds before clearing her throat. "Still, we can't make it painfully public that we are becoming friends again. You know this town can be—gossipy. Therefore, the dinner must be at a place where no one will know we are hanging out. I'm not trying to be on the cover of some tabloid with a dick for brains."

Twitch, twitch, dick, dick.

Shame kink was fully unlocked, and for a second, I almost considered replying with, "Yes, Master," but I went with, "Okay, that works," instead.

"Night," she hollered back, waving me off without looking over her shoulder. For a moment in time, everything was right in the world.

"Good night, Hails."

THIRTY-THREE

Aiden

Aiden: Meet me at 333 N Heights Rd. It's right on the outskirts of town. How about 7pm? I could pick you up so you don't have to come alone.

    Hailee: What do you not get about I can't be seen with you in public?

    Aiden: I can wear a Halloween mask.

    Hailee: Only if you show up as the clown from *IT*. Otherwise, I'll drive myself to the meeting location. I'll see you in a little bit.

    Color her shocked when I showed up at her apartment at 4:40pm wearing an *IT* clown mask.

    When Hailee opened her door, she burst out laughing. "Are you kidding me? Why are you like this?"

    "I just wanted to be able to pick you up for our non-more-date."

    "I was joking about the mask."

    "Well, subtext and sarcasm are very hard to read via text messages. So…" I bowed and held my hand out toward her. "Shall we?"

    She smacked my hand away and chuckled. "Let's get a move on before people think I'm screwing a random clown."

    "You look remarkable tonight, Hails."

She narrowed her eyes. "It's oddly creepy hearing a clown tell me I look good."

"Want to hear a clown joke?"

"I might regret this, but yes."

"Knock, knock."

"Who's there?"

"Boo."

"Boo who?"

"Bootiful you."

She rolled her eyes so hard, and that fact alone made me laugh. She pushed past me and said, "Were you always this cheesy, or is this a new Hollywood development?"

"You might as well call me gouda 'cuz I'm gonna be so gouda for you."

She gave me a blank stare. "It's almost painful how much I hate you right now."

"By hate, do you mean love?"

Her eyes studied me for a moment. Her lips slightly parted, but no words came at first. Then she slugged me in the arm. "Come on, loser. I'm hungry."

I walked her to my car and opened the door for her. She slipped in, buckled up, and I closed the door before heading around to the driver's side. I climbed in, and we took off. After we were driving for a while, I was given permission to take off the *IT* mask. My hair was ruined and sweaty, and I probably looked like an idiot, yet it was worth it when I saw Hailee looking over at me with a goofy grin.

"Do you know that you're ridiculous?" she asked.

"One hundred percent."

We drove a little farther and pulled up to an open field. The sun was setting overhead and looking out toward the field was a picnic spread I'd set up for the two of us.

"You made us a picnic?" she asked, somewhat surprised.

"I figured we could eat and talk and then lay down and count the stars."

"Damn you, Aiden." She shook her head. "You're good."

I hopped out of the car and hurried over to open her door for her. I then went to my trunk and grabbed a picnic basket, chilled champagne, and a few more blankets because I remembered Hailee always got cold.

We sat down and made ourselves comfortable as we began to catch up on the past five years. She told me about some of her worst days and about some of her best. I hated that I wasn't there for both sets of stories. Then she asked about me. About my career. About my major success.

She told me she was proud of me, and that just about did me in. Still, a part of me over the past five years felt empty.

"Your past five years have seemed much easier and more enjoyable than my past five years," she joked as she tossed a grape into her mouth.

"It's not always easy, you know. Life," I told her as I filled up another glass of champagne for her.

She huffed. "Yeah. It must be hard being famous and handsome, and having the world woo over you."

I snickered at her sarcasm. "I'm serious. I get in my head a lot. Almost always. To the point when I don't even know how to be myself anymore."

"What do you do when you lose track of yourself?"

"That's easy. I pick up a new script and become someone else. It's not only for when I'm working either. It's every day. I act as if I'm someone else. Someone people would want to be around, someone people would want to know because—the real me—is a lot sadder than some people would care to be around. People like happy people. People feel uncomfortable around the sad ones."

Hailee frowned. "Aiden?"

"Yes?"

"That's really sad."

"Life can be sad sometimes."

"But most people wouldn't know it if they were around you, huh?"

I laughed. "I guess not."

"Are you acting right now? With me?"

"No. All shields are down right now."

She looked down at the glass of champagne in her hands and bit her bottom lip. I was fascinated by every small movement Hailee made. The way her teeth tugged on her bottom lip made me consider tugging on it, too.

"Tell me something hard for you right now," she said, snuggling up in the blankets.

"Well"—I scratched the bridge of my nose—"the other day, my mom gave me a letter from my biological mother."

Her eyes all but popped out of their sockets. "Wait, what? Oh, my goodness. Are you okay? What did it say?"

"I have no clue. I haven't opened it yet."

"Why not? I know how long you've wanted to know more about her."

"Exactly. So once I open that letter, it's as if everything becomes real, and I'm not exactly sure if that's a good or bad thing."

"Does it scare you? Knowing that she's reached out?"

"Um, it doesn't scare me, but it makes me question the timing. It's no secret that I've been successful. So for her to come around now as opposed to when my career hadn't taken off just rubs me the wrong way. Then again, who knows? I won't really know what she has to say until I read the damn letter. And I'm not ready to read said letter yet."

"If you ever need someone in your corner when you open that up, I can be there for you."

I narrowed my eyes. "Because we're friends again?"

She snickered. "Is it important for me to say that?"

"No, but I think it's important for me to hear that."

She placed her glass of champagne down and looked up at the star-drunk sky. "You never stopped being my best friend, Aiden. I like to think we just had a bad cellular connection over the past five years."

"I told you years ago to switch to Sprint," I joked.

"You know me." She wrapped her arms around her knees. "I'm a terrible listener. What about you and your dad? Have you two talked since you found out what happened all those years ago?"

My jaw tightened at the mention of it. "No."

"Aiden, I know you probably want to stay mad at him for what he did, but I do know that he did it from a place of love."

"Or a place of selfishness and greed. Guess it depends on how you look at it." She went to say something else, but I stopped her. "Conversation shift?"

She took note. I wasn't ready to talk about Dad and what he'd done. "Okay, shift it."

"How have the past five years been for you?" I asked her. "How are you?"

"Okay. I'm okay." She looked up with a soft smile. "I'm good, actually."

"Tell me. Tell me what I missed."

She laughed a little. "Five years' worth of stuff? That's a lot of information."

"I want to know it all. Tell me your story."

She went to college to become a therapist. She was taking a year off before going for her master's degree. A part of me was sad I didn't get to experience the college lifestyle with her. It was another missed opportunity due to my career, but I was glad she seemed to do well in school.

"What's your main focus?" I asked.

"I want to be a child psychologist. High school, as you know, was tough for me toward the end. I never want kids to feel as if they don't belong. I want to help them understand their emotions and help aid them through the dark days. When my parents put me into therapy, it changed my life. Now, I want to pay it forward so kids know they can still have some of the best days of their lives. It's odd to think that, in a way, what happened to me all those years ago put me on my right path."

"Life has a way of putting you right where you're supposed to be."

"Yeah, I think so. Outside of school, though, I'm still the boring girl who reads too much, lift weights for fun, and works at the inn. My life is pretty simple."

"I would kill for a simpler life. And you're happy?"

Her full lips smiled. "I am. I have waves of ups and downs, like everyone, but I am over all happy."

"Good. You deserve it."

"Thank you. Still, even though I'm happy, sometimes I get lonely," she confessed. "A lot of times, I'm fine. I go day by day without feeling that way. But then some nights or early mornings, I feel lonelier than ever. I don't have many friends. That's not a complaint. It's just a fact. No one talks loneliness or how lonely people are forced to lie to themselves sometimes and say they are fine being alone. I think we are met to be around others. Maybe not all the time, but sometimes. And when I'm not, it gets hard. I just do the same things over and over. Wake up alone, go to work alone, come home alone, go to bed alone. I sometimes wish I had someone to do nothing with."

"Why don't you date?"

"Because no one else could ever be you."

I wanted to hug her, but I didn't know where we were on that front.

I wanted to soak up her loneliness and place it inside me. A transfer of hard emotions of sorts.

"I know what that's like...being lonely. Sometimes, I think my life is defined by my loneliness. I'm surrounded by people all the time, but I swear I've never felt so alone being out in Los Angeles. So let me join you," I told her.

She raised an eyebrow, confused by my comment. Honestly, I wasn't certain I understood it completely, either.

"What do you mean?" she asked.

"I mean, let me join you." I leaned in toward her and placed my hands on her kneecaps. "We can be lonely together."

Her eyes fell to my hands on her legs. Was the touch too much? Did she like it? Did she want it? Did I cross a line? I stared at my hand's placement but didn't move them. The heat radiating from her smooth brown skin was sending shock waves of light into me.

A few tears fell against my hands. That made me look up once more to those eyes of hers. Tears streamed down Hailee's cheeks, and she was quick to try to wipe them away. She shifted her legs, making me remove my hands.

"Hails, if this is too much, we can—"

"No." She cut in, shaking her head. "It's just... There's no one in this world I'd rather be lonely with."

We talked for a while longer before lying down to count the stars.

One... two... three...

"Forty-five." Hailee pointed.

"You already counted that one," I exclaimed.

She tilted her head toward me and scrunched up her nose. "I definitely didn't count that one."

"But you did."

"Didn't."

"Did!"

"Is this the hill you want to die on, Walters? After five years of bad cell phone service?" she questioned.

I chuckled and rolled my eyes, looking back up at the night sky. "Forty-five."

THIRTY-FOUR

Aiden

"**H**OLY SHIT!" HAILEE HOLLERED AS SHE WALKED OUT OF the bakery the morning after our two-people-considering-a-friendship-again date, which, by the way, was a success.

"Sorry, did I scare you?" I asked.

"My gosh, Aiden. Are you insane? You scared me shitless!" she said, swatting my chest with her hand. "What are you doing here? How long have you been standing out here?"

"Not long." That was a lie. I'd been there for forty-five minutes. I stood outside of the bakery the following morning with a carrying tray holding two coffee cups. Coffee that was probably cold. In my other hand was a brown paper bag with two croissants. And on my head? The *IT* clown mask. I didn't want to risk her having to be seen with me in public.

"Oh no, I just so happened to be walking by. So weird running into you. I was just picking up my morning coffee and croissants."

She gave me a deadpan expression. "Wearing an *IT* mask?"

"There might have been a small hope that I'd run into you, and I didn't want people seeing us together—per your request."

"That was very thoughtful of you, you weirdo, but I have to get to work."

"Yeah, of course. By all means." I gestured to the sidewalk.

She started walking in the direction of the inn, and I followed alongside her. She stopped her footsteps, and I stopped mine. "What are you doing, Aiden?"

"Walking."

"I see that. Why are you walking near me?"

I shrugged. "We must be going to the same place."

"I'm going to work."

"That's funny. I was just heading to the inn." I lifted one of the cups of coffee and held it out toward her. "Coffee? Is your order still a caramel latte?"

"It is." She narrowed her eyes at me but took the cup of coffee. She started walking again, and I continued next to her for a while. I hummed a tune as I moved beside her. Every now and again, she'd glance at me with that grumpy grump look she loved to sport early in the morning, and then she'd look forward again. That went on for about three minutes before her grumbles grew in volume, and she let out a growl. Was that a growl? Did Hailee Jones just growl at me?

"What are you doing? And no wise-guy stuff, either. Tell me why you're following me!" she ordered.

I cleared my throat. "Well, last night, you said you were lonely. You mentioned you wake up alone, go to work alone, come home alone, and go to bed alone. I just wanted to cancel out some of those lonely moments. And I figured you wouldn't want me to wake up with you, but I mean, if you want me in your bed in the mornings, by all means..."

"Aiden. Focus."

"Right. So since I can't wake up with you, I figured I could at least walk you to work."

She huffed. "That's stupid."

"I'm dumb."

"You're not wrong." Her eyes shifted to the brown paper bag in my hand. "Do you have an extra croissant for me?"

"I just so happen to have one, yes."

"Give it."

"A little demanding, aren't we? You know, some men are into that kind of thing." *It's me. I'm some men.*

She rolled her eyes, and my cock twitched. Geez, this woman didn't even know how much she affected me.

She held her hand out toward me for the croissant, and I gave it to her. As she took a bite, she moaned with delight.

Do that again, Hails.

"You didn't moan like that when I had you on the steps," I complained.

"Yeah, well, you weren't slathered in butter."

"Note to self, bring sticks of butter next time Hailee has me over to her place."

She laughed. "You need to get the idea of us doing the tango together out of your head because it's not going to happen."

"A man can dream. And trust me... I've been dreaming about that a lot."

"Yeah. A few of your fangirls overheard your daydreams."

"How does that feel knowing that I was thinking about you as I did it?"

"I refuse to answer that."

"Want to know how long it took you to mentally get me off?"

Her cheeks rose and reddened. "Having a guy in an *IT* clown mask asking me that question makes it extremely ridiculous."

"Five minutes."

"You shouldn't wear that as a badge of honor."

"What can I say? The Hailee in my mind just turns me on so much that I can't hold out. Just like the one in real life."

"I don't think that's the flex you think it is, buckeroo."

I laughed. "Give me another run at it, and I'll show you how long I can keep going. That was a first time in a long time for me. I had to knock it out."

"I'm sure you've had plenty of women in Hollywood to keep you busy."

"No one since you."

She raised a brow. "I was your first and only back then. I'm sure you've had—"

"No one since you," I repeated, this time a bit more serious.

Her breath caught as she paused her steps. "Say swear."

I stepped in front of her and pulled up my mask so our eyes could lock. "Swear."

"Pinkie promise?"

I linked my pinkie with hers. "Pinkie promise. What about you? How many suitors have been lining up at your door since I left?" The second the question left my mouth, I regretted it. Truth be told, the last thing I wanted to know was how many people she had been with since I'd been gone.

Ask stupid questions, get stupid answers.

Any answer other than none was the wrong one.

"We just renewed our friendship, Tom. Don't push it."

"What can I say?" I bent down and took a bite of her croissant. "I'm a pusher. I'm not going to lie, though. These are some of the best croissants."

"I swear, my parents have the best bread in the world. I know I've never been to Paris, but I bet these give them a run for their money."

Before I could reply, I started greeting and chatting with passersby on the sidewalk, holding full conversations with the individuals. After they left smiling, I turned back to Hailee.

She smiled. "You do that a lot, don't you? Talk to people."

"I find people fascinating."

"Are you looking at us all as some kind of characters you can play one day?"

I laughed. "No, but good idea. Every person is some kind of character, I suppose." I gestured around toward the random people on the street. "We have background characters. Side characters. Main characters. Villains, heroes, fairy godmothers. The whole world is one big film if you really think about it. And a lot of the footage is just mundane stuff, but sometimes, you get some amazing moments that create a great story. I'm still debating if it has a happy ending or if this turns into some kind of zombie apocalypse thing."

She licked her fingers as she finished her croissant and then tilted her coffee cup toward me. "Here's hoping for zombies."

I held out the croissant I got for me to see if she wanted it. She shook her head, so I dove in.

"What kind of character am I?" she asked. "What's my story?"

"You're definitely, definitely the gravedigger. The weird one who lurks in the shadows," I joked. Luckily, she picked up on my teasing and shoved me.

"Jerk."

"A little." I took a sip of my coffee before saying, "Main character."

She huffed. "I'm no main character."

"That's exactly what every main character would say. Any person who said they were the main character would never truly be the main character. They'd probably die in act two."

"Oh, how I wished I would've died in act two." She sighed, tossing her hand up in dramatics.

"Ah, yes. You're the dramatic main character. It's clear as day."

"I know who you are, too."

"Oh? What's my role?"

"You're like the person who randomly gets hit by a bus when they step into the street, and they are never seen or heard from again."

I laughed and hovered over the curb of the sidewalk toward the road. "Don't tease me with a good time, Jones." I hopped off as a car was coming my way, and before it could get too close, Hailee grabbed the sleeve of my jacket and pulled me back onto the sidewalk.

"Are you insane?!"

"Maybe a little. The right amount to make it charming."

"You're not charming. You're annoying. You're like the annoying person who never goes away," she told me. "If America knew how annoying you were, you'd never be Superman."

"Am I giving off Clark Kent vibes? Because that counts, too."

She rolled her eyes, her favorite hobby to do with me. My new favorite hobby to watch. "No. You're more like Goofy from *The Goofy Movie*."

"I know you meant that as an insult, but honestly, that's one of my favorite movies."

"I already knew that."

Of course, she did.

We reached the inn, and I held the door open as she walked inside. "What time are you off work?" I asked.

"You're not walking me home."

"Of course not. To be honest, this was more than I thought you'd allow me to do, but if I just so happen to be walking around the same time you're heading out…"

"For a famous Oscar-winning actor, you sure lack a life."

"It's a moment of stillness."

"And how's that going for you?"

"I feel the best I've felt in a very long time."

"Good." She smiled. "I have to work. Leave me alone."

"Have a good day, Jerry." I opened the door to leave the inn, and she raised an eyebrow.

"Wait. Did you honestly just come all this way with me just to leave right away? You're not going to your room?"

"No. I have a session at the gym in a few. I'm a little late, so I better hit it."

"The gym is right next to the bakery shop where you were."

"Yes."

"Right. Okay." She frowned as if confused by why I'd walk all that way with her only to turn back and leave. She walked over to the counter and pulled out her chair to take a seat. "Six thirty. I'm off work at six thirty."

I tried to hide my thrill from her comment. I nodded once toward her. "I'll see you then."

THIRTY-FIVE

Hailee

FOR THE NEXT WEEK, AIDEN SHOWED UP AT MY APARTMENT wearing that ridiculous clown mask to walk me to work, and then he traveled beside me on the way home. After the first week, I told him to go mask free. It seemed pointless after photographs of him showed up online claiming he had a mental breakdown and he'd been seen walking around in a mask. I guessed it wasn't a good enough disguise.

He didn't seem fazed by the tabloids at all, though. His main objective still seemed to be…me.

He was a persistent man. Each day, he offered to walk me up to my apartment door, but I always declined. Still, he asked. I wasn't ready to have him in my space again. The last time he was on those steps, well… things moved very quickly. I wasn't certain I was ready for things to hit that speed again.

Now, because of my openness, I had the chattiest famous actor walking me to and from work each day. If there was one thing about Aiden, it was the fact that he'd find a reason to talk. He'd talk about anything, too. Most of his thoughts didn't stay in his head—he had a way of spitting out all kinds of things. Some of his random facts were interesting; others were just plain dumb. Secretly, I liked hearing them all.

Walking beside him was odd, though, because our walks were oftentimes interrupted by townspeople coming up to communicate with him. Everyone made it their mission to befriend Aiden, and with the kind of person he was, he welcomed the friendships. He was able to converse with any and everyone who crossed his path. I couldn't help but wonder how much of the interactions were with him, or how many masks he put on daily. How many roles was he playing?

"Great talking to you, Ruby! Good luck at the dog show with your pup!" Aiden waved to Ruby as she walked off with her dog.

"See you later, Aiden!" Ruby waved, grinning ear to ear. That was how most people left his side—smiling.

Whenever people talked to him, they overlooked that I even existed. Aiden made sure to introduce me to everyone who crossed our paths, though, making sure I didn't feel left out. The joke was on him—I wanted to be invisible. It was exhausting when an introvert was befriended by an extrovert. They went out of their way to make you feel included when all you really wanted to do was be invisible, binge-watch some television, and read some books with a dog or cat companion.

One day, I'd hope friends would understand that we introverts were fine not talking. It was literally one of my favorite pastimes.

"I've noticed something about you," I told him as we approached the bakery. "You talk a lot more now to strangers than you did five years ago. I mean, I can tell you still hate it, but you handle it well."

He paused in front of me and gave me that Hollywood smile that made my stomach flip in ways my stomach shouldn't have been flipping for him. "What else have you noticed about me?"

Your eyes.

Your smile.

Your laughter.

Your right dimple that appears when you laugh and smile too hard.

The way your nostrils flares when you're annoyed.

The way you walk in zigzags.

The way you look at me when you think I'm not looking.

The way you chew your gum and blow bubbles with it.

Lots of things, Aiden. I notice a lot.

"Nothing," I lied. "Other than the fact that you're corny."

"Come on, I'm not corny. I'm charming."

I huffed. "Charming? Yeah, right."

"I am. It's true, and I think you know I'm growing on you. I'm like a mushroom."

I arched an eyebrow. "A mushroom?"

"Yeah, you'll see I'm a fungi after a bit of time with me." He laughed so hard that he slapped his hand against his knee, bending over into a giggling fit like a complete goof. "Get it? Fungi? Fun guy?"

I rolled my eyes. "Yes, Aiden. I get it."

He laughed so hard that that silly, cute, adorable dimple of his appeared. That was the real Aiden. He wasn't playing a role or acting as anyone else at that moment. He was being him in his truest, most authentic form.

"Can I tell you a secret?" I asked him.

"What's that?"

"I missed you."

"Enough to invite me up to your apartment?"

"Don't push your luck."

As we were walking that night, the night sky was dark. It was too cloudy to see many stars, but to be honest, I wasn't looking up. I was too busy staring at Aiden. Yet I saw the shift in his personality as he looked down an alleyway. Two men were standing there arguing, one obviously intoxicated as he stumbled back and forth. His face was bloody, and it was clear that the two men had a bad altercation. A very unfair altercation, seeing how one could hardly stand.

The moment I zoomed in, I understood exactly why Aiden's energy had shifted.

"Is that...?" I started.

"Yeah." Aiden sighed, pinching the bridge of his nose. "It's Jake."

Just as we were about to step in, I saw the sober man swing at Jake, and I gasped when he contacted his face. Jake went tumbling into the dumpster before falling to the ground.

"I don't give a fuck why you don't have it. All I know is you owe me my cash," the stranger remarked. As he went to hit Jake one more time, Aiden rushed over and stepped between the two of them.

"Whoa, whoa, whoa, chill out," Aiden ordered the stranger. "I think you've done enough damage here."

"Clearly, I didn't because he's still breathing. And unless you want to look more like this fucker, I suggest you mind your own fucking business."

"You have no clue how much I wished I could, but this is business that I have to mind," Aiden said through gritted teeth. Jake spit out blood, and without thought, I rushed over to make sure he was okay.

"Hails, just wait on the sidewalk," Aiden tried to order me.

"I'm not going to just leave him here," I said, seeing that Jake was beyond stable enough to even sit up on his own. One of his eyes was swollen shut, and he could hardly even form a coherent sentence.

"Hailee!" Aiden barked.

"Aiden!" I barked back, not willing to fold.

He knew I wouldn't give in, so he turned back to the man in front of him. "How much did he owe you?"

"Fifty bucks."

"Seriously?" Aiden grumbled. "You're kicking a drunk's ass because he owes you fifty bucks?" He pulled out his wallet and started going through it.

The moment the man saw Aiden's cash, he narrowed his eyes. "Did I say fifty? I meant two hundred."

"Excuse me?" Aiden cocked an eyebrow. "It was fifty just two seconds ago."

"That was before I realized Jake got blood on my sneakers."

"There wouldn't be blood if you hadn't pummeled his face," Aiden snapped.

"Two hundred bucks and I'm out of your hair."

Aiden muttered something not so nice under his breath but gave the guy the cash. With a smirk and a bounce to his step, the guy wandered off. Aiden rushed over to Jake and me, and he helped me get Jake up to a somewhat standing position as he leaned against the two of us.

"Jesus, Jake. What the hell are you doing?" Aiden mumbled, irritation in every inch of his voice. Not many things rubbed Aiden wrong, but Jake was one of them. Especially in his current state.

"We gotta get him to the hospital," I told him. "He's pretty beat up."

"No hospital," Jake muttered.

"Don't be a dumbass. We have to get you to the hospital," Aiden explained.

"No hospital!" he said again, this time stern. "Take me to your dad's."

Aiden grimaced. "I don't think he'll want you there. You were supposed to be clean."

"I am clean. I am. I just had a bad night. It's fine. Take me to your dad," he ordered, coughing up blood.

"I can drive him over," I offered. "My car's right around the corner at the bakery. It's not a big deal."

"It is a big deal," Aiden said through gritted teeth, but he agreed.

He helped get Jake into my car, and I drove over to the Walters's house. As Jake lay in the back of the car, he mumbled, "I didn't know you were back in town, Aiden. If I did, I would've visited."

Aiden huffed. "Yeah. Just like you did all those other times while I was growing up," he sarcastically remarked.

I was no stranger to the relationship between Aiden and Jake. Or more so, the lack of a relationship. The Walters, or Samuel, thought it was important to keep Jake in Aiden's life. Laurie wanted nothing of the sort. From a young age, Aiden felt special enough to have two fathers. That was until he realized that Jake wasn't the most consistent one in the world. At a young age, Jake would make grand promises about how he'd take Aiden to baseball games. About how he'd always show up for birthdays. About how he'd get sober for Aiden.

Aiden thought it was a big deal—someone wanting to get clean because of him.

Yet Jake always let him down, time and time again.

Some days, when we were kids, I'd show up at Aiden's house and find him waiting on his front porch with a baseball bat and ball because Jake said he'd take him to the dugout to practice batting.

He'd sit there until the sun went down and his parents made him come inside.

Then he'd do it again another day. And another. And another. Until one day, he realized that Jake's words were empty promises that would never come true. If there was ever a reason for Aiden to have trust issues, it was because of Jake Walters. I knew that was why it hurt Aiden to his core when he found out that his father was the reason he and I stopped talking five years ago. Samuel was supposed to be to him what Jake never could've been—honest.

After parking the car, I helped Aiden walk Jake up the steps and waited for one of Aiden's parents to answer the door.

When Samuel appeared, he grew alert when he saw his beat up and bruised cousin Jake standing on the porch. "What the hell happened?" he asked, pushing open his screen door.

"What do you think happened? It's Jake. He did what Jake does best—fucked up. He asked to be dropped off here, so here you go." Aiden lightly shoved Jake into his father's arms and turned to walk away. I felt completely uncomfortable, so I followed his lead.

"Aiden, wait," Samuel said, calling out to his son. "We should talk."

"I don't have anything to say to you."

"Son—"

"Have a good night, Samuel," Aiden said coldly.

I felt the sting from his words as Samuel took a step back. My heart slightly cracked as I watched Samuel shatter within his own eyes. I wanted to give him comfort, but I knew Aiden deserved my gentleness at that moment. Samuel wasn't my concern—his son was.

The two of us got into my car and drove away. The ride was silent, and I wasn't exactly sure where we were heading. Aiden hadn't spoken a word, and his hands were still in fists as he stared with a stern look out the passenger window. His right foot tapped aggressively against the floor mat.

I pulled the car over to the side of the road and placed it in park before I turned to Aiden. "Talk to me."

"I don't have anything to say."

"You didn't have anything to say to your father, which is understandable. But it's me, Aiden. You can tell me everything."

"I sure couldn't for the past five years," he snapped. Then his shoulders lowered, and he cussed under his breath. "Sorry. Didn't mean to say that."

"Maybe you did, and that's okay." I placed my hand against his shoulder and turned him toward me. "You're allowed to be mad at me, too, Aiden. You can say anything to me—even the hard stuff that might hurt me."

"I don't want to hurt you." His blue eyes looked so heartbroken. "You're the last person I'd ever want to hurt."

"Tell me the hard parts, and I'll help you through them."

"Seeing Jake didn't bother me. Don't get me wrong, it was hard and irritating, but that was Jake just being Jake. He'd been that way my whole life. But facing my father? The one who wasn't supposed to be a hot mess? The one who I'd looked up to my whole life and just learned that he lied to me for five years straight? That's the hardest part. Because now it feels as if I'm staring straight into the eyes of a man I never knew."

"You should feel the same way about me, though. I went along with the plan your father made up. I'm the one who actually went through with it. I—"

"Hailee, I know this might be hard for you to understand, but I spent the past five years trying to be mad at you. I've spent over a thousand-plus days trying to be angry with you. I even showed up here trying to ride that hatred roller coaster, and it doesn't work. It will never work. Do you know why I came back to town? Why I decided to stay in Leeks for the holiday season?"

"Why?"

"It was you," he confessed. "I came back for you."

"What do you mean?"

"When we were kids, you told me that if I'm ever in Hollywood and like I'm losing myself, I should come back and find you. For quite some time now, I've felt lost so... I came back."

"To find me?"

"To find you."

My heart would belong to that man for the rest of my forevers.

"Aiden?"

"Yes?"

I bit my bottom lip. "Do you want to see my apartment?"

His whole demeanor shifted with that one sentence. He narrowed his eyes as a sly grin found his mouth. "Is that... an invite to come see your interior design, or is it an invite to come take off your clothes?"

I turned the keys in the ignition and started the car. "I guess there's only one way to find out."

THIRTY-SIX

Hailee

"IF I KNEW MY TRAUMA WOULD'VE GOTTEN ME INTO YOUR apartment, I would've unloaded it earlier on," Aiden joked as we walked into my place. He looked around, slid his hands into his pockets, and whistled. "Whew. This place screams Hailee."

I looked around at my organized to the T apartment. Everything had a label. Nothing was out of place, and it was as clean as ever. The four walls in my living room were covered in bookshelves, and in the middle two of the shelves was a television that was hardly ever on. If anything, it was a decorative piece.

I had plants throughout the space that Mama brought me because she said, "Every home needs a plant because it adds life to a space." And something about helping the oxygen. Sadly, she had more of a green thumb than I did.

My kitchen island had a cake dish sitting there, and on it sat one of Mama's lemon pound cakes. Each week, she'd made me a small cake for me to nibble at throughout the week. It explained clearly why my workouts didn't do much. I lived a balanced life of sweets and squats. Honestly, it was the best of both worlds.

"Your plants are dying," Aiden said as he took off his shoes and made himself comfortable. He walked over to my kitchen, filled up a pitcher, and took on the task of watering said plants. "When was the last time you fertilized?"

I arched an eyebrow. "Since when are you a plant guy?"

"I played a character who was addicted to plants once. These poor things need some tender love and care." He stuck his finger into the soil and frowned. "When was the last time you watered these?"

"Uh, maybe two months ago?"

"Hailee!"

"What? In my defense, I didn't want plants."

"You're killing me, Hails. You're killing me." For the next ten minutes, Aiden went around talking to my plants, singing them lullabies, and telling them they were loved as he watered them. "I'm sorry your mother mistreats you," he told them.

Honestly, I wasn't certain if it was a turn-on or a turnoff.

Then I looked at his biceps as he watered them, and well, yeah. It was a turn-on.

When he finished dusting the plants' leaves, he washed his hands with pride in his eyes. "You are lucky that plants are forgiving. Watch how happy they will look in a few days."

As he walked by my desk, he paused. He tilted his head in amazement as he noticed the items on my push-pin board. Movie tickets to all his films. He looked over at me. "You've seen them all?"

"I saw each one on opening night and own them on DVD. Not to be dramatic, but there's a good chance I'm your biggest fan."

"Hmph. Didn't expect to feel that feeling."

"What feeling?"

"Love."

I smiled. "It kind of sneaks up on you."

"Yeah, something like that." He reached forward and grabbed the necklace that was hanging there. The Jerry necklace he tore off years prior. "Can I?"

I nodded. "Please."

He put it around his neck, and I swore a part of my heart instantly healed.

I curled up on my couch and smiled his way. "Now that you're done distracting yourself, do you want to talk about what happened with Jake and your dad?"

He narrowed his eyes. "I thought you brought me up here to do the sex?"

I laughed. "I never said I was going to do the sex with you."

"Oh. Well. Um, it was nice seeing your place. I better get going—"

I threw a pillow at him. "Shut up and come sit down."

He chuckled and did as I said. As he sat across from me, he sighed. "I know I should talk to him. I'm just not ready. And I know I shouldn't have called him Samuel. That was a dick move. Sometimes I'm a dick. Then I'll replay the dick moment in my head repeatedly and feel bad for my dad even though he did a shit thing."

"People are messed up. We make mistakes."

"I don't think I can handle you siding with my father tonight, Hailee."

I reached across to him and took his hands into mine. "I'm not siding with him, I swear. I'm on your side, through and through. All I'm saying is that I like to believe people make the best choices they know how to make in the moments they are happening. What your father asked me to do back then was wrong—but maybe he knows better now. I'm sure he's sorry. We can't learn from our mistakes if we are never given the grace to show our growth and apologize. I don't want you to carry the regret of never holding that conversation with your father. I don't want that to eat at you for the rest of your life."

His brows lowered. "What if his apology isn't good enough for me to forgive him?"

"Then at least you held the conversation to come to that understanding. You don't have to listen to me. You don't have to talk with your father, but I know you, Aiden. I know this will eat at you forever."

He pinched the bridge of his nose. "Is this my ego? Keeping me from talking to my dad?"

I shrugged. "I don't know. Your decision not to talk to him might be the right one, but you'll always question it if you don't hold a conversation. Maybe it's not your ego. Maybe it's a boundary, but I think it's worth figuring out which one it is."

He scrunched up his nose and locked eyes with me. "How did you get so good at this stuff?"

"Um, a solid five years of therapy did the trick."

"Do you still go to therapy?"

"I do. I wanted to give myself the best shot at being happy after everything that happened with the bullying. I'm still working on the happy thing. One day at a time."

"What makes you happy, Hailee?"

I smiled and pulled my knees into my chest. "Little things or big things?"

"Both."

"When people are walking their puppies, and the puppies have no control on the leash because they are just so excited about everything. Videos of soldiers being reunited with their family members. Hallmark movies. Fireplaces and cocoa in the winter, even though the only fireplace I have currently is the fake one on the television. Children laughing. The stillness of the dawn before the streets get too busy with the morning rush. Doctors who really give a damn about their patients. My mama. Gingerbread cookies. You."

"Me?"

I nodded. "Somehow, you're both a little thing and a big thing." He smiled shyly, and I wanted to remember that smile for a long, long time. It was as if his inner child came out to play for a moment. "What about you? What makes you happy?"

"You."

I smiled. "You can't say me just because I said you."

"I can say you."

"What else makes you happy?"

"You," he repeated.

"Me and me?"

Skip away with me, heartbeats.

He nodded. "You and you."

While that was the sweetest thing, it gave me an idea. I stood from the couch and walked over to my desk, grabbing a notebook and pen. Then, I joined Aiden back on the couch.

"What are you doing?" he asked.

"I'm making us a new list." I began scribbling in the notebook and then held it out to him. His lips turned up as he read the words.

Tom & Jerry's Ultimate Happiness Bucket List

"While I am honored to be the first and second thing on your bucket list, we are going to make a list for more things to try out in order to get you more things on your list of joy."

He chuckled. "You're going to help me get happy?"

I nodded. "I'm going to help you get happy."

"Jerry?"

"Yes, Tom?"

"I'm in love with you."

"I'm in love with you, too." That never stopped. That never went away.

We'd spent the next hour creating the list of things to try over the next few years to help Aiden and me unlock our ultimate level of joy.

- Go skydiving
- Have Aiden take a drawing class for fun
- Build a snow castle
- Travel to see the northern lights
- Take a cooking class
- Say no to more people
- Don't feel bad about saying no
- Travel the world outside of work commitments
- Hailee gets into a master's program
- Get married
- Start a family

As we made the list, we laughed with one another, and it felt as if we were seventeen, sitting between our homes, falling in love with one another all over again. Being loved by that boy felt right.

"I'm a little mad at you," I confessed.

"And why's that?"

"Because you're even more handsome than I remember."

He laughed. "You look better than when I left you, which says a lot because you always looked perfect."

"Screw you."

"Please do."

My cheeks heated. "I'm serious, Aiden. I feel like when we hooked up on the staircase, it happened so fast that I didn't get the chance to do my overthinking thing. Now, we can't hook up again because my thoughts would be too loud. It's not every day you hook up with Superman."

"We can literally make it an everyday thing, Hailee. I promise you, that's an option."

I laughed. "We aren't going to do that."

He moved in closer to me. "You know the best way to get comfortable with someone in the bedroom?"

"What's that?"

"Practice."

I smiled. "Is that so?"

He grew closer, pulling me onto his lap. His mouth grazed against my neck. "Yup. If at first you don't succeed…" He slid a hand between my legs and began rubbing my inner thigh. "Try, try again. I can promise you that you won't be overthinking anything once you let me inside you again and again and…" His lips fell against my earlobe. "Again."

"Well." My heart was racing as my desires grew more and more. "When do we start?"

In the morning, I woke up to a million missed calls and text messages from my parents and Kate. Aiden was still sleeping beside me as a few sunbeams peeked through the window. As I opened the first message, my heart leaped to my throat.

Mama: Don't read the articles.

What?

What articles?

I opened the messages from Kate, and a wave of memories came rushing back to me.

Kate: These people are fucking assholes. Screw them. How did they even get those pictures of you and Aiden? That means there's a rat in town.

Oh no.

I went to the internet search engine and typed in Aiden's name. The first articles that popped up had my face plastered all over them. Just like five years ago. The most unflattering photographs I could've ever imagined with the headlines "From Hollywood Royalty dates Small-Town Nobody."

There were photographs of Aiden walking with me. Aiden laughing with me. Pictures of me walking out of Aiden's room at the inn covered in mustard. Even photographs from the night he and I got into a fight outside the Starlight Inn when Tommy was punched.

How did they get all that footage? Who in town had been following us around?

I felt nauseous as I began to read the comments posted about me. I should've closed the browser. I shouldn't have been allowing those comments into my psyche. Yet I kept reading them. I kept taking in the words that the world had been defining me by.

Fat ass.

Disgusting.

Did you see the size of her thighs?

My tears flooded, but I didn't cry as I kept reading the commentary. Aiden stirred in bed, and I shifted my back to him. He muttered a little before wrapping his arms around me and pulling me into him. I hid the phone beneath my pillow.

"Still sleep time, Hails," he mumbled against my neck.

"Yeah, I have to get into work a bit early. Mr. Lee needs me."

"Oh, okay. Let me get up to walk you." He started to get up, but I stopped him.

"It's okay. I'm okay," I said as I turned to face him.

I'm okay.

I'm okay.

I'm okay.

I kissed his lips gently. "I'll see you after work. Okay? You sleep in a little. You had a wild night," I joked, trying to hide my nerves.

He smirked and stretched his arms out. "Here's to hoping for another wild night with you tonight. Are you sure you don't want me to walk you?"

"It's fine. Rest. I'll see you after work. Just lock up once you leave."

He muttered something I couldn't understand, before hugging his pillow and falling back to sleep. As he rested peacefully, I hurried into the bathroom and locked the door behind me. In that instance. I was transported back to that scared, hurt seventeen-year-old that the world bullied. My chest ached as the emotions fell from me. I choked on my sobs, trying to conceal them so Aiden wouldn't hear. My chest burned from heartbreak. They were still saying all the awful things they'd said all those years before. They were still calling me all the cruel names.

The last thing I wanted was for Aiden to feel bad about what was being said. I knew how deeply it pained him the last time I was viciously attacked online. I didn't want to put him in that headspace again.

I gave myself the space to cry, to feel.

If I'd learn anything from my school studies and my time in therapy, it was that all feelings were valid, and it was best to work your way through them instead of pretending as if they didn't exist. I'd also learned that crying wasn't a sign of weakness, but it was a sign of expression.

Then I took a deep breath, turned on the shower, and undressed. I needed to shock my body and remind myself of my real reality. That I, in my current state, was okay and safe. At that moment, as the water ran over my body, I took deep breaths and I hugged myself. I rubbed my arms up and down to comfort myself. I soothed my mind, my soul, and my body.

"I'm okay. I'm okay. I'm okay…" The water ran over my body as I steadied my breathing. I kept repeating the words until my body began to believe them. I took in heavy inhalations and released them as I brought myself down from the panic taking over me. Then I got dressed and headed into work.

The moment I walked into the inn, Kate was standing at the front desk. She looked over at me with teary eyes.

I sighed and gave her a lopsided grin. "It's okay. Don't cry, Kate."

"Okay," she blubbered, tears already rolling down her cheeks.

That only made it worse for me, because when someone I loved cried, then I'd cry, too. I didn't make the rules of emotions. I just followed them.

She rushed over to me and pulled me into a hug. Comfort was also another thing that made me cry easily. "I'm so sorry, Hailee. These people are assholes."

"It's okay. I'm okay."

I kept repeating that silently, too.

I'm okay.

I'm okay.

I'm okay…

THIRTY-SEVEN

Aiden

WOKE UP TO THE SOUND OF POUNDING ON HAILEE'S DOOR.

I yawned and stretched before pulling myself up from her bed. I tossed on a T-shirt as the pounding continued.

"Cinderella, open up. It's Dad," Karl said.

With that, I tossed on my pants. The last thing I needed was to have Karl catch me naked in his daughter's apartment again. I headed to the front door, opened it, and smiled at Hailee's dad. "Hey, Karl. Hailee is at work already and—"

"What are you doing here?!" he barked, barging into the apartment.

Well. That was a greeting I didn't expect.

"Oh. Well, uh, Hailee and I are back together and—"

"I asked you not to hurt her again," he spat out.

I narrowed my eyes. "Yeah, I know. I haven't."

He huffed. "Bullshit. I've read one too many articles this morning with the media attacking my daughter again like they did five years ago."

My chest tightened. "Wait, what?"

"Article after article attacking her looks and her character. I swear to God, Aiden, you need to fix this. I watched what this shit did to my little girl five years ago, and I refuse to have her go through this again. I refuse to sit and listen to her cry herself to sleep each night or wake up in night terrors. You weren't there. You didn't see her at her worst when you went to California. I was the one who had to soothe her. I was the one who had to help piece her broken heart back together. She doesn't deserve to go through that again. If you are unable to protect her from this kind of cruelty, then you need to leave her the hell alone. She's my baby, Aiden, my world, and she doesn't deserve this."

"Karl, I have no idea what you're talking about."

"Google it!" he hollered, tossing his hands up in irritation as he turned to march down the stairs. "I'm going to find my daughter."

Panic rose in my chest as I dashed over to get my cell phone. I opened my search engine, searched my name, and photographs of Hailee popped up all over the screen. Article after article claiming they knew all about Hailee and explaining who she'd been and commenting on her body.

I swallowed hard as I read the words written about Hailee's character. The false narrative that the internet was spinning about who she'd been.

My mind was taken back to the situation that went down five years ago. I could only imagine what Hailee was going through and how her mind was processing everything if she'd already seen it. Her father was right—she didn't deserve what the world was saying about her.

I tossed on my shoes and jacket before heading to the Starlight Inn to check on Hailee. My nerves were shot as I remembered how she almost spiraled to a very dark place the last time people attacked her. I couldn't have that happen again. I couldn't watch her go through that amount of pressure all because she was seen with me.

When I walked in, Hailee's friend Kate was sitting at the front desk. She smiled my way. I could tell that she knew what happened by the emotions in her eyes. "Hi, Aiden," she said.

"Hey. Do you know where I could find Hailee?"

"She's out back talking with her dad."

I swallowed hard. "Is she okay?"

"I honestly didn't get much of a chance to talk to her with work and all."

I nodded and thanked her. I debated going out to talk to her right then and there, but I knew Karl wouldn't have loved that idea too much.

"Once she's back, do you think you can ask her to come to my room to talk?" I asked Kate.

"Yeah, of course. Not a problem."

"Thank you, Kate."

"Welcome. And Aiden?"

"Yeah?"

"People are dicks online. This isn't your fault."

My brows lowered. "What makes you think I'm blaming myself?"

"Because Hailee has told me a lot about you. If you're the person she claims you to be, which I think you are, then you're blaming yourself."

I gave her a lazy smile and thanked her before disappearing to my room. The moment I stepped inside, I tossed off my jacket and paced my room. I took calls from my public relations team to see how to spin the story. My PR team told me to hold off and wait. To say nothing. Hailee texted me and told me she'd stop by my room during her lunch break.

The waiting was killing me.

It felt like every second that passed, more commentary went live online.

When Hailee finally showed up to my room, I opened the door and felt a wave of emotions as she stood in front of me.

"Hi," she whispered, a small smile on her lips.

"Hey. Come in."

She did as I said and closed the door behind her.

"Listen—" we said in unison. We both chuckled, and she gestured toward me.

"You first," she offered.

"I'm sorry," I blurted out. "I'm sorry this shit is happening again and it's like some weird fever dream. I'm sorry for the nasty shit people are saying online about you. I'm sorry about it all. I've been talking to my PR team, and we are coming up with a plan to—"

"Don't," she cut in. "We're just going to let it be."

My heart sank. "What? No. People don't get the right to talk about you in those ways. I know how hard it was for you five years ago, and your father was right. It's my job to protect you from this kind of stuff. And if I can't do that—"

"Aiden." She walked over to me and took my hands into hers. "It's not your job."

"Yes, it is."

"No. It's not. If you feel as if you need to put out a statement on your behalf, by all means, do it. But if you're doing it because of me, then I urge you not to."

"But…"

"I'm okay," she stated. "Did it shock me at first? Yeah. Was I transported back to those old insecurities that existed when I was seventeen? Sure, for a moment. Then I remember how far I've come. I'm not that young girl anymore, Aiden. I'm not broken and scared of what the world thinks of me, because I know who I am, and I'm so deeply confident in myself that the outside noise is nothing more than a slight buzzing sound."

I swallowed hard. "I just feel bad about the things they are saying, and the only reason they are saying those things is because of me."

She placed a hand against my cheek. "I choose you. Back then, I was blindsided. I didn't know what to expect, but now I've had experience with the media, and I know how it works, how it moves. And this is me saying 'okay' to it all. I choose this life because I choose you. The stories will die down. The internet will find someone else to talk about. We will ignore it all, and we will be okay. We have to unplug from social media and live our lives. That's how we win—by not playing their game."

I swallowed hard and rested my forehead against hers. "But your father—"

"Is human, which means he's not perfect. He reacted from an emotional state and feared watching his daughter suffer again, but I'm no longer suffering. I know who I am. I love who I am. I love this body of mine in all of its glory. I love my hip dips, and stomach rolls, and stretch marks. I don't live in a world where people could create new insecurities for me anymore because my love for self is so loud that it drowns out their sounds. Do you know why I'm able to do that?"

"Why's that?"

"Because of you." She took my hands into hers and guided me to my bed, where she sat me down. She stood in front of me and removed her shoes and socks. She took the back of her hand and caressed her cheeks. "You told me that this was beautiful." She then moved to her blouse and began undoing the buttons, revealing her bra and stomach. Her hands wandered across her arms, across her stomach, across her chest.

Her beautiful, luscious breasts…

I could stare at her body for the rest of my life, and it still wouldn't be long enough.

"You told me to love my thighs," she said, removing her pants. Her hand moved between her legs as she gently brushed against the fabric of her panties. My eyes were dialed into her every movement, as was my hardening cock.

"What else?" I asked her, not removing my stare from her. "What else did I tell you to love?"

She unhooked her bra, dropping it to the floor. Her beautiful breasts released from the fabric, and all I could think about was how I wanted to wrap my mouth around her nipples and taste every inch of them. Her hands cupped her breasts, and she massaged them, making my desire to take all of her right then and there grow even deeper.

"You taught me to love these, and to love…" She took a free hand and slid it into her panties, and within a second, I was beside her, holding her in my arms as my mouth fell against her neck. I moved her back a few feet until she was pressed against the wall.

One of my hands joined hers in her panties. My fingers gently massaged her as her eyes dilated and a quiet moan escaped her lips.

I slid two fingers inside her. "How long is your lunch break?" I whispered against her neck, kissing her, licking her, sucking her.

"Long enough," she muttered, pressing her hips in my direction.

That was a good enough answer for me.

THIRTY-EIGHT

Hailee

I WENT OVER MY LUNCH BREAK BY THIRTY MINUTES, BUT LUCKILY, Kate was more than willing to cover for me. As I got dressed after the most entertaining lunch break, Aiden sat on the edge of his bed, putting on his jeans.

He looked at me and said, "Can I ask you something?"

"Anything."

"How did you do it?" His voice was timid and low as he rubbed the back of his neck.

"Do what?"

"Become so happy with yourself? I see it in you. I see your joy, and I envy that. I see how much you love your life in every aspect. I want that feeling, but it seems so unattainable."

I walked over toward him and sat beside him. "You have to become selfish. You have to decide that your happiness and joy is the utmost important thing in the world, and then you have to do everything in your power to find out where that happiness comes from. For me, it was helping people. For you, it could be anything. The key is to shut everyone else out. That includes your parents, and me. None of our input matters at this point. The world is so loud with their opinions, that it makes it difficult for us to hear our own thoughts. You have to take control of your ship and steer it to shore, because no one else knows how your boat works. You have to become so dedicated to yourself that the outside noise becomes nothing but a whisper."

"How do I do that?"

"Think back on the times you felt happiest. What were you doing? What were some things you loved to do?"

"I loved to draw. I haven't done it in a while, due to my career, but I did love it, and it was something I did for myself. Most people didn't even know it was a hobby of mine."

"Do that more. Then try new things, try old things, try everything. Then, one day, you're going to wake up, and the sadness you have right now will feel like nothing more than a distant dream. Aiden…" I placed my hand in his and squeezed it lightly. "You don't have to be sad forever, but even if you were, you won't be alone with your sadness. I'll be here with you throughout every single step of your journey."

"I don't deserve you," he confessed.

"That's the funny thing about self-doubt. It lies to you all the time." I leaned in and gently kissed his lips. "Because the truth of the matter is that you definitely deserve me, and I deserve you, too."

After our talk, I gathered my things from Aiden's room and slipped out just in time to come across Marna and Violet, who were wandering the hallway like the snakes they'd been.

I gave them a bright smile. "Ladies, good afternoon."

"Hi, Hailee. Did we just see you come out of Aiden's room?" Violet asked with narrowed eyes.

I nodded. "I think you already knew that. Do you two have a minute for a chat?"

They glanced back and forth toward one another before saying, "Sure, okay," in unison.

I led them downstairs and sat them on the couch in the reading room. I took a seat on the coffee table in front of them and crossed my legs.

"I think it's time for you ladies to check out of Starlight Inn," I stated matter-of-factly.

Marna arched an eyebrow. "Excuse me?"

"We're terminating your reservation at this time. You can take the next thirty minutes to gather your belongings, but it's time for you to go."

"What?!" Violet gasped. She sat up straight and grimaced. "You can't do that. We are paying customers."

"Yes, but as our policy states, if you become a bother to our other customers, we reserve the right to remove you from our premises."

"But we haven't done anything!" Marna remarked.

I smiled and leaned in toward her. I tapped her wrist. "That's a beautiful charm bracelet." I pulled out my cell phone and showed her a photograph I'd saved earlier that morning from the tabloids. In the image of Aiden and me was also a stretched-out arm with a charm bracelet that was remarkably like Marna's.

Her face dropped. "Oh fuck."

"Oh fuck indeed," I agreed.

"You were supposed to double-check the pictures before sending them in!" Violet scolded her friend.

"I know, I know. My bad." Marna gave me a wide-toothed grin. "They paid good money for those pictures. And on the plus side, aren't you happy it's out in the public now? Honestly, we did you a service."

"And now, you'll be doing me another service by packing up your bags and leaving town."

Violet shrugged. "Valid request." They stood, whispered between one another, and then Violet turned back to face me. "Do you think we can get a picture with Aiden before we leave?"

"Go!" I shouted, making them scurry away like the little rats they'd been. Then I returned to my life because I refused to let the world steal any more moments of my happiness.

The greatest thing a person could ever do to be happy was to shut out the opinions and judgments of the outside world.

THIRTY-NINE

Aiden

FOR THE PAST FEW WEEKS, HAILEE AND I KEPT FALLING MORE and more for one another.

I felt the happiest I'd been in a very long time, and I knew that was because of the freckle-faced girl who let me back into her life. When we weren't making love to each other's bodies, we were making love to one another's brains. The conversations with Hailee came as easy as ever before.

My father and I hadn't spoken much, except on the surface level at Thanksgiving, and I only did that to please my mother. She didn't push for me to reconnect with Dad because she knew how much damage he'd done with the choices he made.

On Thanksgiving Day, Jake came to dinner, and Dad gave him money again. Something I'd never understood. Jake asked me for a hand-out, too, but I was beyond the point where I felt as if I owed that man anything. Of course, Jake made a big scene about it, calling me a famous selfish asshole. Saying that I had more than enough to help family.

I knew enough that family was much more than Jake had ever been to me. Still, for the life of me, I couldn't understand why Dad kept feeding the beast. He'd given him more money through the years than made sense, and it only went to feed Jake's bad habits. At that moment, when Dad pulled out his wallet on Thanksgiving Day, I realized how toxic love could be. My father gave and gave to his cousin and never got anything but disappointment back from him. Each time he gave to Jake, it was as if he was breaking a piece of my mother's heart. She didn't speak about it much, but it was easy to see if my father took the time to look into her eyes.

"Sometimes he feels like a stranger to me," she confessed on Thanksgiving evening after one too many glasses of wine. "Like the man I once married was a completely different person."

I couldn't blame her.

He felt different to me, too.

He tried to force me to talk to him, but I set a boundary and said I'd come to him when I was ready. I wasn't to the point where I wanted to converse with him about what he'd done.

December brought cooler temperatures with it, along with our first snow. The closer I grew to the new year, the more I started overthinking my return to Los Angeles. How was I going to leave this small town where the woman I loved resided? The break from the Hollywood world felt much better than I'd ever thought it would've felt. A huge part of me didn't want to go back.

One afternoon, my father kept calling me repeatedly as I walked beside Hailee to take her home after her workday. It was damn near a blizzard, and truthfully, we would've been better off driving. Her rosy cheeks were damn near frozen as I wrapped my arm around her to pull her into my side, trying to keep her warm.

"I think it's rude that you set a boundary with your father, and he keeps reaching out to you," Hailee said.

"Yeah, well. My father never really was good at having boundaries set against him."

"You know what they say, those who struggle the most with the boundaries you set were probably the ones benefiting the most from you when you didn't have them."

I smirked as I kissed her forehead. "Oh, yes, Hails. Talk therapist to me. It turns me on."

"You're ridiculous, but I adore you, so it's fine."

She asked if I was staying the night, but I had some work to do back at the inn, so after I dropped her off, I headed back to the Starlight only to find my father standing inside the lobby, waiting for me.

My gut tightened as annoyance found me. "Dad. What are you doing here?"

"I've been trying to call you."

"Yeah. I told you. I needed space and time. I'm not ready to talk."

"I know, but...it's just. Your mother and I got into a fight tonight. We were arguing about Jake and how I've helped him financially all these years. I know it's a tricky subject, but me helping him comes from a place of love. Your mother doesn't see it that way."

"Can you blame her? At some point, it feels like you're feeding his bad habits."

"I know...it's just...he's done a lot for me. For us."

"A person doing a good thing once doesn't give him the right to forever abuse you."

He grimaced. "I know. I know." He slid his hands into his pockets. "That wasn't the only thing we were arguing about."

"What else?"

"Your mother mentioned that she gave you a letter from your biological mother."

I tensed up. "Yeah, she did."

"What did it say?" he asked, concern dripping in his tone. "What did she have to tell you?"

"I don't know. I haven't read it yet."

He pinched the bridge of his nose and nodded. "Don't read it, Aiden."

"What?"

"Don't read that letter. Nothing good can come from it. It would only end up hurting you and causing more trauma or hurting your mother and making her feel like she's less of your mom. No good can come from reading those words. Do you understand me?"

I didn't reply. I didn't know what to say. "I need to get some work done," I told him.

"Yeah...okay. Right. I'm actually staying in a room here tonight. Your mother didn't want me at home. If you want to talk more, I'm in room fifteen. You have a good night. I'll talk to you later."

He headed to his room, leaving me standing there with an odd amount of doubt. Even though I had work to do, I knew I wouldn't be able to focus if I didn't first make sure Mom was okay, so I headed over to check in on her. The argument must've been worse than Dad made it seem if Mom had him staying at the inn for the evening.

When I showed up, Mom opened the door. She smiled, but I could tell she was hurting. We walked inside and I pulled her into a hug, and she sighed. "Did he tell you about the argument?"

"He did. About Jake."

"It wasn't only about Jake…" She sighed and shut her eyes. "Aiden…I told him I wanted a divorce."

"What?"

"I told him I wanted out of the marriage. The truth is, we haven't been happy in a long time. I thought that if I ended things, I would be breaking up this family that I've prayed for the longest time. But I just can't keep pretending that I'm happy with him. He's not the man I thought I married, which is fine. But I just…" She closed her eyes. "I can't keep lowering my standards in hopes that he will rise to higher ones at some point. I feel like an awful mother for breaking up our family."

"No," I scolded her as I led us to the living room to sit on the couch. "You have been nothing but the greatest mother in this world. I don't want you to ever doubt that. You staying in an unhappy marriage is the last thing I'd ever want you to do. Your happiness has to come first, Mom."

Tears rolled down her cheeks. "Thank you. I needed to hear that. I just worried that you'd think differently of me."

"Never." I squeezed her hand. "Which is why I know Dad was right about the letter."

"What do you mean?"

"He told me not to read it. That it would harm you too much and make you doubt our relationship. So I'm not going to read it. I don't need to know who my birth mother is…you're the only one who truly matters."

"Aiden." She took my hands into hers and locked her eyes with mine. "Don't you dare avoid reading that letter. I need you to go home and read it. I would never feel any kind of way about you knowing what that note says. I know my place in your life. I know our love. I know our strength. So don't you listen to your father. Promise me the moment you leave here, you'll open that letter."

"Mom—"

"Promise me, Aiden."

I sighed, but I made that promise.

After my visit, I headed back to the inn before hopping into my car to drive over to Hailee's place. When she opened her door, she could tell something was off.

"What's going on?" she asked.

"Do you think you can do a favor with me tonight?"

"Anything. What do you need?"

"Someone to be there beside me as I read the letter from my biological mother."

Her eyes grew somber, but she was alert and quick to reply. "Of course. I'm here."

She led me up to her apartment. I felt like an idiot for being so nervous. It was just a letter. Nothing more, nothing less. Still, it felt like the weight of the world was sitting within that envelope. It felt like every key to my past was written in ink.

"Are you ready?" Hailee asked.

I sat down on the couch beside her. "Absolutely not, but I doubt I'll ever be ready. Here goes." I opened the envelope and unfolded the letter, unfolded my past. Unfortunately, it wasn't a long note. It seemed my biological mother wasn't much of a talker—or writer I guess. My eyes danced across the few paragraphs in a bit of misbelief as I read the words.

"What is it?" Hailee questioned. "What does it say?"

I passed it over to her and stared forward, unsure how to feel. How to react.

Hailee began to read it out loud. *"Aiden, first and foremost, I'm glad to hear your father kept your name. When I found out I was pregnant with you, I flipped through a name book for a week. I knew I wouldn't keep you, but when I saw the name Aiden, I knew it was yours. It means little fire. It described what I did and probably still do throughout my life. I leave little fires everywhere I go, and I never extinguish them. I make people's lives harder than they have to be due to my selfish ways. So I stayed away from you. You were the little fire I kept safe from spreading too far. You were contained and controlled, placed into a stable family unit. Which, oddly, is probably the most successful thing I've ever done.*

"I saw you at the Oscars. I've also seen every single one of your movies. Bravo, Aiden. Bravo. Selfishly, I like to think you have my eyes, but I know they are much more like your brother's.

"Which brings me to the next point: You have a brother in California.

"His name is Damian Blackstone. He just recently learned about me. While I have no desire to formally meet you because I know that meeting with me will only spread your little fire, I think I's fair that you know your blood brother. On the back of this letter, I'll put the location of his place of employment. You can do with it as you wish.

"I wish you the best, Aiden. I would call you son, but I know that title belongs to someone else. Take care of those who stayed beside you. They are worth keeping safe. -Catherine."

Catherine.

Her name was Catherine.

"A brother?" Hailee questioned. "You have a brother?"

A brother named Damian Blackstone.

FORTY

Hailee

HE HAD A BROTHER.

      I still hadn't wrapped my mind around that detail, and I was certain Aiden hadn't either.

Aiden didn't sleep much. When he woke up, he didn't mention the letter at all. He simply headed to the gym to get a workout in. I'd messaged him a few times throughout the day but didn't get much of a reply. I knew him well enough to know that he was in his head. I wasn't going to push him to express himself, though. Sometimes people had to work things out in their heads before they were ready to talk about it.

When I was on my lunch break, I texted Laurie to see if she was at home and available for a conversation. I was relieved when she messaged me back, telling me to come over, so I headed straight to her.

"Hey, Laurie, how are you?" I asked as she opened the door. She smiled and gave me a hug. I knew it sounded odd, but I swore her son had her smile. The kind of smile that made every single heart feel loved.

"I'm doing okay, sweetheart. Did Aiden read the letter?" I nodded. She sighed. "How's he doing? Did it give him the answers he was looking for?"

"I'm not sure. She didn't seem interested in meeting him, but she dropped the bomb that he has an older brother."

"A brother?"

"Yup. His name is Damian, and he lives out in California. I guess he's a big successful real estate agent."

"Aiden always wanted a brother." Her eyes glassed over, but she didn't cry. "He's sad, isn't he?"

"Yes. And confused."

"I talked him into coming back home for a few months because I noticed how unhappy he'd been. I knew his mind was going to those dark places that he doesn't speak about. Most people can't see it, but I know you can, Hailee. So can you do me a favor?"

"Anything."

"When you see him getting lost in himself again, when you see him going down the road of darkness, I need you to help bring him back. I need you to keep my son safe."

My eyebrows lowered. "Yes, of course. How do I do that, though?"

"The same way you brought him back these past few months…you show up. You stay. You're his true north, Hailee. When you're around him, he'll always find his way back."

That night, I stayed late at the inn, waiting for Aiden. When he did show up, his eyes were bloodshot, clear signs that he'd been emotional, but I didn't call him out on it.

"Hey. You didn't answer your phone today," I mentioned.

"Yeah. Sorry. I just feel as if I needed some time alone."

I went to hug him, and I could smell the bourbon when I got close. "Let's go upstairs," I offered. He didn't decline the request as he led me to his room. Once we were inside, he closed the door behind him.

"Are you drunk?" I asked.

"Yes."

"You're sad."

"I'm fine."

"You're sad," I repeated.

He grimaced. "It's fine. I was about to go to sleep, so—"

"Okay," I replied, climbing into his bed without an invite.

"No, Hails. I don't think you understand. I want to be alone."

"Yeah." I nodded as I took off my shoes. "And you will be," I agreed as I pulled back the blankets on his bed and climbed inside. "I know sometimes, you'll want to be alone, and I'll respect that. But not tonight, Aiden. Not after the few hard days you've had. So tonight we are going to be alone together." I patted the spot beside me.

He sighed a little but walked over to me. He climbed into the bed, and the second he was settled, he wrapped his arms around me and pulled me against his chest. My perfect puzzle piece.

He placed his forehead against mine. "I'm sad and confused."

"You have every right to feel that way."

"I just keep going back and forth about what to do. Am I supposed to meet this guy? What if I do, and it's a letdown? What if I meet him, and he's just like Jake, or worse. What if he adds more drama to my life?"

"Yeah. I get that. Or what if it's better than you could imagine?"

He didn't reply, but I felt his body relax from the idea of it.

"Hailee Jones?"

"Yes?"

"Thank you for being alone with me." He kissed my forehead and pulled me in closer, wrapping me in his embrace. "I really needed to be alone together."

Aiden stayed at my place for the next few days, so I could make sure he was doing all right. The morning of Christmas Eve, I woke up expecting him to be beside me in the bed. Instead, I found a little note.

Hails, I made a rushed decision and booked a flight to Los Angeles to meet my brother. I'll be back in the morning for Christmas. I love you. -Tom

I read his words repeatedly, feeling my heart racing faster and faster. He was meeting his brother. I wished I could've been on that flight with him, but perhaps it was something he had to do on his own.

I kept myself busy, but my phone near if Aiden needed to call me for reassurance in any form that everything was going to be okay.

I headed over to my parents' house to help Mama and Laurie prep the food for this evening and for tomorrow's big dinner. Laurie let Samuel move back into the house, but I could tell the tension between them was still there. It grew even worse when Jake showed up for Christmas Eve dinner, uninvited.

Laurie didn't send him away even though she'd clearly wanted to. I felt bad for her. She wanted nothing to do with that man. Samuel seemed to have reached his breaking point with his cousin, too, taking him outside for a conversation.

"Hailee, can you take the trash out? It's full," Mama asked me after I'd finished chopping up vegetables. I agreed, grabbing the trash bag from the bin.

I headed out to the backyard to toss the trash away, and as I approached the bins, I heard yelling from next door. I paused as I hid behind the wall of my parents' garage and listened.

"I don't give a fuck, Jake. You can't be here. My wife is saying she wants a divorce. I'm done giving you handouts," Samuel told his cousin.

My heart was in my throat as I listened.

"You owe me! Or are you forgetting why you even have a wife still to this day? If Laurie knew the truth, she would've left your ass years ago. I just need a few hundred dollars and—"

"No, Jake. We're done here. I've more than paid you back for what you did. You can't keep showing up like this."

"I can, and unless you give me what I want, I'll tell Laurie what happened. How you came out to visit me in Los Angeles—" he warned.

"Stop it, Jake," Samuel cut in.

But he didn't stop. The more Jake talked, the more my heart pounded in my chest.

"The way you were supposed to be auditioning, but you got so wasted that you missed the audition. The way you fucked a woman on my couch and got her knocked up. Who cleaned up that mess for you? Who came up with the plan of lying so your wife wouldn't know you cheated? That was me! You wouldn't have this life if it weren't for me pretending to be Aiden's father, so you wouldn't look like the bad guy. So until I get what I want, I will keep showing up and—"

I dropped the bag of trash, causing a loud bang.

The two men went quiet.

"What was that?" Samuel asked.

I covered my mouth with my hands and tried to be as quiet as possible, but when Samuel and Jake rounded the corner to see me, I panicked.

"Hailee," Samuel said.

"Oh shit," Jake muttered, running his hands through his hair. "You think she heard anything?" he asked his cousin.

"Are you fucking stupid? Of course, she did," Samuel snapped. "Leave, Jake."

Jake stood straight. "What about my money?"

"Leave," Samuel barked. Jake grumbled a bit and stumbled off, leaving me there with Aiden's father.

His father.

His biological father.

Oh my gosh.

Samuel grimaced and pinched the bridge of his nose. "Hailee, I…"

"You're his dad," I gasped. "You're Aiden's biological father."

"You can't tell anyone," Samuel ordered, leaving me in shock.

"What?"

"You can't tell Aiden this. You must keep this between you and me. Otherwise, it would ruin his life. You cannot tell a soul about what you overheard."

Just like that, I was transported five years prior. I was that scared teenager afraid of ruining the love of my life's world. Samuel was asking me to betray Aiden all over again, only this time, I knew better. I was smarter and wiser and wasn't the scared little girl I'd once been.

"No," I replied.

He stared at me, flabbergasted. "Excuse me?"

"I said no. I'm not going to keep this from him. I love him, Samuel, and years ago, you convinced me that if I loved him, I'd lie to him and tell him I didn't have feelings for him to convince him to go after his dreams. I lied to him and broke my own heart in the process of trying to do what I thought was right. I was just a kid who wanted the best for him. But I refuse to listen to you anymore. Back then, I thought your choices were being made for your son's best interest, but now I see they were just for you. You are a selfish, cruel man, and I will not keep this from Aiden. The second he returns, I'm telling him."

"I'll tell him first," he swore. "The moment he gets here, I'll tell him the truth. Just let it come from me. At least give me that chance."

I didn't want to give him any chances. I didn't want to be anywhere near him. He'd used and abused his son throughout the years, shaping

Aiden's life into Samuel's dream world. He'd watched how his son struggled and cried over a bad relationship with Jake. He sat through Aiden's panic attacks as a kid about Jake not showing up for him only because he didn't want to look like the bad guy.

He allowed his son to experience trauma because he was too selfish to tell the truth.

This time, I wouldn't be his scapegoat.

This time, he couldn't keep paying Jake off to keep his mouth shut.

"Please, Hailee," Samuel begged, tears flooding his eyes. "Aiden is possibly meeting his brother right now, which has to be hard on him. I don't want this to mark our Christmases for the rest of our lives. Give me until the day after Christmas. Then I'll tell him. My world is about to be set on fire. At least give me the respect to be the one to light the match."

I grimaced as I crossed my arms and stood tall. That man would never make me feel small again. Still, I didn't want all the Christmases moving forward to be scarred with these details of Aiden's father being his... father. That was a different kind of trauma to unpack.

"You have until the twenty-sixth. I'm not going to wait a second after that."

He sighed and pinched the bridge of his nose. "Deal."

FORTY-ONE

Aiden

DAMIAN BLACKSTONE WAS A MUCH COOLER NAME THAN AIDEN Walters.

There was no getting around that fact. I did an engine search on him, so I'd know what he looked like, and well… he looked like me. That was weird. Catherine was right—I had his eyes.

When I walked up to his office, I'd paced back and forth for a good while. I could see him up in his office space working. The way I was lurking outside of his building made me feel like a stalker. I hadn't built up the courage to walk inside to converse with him. My nerves were too shaken up for that.

So it was a knock to my system when Damian came out. I panicked as he was locking up the door, and I called out to him. "Hey, Damian? Are you Damian Blackstone?"

He turned around to look at me. He seemed confused at first but stood tall and confident. "Yes, I am. Do I know you?"

I laughed nervously, probably looking insane as the palm of my hand rubbed my neck. "No, you don't. Well, I mean, shit." I was fumbling my words, making the situation more awkward than it had to be. "Honestly, I didn't even know you existed."

"Then why are you here?"

"It's insane, actually. I should be back in Chicago with my family getting ready for the holiday tomorrow, but I had to fly out here. A few weeks ago, I received a letter from a woman named Catherine. She told me about you, and then told me about...me. I guess what I'm trying to say is I'm Aiden." I took a deep breath and tossed my hands up in surrender. "Your younger brother."

Damian blinked a few times in disbelief before muttering to himself, "Fucking Catherine." He pinched the bridge of his nose and looked at me. "So we're kinfolk?"

"I suppose so."

"A brother?"

"Yeah."

"Oh." He cleared his throat and had a somber look as he stared my way. Same blue eyes. Same nose, too. "I'm not good at this kind of shit. Emotions and stuff. Or being blindsided," he confessed.

My heart sank a little. It was clear that my surprise attack was the wrong idea. "No, totally. I get it. I'm sorry. It's also Christmas Eve, and I'm sure you have stuff to do. I'll let you be." I turned and started to walk away.

"Aiden."

I turned back toward him. "Yeah?"

He slipped his hands into the pockets of his peacoat. "I wasn't done."

"Oh..."

He walked in my direction. "I'm not good with emotions and shit, but I have a house full of people who are better equipped to help us figure this out. Do you have plans tonight?"

"Um, this interaction was my only plan."

"Good." He patted me on the back. "I've got three women back home cooking enough food for an army, two best friends who are in touch with their emotions—well, one at least, and a spare bedroom with your name on it. Let's go, brother."

Brother.

He didn't know how much hearing that word leave his mouth healed the panic attack I was in the middle of.

"You always have those?" he asked.

"Have what?"

"Panic attacks?"

How did he...?

"Don't overthink it," he said as he reached his car. "I'm just really fucking good at reading people. You can follow me to my place in your car."

Damian lived on a huge coastline property, with a massive mansion, tennis courts, basketball courts, and a gigantic swimming pool. The landscaping was stunning, and even though the property was large, it had an odd warmth to it. You could tell it was an actual home as opposed to a mansion. There was a lot of love within those walls.

Cars were parked all around his driveway as we pulled up, and after we parked, he looked over at me. "Are you a people person?" he asked.

"Yeah. I can be."

"What are your thoughts on kids?"

"I love them."

"Good, because there are like fifty million rugrats running through this place, a hormonal pregnant wife named Stella who will probably cry when she sees you, and our two best friend couples who have a collection of their own kiddos."

"Sounds like a good time."

"Or a circus, depending on how you look at it. Come on." Damian walked me up the front porch, and when he opened the front door, two kids went dashing through the space. "Slow down, jerks!" Damian hollered.

"Sorry, Uncle Damian!" the girl shouted.

"Yeah, sorry, Dad!" the boy responded before they continued their journey.

"You're home!" a beautiful woman said as she walked over to Damian. She gave him a kiss and then turned to me. "And you brought a...friend?" she questioned, smiling my way.

"A brother," Damian corrected. He gestured toward me. "This is my brother Aiden."

"Brother?" Stella asked, stunned.

"Apparently good ole Catherine had another kid," Damian explained. "You know how good she is about keeping shit to herself."

Stella's eyes glassed over as emotions hit her fast. Her hand covered her mouth. "Oh my goodness, you have a brother!" she exclaimed, tears rolling down her cheeks.

"Don't be dramatic and cry," Damian told his wife.

"Don't call me dramatic!" she replied, hitting his chest. Then she turned to him and cupped his face in her hands. "You always wanted a brother."

"Yeah," he agreed. "I know."

She kissed her husband, and then turned to me. She rushed over and pulled me into a hug and welcomed me with arms wide open. She then cupped my face and smiled. "He always wanted a brother."

I smirked. "I did, too."

"Oh my goodness. You two look remarkably similar. This is wild."

"What's wild?" someone asked as they walked into the room. The moment he saw me, he almost dropped the glass in his hand. "Holy shit."

"What is it?" Damian asked.

"What is it?! Dude! Why the hell is Superman standing in your living room?!" he asked. "Holy shit!"

Damian raised an eyebrow. "Superman?"

"Dude. Are you shitting me right now?" The guy rushed over to me and began shaking my hand. "Aiden Walters, right? I'm Connor. I'm a massive fan of your work. You are fucking amazing. I mean, don't get me wrong, I'm more of a Marvel guy over DC, but you are going to make an insanely great Superman. It's a franchise I'm excited about, and holy shit! Why is Superman in your house?!" he exclaimed, making me laugh with his confusion and excitement.

"Aiden, this is my best friend, Connor. Connor, this is Aiden...clearly, you already know him," Damian explained.

"Hell yeah, I know him." He patted me on the back as if we were the best of buds. I wasn't going to lie. The welcome party eased a lot of my worries away.

"He's also my brother," Damian added.

Connor's eyes widened. "Your brother?"

Damian nodded. "Yup."

"Your brother's Clark Kent?"

"I suppose he is."

Connor groaned and tossed his hands up in the air. "Why does all the cool shit happen to you? You got a free mansion from your dad, a shit ton of money, and now Superman is your brother? This is unbelievable. Wait until I tell Aaliyah about…oh shit." He looked at me as a flash of panic hit his stare. "You can't be here."

"Excuse me?" I asked.

"Connor, what do you mean?" Stella questioned.

"No, don't get me wrong. You're amazing, and I am a big, big fan. But my wife, Aaliyah? She's next-level obsessed. You're her hall pass."

"Hall pass?" Damian asked.

"The one celebrity your spouse is allowed to sleep with if they were ever given the chance," Stella explained.

"Oh. Wait. Do we have hall passes?" Damian asked his wife.

"No, sweetheart, we don't. Well, you don't. I do," she said matter-of-factly.

"What? Who's yours?" he asked.

"Chris Evans," Connor and Stella said in unison.

"How did you know that?" Damian asked.

"Most women say Chris Evans. He was second on Aaliyah's list after…" Connor glared at me. "Dude, seriously. You have to go. It was fine for her to call you her hall pass because I was almost certain we'd never cross paths, but now that we have, you have to leave before my wife—"

"OH MY GOSH, IS THAT AIDEN WALTERS?!" was screeched as a woman walked out of the kitchen. She had her hair up in a messy bun, and her apron was covered in flour. "OH MY GOSH, YOU'RE AIDEN WALTERS!" she exclaimed. Before proper introductions could made, Aaliyah was wrapping her arms around me as if she was a kid on Christmas morning. "Oh my gosh, you smell like oak and heaven. Connor, look! It's Superman!"

"You don't even like DC comics," he muttered. Connor sighed and tossed his arms up. "I'm going to need more bourbon to make it through tonight."

"Did someone say bourbon?" A tall, built man walked through the front door with a bag of liquor. He pulled out a bottle and held it up. "Because I have bourbon."

Connor shot over to him, grabbed the bottle, and opened it.

"Thanks, Jax. My wife's about to leave me for another man, so I could use a shot." He chugged from the bottle.

Jax looked around, confused as ever. "What did I miss?"

Connor, Damian, and Jax all took me out to Damian's man cave, which was just a basement with a ridiculous amount of beer and a pool table. We'd been sitting around drinking old-fashioneds that I was tasked with making due to my Wisconsin roots.

Connor and Jax were exactly as Damian described them to me. Connor was the friendly sunshine one of the group while Damian and Jax leaned more toward the mysterious dark side. I probably leaned more toward Connor's persona. Jax said that was a good thing—they needed to balance it out.

"So you had no idea that you had a brother, huh?" Jax questioned. "None?"

"Not at all. Not until Catherine sent me that letter," I told him as I handed out another round of drinks.

Connor raked his hand through his dark brown hair. "What's crazy to me is that I've seen all your movies, seeing how my wife is obsessed, and I never noticed it before, but you and Damian look insanely alike. It's almost scary, and it also makes me fear that my wife might have a crush on Damian, too."

"Could you blame her? I am remarkable," Damian dryly replied, making me smirk.

"You two do look alike," Jax chimed in.

Damian and I stared at one another and blinked before shrugging. "I don't see it," we said in unison.

"You two could be twins." Connor laughed.

Just then, a little girl came in with a box in her hands. She set it in front of me and waved. "Hi, who are you?"

"I'm Aiden, Damian's brother."

"Uncle Damian, you have a brother?" she exclaimed.

"Yup, sure do."

"I'm Elizabeth. That's my daddy, and my mom is helping cook."

She pointed at Jax before opening her box and pulling out some makeup. "Can I do your makeup and nails now?"

"Oh, uh, sure?" I questioned, uncertain what to say.

"Elizabeth, what did I tell you about using makeup on strangers?" Jax called out.

"Only use non-waterproof mascara, and use a beauty blender to add highlights," she replied.

"Exactly." He held his hands up to show his hot pink=painted nails. "She wants to open her own makeup and nail salon when she's older. I'm test dummy number one."

Connor held up his neon green nails. "Two."

Damian held up his black nails. "Three. Think of it as your pledge to become a part of our self-made fraternity."

"Well, by all means, beautify me," I told Elizabeth. She went to work as the guys taught me all about themselves. Connor and Damian were in the real estate business, and they were slowly but surely trying to convince Jax to take on the role at their real estate branch in the south.

"I'm a plumber," Jax argued. "I don't sell toilets. I unclog them."

Fair enough.

After my nails were properly painted and everyone was juiced up for the night, Damian took me to the spare room I'd be staying in. "Thanks again for letting me stay here."

"Of course, it's not a problem. Also, Stella would've killed me if she knew I had you stay at a hotel."

"She's a good one."

A small smile slipped out of Damian. The first smile I'd seen him give. "The best one. Let me know if you need anything. My room is two doors down."

"Thanks. I do have a question for you, though."

"What's up?"

"Do you happen to know where I could find Catherine? She didn't leave an address or anything, but I figured I could see her in the morning before I head to the airport maybe."

His brows knitted, and he grumbled to himself. "You sure you want to do that?"

"I just feel it's a part of my story, and once I face her, I can officially close out my past."

"Yeah." He blew out a hot cloud of smoke. "I get it. Lord knows I had to take on my own adventures of shit in order to get to this stable place now. Do what you need to do to get closure. I'll get you her phone number, and you can reach out. Can I give you a word of advice as your older brother?"

"Go for it."

"Catherine is, to put it nicely, a bitch."

"That's putting it nicely?"

"Trust me, it is." He cleared his throat. "Just don't get your hopes up, kid. Know that your story is yours, not the ones who gave you up. No matter what, you get to make a good life for yourself. If you need to see her in order to make your life better, do it. But don't expect much of her being a part of your happy ending. She's not built that way."

I thanked him for his advice.

He scratched at his hair. "We aren't like, hugging brothers, are we?"

"I mean, we could be if—"

"I don't like hugs," he cut in.

"Oh. Well, okay."

He held his hand out toward me. "Handshake?"

I shook it. "Night, Damian."

"Night, brother."

That morning, I called Hailee to wish her a Merry Christmas. "I'll be home in no time," I told her.

"I'll be waiting here," she replied.

I woke up early, but clearly so did the rest of the household. Kids were screaming downstairs with excitement. Santa must've come that morning. As I collected my things to leave, I walked downstairs and came into the living room with three families dressed in matching pajama sets.

"Merry Christmas!" everyone shouted the moment they noticed me. Connor gave me a hug, Jax and Damian kept with their handshakes, and it felt oddly normal being in a household with strangers who made me feel like family.

I was, after all. I was their family.

"Nice pajamas," I told Damian with a smirk. He was wearing a red set with reindeer all over it. Funny enough, I doubted that was his normal go-to attire.

"Don't laugh too hard. This will be your future one day."

Oddly enough, that didn't freak me out.

"Did you hear from Catherine?" he asked, walking me to the front door.

"Yeah. I'm going to meet her for coffee before my flight."

"Just be careful, all right?"

"Will do. Thanks for your hospitality. It's been great meeting you and your whole family."

He gave me another smile. "Stella wasn't lying. I've always wanted a brother. You have my number now. Use it."

"I will. It goes both ways."

"When you're back in Los Angeles filming, we'll meet up again." He took my hand for a shake and pulled me into a hug.

"I thought you didn't do hugs?"

"Whatever. It's Christmas."

I thanked everyone for a final time before heading out to my car and driving to meet up with Catherine. My nerves were shot, and I wasn't quite certain how to deal with the anxiety I'd been feeling. As I parked the car, I climbed out. Standing in front of the shop was a woman in a luxury coat and red bottom heels. She looked at me, and my stomach knotted up.

"Catherine?" I asked.

She blinked, and I saw pieces of me in her expressions. "Aiden, yes. Hello."

She seemed nervous, but I couldn't blame her. I felt it, too.

"Do you want to head in and get coffee?" I started to open the door and she stopped me.

"No, not really. I just wanted to meet to get it out of the way. It seemed important to you, but I don't want to give you false hope. From what I can tell, you have a good life now. I don't want to interfere with that, and honestly, I'm not interested in being involved in your life."

The coldness of her words stung. I couldn't say that Damian didn't warn me.

"No, I get it. I guess I don't know why I wanted to meet you."

"So you could look at me and realize you already had the best parents. It's fine. Consider this my Christmas gift to you."

"Thank you."

She nodded. "Whoever thought that Samuel and I would make something this talented?"

I blinked. "What?"

"Did I say something wrong?"

"Yeah. You mean you and Jake. Not Samuel."

She narrowed her eyes. "Uh, no. I think I know whose baby I carried. I don't even know who this Jake person is that you're talking about."

I felt nauseous. As if I'd been sucker punched in the gut. "Are you sure?"

She sarcastically laughed. "Yeah, I'm certain. One doesn't easily forget the man who messed up your body for nine months."

My mind was spinning, and I felt faint. I wasn't certain what to do, so I excused myself from the situation. "It was nice meeting you, Catherine, but I have to go."

FORTY-TWO

Hailee

I'D BEEN COUNTING DOWN THE HOURS FOR AIDEN TO MAKE IT
home. Mama and Dad had been slow dancing around the Walters's
living room with Laurie, laughing up a storm while Samuel kept to
himself for the most part. I still couldn't stomach what I'd overheard
the night before, and I was more than ready to tell Aiden if Samuel
didn't step up and handle the issues at hand. It'd been eating at me
since I'd heard Jake confess everything.

Aiden sent me his location as he was driving home from the airport,
and I felt the same excitement I had when I was a kid whenever he'd
come back home to me. I dashed outside the second I saw his car was
pulling into the driveway, and I rocketed straight into his arms.

"Merry Christmas," I whispered against the nape of his neck as he
held me.

"Merry Christmas, babe." He pulled back and kissed me. I could
feel the tension against his lips.

"What is it?" I asked as we disconnected. "What's wrong?"

"Nothing. Come on. Let's go inside." He took my hand into his,
and I followed. The second he was through the door, and laid his eyes

on his father on the living room couch, his nostrils began to flare. He dropped my hand.

"Aiden, what is it...?" I asked, but he ignored me as he marched over to his father.

"Is it true?" he blurted out. The music on the record player kept playing, but Laurie and my parents stopped their movements. "About Catherine and you?"

Samuel stood from the couch with a look of shock in his eyes. Then his stare moved to me. "You told me you wouldn't say a word."

Oh no.

Aiden's eyes met mine, and the look of hurt and betrayal that washed over him made me want to vomit. "You knew?" he asked as tears flooded his stare.

I shook my head and reached out to him. "No, Aiden, it's not what you—" He shoved my hand away from him.

No, no, no...

"What's going on?" Laurie asked.

"Now, listen, son..." Samuel started to step toward Aiden, but he was instantly stopped.

"Fuck you!" Aiden hissed at his father as he shoved him hard against the chest.

"Whoa, whoa, whoa, what's going on?" Dad asked, stepping between the two men to make sure it didn't escalate. "Aiden, what are you doing?"

"What am I doing? How about you ask what he's been doing," Aiden muttered. He flung his hands in irritation as he looked at Samuel. "How about you tell the crowd the truth, huh? How you aren't the stand-up man you've always made yourself out to be."

"Samuel, what is he talking about?" Laurie asked, walking over to her son.

"I, he..." Samuel shut his eyes, and when he opened them, he didn't say anything.

He couldn't bring himself to tell the truth. It sat tangled behind his tongue, a web of lies and deception. He was a coward because he still wouldn't say it. He wouldn't tell the truth even though it had already been revealed.

"He got Catherine pregnant all those years ago, not Jake," Aiden said, airing all of Samuel's dirty laundry. "He made Jake pretend that he was the father after Catherine gave up her rights. He made it all up, so he wouldn't have to face you, Mom, with the truth. And ever since then, he'd been pretending to be something he's not. Is that why, Dad? Is that why you kept helping Jake? Because you feared he would tell your little secret if he didn't get money from you?"

"Oh, my goodness," Mama mumbled as she stood beside me.

Samuel's eyes released tears as his voice cracked. He turned to his wife. "You don't understand, Laurie. You and me… we never saw each other. There was no romance between us. I was struggling being in Los Angeles alone…"

"Ha!" Mama laughed sarcastically at Samuel's pathetic attempt to explain.

"I didn't mean for it to happen, Laurie, I swear, I didn't. I was just flying out to Los Angeles for an audition and ended up, well, it was a mistake, okay? I fucked up. But, look at the miracle it brought us." He reached for her hand and squeezed it. "We have our son because of my mistake. He's our miracle baby."

What was wrong with that man?

Laurie ripped her hand away from her husband's and held a hand up to him. "No," she ordered. "Get out."

Samuel shook his head. "No."

"Get. Out," Laurie hissed as she shoved him hard against the chest. "Get out, get out, get out!" she screamed as tears fell down her cheeks. Her heartbreak began to unleash from her vocals as she cried and slapped Samuel against his chest.

Dad had to remove Samuel from the house. He physically lifted the sobbing man and took him outside. When he came back, we were all still frozen in place. Laurie looked around and choked on her sobs.

"I'm fine," she swore.

Mama went to step forward to comfort her best friend, but Aiden was already wrapping his arms around his mother.

"We should give these two some space for a little while," Dad said, nodding to Mama and me.

I didn't want to leave them, but I knew it was the right thing to do. That mother and son needed one another right then and there.

Still, I wished I could've been there for Aiden the way he was for his mother.

I knew he needed the comfort, too.

Later that night, I saw Aiden's bedroom light turn on. I instantly crawled out of my bedroom window and knocked on his.

He saw me and sighed before turning his back on me.

I knocked again.

And again.

And again.

I pounded on that window repeatedly until a grumpy Aiden appeared and pushed it open. "What, Hailee?" he snapped. "I need space right now."

"No."

"Excuse me?"

I climbed into the window and stood stern in front of him. "I said no. You don't get space right now because this whole situation is a mess. And just to be clear, I was going to tell you. I found out about the whole thing while you were gone and was waiting for you to come home, but he said he'd tell you first thing. It turned out you already knew. It's important for you to know that I have not been sitting on this big secret for a long time, Aiden. I didn't know."

"I hear you. I do, but—"

"No buts. You don't get to push me away right now, okay? Because, like it or not, you need me just as much as I need you, so I'm not going anywhere. I'm staying right here."

"Hailee—"

"Be pissed off. Be pissed off at the world. Be pissed off at everything that exists. Heck, you can be pissed off at me, too, but you can't push me away, Aiden. I refuse to be moved. We aren't doing that."

"Hailee—"

"No. I've read enough romance novels to know how this is supposed to go. We are supposed to fight and break up at this point in our story, but I refuse to do that. No third act breakup, okay?" I took his hands into mine. "We are not going to have some dramatic fight between us and a breakup for a short period of time to just come back together to be happy. We already did that part, Aiden, okay? We are happy. You and me… we are good. It's the rest of the world around us that sucks. So we aren't going to screw this up because of them. I've already lost five years of you due to that man. I refuse to lose one more second."

He shut his eyes and rested his forehead against mine as he pulled me against his chest. "I'm sorry. My emotions are jacked up."

"It would be weird if they weren't. But you don't have to figure them out alone, right? I'm here."

"I feel as if I'm too much for you right now. You've spent the past five years facing your shadows and growing. I've been running from them. Now, I have even more shit to face, and it's not fair of me to ask you to stick around as I deal with my issues."

"Hey, stop it." I pulled back and placed my hands against his face, locking my eyes with his. "You don't have to be perfect to be loved by me. That's not how this love works. I don't only love you on the good days. I love you on the hard ones, too. Be broken, be raw, be damaged. And still, I'll stay."

"Hailee?" he whispered.

"Yes?"

His lips brushed against mine ever so gently. "You are the greatest thing that's ever happened to me."

FORTY-THREE

Aiden

THE NEXT MORNING, I SAT ON THE FRONT PORCH FOR A WHILE, getting fresh air when the front door opened and Mom appeared. She'd been sleeping for hours. I didn't blame her.

"Hey, Mom."

She smiled and stepped outside. "Hey, you."

"Last night was crazy."

"That's putting it mildly." She snickered.

I lowered my head and grimaced before looking back up at her. "Have you talked to Dad since everything unfolded?"

Her small smile faded a little and I saw the hurt she was trying her best to hide from me. I wondered how many times I'd missed seeing that. I wondered how many times my mother hid her hurt. "I did. He's staying at a hotel for a few weeks."

She walked to the top step of the porch and took a seat. I clasped my hands together. "Are you okay?"

She lightly laughed. "Define okay. Don't worry about me, though. I'll be okay. How are you?"

"I'm always going to worry about you. You're my mom." I took my hands and placed them on her shoulders. I wanted her not to only hear me but to also feel my words as I looked into a pair of eyes that looked nothing like mine, but her heart? It beat like mine. It was because of her heart that my heart knew how to love. "You're my one and only."

"Oh, Aiden..." she whispered with a shaky voice.

The tears sitting at the back of her eyes finally began to fall, and I pulled her into a hug. "My mother."

"My son," she replied, holding me tight.

I wasn't certain who needed the hug more, me or her, but we held one another for a few minutes. When she fell apart, I was there to hold her, and I needed her to know that I'd always be there for her, in her corner, for the rest of my life. Maybe unlike my father, I didn't stand at an altar and make those vows to her, but I held them close to my heart. The moment my mother chose me as hers, I chose her as mine. From my first steps to my last, I would always be her son, and I was the lucky jerk who would always have her as my mother.

Once she pulled herself to a more stable state, we separated our embrace. She wiped at her eyes, then placed her hands in her lap and said, "You know the worst part of it all?"

"What's that?"

"I can't hate your father. I want to, God knows what that man has put me through over the years, but I can't... because I know what would've happened if I found out the truth all those years ago. I would've left him. He knew that, too. And, if that happened, if I would've left your father when I found out he got another woman pregnant, I would've never become your mother. That thought breaks my heart because the greatest part of my life, has been becoming your mom. I would go through all this again if it led me to you."

The new year came in, and I was having a hard time feeling festive. I had to leave Leeks soon enough to start filming, and I felt like my world was still upside down. Dad, or Samuel, or whatever the heck I was supposed to call him nowadays, kept trying to message me to communicate. Needless to say, he was fired as my manager and fired as my mother's husband. I was still debating how to cut him loose from the fathership role, too. I wasn't ready for that conversation. Each time I considered it, I'd talk myself out of it because of my anxiety. I hated confrontations. If it were possible, I wished I could simply ghost my own father, disappearing from his life like I'd never been a part of it.

The more I sat on what he had done, the more pissed off I'd become. The number of times I'd cried to him about Jake as a child. The number of times he'd watched me sit at holiday dinners uncomfortable as Jake was drunk off his ass. The times he'd watch me sit on the front porch with a baseball glove and a ball, waiting for Jake to pick me up, then instead of offering to toss the ball with me, he'd take me inside, set up a camera, and have me film audition pieces.

I was never his son. I was his puppet. I was his meal ticket. I was the dream he'd never discovered himself. It was messed up because he knew I'd do anything to make him happy, so he abused that privilege. He also abused my mother's love, knowing she'd never leave him because she wanted to give me a stable home.

Samuel Walters was not a good man. And now I knew the blood in his veins coursed through mine. That was doing a number on my thoughts, on my mental health. How could such a liar, such a conman, be the same as me? A part of me would've rather taken Jake, because at least I could understand how drugs and alcohol could jade a person's choices. What I couldn't understand was Samuel's darkness. Was it all greed? Selfishness?

It got to the point where I had to hold a conversation with him. Before I could move forward in my life, I needed to close that door with my father.

I met my father at a hotel in Chicago. He'd knew staying in Leeks wouldn't have been a good idea. I was thankful for him removing himself from town. It would've been hard to see him walking around Leeks.

We went down to the restaurant in his hotel and sat down for a cup of coffee. He asked me if I wanted lunch, but I had no desire to stay too long.

I crossed my arms. "I don't want to drag this out. I just want you to know what's been going through my head."

"I'm all ears."

"My whole life, all I wanted was for you to be my father. I did everything in my power to make you proud of me because I wanted to feel closer to you. I took on an acting career, even when I didn't want to do it any longer because I saw how much it meant to you. Everything I've ever done was because I wanted you to be happy. It breaks my heart knowing that you wouldn't have done the same for me. You chose yourself day in and day out."

"That's not fair, Aiden. You've had the greatest life because I fought for you to make it in the acting industry. I went hard for you because—"

"Because you craved being in the industry yourself, and you used me to get as close as you could. Don't pretend that you did any of this for me."

"So, you're truly saying I'm a selfish asshole, huh? Is that what you truly believe? After having me in your life for twenty-three years?"

I shook my head. "I don't have any words to describe what I think you are. I just know I don't want to be a part of it."

He grimaced. "Then why show up here? Why come talk to me?"

"Because I wanted to look into your eyes and tell you straight out that I'm taking a note out of your book. I am choosing myself from this point on. I wanted it to be clear that this relationship between us is over, and I don't wish to drag it out. You're free to go on and chase any dream you might have in your life. You just no longer get to use me to have them come true."

With that, I closed the biggest chapter of my life as I walked away from the man who raised me, the man who brought me into the world. Even as I walked away, though, my heart still felt heavy.

It turned out that closure didn't always feel good. Sometimes, it just felt so uncomfortably final.

FORTY-FOUR

Aiden

EVERY PIECE OF ME FELT A BIT OFF-KILTER SINCE I'D FACED MY father. I didn't know who to turn to, but somehow, a certain person knew how to show up exactly when I needed them the most.

"Hello, brother."

Damian Blackstone was standing on my front porch, dressed all in black.

How the hell did Damian Blackstone find out where I lived?

"Damian. What are you doing here?" I asked, stunned to find him standing in front of me. "How did you find me?"

"They call me the gravedigger. I'm good at digging up information on people," he said, slinging his duffel bag over his shoulder. "You got a spare room for a few days?" Without thought, I pulled him into a hug. He grumbled. "The hug thing was only for Christmas Day."

"Yeah, well, I've had a shitty go at things. I could use the hug."

"Fine. Only this once." He hugged me back, and I was thankful for the comfort. The moment he let me go, he stood tall. "So what do people do in Wisconsin other than freeze their ball sack off?"

✦

"Cheese curds?" Damian asked as we sat at the counter of the local bar. "You deep-fried cheese?"

"You've never had a cheese curd?" I gasped. "Your life is about to be forever changed. These are the best ones in town. They make their ranch homemade, too. Trust me, that matters."

Damian picked up the cheese curd and pulled it apart, showcasing some solid cheese pull action. Then he dunked it into the ranch and tossed it into his mouth. He sat back in his chair, a bit amazed. "Well, fuck," he moaned. "I didn't know your food had drugs packed in it."

"What can I say? We do a few things well. The Bucks, cheese curds, and Spotted Cow beer. You won't find this goodness anywhere else."

"Speaking of good." He snapped his hand in the air. "We are going to need more of these cheese balls and more Spotted Cows, stat."

Damian turned to me and gave me a bit more serious look after he tossed a few cheese curds into his mouth. He wiped his hands off and his brows were knitted as he looked my way. "Rumor has it that your father's a dick."

"How did you find out?"

"Hailee reached out to me on social media. She said you might need a brother, so here I am."

Of course, she did.

"She's the best person I know," I confessed.

"That's funny. She said the same thing about you," he said. "I am sorry about your father. I honestly don't know why he'd even go that far to keep it a secret."

"He knew he would've lost the best thing that ever happened to him—my mother. Turns out all these years later, he still lost her."

"Karma catches up, no matter how long it takes."

"I hate him. He watched me throughout the years struggle with Jake and still made these choices. He's the only reason I even did this acting thing, because I wanted to make him proud. I dreamed of him being my biological father my whole life. I thought I was making it up that we had characteristics that matched. I was convinced that I was insane for thinking those things. Now, when I see him, all I feel is hatred."

"I get it, man. My dad was a dick and played mind games with me, but it led to me finding Stella, so I'm kind of thankful for him, too, the asshole."

"Are you two closer with one another now?"

"Nah, he croaked," he said with a deadpan expression.

"Oh shit. I'm sorry. I didn't know."

"How would you know? We'd just met."

It didn't take long for me to realize that Damian was a very straight-forward guy. He was the opposite of his best friend, Connor. Yet a little more like Jax. The three of them were such an odd pairing, but somehow it seemed to fit together. They balanced each other out completely.

Damian took a drag of his beer. "The way I see it is if the old man didn't croak, I would've never met Stella, so it feels like an even trade. An asshole father drops dead, and then you end up with the love of your life? Sign me up."

I sat there completely stunned by his comments.

He looked over to me and released a weighted sigh. "I went too dark, didn't I? Stella always tells me my dark humor would be the death of me. At least if I died, I could join my dad in the great downstairs and tell him how big of a dick he is. My biggest regret is not telling more people to fuck off."

I snickered a bit and held my glass up. "Hear, hear."

"Most people would tell you that time heals all wounds and that you should forgive your father. But do you want my advice?"

"Shoot."

"Fuck him. You owe him nothing. Not your kindness, not your for-giveness, and not your presence in his life. He made his bed, and now he gets to sleep in it. A father isn't defined by blood, it's defined by the man who does right by you. Still, you can silently thank him for the things he did give to you. Like your mother."

I sighed. He was right. If it weren't for my father's lies, I wouldn't have my mother.

I whistled low. "A lying asshole in exchange for the best mother in the world?"

Damian grinned a little and popped more cheese curds into his mouth. "Feels like an even trade."

He shifted in his chair and said, "Truly, though. If I learned anything in life, it's the fact that family isn't about blood ties, it's about loyalty. It's about the people who love you and are honest even when it's hard. It's about the people who show up day in and day out to help make you the best version of yourself. It's about being in a place where you can be authentically yourself and not feel shamed for it. It's having dreams and having people to cheerlead them. They say blood is thicker than water, but water is a lot smoother going down. It refreshes you and nourishes you. It's good for your body, good for your spirit. Don't take shit in that makes you feel heavy. Only accept love that feels good to the soul and give that love back tenfold."

"For a man who claims to be tough and cold, you sure give good speeches."

"Having kids softened me. I had to be a better man for them. It comes with the job title."

"Lucky kids."

"Lucky Damian," he corrected.

"I think I'm going to like this having a brother thing."

"You're not too much of an annoying shit, so that's refreshing."

"I still can't believe you flew all the way out here to check on me."

"We're family. That's what family does. Looks out for each other. So"—he clapped his hands together and smirked—"when do I get to meet this special lady of yours?"

"She's at her parents'. I had her mom and dad invite her over for a movie. After we are done here. I was hoping I could have your help with something if you're up for it."

"What do you have in mind?"

FORTY-FIVE

Hailee

MOVIE NIGHTS WITH MY PARENTS WERE ONE OF MY FAVORITE things. Except for the fact that Dad had a way of talking all the way through it and asking questions about the movie as if Mama and I knew better than him what was going on. Mama always ended up throwing popcorn at him, telling him to shush.

"Did you hear that Laurie is selling the house?" Mama asked me after the movie went off. The past few weeks have been crazy. Aiden was heading back to Los Angeles soon, which broke my heart a little, and Laurie's whole world had been turned upside down.

"Is she?"

"Yeah. Figured it was about time. Samuel told her she could keep it, but she felt as if she needed a fresh start. Which I can understand. That brings me to the next topic at hand." Mama took Dad's hand into hers and they smiled my way. "Since our bakery has grown so much over the past few years, we have made more money than we've ever imagined. So we have decided to sell our house too and get our dream home."

"What?!" I gasped, shocked. "You're selling this home?" I didn't know why, but that fact brought tears to my eyes. Mama already had a tissue ready to hand my way. I took it and wiped my tears away. I was currently sitting in the house that raised me. It was the only home I'd ever known. Those four walls, that roof, those doors and windows… they all told the story of my life. It was within that home where I met my best friend. My person. My Aiden.

I looked around the living room and kept swiping at my overflowing tears.

"It's okay," Dad said, putting a comforting hand on my knee. "Feel all of the things you need to feel about this."

"It's just… I'm happy for you both. This is a good thing. This place has so many of our stories in it. It's just odd to think—"

Before I could finish the thought, I heard knocking.

I sat up straight. "Is someone supposed to be here?" I asked.

"Not that I know of…" Mama looked at Dad. "Did you invite someone?"

"You know I don't like people," Dad joked. "But it sounds like it's coming from your bedroom, Hailee."

Strange.

The three of us stood from the couches and headed to my bedroom to find out what was happening. The moment I turned on my light, I saw a stranger standing outside my window, knocking.

I walked over to the window, taken aback, but when I saw those blue eyes, I felt as if the stranger was so familiar. He gave me a halfway grin and gestured for me to open the window. I glanced back at my father, and he shrugged.

"Open it. I got your back," Dad said, giving me reassurance.

I opened it, and the guy held his hand straight out to me. "I've heard a lot about this window. You must be Hailee. I'm Damian. Aiden's brother."

Of course, he was. He looked remarkably like Aiden. The blue eyes should've given him away. A sigh of relief hit me as I reached out to shake his hand.

"Goodness, hi. It's nice to meet you…at my window."

He chuckled slightly. "I came into town to see Aiden. I'm staying at his place with him and his mom. He told me how you and he climbed out of windows and shit to see each other." He glanced past me and nodded in the direction of Mama and Dad. "You're Hailee's parents?"

"We are," Mama said.

"Sorry for the foul language, ma'am," Damian said. He turned back to me. "Anyway. I'm shocked you guys don't need back surgery from bending out of these windows. I almost got stuck, but I wanted to come meet my new sister-in-law before I headed back to Los Angeles."

"Oh, no. Aiden and I aren't married. We're just dating."

Damian arched an eyebrow. "Are you sure about that? Because there's a man on a bent knee right over here hoping that that fact would change sooner than later." He gestured behind him and revealed Aiden, down on one knee, with a box in his hands.

"Oh, my goodness," I gasped. I had more tears, but these ones were happy.

Damian held his hand out toward me to help me step through the window. He led me over to Aiden, who had the biggest smile resting against his face. That smile controlled my heartbeats.

"Hey, you," he whispered.

"Hey, you," I replied, stepping in front of him.

"You know, I've practiced this speech many times throughout the years, but actually doing it is another thing." Aiden nervously laughed as the ring box shook in his hand. The ring box. The ring. It was the most beautiful ring I'd ever seen in my life.

He continued speaking as my tears continued to flow. "Hailee Jones, you are my person. The reason I believe in destiny, the reason I believe in love. I've played many different characters in my life, but the best leading role I've ever played was the one where I had the privilege of being your best friend. You are my morning coffee and my bourbon at night. You are the Jerry to my Tom. You are my north star that guides me home each night. I know people say you're supposed to fall in love, but the truth is, I was born in love with you. From the moment I took my first breath, my heart longed for you. So marry me, Hailee. Marry the good parts of me and the messy ones, too. Marry my confidence and my insecurities. Marry me. Marry all of me, the good and the bad, and give me the joy of loving you more and more until the day I die. Will you marry me?"

I lowered myself down to his level, sitting on my knees in the snowy grass right beside him. I placed my hands against his cheeks and smiled. "Yes." It was the easiest yes I'd ever spoken. Being loved by Aiden was a gift. Aiden Walters was the kind of man a woman never truly got over.

I was given a second chance with his love, with his heart, and I swore for the remainder of my life, his heart would remain in my protection.

I kissed him long and hard as our families cheered from behind. Laurie had a camera in her hands taking photographs while Mama and Dad snapped their own. The proposal taking place in the exact spot where I'd first fallen in love with him felt like kismet.

I was going to marry Aiden Walters, and he was going to be mine forever.

He was going to marry me, and I was going to be his always.

For as long as we both shall live.

"Can we just live in the part of wedding planning where we sample cake flavors for the rest of our lives?" I asked Aiden as we sat in front of eight different samples of cakes. It was fair to say that picking out a cake had been my favorite part of the wedding planning process.

He wiped his finger into the chocolate buttercream frosting and stuck it into his mouth. "I think that's the greatest idea you've ever had."

"Now, this one is an orange peel cream. The cake is a white cake with a hint of lemon zest. Not to toot my own horn, but it's astonishing," Mama said as she brought out yet another piece of cake for us to try. We'd been sitting in Hailee's Bakery for the past two hours trying cakes, and I wasn't complaining one bit.

The fact that Mama oversaw the sweets for the wedding, and Laurie was in charge of the elegant meals felt so exciting to me. It was the best of both worlds. Our mothers were masters in their fields, and they were bringing out their best for Aiden's and my wedding.

Aiden and I took a bit of the orange peel cake, and we moaned in unison.

"Holy," Aiden groaned, shutting his eyes as he fell into euphoria.

"This is the one." I nodded. I looked to Aiden. "Isn't this the one?"

"This is absolutely the one. Penny, I don't know how you did this, but I'm so glad you did. This is it."

Mama grinned ear to ear. "Trust me, I already knew."

Aiden gave Mama puppy dog eyes. "Do you by chance have any more samples of it in the back so we can be extra sure?"

"I think I can manage grabbing a few more bites for you." She headed to the kitchen, leaving Aiden and I in cake heaven, finishing up all the bites we didn't finish previously.

As we were eating, my phone dinged with a new email. I went to open it, and my eyes instantly watered over.

"What is it?" Aiden asked, becoming concerned with my expression.

I turned to him as I choked on my next words. "I got in."

"What?"

"I got into the master's program of psychology at Adler University in Chicago," I breathed out as my heart pounded wildly within my chest.

"Holy shit!" Aiden remarked, leaping up from his seat. Within seconds, he yanked me from my chair and began spinning me around in circles. The moment he placed me on the floor, I saw the tears falling from his own eyes. Because when I cried, he cried. When I celebrated, he celebrated.

"You did this, Jerry!" he remarked, pulling me into the best hug of my life. "Your hard work did this. I'm so proud of you."

Mama came out with two more pieces of cake and paused when she saw our emotions. "What's going on?"

"Hailee got into the master's program at Adler," Aiden said with so much glee in his voice.

Mama's eyes widened as she shouted with excitement. "Oh, my goodness! Let me go in the back and bring out the whole freaking cake. Karl! Get out of the office! We are celebrating!"

Dad came out right away and when we told him the news, he started jumping up and down with joy, too. When Aiden let me go, I fell into Dad's arms. The first man who'd ever taught me what love looked like, what it felt like.

"I had no doubt in you and your abilities. I'm so proud of you, Cinderella," he whispered as he kissed my forehead. "I love you forever."

"I love you longer than that."

FORTY-SIX

Aiden

One Year Later

I WASN'T HAVING A PANIC ATTACK.

Truth be told, I hadn't suffered from a panic attack in a while. Not since Hailee helped me discover paths to my happiness, and I got into therapy. It turned out, getting help could lead to a happier life.

And my life was becoming happier and happier each day.

That morning, I felt the calmest I'd ever felt in my life. It was the day of my wedding. The day I looked at my very best friend and said, "I do", and I'd never felt surer about anything in my whole life.

Loving Hailee was something I'd do for the rest of my life, and it felt like an honor to say those two words to her when we'd reach the end of the aisle in front of our family and friends.

"You look good," Damian said, walking over to me as we waited in the dressing room. The ceremony was going to be starting any moment, and I had my three newest brothers with me as groomsmen. Connor, Max, and Damian became instant brothers to me. They were the definition of family and they welcomed me with open arms.

Damian straightened out my bow tie and I smiled. "You don't look half bad yourself."

"Must be genetics," he joked before patting me on the back.

"Okay, Connor, Jax, the photographer needs you all out in the hallway," Mom said as she walked into the dressing room. The moment she saw us all she teared up. "Handsome, handsome men," she mentioned. Connor and Jax headed out for the photos as Mom walked over to Damian and me. She stood on her tiptoes and kissed my cheek and then turned to Damian and kissed his as she placed her hands against his cheeks. "You look amazing, son."

Damian was a tough guy. He didn't show much emotion, but in that moment, I thought he was on the brink of tears.

"What is it?" Mom asked him.

He shook his head a little as a half-smile slipped out. "Nothing. It's just... You called me son."

"Yes. That's what you are to me."

He cleared his throat and stood straighter. "I just always wanted that."

"Wanted what?"

He sniffled, trying to stay strong. "A mom."

Mom smiled. "I always wanted another son for my Aiden, so I think it works out perfectly. Meet Jax and Connor outside for pictures in a minute, okay?" She gave Damian another kiss on the cheek before leaving the room.

I smirked as I looked at my brother.

He grimaced and brushed away his tears. "If you ever mention me crying to anyone, I will punch you in your balls," he grumbled.

I tossed my hands up in surrender. "Your secret is safe with me."

He patted my back one more time before leaving the room to join Connor and Jax for photographs, leaving me alone with myself and my thoughts.

I stood in front of the mirror, smoothing out my suit, thinking about how I was minutes away from the biggest moment of my life thus far.

"You look good," someone said from behind me. I turned to see Karl standing there in his own tuxedo.

"You don't look that bad yourself."

"What can I say? This old man knows how to clean up well." He walked over to me and brushed his thumb against his nose. "Are you nervous?"

"Not at all. Just ready."

He smiled. "That's how I felt on my wedding day to Penny. Just ready. When you know you're marrying your person, there's a calmness that comes over you." He glanced at his watch. "I must get to Hailee to get ready to walk her down the aisle, but I wanted to stop in quick and let you know that I couldn't think of a better man to be marrying my daughter. I've seen the way you love her, and that only makes me love you more. It is an honor to be your father-in-law, but if you'd like, you are always more than welcome to call me dad."

I was seconds away from crying like Damian. Who knew a heart could feel more and more happiness with every passing second?

Karl patted my shoulder before he pulled me into a tight hug. "I love you forever, son."

He used the saying I'd heard him use with Hailee my whole life growing up. I choked on my words but managed to get them out. "I love you longer than that," I replied.

Hailee

I had the wedding of my dreams with the man of my dreams. I couldn't imagine a better way to celebrate the love that Aiden and I had for one another. It was a night filled with love, with laughter, with joy. There was something so refreshingly wholesome about watching everyone come around to witness my happily ever after. I'd never felt more loved than I had that evening.

The champagne was poured all night long, leaving everyone in a giggling fit as we sang and danced the night away. Mr. Lee brought a plus-one to the ceremony, his son Lin. Lin was in his mid-sixties and was considering moving to Leeks, Wisconsin to take over his father's business. He was such a dapper, kind man, and I couldn't help but take note of the way he'd spent the whole night complimenting Laurie.

As Aiden and I slow danced, I gestured toward Lin and Laurie who'd found their way to the dance floor, too. "What do you think of that?" I asked him.

He looked over to his mother and raised an eyebrow. "Is he hitting on my mom?" he asked, alert. "I'm going to go stop him."

Before he could pull away, I tightened my grip on him. "You most definitely will not. Look at her. She looks happy."

Aiden grumbled. "Yeah, she does. But if his hands move any lower, I'm going to rip them off."

Overprotective son was in full force. "You're ridiculous."

"And yet you still married me," he joked, kissing my nose. "Hey, you want to do something with me? You want to get out of here?"

I narrowed my eyes. "Out of our wedding?"

He nodded. "I bet no one would notice we were gone. Everyone's too champagne drunk. Besides, I want to go somewhere with you. I think it will be nice. Just say yes?"

I glanced around, took a deep breath and shrugged. "Yes."

Wherever he would lead, I would follow.

He took my hand, and we snuck out of a backdoor without anyone noticing us. Then, we began walking down the streets of Leeks, under the perfectly clear sky. It was a beautiful night, and the weather was more than perfect for a scroll in an expensive tuxedo and a stunning wedding gown.

As we reached our destination, my heart smiled almost more than my lips had.

We stood at the spot between the two homes that raised us.

The for-sale signs sat in front of both houses, and our parents had moved most of their things out from the homes.

"In a little while, these houses will be places for someone else to create memories, but I figured maybe we can have one last night of counting the stars," Aiden explained as he walked me to the space between our two childhood windows.

The love I had for this man was unmatched.

We lay between the trees, and I cuddled up closely with him. He held me close and kissed my chin before he gestured toward the sky. "One…two…three…"

EPILOGUE

Hailee

Three Years Later

"**K**ENNEDY AND AALIYAH, WE NEED BOTH OF YOUR INPUT quick. Stella and Hailee can't be involved because they will be biased." Aiden hopped off the tree stump he was sitting on and hurried over to the front yard where us women were hanging out with all the kids. The three girls were giving me notes on what to expect when expecting, seeing how I had a bundle of my own on the way.

Damian followed his brother, walking in our direction.

The two men stood next to one another, Aiden towering over Damian with a few inches. They crossed their arms in sync and wiggled their noses at the same time. Their blue eyes matched the sea at dawn, and they cleared their throats in harmony. They were brothers, all right. No getting around that. Discovering their matching mannerisms was one of mine and Stella's favorite pastimes.

"We've been going back and forth all morning about this, and we need your vote," Damian explained.

Kennedy raised an eyebrow. "What's the question?"

"Who's better looking, Damian or me?" Aiden asked.

"That's not fair, Aiden was Aaliyah's hall pass," Damian chimed in. "You already know who she's going to pick. This isn't a fair study."

Aaliyah frowned. "You know what…the more I hang out with him, the cornier he becomes and now he feels like a little brother, so the thought of it is…" She shivered in disgust.

I smirked. "This is why they say you shouldn't meet your idols. You always end up disappointed."

"So you're saying I'm the more attractive brother?" Damian asked, arching an eyebrow.

"Actually, you're both equally hideous," Kennedy remarked.

"Yeah, it's like God took his paintbrush, dipped it in black ink and instead of making a masterpiece, he drew two stick figures and went 'meh that will do,'" Aaliyah added in.

"Exactly! Like he got lazy the day you two were created," Kennedy agreed.

Aiden pouted. "Jax and Connor, your wives are bullies."

"Don't ask silly questions unless you want sassy answers," Jax hollered as he and Connor sat with fishing rods at the back of the property. We were right on Lake Michigan, celebrating the Fourth of July.

We'd been working on our dream property for a while in Leeks. When I brought up the idea of building our home, Aiden was too excited about it. He still had one final Superman movie to complete with his contract, but then he'd be back on his way to moving to Leeks full time with me and our bundle of joy that was on the way.

The movies had all been great successes, which wasn't shocking. Aiden was remarkable at everything he'd done. But his passion for acting wasn't there, and it never had been. Once he let his father go from his life, he felt as if he, too, could let go of the dream that was never his to begin with.

He went to college. He was still trying to figure out exactly what he wanted to do, what he wanted to be, but I loved the joy that it brought him—the possibilities. The world probably thought he was insane for giving up his acting career that was filled with success, but that was never his dream. It was Samuel's. I could see the joy in Aiden's eyes as he talked about the possibilities of our new future that we were building from the ground up.

As nightfall grew upon us, Mama, Dad, and Laurie came over for our cookout. Later, Kate and Henry showed up, too. Even Mr. Lee came through for a plate of barbecue and some fireworks over the lakefront. Mr. Lee also brought his son, Lin, who'd moved into town not that long ago. He seemed to be making Laurie laugh harder than I'd ever seen her laugh before. My romance novel loving heart was strongly hoping that there could've possibly been a love connection there. Laurie deserved a happily ever after, and the way Lin was making her smile made me think that perhaps he could lead her down that road.

Aiden and I were surrounded by love, and everything felt right in the world. I couldn't wait for our kids to be running around with their cousins on the lake when they'd come visit in the summers. Damian said he'd only come during summertime because winters in Wisconsin were made for insane people. Fair enough.

We were lucky the builders even allowed us to have a small gathering while it was still in the process of becoming our forever home, but fireworks over the lakefront in Wisconsin were unmatched.

The house was nowhere near done. We only had the foundation up. The bones were there, it was just time to add the meat to it all. We still had to have the insulation put in, along with the walls, the roof, and the brick stones. I wasn't too concerned with how much time it would take. We had a solid foundation, Aiden and I. Everything else would come into place right as it was meant to be.

As the fireworks began, everyone rushed over to the water to watch them explode in color. All but Aiden and me.

He took my hand and walked me into our home. He led me to what would one day be our living room where we'd make a million memories together with our children. We laid down on the floor and looked toward the sky, since there was no roof blocking our viewpoint just yet. As the sky exploded in color, my heart burst with a level of joy I never thought I'd experience.

Aiden took my hand into his. "Look at the stars, Hails," he whispered, pointing up to the sky.

I tilted my head toward him and smiled. My Tom. My lover. My very best friend. "Yes," I said, snuggling against him, feeling his warmth, feeling his love. "Look at the stars."

#

Four Years Later

"Daddy! Look! It's Mommy's turn!" DJ said, pointing to the stage. DJ was short for Damian Junior—named after the brother who came into my life and showed me what it meant to be family. I felt as if I'd been cheated out of having Damian in my life for so many years, but he told me that we had the rest of our lives to annoy the living hell out of each other, so that felt promising.

"Yeah, look at her go!" I said, pointing to the stage with my left hand as I held baby Luna in my arms. She was only four months old, and in a deep sleep, even with all the noise surrounding us in the auditorium. I glanced down at the seats that were filled beside DJ and me with all our family members. Damian, Connor, Jax and their crews all came out for the celebration. Along with Kate, Mr. Lee, my mom, and Hailee's parents. We were a lively bunch, and Hailee's biggest fans.

"Doctor Hailee Jones-Walters," was called out by the speaker. Our three rows of individuals began to cheer as loud as we could as Hailee walked across the stage to get her Psy.D degree. After years and years of hard work, she'd collected her Doctor of Psychology degree.

The smile on her face as she collected her degree said it all. When she turned toward us, she held the diploma in the air and grinned ear to ear.

"ILY," I mouthed to her.

"ILYT," she mouthed back.

My eyes grew misty as I stared up at the love of my life. Even when the stars didn't align for us, we created our own galaxy. Our own happily ever after. Hailee Jones was a remarkable being. She was the perfect partner, the perfect mother, and the perfect friend. On top of that all, she was now a doctor who was going to save the lives of so many individuals—the same way she saved mine.

I could say with confidence that my life wouldn't be as great as it was without that strong woman by my side. She was there when I got my degrees in illustration and animation. It turned out, I still wanted to be in the entertainment field, but not in the form of acting. I returned to my love of drawing and illustration, which opened a wave of possibilities for me. Hailee was my biggest cheerleader throughout my search for myself. She was the brightest star in my life. She was my north star, and she led me home time and time again.

She was victorious in everything she did in her life. Her goals always reached completion because giving up was never an option. She was my heart, my soul, and my very best friend. My pride in her success was infinite. It was a gift and the greatest privilege in the world to watch her shine.

And oh, how brightly she shined.

Printed in Great Britain
by Amazon

13249135R00180